AND THEN THERE WAS ONE

"What about it?" Dodie asked Lily. "Could you marry this rogue in gilt wrapping?"

"I'm sure any woman could marry Zac," Lily said. "He's very nice and really sweet when he wants to be."

"The girl is bewitched," Sarah Thorogood exclaimed. "You must have doped her."

"I did not," Zac exclaimed. "I don't want her to marry me, remember!"

"Would it be so bad to be married to me?" Lily asked.

"It would be terrible," Zac said. "You'd expect me to get up early and learn to milk some damned cows you're bound to come up with sooner or later. You'd sing and dance until every man in the place was ready to shoot, knife, or bite his neighbor just to get a smile from you. You'd have this bloodsucking preacher and his passel of furies yapping at my heels, invading my bedroom, accusing me of things I've tried my damnedest not to even think about doing. You'd have me going crazy trying to fight the lot of them to keep you to myself."

"It sounds like love to me," Dodie said. "I say we call for a preacher and do the deed."

LEIGH GREENWOOD'S
SEVEN BRIDES

LILY

LEISURE BOOKS   **L**   **NEW YORK CITY**

*To my mother and father, both of whom were born
into families of seven.*

A LEISURE BOOK®

September 1996

Published by

Dorchester Publishing Co., Inc.
276 Fifth Avenue
New York, NY 10001

Printed in the United States of America.

WILLIAM HENRY RANDOLPH (1816-1865)—AURELIA PINCKNEY COLEMAN (1823-1863)
m. 1841

George Washington
b. July 14, 1842
m.
Elizabeth Rose Thornton
— William Henry '67
— Aurelia Coleman '71
— Juliette Pinckney, twins
— still-born son '74
— Elizabeth Rose '77

James Madison
b. Feb. 14, 1845
m.
Fern Sproull
— James Madison II '72
— Robert Tazewell '74
— John Tucker '76
— Alexander Stuart '78
— Carter Harrison '80

Thomas Jefferson
b. Nov. 12, 1843
m.
Violet Goodwin
— Thomas Jefferson II '81
— Dorothy Ankum '82
— Catherine Ward '84
— Margaret Anne '86

Juliette Coleman
b. May 21, 1847
died in infancy

James Monroe "Monty"
b. Sept. 16, 1849
m.
Iris Richmond
— Susan Irene '81
— Helena Grisham '84

John Tyler
b. June 17, 1853
m.
Daisy Singleton
— Lillian Diana '81
— John Tyler, II '82

William Henry "Hen" Harrison
b. Sept. 16, 1849
m.
Laurel Simpson Blackthorne
— Adam Blackthorne (6-addopted '77)
— Jordy McGinnis (9-adopted '77)
— William Henry Harrison II '79
— Peter Nathaniel '81
— Stephen Curtis '83
— Judith Grace '84

Zachary Taylor
b. Aug. 2, 1859
m.
Lily Sterling
— Jasmine '86

Chapter One

San Francisco, 1885

Lily Sterling paused to offer a silent prayer to the angel responsible for waifs and homeless children. She knew she didn't qualify for either category, but if he'd just watch over her for the next few minutes, she'd never so much as whisper his name again.

Nothing in her nineteen years had prepared her for San Francisco and Pacific Avenue at 6:37 P.M. The street teamed with men. All kinds of men. All in a hurry. Many wearing guns. Some of them drunk. All of them strangers.

With them were women unlike any Lily had ever seen. Most wore brightly colored dresses cut to reveal so much of their bodies it made Lily blush. Their hair and skin had been dyed and painted until their faces looked like masks. They were nearly as loud and as drunk as the men. Lily had never seen a drunken female before. She didn't know it was allowed.

The boardwalk was crowded with buildings of every description, spilling bright light, music, and the noise of human revelry into the night. Lily had never heard such a racket, not even at last summer's campground revival attended by more than two thousand people.

She stared up at the facade of the Little Corner of Heaven Saloon. It looked more like the Devil's front door. The building had been built of brick, but everything was red and gold, even the curtains at the windows.

Lily couldn't see through the etched glass panes in the doors, but every so often someone would leave or enter, offering a brief glimpse inside. Tobacco smoke hung over the room like fog in a valley on a crisp fall morning. The smell of whiskey was so strong, she could almost taste it. She felt the heat from the press of so many bodies, heard the music, women singing and dancing, felt the energy of the life that throbbed so vibrantly inside the saloon.

Nearly every evil her father had warned her about since she was a little girl had come together in this place. Yet she was fascinated by the flashes of bright color, the brash energy of the music, glimpsed smiles, voices raised in laughter, the sheer energy that flowed from that room. For the first time in her life, she was seeing sin and temptation up close, and it didn't seem half bad.

She shivered even though it was July. The wind off the bay chilled her to the bone. She took a deep breath to calm her nerves, but it didn't help. What would Zac Randolph say when she walked in and announced that she had come to live with him? He had invited her, but she was certain he had never expected her to take his invitation seriously. She took another deep breath, but her heart still pounded like the hooves of a team of horses trying to outrun a stagecoach going downhill.

She unclenched her hands and automatically smoothed her dress. There was one good thing about wearing black. It might show dust and lint, but it didn't show soot. After a week on a train, plenty of that had settled on her. She just hoped there wasn't any on her face.

She pulled her veil down, but it fluttered so much in the wind that she put it back up. She'd never been in a place as windy as San Francisco, not even her mountain valley home in southwestern Virginia. She knew she must look untidy, but she had too little money to rent a room for the sole purpose of making herself more presentable. If Zac couldn't take her in—if he *wouldn't* take her in—she'd need every penny to keep body and soul together until she found a job.

That was another thing that concerned her. From birth she had been destined to be the wife of a preacher. Aside from being able to run a household, quote the Bible, and smile comfortingly, she couldn't do much. From what she had seen so far, she doubted her smile or her Biblical quotations would be much in demand in San Francisco.

It was too late to start thinking about that now. The die was cast. It was time to face Zac.

But her feet wouldn't move.

Lily told herself she was merely postponing the inevitable. Her father had often told her that only made things worse. It was time to face the issue squarely and be ready to deal with the outcome.

But that was more easily said than done. She couldn't go back home, not even if she had the money, which she didn't. Her father would kill her. There wasn't any doubt in her mind. He'd simply wring her neck and throw her body down the mountainside.

Lily nervously plucked at her veil. In her mind's eye, she saw herself, a thin female clad in black from head to foot. She must look as if she were dressed for a funeral. Those brightly colored females inside would laugh themselves silly.

With sudden decision, she untied the bonnet strings and pulled the hat and veil from her head, removed the pins that held her hair in place, and dropped them into her purse. She shook her head to loosen the hair she had so carefully hidden under her hat early that morning. A mantle of white-blond hair tumbled down her back, around her shoulders, and over her breasts.

Lily became aware that the steady flow of men all around her had slowed. Looking up, she saw men staring at her from all sides.

"Jesus, Joseph, and Mary!" one man, unsteady on his feet, exclaimed to his companion. "It must be the angels come for me."

"Ain't no angel stupid enough to set foot in San Francisco," his slightly more sober friend said. "It must be the whiskey."

The first man drew closer until he could reach out and touch Lily. "She's real!"

"That's it," his companion said. "No more whiskey for you. From now on we stick to opium."

Petrified she would attract even more unwanted attention, Lily gave her hair a final smoothing, took a deep breath, picked up her suitcase, and stepped inside the Little Corner of Heaven.

Zac felt Dodie Mitchell's grip on his shoulder tighten. She was standing behind his chair as she often did. He flexed his muscles as a warning. He had been a gambler too long, had played too many games with thousands of dollars at stake, had bluffed too many times when holding nothing more than two pair, to let his own excitement betray him. He'd be damned if he'd let Dodie's do it.

But he understood. For the first time in his twenty-six years, he held a spade flush, ace high. With no cards wild, he would take the pot no matter what they threw on the table. It wasn't the money or the game. It was the hand, and he'd drawn it. He didn't need to discard. It was perfect. Most gamblers went through their entire lives without seeing a hand like this.

He glanced up at the other men at the table. They all had good hands. He could tell.

Bob Wilkerson thought his demeanor was impenetrable,

but his left eyebrow bunched ever so slightly. Asa White's eyes glazed over. Eric Olsen tapped his boot against the table leg. Heinrich Beiderbecker had no control at all. He grinned like a bear in the middle of a trout stream during a spawning run. When he had a good hand, everybody knew it.

Only Chet Lee could match Zac's poker face. But then Chet always had a good hand. Zac was certain he cheated, but he'd never been able to catch him. Tonight it didn't matter.

Zac settled back and the betting began. It wasn't until the pot topped twenty thousand dollars that he became aware of a ripple in the noise that surrounded him. He ignored it.

He enjoyed gambling even more than his customers did. His employees were under strict orders not to bother him unless it was a life-threatening emergency. But there was something different about this sound.

In a city of more than two hundred and fifty thousand people, all of them seemingly addicted to gambling, even the biggest gambling saloons were always crowded and noisy. That's what was wrong. The noise was dying down. That never happened. If the mix of men, whiskey, gambling, and women could guarantee anything, it was noise. It needled at Zac's mind until he looked up.

At first, he saw nothing to account for the change. The men around him were concentrating on their games, shouting their pleasure or bellowing their fury. He started to turn back to his game.

Then he saw her.

She was dressed in black from head to toe. As she crossed the brilliantly lighted room, all sound and motion stilled. Like the hand of an angry creator quelling an annoying din, she left the men and women dressed in gaudy colors staring after her in bemused, immobile silence.

She seemed to float, the only evidence of physical movement the gentle sway of the stiff material of her skirt. The warm, creamy softness of her skin, the moist vermilion of

15

her lips, the robin's-egg blue of her eyes stood out in stark contrast to her black dress and gloves. But even they paled in comparison to the shimmering halo of white-blond hair that fell across her shoulders and over her breasts. She looked like a figure from a Botticelli painting.

Zac watched as she threaded her way across the room until she came to a stop before his table.

"Hello," she said.

Her voice was soft and clear. There was only a trace of the drawl that betrayed she had lived in Virginia's Shenandoah Valley.

"Hi," Zac replied, having no idea what he was supposed to do for this woman. She looked vaguely familiar, but he couldn't remember having met a female all decked out in black since meeting those Civil War widows when he visited his brother in Virginia. Not one of them was under the age of forty. This woman was hardly out of her teens.

"Who are you?" Dodie demanded.

Dodie sounded possessive, and that irritated Zac. He liked Dodie as much as he liked any woman. She took good care of his girls and kept the saloon running smoothly, but he didn't want anybody thinking Dodie had a claim on him, not even this stray from a Salvation Army mission.

"What do you want?" Zac asked.

The quiet serenity of the young woman's face relaxed into a smile that caused the men near her to forget there was anyone else in the room. If ever there was an angel come down to earth, it was this woman.

Zac had a sudden apprehension that his time was up, that she'd been sent to fetch him to some eternal reckoning for a life thoroughly enjoyed but badly misspent. It wasn't fair. His brothers had all had time to grow older and repent for their earlier indiscretions. He had a long list of indiscretions still waiting to be committed.

"Don't you recognize me?" the vision asked. "I'm your cousin, albeit a distant one. I've come to stay with you. You invited me," she added when Zac seemed unable to answer.

16

The denizens of the Little Corner of Heaven were not yet aware that a dividing mark in the annals of their lives had just occurred, but they observed its coming with an appropriate hush.

"I wrote," the vision explained, "but I got no reply. I thought you were still in Virginia City. But when I got there, a very nice young man told me you'd moved to San Francisco. He found my letter slipped down in a crack."

"You can't be any relation of Zac's," Dodie said, her red-blond hair quivering from agitation, her voice harsh and urgent. "He's as dark as you are fair."

"It's not very close. My grandmother was a Randolph."

"Where is your family?" Zac asked, ignoring Dodie.

"They're still in Virginia." She laughed softly. "Papa doesn't approve of you. Neither does Mama."

Zac could tell the laugh was forced. She was scared stiff.

"You'd better sit down so these fellas can breathe," he said. "What are you doing here in San Francisco?"

She remained standing, a look of anxiety flaring in her eyes. "I just told you. You said if I ever got tired of Salem to come see you, so here I am."

"I don't remember inviting you," Zac said, wondering how he could have forgotten such a stunning young woman.

"You invited me four years ago when you were visiting your brother in Virginia," she said shyly. "I guess I've changed some since then."

It had been the first time his entire family had gotten together in twenty years. They had come from Texas, Colorado, Wyoming, and California to gather at the home they'd been driven from in 1860. For George and Jeff, it was a vindication. For Zac, it was too many people in one house.

He remembered the shy, elfin creature who'd followed him everywhere, asking endless questions about the places he'd been and the things he'd done, until her father dragged her off with a particularly offensive warning to beware of lechers parading as gentlemen.

"I'm Lily," she told him. "Lily Sterling."

Lily! Hell and damnation! All six of his brothers had been corralled by women with flower names.

His mind went blank, his muscles went slack, and his cards spilled onto the table.

"Holy hell!" Asa White cried. "Do you see what he's holding!" He threw his cards on the table. "Nobody can beat that."

One by one the players abandoned a game they couldn't win.

Zac leapt to his feet, his brain and limbs finally released from immobility. Though the men in the room had resumed their normal breathing, no one spoke except a brightly painted girl in purple net, who asked in a voice perilously close to a squeal, "Who'da thought Zac could be related to anybody like her? If I didn't know better, I'd swear I was back home in Massachusetts."

As though released from a spell, they all started talking at once.

"Introduce us, Zac," Eric Olsen said, the card game forgotten.

"You got no call to be getting familiar with a gal like her," Dodie said. "What are you gonna do with her?"

"You just introduce me. I'll figure something out." Eric was young, beardless, and thin to the point of gauntness, but there was strength in his gaze and confidence in his voice.

Chet Lee and Heinrich Beiderbecker stood up. That seemed to bring Zac out of his trance. "Where are you going?" he demanded. "The game's not over."

"It sure as hell is!" Chet said, pointing to Zac's hand laid out in front of him.

Zac looked at all his lovely spades lying face up on the table, his wonderful secret exposed, and he felt furious enough to strangle someone.

"Who turned them over?" he demanded. It was an unspoken rule of the game that no man touched another player's cards for any reason.

"You did," Chet said.

"P-probably when you g-got a good l-look at your *c-c-cousin*," Heinrich Beiderbecker stammered around his thick German accent.

Zac looked at his cards, then at Lily, then back at his cards. He should have expected it. Women named after flowers had spelled disaster for each of his brothers. What had he been thinking of when he invited Lily out West? She might have been a young girl at the time, but surely he knew she would grow up and become a potential hazard. She had calamity written all over her.

Just look at the men, staring at her as if they'd never seen a woman. Not a one of them gambling or drinking, just staring at her as though Dodie and the other girls weren't females, too. She was big trouble he needed to head off before he found himself surrounded.

He rose to his feet and with his customary calm said, "Gentlemen, this young lady is my cousin, Miss Lily Sterling. She will be staying at Bella Holt's tonight and leaving on the first train headed east in the morning. She regrets she doesn't have time to get to know you, but it's late and she has to go to bed." Zac walked around the table and took Lily firmly by the elbow. "Say good night, Lily."

"Good night," Lily said with an entrancing smile that encompassed the whole room. "I hope to see you again soon."

"She wishes she could, but she can't," Zac corrected. Keeping a firm grip on her elbow with one hand and picking up her suitcase with the other, he escorted her from the saloon, refusing to acknowledge the chorus of groans and complaints about his selfishness. He had no idea how heated he had become until he stepped outside. The cold that raced through him when the fog-dampened air came into contact with the thin film of moisture covering his body caught him by surprise.

Just his luck to catch a chill and come down with pneumonia all because some blond enchantress didn't have enough sense to stay in Virginia and limit herself to driving farm boys and any married man this side of death out of their minds.

"Does your father know where you are?" Zac demanded as he propelled Lily along the boardwalk, away from at least a dozen saloons and gambling parlors. He could imagine all too vividly the fire-breathing Reverend Isaac Sterling coming after him with a Bible in one hand and a shotgun in the other.

"Not exactly," Lily answered.

A past master at manipulating the truth, Zac knew what *not exactly* meant.

"In other words, you didn't say a word to the old devil."

"He's not a devil," Lily said, "but he wouldn't understand."

"I guess not," Zac said, "especially if you don't explain anything to him."

"I tried. He doesn't want to understand."

"I don't know why I should expect him to. I don't understand myself."

"Of course you do," Lily said, trying to twist around so she could see his face. "You're the black sheep of your family. You told me so yourself. You have defied tradition, tossed your brothers' advice in their faces, and gone into the world to do what you pleased."

"Sounds like I really shot my mouth off," Zac said. "I can't think what go into me."

"It was after lunch. Jeff had been lecturing you about your responsibilities to the family. You came storming out into the garden and told me no matter what I did with my life, I wasn't to waste one minute of it trying to satisfy a bunch of relatives. Far better, you said, to dash out into the night and howl at the moon."

"I never was very good with children," Zac observed in a tone that implied it wasn't a problem likely to keep him awake nights. "Never did know what to say to them."

"I wasn't a child," Lily declared. "I was fifteen."

"If you paid attention to anything I said after being lectured by Jeff, you were thinking like a child. Everybody knows he can make perfectly saintly people start searching for a really hot place to shove him."

"That may be," Lily said, her chin jutting doggedly, "but there's no point in discussing it. I'm already here." She stopped and whirled to face Zac. "Why can't I stay with you until I get settled?"

"Your brain must have been eaten away by all that smoke on the train!" Zac exploded. "You can't stay with me."

"Why not?"

"The saloon is no place for a woman. Even Rose won't go there. You'll never survive here on your own. You ought to go straight back home."

He turned her around and headed her down the boardwalk once more.

"I've seen quite a few women since I arrived, many of them mothers and young girls. I don't see why I can't succeed if they can. Is there some weakness you see in me I don't know about?"

Flower women, Zac thought angrily to himself. All you had to do was name them for something that smelled good and looked pretty and they thought they could do anything.

"You'll have to take my word for it," Zac said. "You don't know the West. I do."

"You're just like all the Randolph men I ever knew," Lily said without heat. "You think all you have to do is make a pronouncement and women will hop to obey. My mother is like that. I don't doubt yours was as well. But I'm a Sterling, and I don't hop for any man. If you wish me to give your opinions any consideration, you'll have to give me some facts."

He could do that. She needn't think her angelic face was going to paralyze his brain.

"Fact number one: You don't have a job. I'll lay odds

you're broke. I'm certain you used nearly every cent you had to get out here. Fact number two: People get killed out here for no reason other than being in the wrong place at the wrong time. You could get shanghaied off the street and end up in a brothel on the other side of the world. Fact number three: You know nothing about the West, its people, or what it takes to stay alive here. Beautiful women get used up overnight. Young ones simply disappear. Fact number four: You'll hate everybody and everything you see. Your rigid Virginia morals will be so outraged, you'll be begging to go home inside a week."

"In that case, you can stop worrying about me. Surely I can survive seven days on my own."

But Zac wasn't certain. From what Jeff had told him, the Salem branch of the Sterling family was a rigidly moral bunch who had no tolerance for behavior that didn't conform to their standards.

She wasn't his responsibility. Their relationship was a fact of birth, not of choice. He had never taken responsibility for anyone, and he wasn't about to begin with an innocent, narrow-minded, ignorant female from Salem, Virginia.

"You don't have to worry about me," Lily said, pulling her elbow from Zac's grasp. "I can stay in that young ladies' hotel."

Following the direction of her gaze, Zac found himself staring at the elegant facade of Salem House, the most expensive and most exclusive house of prostitution in San Francisco.

Chapter Two

Salem House had a summer ritual known to every man in this part of San Francisco. Each evening, promptly at six-thirty, six of the girls would come out on the porch. They would talk among themselves, even have tea on occasion, but they would ignore the men in the street. At seven o'clock, the girls would go back inside. That was the signal that Salem House was open for business.

Zac took Lily by both elbows and started her moving again.

"That's not a rooming house."

"It looks like one."

"It isn't."

"How do you know?"

"Because I've been . . . I just know. Besides, it's full."

"How do you know?"

"A place like that is always full on Friday night."

Lily looked over his shoulder at the pretty girls in the lovely dresses. "They look very nice."

"They're paid to look nice."

"Maybe I could get a job there."

Zac hurried her along. "You don't need a job. You're going back to Virginia on the first train."

"I can't," Lily told him. "I don't have enough money."

He was prepared for that. "I'll buy your ticket."

"I can't let you do that. It's not proper."

"It's a damned sight more proper than you trying to get a job in that *lady's boarding house.*"

"It's not proper to curse, either. Papa says it's a sign of an unprincipled heart and a limited intellect." Before Zac could return the scalding retort that sprang to his lips, she continued, "I know that's not true of you. Everybody says you're as crafty as a weasel."

"What bastard said that?" Zac thundered. "And don't tell me I'm cussing. I know it."

"One of your brothers. I can't recall which. Rose said you used to be a little devil. She also said you hadn't changed much."

Zac had regretted attending that family reunion from the moment he stepped through the door. His brothers had spent most of their time criticizing him and insisting he *reform his character* and *amend his way of life.* By the time he stalked out, he was so blazing mad that he'd poured any number of ill-considered remarks into this female's ears and topped off his folly by inviting her to come see him.

"Let that be a lesson to you," Zac said. "Never go to a family reunion unless you want to have your shortcomings served up as the main course at breakfast, lunch, and dinner to be discussed in great detail and lamented at great length."

Lily laughed. "I don't think your brothers would approve of your saloon."

Zac chuckled. "Monty would, if Iris would let him."

"I liked Iris," Lily said. "Monty, too."

Zac felt a chill settle around his heart that was more icy than the fog drifting in off the bay. The name Lily reverberated in his head. It didn't matter that he didn't want to get married, that he had no desire to fall in love. None of his brothers had wanted to get married, either.

"Turn here," Zac said, directing Lily's footsteps up a steep street. "Bella Holt's rooming house is at the top."

At first Zac was surprised at how easily Lily climbed the hill. She actually reached the top a step ahead of him. Then he remembered Salem was in the mountains. She probably didn't know how to walk on flat land.

"This is not nearly as pretty as the house with the women on the porch," Lily said when she came to a halt before Bella's steps.

Unlike Salem House, Bella's home was a tall wooden structure of three floors and a basement built in the Italianate style with bracketed cornices. Not quite two full rooms wide, a circular bay on the front projected out from the house the same distance as the steep stairs leading up from the street. The orange-brown paint did nothing to enhance its appearance.

"Rooming houses aren't supposed to be pretty," Zac explained as they mounted the steps, "especially if they cater to young ladies. They don't want to attract attention to themselves."

"I shouldn't think it could be called attracting attention to oneself not to look like a dreary bird," Lily said.

Zac smothered a chuckle. "I wouldn't mention that to Bella. She's quite proud of her house. Besides, you shouldn't complain. You're dressed all in black."

"Papa says bright colors and fancy dresses lead to dangerous frivolity. He said it encourages young girls to give too much consideration to physical appearance and not enough to spiritual being. He said it encourages young men to do pretty much the same thing."

"That's bad?"

"Of course. A person can't be solely concerned with himself without becoming thoroughly selfish."

Zac was sure her words had been meant for him.

"Of course, I haven't always agreed with Papa. He thinks people who allow themselves any sort of fun are pawns of the Devil. Do you believe that?''

''Hell, no! If everybody thought that, I'd be out of business.''

''Papa says—''

''I don't want to hear any more of what your Papa says.'' Zac knocked on the door. ''He sounds too much like Jeff.''

''I like Jeff.''

''Well you wouldn't if he was forever calling you a wastrel, a good-for-nothing likely to end up in an alley with some unmentionable disease.''

''No, I don't think I'd like that.''

Zac was feeling more charitable toward her until she added, ''Even if it were true.''

''Well, it's not,'' he snapped, wondering whether it might not be better if he put her on a train tonight.

''Of course not,'' Lily agreed. ''I never thought it was. I just meant one wouldn't like to hear that even if it were true.''

Zac decided their conversation was beginning to coil around him like a snake. He was greatly relieved when Bella's maid opened the door.

Zac launched in without preamble. ''This is my cousin. She needs a room for the night.''

The girl stared at Zac, her eyes wide with curiosity. He couldn't tell whether she believed Lily was his cousin, but he doubted it. Probably too many men came here claiming to be looking for lodgings for cousins, nieces, aunts, daughters, and sisters-in-law.

''If you'll step into the parlor, I'll let Mrs. Holt know you're here.''

Zac could tell Lily didn't like the look of the place. She looked as if she thought something was about to jump out at her from behind one of the chairs. Come to think of it, he didn't like it much, either. Too dark and gloomy. With all the overstuffed chairs, shawls draped over everything, and dreary pictures staring at you from the walls, you'd think Bella was running a funeral home.

"You may as well have a seat," Zac told Lily. "No telling how long it'll take Bella to make herself presentable."

Lily didn't move. "I don't like it here," she said. "It's dark and stiff and mean looking."

"Sounds like the kind of place your father would approve of."

"Maybe, but I'm the one staying here, and I don't like it."

Zac chose a chair and sat down. "Meet Bella first. She's not a cheery woman, but she's probably your sort."

"If she chose the furnishings for this room, she's definitely not my sort," Lily replied. "Can't we go someplace else?"

"There aren't many places for a respectable single woman to stay," Zac said. "And don't mention that house with the pretty women again. If you must know, it's a place where men go when they don't have wives to go home to."

Lily regarded him in silence for a moment. "Or where they go when they have wives they don't wish to go home to?" she asked with a raised eyebrow.

"That, too, I expect," Zac said, not entirely pleased with Lily's quick understanding. "Now sit down and stop asking so many questions."

But Lily didn't sit. She made a slow circuit of the room, subjecting everything in it to close scrutiny. Zac had no desire to make an inventory of Bella's taste, but he found his gaze following Lily as she moved about the room.

She might say she was fed up with her tiresome Papa and wanted a bit of fun, but Zac recognized her type. Her bit of fun would hardly be a bump on what he saw in a single night. She wasn't the kind to like some man for a time, then effortlessly transfer her affections to another when he disappeared or looked elsewhere. No, once she loved some man, she'd love him forever.

That was the most dangerous kind of woman in the whole world: faithful, loving, and virginal. Zac was more determined than ever that Lily should leave town as soon as possible.

But as his gaze continued to follow her around the room, he realized that until now he hadn't really noticed any aspect of her appearance other than her face and hair. The rest of her was equally eye-catching. He didn't know what maggot had gotten into her father's head to make him think black bombazine could obscure the fact that she had a tantalizing figure. He was certain all those mountain boys had noticed.

She had a slim waist, the kind that made a man want to reach out and put his hands around it. But its real significance was that it drew attention to her bosom, a thing not easily ignored. Not by Zac anyway. He could easily imagine its softness and warmth, the feel of her breasts as he kissed her nipples to hard peaks.

Zac had seldom been called upon to rely only on his imagination in situations such as this. By the time Bella arrived, he was squirming in his seat.

Bella didn't look happy to see him. She didn't look any more delighted with Lily. The more closely she looked at her, the more unhappy she seemed.

"Ellen tells me you're wanting a room for your cousin." She raked Lily with a searing gaze. "Is this the *cousin* you had in mind?"

Bella quickly discovered she'd said the wrong thing.

"The Bible says, 'Judge not lest ye be judged,' " Lily quoted, her expression stern.

"If I didn't *judge*," Bella replied, not backing down an inch, "no telling what kind of female I'd have trying to put up here."

"I have no fears on that score," Lily answered, her expression unrelaxed. "I doubt much gets by you."

Lily's remark seemed to gratify Bella a little, but not enough to ensure her wholehearted acceptance.

"You'll forgive me if I'm not as accepting as you'd like, but your cousin keeps some questionable company."

Zac was irked at Bella for acting the stiff-necked moralist.

She damned well ought to know the girls who worked in his saloon were honest and hardworking. She used to work there herself.

"You shouldn't judge Zac by the company he keeps or the women by their jobs," Lily said. "I imagine many of them had little choice."

Bella threw Zac a glance full of resentment. She still looked as if she smelled something bad, but she forced herself to smile. Smart woman. She'd better not push him too far. There were lots of people who'd be very interested in knowing what Mrs. Bella Holt had done before she opened this boarding house.

"What you say is very true," Bella said. "But you must understand that in my position I have to be very careful."

"I'm sure you do, but I'm certain Zac respects you too much to take advantage of your trust."

Zac nearly laughed aloud. That ought to have pulled the last of Bella's fangs.

Bella's smile was strained, but it was a smile.

"My name is Lily Sterling," Lily said, taking control of the conversation. "I arrived only this evening. I'm sure Zac would have reserved a room ahead of time, but my letter got lost in Virginia City. He was even less prepared for my appearance than you. I do hope a room can be readied without too much trouble."

"My rooms are always ready," Bella replied. "They're as clean and neat as any you'll find, even in those grand hotels downtown."

"I need only a modest room," Lily said.

"Give her your big one on the front," Zac said. "I don't want anybody saying I put my cousin in a poky little hole."

"I don't have any *poky little holes*," Bella snapped, happy to vent some of her irritation at Zac. "It'll cost extra."

"When it's family, cost is no object." Zac swallowed hard. He'd never said anything like that in his whole life. No telling what Bella would charge him now.

Bella smiled like a self-satisfied cat. "Is that bag in the hall all you've got?" she asked Lily.

"No. I have a trunk that went to Sacramento by mistake and a larger suitcase still at the ferry landing."

"What?" Zac said, sitting up with a start.

"You can't expect a respectable woman to dress herself out of a single bag," Bella said, apparently reassured by the quantity of Lily's luggage. "You have a seat," Bella said to Lily. "I'll have Ellen bring you some coffee. Have you had anything to eat?"

"I'm afraid not. With the excitement of arriving and trying to find Zac, I forgot all about food."

"We've got some pork roast. It won't take but a minute to heat it up along with some potatoes, peas, and pan bread."

"You sure it won't be too much trouble?"

"I'm paying her to take the trouble," Zac said.

Bella smirked at him. He made a mental note to have a talk with her once he hustled Lily back to Virginia.

"You settle with Zac about the luggage," Bella said to Lily, "and I'll be right back with your dinner. Then you'll have to leave," she said to Zac. "I don't allow men in my house after dark."

"You never told me you had more luggage," Zac said as Bella left the room.

"I might be a preacher's daughter, but I do have more clothes than I can stuff into one small suitcase."

Zac thought it looked like a rather large suitcase, but he abandoned the topic. It was much more important that he convince Lily to go back to Virginia.

"It's just as well the suitcase is at the dock. All you'll have to do is have them reload it on the ferry. I'll get Dodie to find the schedule. I've got one somewhere. If not, Tyler will have one. When you run the biggest hotel in town, you have to know the exact departure and arrival time of every train, ship, ferry, and stagecoach that serves San Francisco."

"I have no intention of returning to Virginia tomorrow,"

Lily stated, her chin assuming an alarmingly obstinate tilt.

"Well you can't stay in San Francisco," Zac said, his patience at an end. "And don't start yammering about me inviting you. Anybody with a grain of sense would know I was in a temper and didn't know what I was saying. Besides, nobody but a simpleton would head off to Virginia City just like that." Zac snapped his fingers. "You could have been dead by now."

"I'm not."

"And wipe that wounded expression off your face. It won't do you a bit of good. Good God, girl, don't you know what kind of reputation I have? I'm the last person you should come to for protection. Didn't you listen to a word Jeff said?"

"But you said it wasn't true. You said—"

"Of course I did. Do you expect me to stand around letting that sanctimonious blockhead call me a layabout and not call him a liar? I've got my pride."

"But—"

"Don't start butting. I'm a gambler. I run a saloon. I consort with the worst elements of society. Your mother would probably cross the street to keep from meeting the women I employ."

"If I don't do anything disgraceful—"

"You don't have to *do* anything, just have people think you do. If you have anything to do with me, they'll think plenty."

"Are you so terrible?"

Her question surprised him. He let out a crack of laughter. "I guess I did make myself sound right awful."

"Yes, you did," Lily agreed, her smile uncertain.

"I'm no criminal, but I might as well be as far as you're concerned. Now be a good girl. Eat your dinner, have a good night's sleep, and we'll get you across the bay and on the train first thing in the morning."

Lily looked him square in the eye. "I'd have to be the simpleton you think me, and a great coward as well, to ignore my family's wishes, travel three thousand miles, then turn around and go back after less than a day. I appreciate your finding me a place to stay. However, if you wish to wash your hands of me, I will manage on my own."

"Haven't you been listening to a word I said?" Zac demanded.

"Of course I have. You think I know nothing about getting along in San Francisco, and you believe being seen in your company would ruin my reputation."

"That's not enough for you?"

Lily smiled at him. "When you decided to become a gambler, did your family approve?"

"Are you kidding! They did everything they could to stop me. George even cut off my allowance. I had to run away."

"Did you ever doubt you were doing the right thing?"

"Never."

"Then you should know exactly how I feel."

"But you aren't wanting to do anything disgraceful."

"My family will think so. I'm actually in very much the same boat you were in years ago."

"But you're a woman."

"I'm glad you noticed."

"Don't get smart with me. Men can do lots of things women can't."

"I know that, but I'm here now. I've got to at least try to be a success. If I'm a total failure, I promise I'll go back."

Zac eyed her doubtfully. "I don't believe you."

"You're not a very trusting man, are you?"

"No. It only gets you in trouble."

"Even with women?"

"Especially with women."

"Well, you can believe me. No matter what happens, I won't expect you to take care of me."

Zac cursed roundly. "See, that's exactly what I mean."

"I don't understand," Lily said, confused.

"You say you won't expect me to be responsible for you, but I'll have to be."

"No, you won't."

"What kind of bastard would I be if something happened to you because I turned my back? I said I was a gambler. I didn't say I was a misbegotten scoundrel and a yellowbelly rolled into one."

Lily laughed. It was a light, bell-like sound, but it didn't make Zac feel a bit like joining her.

"You're shot through with Southern chivalry."

"Don't go nosing that around," Zac snapped. "It's not true. I just can't chuck over relatives, that's all."

"Well, you can cross me off your list. I'm certain Mrs. Holt will help me find a job."

"And no doubt broadcast it all over town that I abandoned you."

"I won't tell anyone I know you. You just said it would prejudice my chances of getting a job, didn't you?"

Zac glared at Lily. "Why don't I trust you?"

"I have no idea."

She smiled at him, innocently and demurely. That made him trust her even less.

"I'll come around tomorrow," Zac said. "We can talk about it again."

She looked fragile, Zac thought as he went down the steps, but she gave every indication of being tough-minded. That's what came from having a father who was convinced every thought that popped into his head had divine sanction. Some of the attitude was bound to rub off.

Zac had to admit he'd never seen anybody quite as lovely, even dressed in black. And that hair! It made him think of a statue that occupied a quiet niche in the chapel where he had gone to school. The headmaster had forced Zac to attend services despite his vigorous protests. He'd spent many hours looking at that angel, thinking thoughts that were far from angelic.

Lily had much the same effect on him.

Zac shuddered. He liked his life the way it was. He liked sleeping when, where, and as long as he wanted. He liked having meals cooked to his tastes and served at any hour of the day. He liked having his pick of women. He also liked having his clothes closet and his mirror to himself.

Maybe it would be better if he didn't meet Lily tomorrow. Maybe he'd send Dodie.

No. With his luck, they'd put their heads together and come up with something that would turn his hair gray. He might have to be very firm, even forceful, but she was going straight back home.

All the same, it was a shame she couldn't stay just a day or two. He liked her slow, unhurried way of talking, the way she drew the vowels out just a little longer than usual. After all the noise and energy of the saloon, listening to her had a wonderfully soothing effect on him.

Or maybe his calm was the aftermath of his excitement over the spade royal flush. Or the shock of looking up, seeing a woman who looked like angel, and fearing God had decided that after such a hand, he had nothing left to accomplish.

Zac turned the corner, saw the lights and heard the sounds coming out of the saloons and gambling halls, and the familiar excitement began to surge within him. His doubts faded as he started to feel like himself again. It had to be Lily and the royal flush. They had upset his equilibrium. The game was over, and Lily would soon be gone. Everything would be the way it used to be.

But for some reason, that didn't seem like a perfect solution.

Chapter Three

Lily closed the door to her room, effectively bringing to a close the most momentous day of her life. Well, maybe the day she packed her trunks and left Salem while her parents were away at a two-week revival meeting was more momentous, but everything had gone according to plan that day. When the train pulled out of the station, she had actually experienced a tiny feeling of anticlimax.

Today things had gone wrong from the start. From discovering that her letter to Zac had gone astray to convincing her cab driver that she really did want to be taken to an address on the edge of the Barbary Coast district, everything had been a struggle.

Then there was Zac's refusal to honor his invitation.

Well, he hadn't exactly refused. He had found a room for her, and he would probably keep an eye on her. But he clearly intended for her to go back to Virginia at the earliest possible moment.

Lily had no intention of going home. She wasn't sure her father would let her. That saddened her, but she knew it couldn't be helped. They had never understood each other. There was no use pretending they had.

Neither was there any use pretending she'd be happy married to Hezekiah and helping him minister to his flock. She'd tried to explain to Hezekiah why she didn't want to marry him, but he believed a woman's marriage should be settled between her father and her bridegroom. Once that was done, it was the woman's duty to accept her lot and do everything in her power to make her husband happy.

Lily had decided that arrangement was stacked in favor of the groom. She had no faith that a man who could ignore her wishes before the wedding would pay them any attention afterwards.

She took off the black dress, undid the laces of her corset, and heaved a sigh of relief as the whalebone cage dropped to the floor. She quickly changed from her petticoat and chemise into her nightgown and robe. She looked at herself in the mirror. She looked pale. No wonder Zac had acted as if he'd seen a ghost.

She smiled to herself when she thought of Zac Randolph. He had to be the most handsome man in the world. He looked as though he could be dangerous under the right circumstances, but there was still a vulnerability about him. He was exactly the kind of black sheep who appealed to a woman's fancy.

Despite her father's dire warnings, Zac didn't seem to be doing anything very bad. He was gambling, but since he wasn't married, he wasn't taking food out of the mouths of his wife and children. He wasn't drinking, he wasn't wenching—though she didn't imagine he'd be doing that in the middle of a saloon anyway—and he wasn't blaspheming. A black sheep who passed up all those things couldn't be any darker than medium grey.

When he smiled, she felt sure light grey was probably a more accurate assessment. No man who looked as good as he did could be evil.

Lily pulled back the covers. It was wonderful to climb

into a real bed instead of a train berth. It was sheer luxury to stretch out, to be able to turn over without fear of falling out of bed. It was wonderful not to hear the incessant scream of iron wheels on steel rails, not to feel the incessant rocking and swaying, not to have the acrid odor of soot and smoke constantly in her nostrils. It was heaven to know she was safe from the wandering hands of male passengers.

She had traveled by train before, but always with her father. She hadn't known there were so many dangers. Nor had she been prepared for the differences between western men and those she'd grown up with in her small Virginia town. Still, she hadn't been frightened.

She was fascinated. She'd been told saloons were the haunts of the devil. She'd almost expected hideous creatures with horns and tails to snatch innocent passersby off the streets and carry them down into the bowels of hell. Instead she'd seen a room full of people having a good time and in no danger of being whisked off to some nether region.

It seemed her father was mistaken about saloons. He might be mistaken about Zac as well. She hoped so. She liked Zac. She liked him a lot.

But her father wouldn't.

Lily sat up in bed. She hadn't written to her parents. They wouldn't return from the revival for another week, but she wanted the letter to be waiting when they got back. She didn't want them to worry about her.

She got out of bed. She saw writing materials on a small table by the door. All she had to do was sit down, write the letter, and post it tomorrow.

But what to write, what to say? No one had ever defied her father, not even her brothers. That his daughter should challenge his authority would be beyond his comprehension. He didn't understand that she had beliefs of her own and the right to have her wishes considered. She was *his* daughter; she should do what *he* wanted; she should make *him* proud.

He had pushed her into leaving, but he would see it as

willful disobedience. He might not even want to know
where she was or care whether she was safe. He might not
even love her anymore.

That thought pained her. Though she disagreed with her
father, she loved him deeply. He had protected her, sheltered
her, taught her, loved her.

But there was no use thinking about it. She'd done little
else for months. She drew the paper to her and dipped her
pen in ink.

Dear Papa,
You're going to be very angry when you read this letter. I'm sorry. I know you don't understand. I could
never be the kind of daughter you wanted, so I thought
it would be better for me to go away.

Tell Mama and the boys not to worry. I'm staying
in a very nice boarding house for young women. You
don't have to worry that I don't have money. I used
Aunt Sofia's money to get here. Tomorrow I will get
a job, so you see I will be quite self-sufficient.

Lily had to stop to wipe her eyes. Just thinking about her
mother caused her to tear up. She would miss her family.
They didn't understand her, but they were very dear to her.

I'm in San Francisco. Zac Randolph is here, too. I
know you don't like him, but he has been very nice.

Tell Hezekiah to be glad I wouldn't marry him. I
would not have made a good wife. He'd have been
truly unhappy.

I'd better go now. I'm tired from the train ride. It
was exciting, but I miss my own bed. I would very
much like a letter now and then to let me know you
are doing well. Even though I don't agree with you, I
love you.

Lily had to stop. She was crying so hard the tears were running down her cheeks. She was determined none of them would drop on the letter.

Please write. I miss you already.

Love, Lily

Lily addressed the letter and sealed it. She would mail it first thing in the morning.

The next morning Lily was dressed and downstairs before Bella.

"I wasn't expecting you out of bed before noon," Bella said. She looked uncomfortable at being caught in her worn robe, her hair in curler papers.

"At home we were always up by six, finished breakfast by seven," Lily said.

Bella winced. "That won't make you very popular in San Francisco. There's nothing to do at this hour unless you're the milkman." After a moment's silence, Bella asked, "Would you like something to eat?"

"Yes, please. My father always insisted we have a big breakfast. He said it was the most important meal of the day."

Bella winced again. "You're going to have to do some adjusting before you'll feel comfortable here."

"I know. I plan to start today."

"How?"

"I'm going to see as much of San Francisco as I can. Then I'm going to Zac's saloon. I'll probably be gone all day."

Lily found the streets virtually empty. She couldn't imagine how so many people could live in one place and nobody be out before eight o'clock. At home they would have completed half a day's work by nine o'clock. Apparently San Francisco didn't get started until then.

39

Lily stopped to look back at the view out over the bay. She was used to mountains, but at home there was nothing to compare to the view of the bay and the sea beyond the headland. Merely by turning a quarter of a circle, she could look out over the Golden Gate and watch the magnificent sailing ships coming in from distant ports all over the world, their sails bulging with the wind that had carried them thousands of miles over the limitless sea.

The tang of the salt air was even more invigorating than a mountain breeze. She couldn't imagine how anyone could stay in bed.

Lily left the serene row of respectable houses and entered a street that seemed to be lined with businesses. She didn't see a single person. She turned onto Pacific Avenue, and everything changed.

Only a few buildings were as grand as the Little Corner of Heaven. Most were squat buildings of poor construction and discouraging appearance, almost all of unpainted wood. Signs invited patrons inside to partake of various pleasures, the nature of which Lily sometimes couldn't even guess.

Salem House looked just as grand as it had the night before, but today the curtains were drawn and no lights shone from the windows. A man came out of a side door, looked nervously up and down the street, then hurried away in the direction from which Lily had just come.

Something about his furtiveness made her feel uneasy until she reached the Little Corner of Heaven. Relieved, she stepped inside.

The saloon didn't look at all as she remembered. It was as empty and silent as the streets outside. The tables had been wiped clean and the chairs stacked neatly. All the cards had been cleared away, the chips and dice boxed up, the wheels stilled, tables stripped of their green cloths, and the machines with the handles covered. Even the floor had been swept clean. Only the smell of whiskey and smoke kept Lily from thinking she had imagined the whole scene of the night before.

And Dodie. Lily found her sitting in a corner, a cup of coffee in one hand, some sort of book in the other. She wore a faded green velvet robe over a cream-colored silk nightgown. Pink puffballs on her slippers clashed violently with the rest. She smoked a long, thin cigar, smoke drifting lazily from her nostrils. Even at this hour, her face was hidden behind powder and paint.

Lily walked toward her, relieved at last to find someone she knew.

Dodie looked up. "What are you doing here?" she asked. Lily supposed she wasn't trying to be rude, but she clearly wasn't happy to see Lily.

"I came to see Zac."

"He said you'd be leaving on the first train. You ought to be packing."

"I'm not going anywhere."

"He said you were."

"I told him I wasn't."

That appeared to give Dodie pause. She took a swallow of coffee, puffed on her cigar, and motioned for Lily to take a seat.

"I'm never at my best in the morning. Having to look up at your hideously beautiful face is making it a lot worse."

Lily sat. "Why do you say my face is hideously beautiful? I don't see how it can be both."

"Any fool can see you're beautiful. It's hideous because I can't stand to look at anybody as beautiful as you."

"But you're beautiful, too," Lily said.

Dodie swallowed some more coffee and took another puff from her cigar. "You see this mess all over my face?" Dodie smeared her lipstick with her index finger. "That's how I do it. Are you wearing paint?"

"Of course not," Lily declared, startled by such a notion. "Papa wouldn't allow it."

"That's why I think you're hideous," Dodie said. "You get out of bed looking like that. I spend hours on my face, it costs a fortune, and I still don't look half as good."

41

"You've got more color than I have," Lily said. "I look so pale, people think I'm unwell."

"I bet you get lots of young men offering to bring you water or to hold your hand until you feel better."

"Not in Salem. Papa says no decent female wants a lot of idle young men hanging about. He sends them about their business."

"I'm sure he does," Dodie said between a swallow of coffee and another puff on her cigar.

"Papa says—"

"Spare me any more of your papa's sayings. I can imagine what they are. He sounds very much like my own father."

"Was he a minister, too?"

"That's what he called himself, but it's not how most people described him."

"I know what you mean. People sometimes say unkind things to Papa when he points out the error of their ways."

"My father's problem wasn't expecting too much of others. It was requiring too little of himself."

Lily wasn't sure she knew what Dodie meant. She was beginning to understand that people in San Francisco were different from people back home. She decided it might be wise not to pry until she understood more.

"Why did you come here?" Dodie asked.

"I told you, to see Zac."

"I mean why did you come to San Francisco?" Dodie said. "You're a country girl. You don't belong in a place like this."

"I imagine you were a country girl once."

"What makes you say that?"

"You don't want me here, but you haven't thrown me out. You know what it's like to be a stranger."

Dodie's gaze became more intense. "Some of us didn't have as far to go as you."

Lily refused to give ground. She knew Dodie didn't like

her, probably distrusted her, but she refused to be intimidated.

"Maybe, but I'll still succeed. I mean to get a job and support myself. I won't be a burden on Zac."

"What can you do?"

"I thought maybe I could help in the saloon."

Dodie nearly choked on her coffee. As it was, she got it all over the table. A bit dribbled down her chin onto the front of her robe.

"I can't dance, at least not the way I saw them dancing last night," Lily confessed, "but I can sing. I've been singing in the church choir since I was fourteen. Everybody says I have a pretty voice. I sing country songs—I guess you'd call them mountain songs—but people generally like them a lot."

Dodie finished cleaning up her coffee and tossed the damp handkerchief down on the table.

"We're full up with dancing girls and songbirds just now. We generally don't get much call for mountain songs."

"I could help with the serving," Lily offered. "I used to help Mama with all the meals."

"I don't think so."

"Why not?" Lily wasn't pleased that Dodie should disparage her singing without having heard it, but it was insulting to think she couldn't serve food.

"Our girls serve mostly whiskey," Dodie explained. "They wear dresses hemmed so high and cut so low you'd probably catch pneumonia."

"I could—"

"Then there's the matter of make-up. You'd have to wear it thick all over your face like I do. The men like it. Besides, it's so dark in here at night you'd look like a ghost if you didn't."

"I don't think—"

"I almost forgot to mention the pinching and hugging, and men dropping coins down the front of your dress and then wanting to fish them out again."

"They would not!" Lily gasped. "If any money were to become lost in my clothes, it would remain lost to that man forever! Papa would—"

"What your papa would say or do is of no consequence," Dodie continued relentlessly. "He'd be three thousand miles away, and you'd be here by yourself."

"Zac wouldn't allow anyone to manhandle me for the sake of a few coins."

Dodie got up and picked up her coffee cup. "You've got a few things to learn about Zac. Would you like some coffee?"

"Yes, thank you."

"Anything in it?"

"Lots of cream. About half, if you have it."

"If I drank that much cream, I'd soon look like the cow giving it," Dodie grumbled on her way out. She came back with two cups of coffee. She set one in front of Lily that looked as if it was at least ninety percent cream.

"I put in a little extra. I don't think the cow had her heart in it this morning," she explained.

Lily took a sip. It was too hot to really taste, but she could tell it was too strong for her liking. She was glad of the extra cream.

"Papa would say you're spoiling me," Lily said, "but I appreciate it."

"Do you always quote your father? Doesn't anybody else talk in that town you come from?"

Lily felt herself blush. "I suppose they talk quite a lot, but not when Papa's around. He always has so much to tell people that by the time he's done, there isn't time for them to say much."

"They're probably so glad to get away, they don't open their mouths for fear he'll start in on another sermon," Dodie said.

Lily surprised herself by smiling. "I've done the same thing myself. Papa hates it something awful when people

44

run away from a recital of their shortcomings. He says it shows a want of backbone.''

"Well, you're going to need all the backbone you can come up with if you're going to survive in San Francisco,'' Dodie said, getting back to the original subject. "Tell me what you can do, besides milking cows and serving a country breakfast.''

"I can cook, sew, clean, and manage a household well enough to leave the man of the house free to pursue his responsibilities.''

"It sounds as though your papa had you learn that by rote to impress your suitors.''

"Papa says it's unbecoming for a young woman to take pride in her accomplishments,'' Lily said, flustered. "It's a father's duty to inform the young man of how useful a woman can be to him.''

"He makes you sound like a servant,'' Dodie said. "But that's men all over. Wanting to know what you can do for them. Never a thought in their heads as to what they can do for you.''

"Does your young man do that?'' Lily inquired with a candidness that seemed to rattle Dodie.

"I don't have a young man,'' Dodie said, rather too loudly to be convincing. "I haven't found one worth the trouble.''

"I thought you might be talking about Zac.''

Dodie actually turned red under her makeup.

"For a naive mountain girl, you sure see to the heart of things on occasion,'' Dodie said, not sounding the least pleased with Lily's shrewd insight.

"Milking and sewing aren't very hard. They give you a lot of time to think. And some of us country girls actually learn to read by the time we're old enough to be married.''

Dodie looked as if she was about to get angry, then she suddenly burst out laughing. "I like you. I don't know why the hell I should, but I do. You're going to have an awful time if you decide to stay. I'll give you a hand now and

45

then if you're not too much trouble. But we're going to fall out if you start showing up before I've had my coffee and had a chance to go over the books. Ten o'clock is plenty early.''

Lily smiled. ''I'll try to remember. But I'm used to getting up at six.''

''Lord!'' Dodie exclaimed, shaking her head in amazement. ''Would you believe I used to get up that early? I hated it. The world is in a hell of a mess. It takes God several hours to dry it out, warm it up, and get things going. I figure it's best to stay in bed until He's done. That way I don't get in His way, and He doesn't get in mine.''

Lily tried to hold back the laughter, but it was impossible. ''If Papa ever heard you say that, he'd have apoplexy.''

''Then let's hope he never comes to San Francisco.''

Lily sobered quickly. ''He won't.''

''I bet he's on a train right now.''

''He doesn't know I'm gone yet, but he still won't come. He'll probably tell everybody I'm dead. He'd prefer it that way. Papa says places like this are cesspools of iniquity.''

''That doesn't mean he'd let you sink from sight without lifting a finger to prevent it.''

''I don't mean to sink from sight,'' Lily said.

''I hope you succeed, Lily, I really do. Just don't pin your hopes on Zac. And make sure you don't fall in love with his handsome face and start having notions of him settling down and giving you a house full of kids.''

''I'm not interested in getting married just yet. If I had been, I could have been married a dozen times in Salem.''

''Goodness, wouldn't your father have been pleased about that.''

They both laughed.

Dodie sobered first. ''You implied earlier I was in love with Zac. I was in love with him once, desperately, but I got over it. Every female who sets eyes on him thinks she's died and gone to heaven. If he speaks to her or gives her a smile, she's ready to go off into a swoon. I'll probably work for him as long as this muck can make me look half decent," Dodie said, indicating her makeup, "but I discovered long ago that he's the most selfish human being on the face of the earth.

"Take my advice. Use him to get you settled in and set up. Hell, if he's your cousin, use for him anything you can. But don't ever—no matter how often he smiles at you, no matter what he says—let yourself fall in love with him. He'll break your heart and not even notice." She spoke almost without passion, as if Zac's selfishness were something she had accepted long ago.

"Do you still like him?"

Dodie dropped her gaze. "Everybody likes Zac. It's impossible not to like a rascal that good-looking. Besides, he can be as sweet as a lamb and as charming as a snake oil salesman when he wants."

Lily couldn't help but smile. She had known that from the beginning. He had been so sweet and charming to her all those years ago that she almost felt disloyal talking about him behind his back.

Dodie looked up. "But he still can't think of anybody but himself."

"Doesn't he have lady friends?" Lily asked.

"Every woman he ever met," Dodie said. "But Zac's in love with only one female."

That surprised Lily. She hadn't known Zac's affections were engaged. "Who's that?"

"Lady Luck. So far, she's been mighty faithful to him." Dodie pushed herself up from the table. "Now it's time for me to get about my business. You'd better go on back to Bella's. I'll tell Zac you want to see him."

"I don't mind waiting," Lily said. "When do you expect him back?"

"He hasn't gone anywhere. He's still in bed."

"But it's past nine o'clock."

"Child, the man never gets up before five. Why should he when he's got me doing his work for him? He says he needs his beauty sleep. How do you think he keeps himself looking like some Greek god?''

"Where is his rooming house?" Lily asked.

Dodie laughed again. "When he bought this place, he had three rooms knocked into one. He turned them into a suite right and proper. He's upstairs now, just about above your head, snoring away."

"It's time he got up," Lily said. "It's ridiculous to sleep away the best part of the day."

"Zac thinks the best part of the day begins at dusk."

"That's because he hasn't seen enough of the morning."

Dodie laughed. "This is San Francisco. Nothing important happens before nightfall."

"It certainly won't as long as everybody spends the day in bed." Lily got to her feet.

"What are you going to do?" Dodie asked.

"I'm going to wake him up."

"Nobody wakes him. He'll shoot you if you try."

"Not if he's too sleepy to tell whether I'm his cousin or a curtain flapping in the breeze."

Dodie started to step in front of Lily, but she paused, smiled, and stepped back. "Maybe you'll be the one," she murmured, half to herself.

"The one what?" Lily asked.

"The one who can wake him without getting shot."

Chapter Four

She should have asked Dodie for directions to Zac's room. The upstairs covered more area than the saloon and was cut by several long, narrow halls into blocks of rooms. Numerous doors, all closed, opened off each hall. No sound came from behind any of them. There were little pieces of pasteboard tacked to each door with names on them. At least that's what Lily thought they were. She wasn't sure. Nobody in Salem had a name like Morning Dove, Long Stemmed Mabel, or Weasel Annie.

She was soon lost in the maze of hallways. She finally gave up and knocked on the door of a young woman called Leadville Lizzie.

She got no response. Lily knocked again. Still no response. She knocked louder. She heard someone mumbling, but the door remained closed.

Lily tried the knob. To her surprise, the door was unlocked. It opened without a squeak.

The room was small, but decently furnished with a bed, table and chair, wardrobe, and a dressing table with a mirror.

Brightly colored dresses, shoes, and other items Lily couldn't readily identify lay scattered about on the floor, on chairs, half out of the wardrobe. The female occupant was asleep, mostly hidden under a vile greenish-yellow bedspread.

Lily decided that Lizzie must be color blind.

"I hate to disturb you," Lily said softly, "but I can't find Zac's room."

The young woman sat up in bed, exclaiming a sharp epithet Lily refused to admit she had heard.

"Who are you?" she demanded, peering at Lily through barely open eyes.

"I'm Zac's cousin, Lily Sterling. I came to wake him up, but I can't find his room."

"What time is it?"

"It's nearly ten o'clock."

"He'll kill you."

"He promised to help me look for a job."

"Zac wouldn't get up this early for his mother's funeral. Now go away."

Leadville Lizzie burrowed under the covers, but Lily didn't budge. This constant criticism of Zac was beginning to irritate her. "I don't know why everybody is so eager to convince me Zac is mean and thoughtless," she said. "He promised to help me today, and Zac keeps his promises. Now are you going tell me how to find his room, or do I have to ask someone else?"

Lizzie surfaced again. "You're serious, aren't you?"

"He can't very well help me find a job while he's in bed."

Lizzie smirked. "Sure he can. He'd just love to . . ." Her gaze narrowed. Her smirk faded. "Naw, I don't suppose he would. Not with you."

Lily wasn't interested in Lizzie's mental meandering. "Go back to sleep. I'll ask someone else."

"No, I'll take you," Lizzie said, preparing to get out of bed. "This I've got to see."

50

"You don't have to get up. Just tell me where I can find his room."

"You'll get lost." Lizzie pulled on a screamingly pink velvet robe with tufts of velvet missing. She stuffed her feet into high-heeled slippers an equally virulent shade of orange.

Now Lily was certain that Lizzie was color blind.

"Zac's suite is in the back corner," Lizzie said. "He likes to be away from the noise. Just remember to take two lefts and a right when you come up the stairs, and you'll find it every time."

Lily doubted that. Right now she wondered if she'd ever find her way back downstairs.

Lizzie threaded her way through the maze of halls, knocking on a half-dozen doors as she passed, saying, "This gal is going to roust the boss out of bed. You gotta see this." By the time they reached Zac's door, a covey of half-awake, brightly colored birds trailed behind them.

"There it is," Lizzie said, pointing to a door all by itself on one side of the hall. "Go ahead. Knock."

The presence of the girls made Lily nervous. Seeing Dodie peering at her from around the corner didn't make her feel any better. Obviously everyone expected an explosion, and they didn't want to miss it.

Lily felt a very strong desire to go back to Bella's and wait for Zac to come to her, but she decided against that. No matter how unsteady her legs might feel at the moment, she was not a coward. Besides, after all the things she'd done in the past week, waking Zac up ought to be easy.

She knocked.

No response.

She knocked two more times with the same result.

"He sleeps like the dead," Lizzie said.

"I guess I'll have to shake him awake," Lily said. She opened the door and stepped inside.

It was nearly pitch black inside the room. She stood still for a moment while her eyes adjusted to the dimness. At first she could see only the outlines of a huge, four-poster bed. Gradually she could make out the shape of someone in it. She noticed a lamp beside the table. Matches lay next to it. She decided to light it before trying to wake Zac.

Removing the globe, she struck the match and lighted the lamp. As she blew out and discarded the match, she turned up the wick. Soft light flooded the room.

She stifled a soft gasp. Zac lay in the middle of the bed, bedclothes twisted about his body, which was naked to the waist. Lily was frightened he'd wake up, see her staring at him, and draw the wrong conclusion. But he continued to sleep as peacefully as ever.

Her courage slowly returning, Lily drew closer to the bed. Even in sleep, Zac was breathtakingly handsome. It was hard to believe this man could be selfish. He looked too sweet and adorable.

Lily smiled to herself. She doubted Zac would appreciate being described like that. He'd probably prefer dangerous and virile.

Lily hadn't forgotten the electricity that seemed to emanate from him last night. She supposed some people could dislike Zac, but no one could be unaffected by him.

Her gaze was drawn to the mat of ebony hair that covered his upper chest and spiraled down toward his waist. She'd caught glimpses of her father and brothers as they washed, but they were blond and hairless. She'd never seen a man with hair on his chest, and it fascinated her. She wanted to reach out and touch it. Was it soft and springy or coarse and brittle?

The inclination to touch it was almost irresistible. It looked as soft as lamb's wool, but Lily thought it would be better if she managed to resist. If Zac should wake up and find her fondling his chest—well, she doubted she'd be able to come up with an acceptable explanation.

She forced herself to look at his face. That was safe. Everybody looked at his face.

His hair, brows, and lashes were of the same glossy black

color. His brows were thick and heavy, almost joining. His lashes were sinful. They were too long for any man. His hair was bushy and curled about his head in artful disarray. He had a strong, straight nose, generous lips, and a firm chin. His heavy beard gave his face a dark mask. Undoubtedly any woman who tried to kiss him before he shaved would be badly scratched.

Lily was surprised at herself for thinking such thoughts. It was exactly the kind of thing her father had warned would happen if she allowed herself to be alone with a man. But it didn't feel bad to think about kissing Zac. In fact, it was quite pleasurable.

It was impossible not to think of being held in his powerful arms. Such a thing had never happened to her. Every young man within a hundred miles of Salem knew her father would consign his soul to the fiery pits of hell if he so much as touched Miss Lily Sterling.

Lily had once spied Mary Beth Parker and Sam Lofton sitting on a log by the big pool the boys used for swimming in summertime. Sam had his arm around Mary Beth and was holding her close. Mary Beth had seemed quite happy in his embrace. Lily had asked her mother about it. Her mother said proper men and women didn't do such things, that Sam and Mary Beth were bound to get themselves in trouble.

Lily thought it looked quite nice. Besides, what trouble could you get into just sitting next to a fellow? She wondered if Zac would put his arm around her if she asked, just so she'd know what it felt like.

"Psst!"

Lily whipped around to see Leadville Lizzie peering around the door. "What are you doing, counting the hairs on his head? Wake him up if you're going to."

Lily motioned for Lizzie to get back outside, then turned back to Zac. "It's time to get up," she said in a normal voice.

No response.

"Zac, it's time to get up. It'll soon be ten o'clock."

Still no response.

She picked up the lamp and held it close to his face. His even breathing continued without pause. She put the lamp back on the table, reached out, and patted his arm.

"Wake up!"

He moved. She jumped back, but he simply turned over.

"I told you he slept like the dead." It was Lizzie again, her head back through the door.

"Get back outside," Lily hissed. "If he finds us both here, he's liable to be quite angry."

"I'll say," Lizzie said smiling wickedly. "He'd probably toss us out the window."

Lily felt stupid, standing in a man's bedroom carrying on a conversation while he was sound asleep. She dared not think what her papa would say.

"Shake him," Lizzie said. "You'll never wake him whispering in his ear."

"I never did any such thing!" Lily exclaimed.

Lizzie giggled.

Taking a deep breath, Lily put both hands on Zac's shoulder and shook him gently. He didn't even move. She shook harder. He groaned but didn't wake up.

Giggles from the doorway told Lily she still had an audience. She couldn't stand here all day shaking him like an apple tree. She walked around the bed and pulled open one set of curtains. Morning sunlight poured into the room. She didn't stop until she'd opened them all. Then, grabbing hold of Zac's shoulder, she pushed with all her might until he rolled over and sunlight streamed into his face.

"Wake up!" she practically shouted into his ear. "You should be ashamed of yourself, sleeping away half the day. The Bible says—"

Zac sat up in the bed like a man waking from a nightmare. "What the hell!" he demanded, looking wildly about the room.

Lily was only faintly aware of the giggles from the doorway. The sheet had fallen away, exposing all of his torso and part of a thigh. She was horrified to discover he was entirely naked. She knew she should look away, but she couldn't. He was the most beautiful creature she'd ever seen. He hardly even looked mussed, just sweet, adorable, and terribly confused.

"I came to wake you up."

Zac seemed to have trouble focusing. He stared at Lily without recognition. "Who the hell are you, and what are you doing in my bedroom?"

"I'm Lily, remember? I arrived last night. You said you'd help me find a job today. Well, I'm here."

Zac whirled about and stared at the sunlight pouring in the three windows as though it were a phenomenon he'd never witnessed before. "What time is it?"

"About a quarter to ten. I know it's rather late, but if we hurry, we—"

"Late! Dammit, girl! I didn't get to bed until six!"

The giggles were louder now.

Lily was about to reprove Zac for cussing in her presence, but she was so startled that anyone would actually stay up until six o'clock that she completely forget her rebuke.

"That would never do on a farm," she said. "You'd have to milk the cows."

"That's why I don't live on a farm. I'd kill any damned cow that wanted to be milked at that hour." He threw back the covers and started to get out of bed.

Lily shrieked and clamped her hands over her eyes.

"Hell and damnation!" Zac cursed.

The giggles from the doorway turned into shrieks of laughter.

A rustling of the covers and more curses told Lily that Zac was covering himself.

"You deserve to be scandalized," Zac said, "bursting into a man's bedroom when he's sound asleep. Oh, for God's sake, open your eyes. I've covered up everything that's interesting."

Lily peeped through her fingers, then lowered her hand. "I've never seen a man naked."

"Sorry, but you're not going to start with me."

"I didn't mean that I wanted to, just that I hadn't."

Zac slid off the bed. Holding the sheet in place with one hand, he used the other to grab Lily by the shoulder. "You shouldn't be in a room alone with a naked man." He spun her around. "Especially me. Your reputation will be ruined if this ever gets out." He pushed her toward the door. "Go back to Bella's. Ask her to make you a nice hearty breakfast."

"I've already had breakfast."

"Before ten o'clock!" Zac grimaced.

Zac reached the door to find a dozen females clustered in the hallway. "What is this, a conspiracy?"

The girls backed up a few steps but showed no inclination to leave.

"We just wanted to see what would happen," Lizzie said.

"Take her and tie her in a bed until a decent hour." Zac disappeared into the room and slammed the door behind him.

Mortified at being hustled out like a child, Lily reached for the doorknob just as she heard a key turn.

"He's locked the door," Lizzie said.

Lily knocked on the door. "You can't go back to bed. You promised to help me find a job."

"Ask Dodie," Zac shouted through the door. "She knows what goes on around here in daylight hours."

Lily knocked again.

"You can stop knocking," Zac said, his voice sounding farther away. "I'm putting the pillows over my head."

"That's that," Lizzie said. "Once he gets them pillows over his head, even an earthquake wouldn't wake him."

"But what am I going to do about a job?" Lily asked. "I can't sit around waiting until dark."

"You girls go on back to your rooms," Dodie said. "If

56

you don't get some rest, it'll take an extra layer of paint to make you look decent.''

She waited until they had left the hall. ''Do you want to get back in that room?'' Dodie asked, lowering her voice.

''He locked the door.''

''I know another way in. But if I show you, you've got to promise you won't let him push you out the door again.''

''He's bigger than I am.''

''If you're going to back down from people just because they're a few inches taller or a few pounds heavier, you'll never get anywhere in this town.''

Lily liked that philosophy. It made her a little nervous to think she was the one designated to put it into practice, but she was heartened by the fact that the Bible was full of instances where people had faced great challenges and succeeded. Maybe Zac Randolph was her Goliath.

''I promise to kick and scream loud enough to bring the entire police force before I let him throw me out,'' Lily said. ''Show me that door.''

''There,'' Dodie said, pointing to a door at the end of the hall. ''It goes into his closet. That leads into his bathroom, then into the bedroom.''

Lily had no trouble making her way through the dark rooms. Her father didn't believe in lighting a lamp unless it was to study the Bible. She'd spent half her life in shadows.

Zac was back in bed when Lily entered his room, the curtains drawn, the lamp out. She paused to consider how best to approach him. It wouldn't do to snatch his covers away. The moment she did, she'd have to clamp her hands over her eyes, and he'd push her right back out the door.

She could dash water in his face, but she feared he'd probably throw her into the bay in return. Maybe if she just dribbled a little on him. She approached the bed on tiptoe, which she told herself was stupid since she was trying to wake him up. He was asleep. She found it hard to believe anyone could drop off to sleep so quickly.

She opened the curtains again. Zac didn't stir. She went

to the bathroom, poured some water into a shaving mug, and carried it back to the bedroom. Holding the mug over the bed, she had just dipped her fingers into the water and was about to dribble some onto Zac's forehead when he opened his eyes.

"Don't you dare!"

Zac's speaking so unexpectedly caused Lily to jump. One hand flung drops of water all over his face. The other let go of the mug, which spilled water all over the sheet, the pillow, and Zac.

He rose out of the bed like an erupting volcano. He didn't seem to be aware that he didn't have a stitch of clothes on his body. Neither did he seem to care that he was assaulting Lily's ears with a torrent of words she'd never heard in her life. She didn't have time to puzzle out their meaning, but she felt safe in concluding that her life was in the gravest danger of ending right there and then.

"You're still naked!" she cried as she ran behind a sofa to avoid being strangled, her gaze only partially averted.

"Of course I am," Zac shouted. "How do you expect me to sleep?"

"In a nightshirt, like any normal Christian man," Lily answered, her eyes still averted. "Cover yourself. With all the noise you're making, people could start bursting in here any moment."

"Hell and damnation!" Zac flung himself at the bed, rolled up in a sheet, and sat up again, all in one fluid movement. He glared at Lily. Then, sliding off the bed, he started toward her with slow, menacing steps.

Lily's concentration was divided between the immediate danger to her well being and the wet spot in the sheet. It extended from Zac's shoulder down his side to cling provocatively to one well-rounded, cleanly-muscled buttock.

Lily had long been aware of the attractiveness of the male physique, but she'd never seen a specimen so clearly, so close up, or under such circumstances. The effect was hypnotic. The realization that the damp reached almost to his groin was paralyzing. Fortunately, since Lily was feeling decidedly faint, the rest of the sheet was dry and opaque.

"Why aren't your hands over your eyes?" Zac growled, his black eyes boring into her like those of a stalking cat. "Why aren't your knees shaking and your stomach doing somersaults?"

Lily's grip on the sofa back tightened. "My stomach is a bit jumpy and my legs don't feel at all dependable, but I don't dare cover my eyes for fear you'll grab me and do something terrible."

"I ought to throw you out the window." Clutching his sheet with one hand, he continued to advance in a melodramatic fashion. She didn't think he was serious—he looked perfectly ludicrous trying to intimidate a fully dressed woman while preserving his modesty with a sheet—but she didn't trust him. He might really mean what he said. She was in the room alone with him, with the door locked, and no way for anyone to get in to help her.

"Did you like dressing up for Halloween when you were a young boy?" Lily asked, desperate for something to distract him.

"What the hell are you talking about?"

Zac looked like he thought she was crazy, but Lily didn't mind. He was no longer advancing toward her. "You look like a ghost. I always wanted to be a ghost, but Papa wouldn't let me. He said it was a heathen custom."

"I think you and your papa are nuts," Zac said, abandoning his attempt to scare Lily. "Now get out of here and let me sleep."

"You can't go back to bed," Lily said, taking care to keep out of his reach. "You promised to help me find a job. I'm not certain what people do here in San Francisco, but I doubt I know much about it. It may take several days to find something I can do. I only have enough money for a week. Less, actually. So you see, we've got to get started right away."

"Do you always chatter on like a magpie, making no sense at all?"

"Only when I'm nervous. Or caught in a room with a naked man," she added.

"Does it happen often?"

"All the time. Everybody is nervous when they're around Papa."

"I mean getting caught in rooms with naked men."

"I'm never caught in rooms with naked men—I mean, a room with a naked man. It's making me jittery. I can't see why anyone would like it."

That wasn't entirely true. She had a distinct feeling that being caught anywhere with Zac would be exciting, but she wasn't about to tell him that. She knew well enough what happened between the male and the female of the species, but she had also been taught that doing anything like that outside the bounds of holy matrimony would cause her to be swallowed up by fire and brimstone. She didn't think she believed that, but she wasn't anxious to test her theory.

"Men like it. Quite a few women do as well." Zac approached a little closer. "Would you like me to explain why?"

A mental image of Zac bursting out of his bed—nude as the day he was born but looking quite a bit better for the passage of twenty-six years—sprang into her head. "I can guess," she said, her voice barely audible.

"I could erase all doubt if you would like."

"What I would *like* is for you to put on your clothes and help me look for a job."

They circled the sofa like dancing duelists.

"What an uninteresting way to spend a morning. If I must be up, and it appears that I must, at least there ought to be some reward for my labors."

"You'll have the satisfaction of knowing you helped me get a situation."

"I was hoping for something a little more concrete." He moved closer.

Lily slipped well beyond his reach behind a table and a pair of chairs. "I realize you're teasing me, trying to pay me back for waking you up. I know you wouldn't do anything unkind, but I really wish you'd stop saying those things, even in fun. It's making me very anxious."

Zac stopped. "How can you wake me up at this unholy hour and accuse me of having fun? How did you get in here? I thought I locked the door."

He walked to the door and tested the knob.

"It *is* locked," he said, advancing on her again. "How did you get in?"

Lily's gaze went involuntarily to the bathroom door.

"How did you know about the other door?"

"It was there, at the end of the hall." Lily backed around a table. "It had to go somewhere."

"Who told you?"

He was stalking her again. She backed away.

"Why should anybody have to tell me?" She backed around the sofa and found herself practically on top of the rumpled bed. She scurried to the other end of the sofa.

"Tell me, or I promise to throw a whole pitcher of water over you."

Lily smiled in spite of herself. "Dodie told me. I think she wanted to see if I could wake you up without getting killed."

"I ought to strangle you both," Zac said, looking as though he was seriously considering the possibility.

"While you're making up your mind, maybe you ought to get dressed. I doubt people who strangle other people normally do it wrapped up in a sheet. How would it stay up with both your hands around my neck?"

Zac let out a crack of laughter that made Lily jump.

"You're insane, and I must be crazy even to talk to you. However, I'm wide awake. Why don't you go downstairs like a good little girl while I get dressed?"

"I'd rather wait here, if you don't mind."

"Supposing I do mind?"

"I don't see why you should," Lily said, avoiding his eyes. "You'll be in your bathroom, and your clothes are in the room beyond that. You won't even see me again until you're completely dressed."

"That's not the real reason, is it?"

He was advancing on her again. Lily backed away. She didn't know what she expected him to do if he got his hands on her, but she didn't want to find out.

She wanted still less to find out what she would do. The idea of his hands on her was becoming more intriguing as the minutes passed. She had never been so aware of a man's body before. Nor had she any idea how stimulating that awareness could be. Her father had warned her to avoid all situations such as this, but she had a strange, unaccountable desire to stay and see just what would happen.

She thought of his naked body again.

Well, she didn't want to see *everything* that could happen. She knew about part of it. But there must be a great deal more. She knew people who'd been engaged for several years before they got married. Surely there was something they could do to fill up that time, except . . . except . . . well, if there wasn't, there ought to be.

Zac reached out his hand to her. "If you're going to stay, you can help me take a bath. I could use someone to scrub my back."

That "except" looked far too close for Lily's comfort. "I'll wait downstairs," she said as she dashed for the door.

Chapter Five

Zac laughed. He was so tired and sleepy, he didn't know what he was feeling or why, but he couldn't go back to bed. The little minx had ruined his sleep.

He closed the door behind Lily and headed for the bathroom. He dropped his sheet, took out towels, and stepped into the bath. He hoped they had heated plenty of water this morning. He couldn't remember if anyone except Dodie ever took a bath before noon.

The water came out hot. He adjusted it to his satisfaction and began to soap his body while the tub filled. He'd have to make sure Lily didn't find her way into his bedroom tomorrow. Maybe if he got her a job, she'd be too busy to bother him. That thought made the prospect of prowling the streets less onerous.

He leaned back and let the water rinse the lather off his body. He didn't often feel grateful to his brothers, but he was glad Tyler had insisted that he install hot water for his bathroom. Zac remembered Rose heating water on the stove when he lived on the ranch and his taking a bath in a tub in front of the kitchen stove. A tub full of hot water in his own private bath was a luxury he didn't intend to do without.

He wondered if Lily had ever had a bath in such a tub. He'd have to ask her. Maybe he'd offer to let her use his bathroom. He laughed. She'd most likely recoil in horror. She probably thought there was something about a male that could rub off in a bathtub. He wouldn't put it past her crazy old father to have told her some such nonsense to keep her away from men.

Which was probably a good idea. Any woman who looked like Lily was bound to attract men. Lots of them. "Damnation!" he said aloud. There was no place on earth where she could attract more of them than San Francisco.

He hurried to rinse the last of the soap from his body. He stepped out of the tub and began to towel himself dry.

It wasn't just that she would attract men. She'd attract the wrong kind. There wasn't much else in San Francisco. That was why he'd moved here and spent a fortune building the largest and fanciest saloon in the state. He was counting on there being an endless supply of exactly the kind of men he didn't want having anything to do with Lily.

After putting on his underclothes, Zac picked up his shaving bowl and began whipping up a lather. Soon his face was covered in snowy foam. He shaved with his usual care. It was never wise to hurry with a straight razor.

As soon as he finished shaving and burning himself with aftershave lotion—he hated that part—he reached into his closet for his clothes. Something sober and businesslike. It wouldn't help Lily get a job for people to see at a glance that she was in the company of one of San Francisco's best-known gamblers.

When Zac came downstairs, several of the girls were trying to teach Lily to dance. It was an incongruous sight. Dodie was plunking out a tune with one finger and slapping the piano with the palm of her hand to keep the rhythm; the girls in a kaleidoscopic array of brightly colored robes, all clashing with each other and overwhelming Lily's black dress; their hair up in curlers or tied up under scarfs while Lily's silver-blond tresses fell down over her shoulders like a shimmering cape; Lily's tentative steps so much at variance with their practiced precision.

A swan among ugly ducklings.

She had a radiance the others lacked. It wasn't just the color of her hair or the purity of her skin. Nor was it the brilliance of her smile, the sparkle in her eye. Part of it was the sheer pleasure she found in what she was doing. Part was the way she concentrated, trying so hard to master steps unfamiliar to her feet. Another part was the way she had drawn these girls into the friendliest gathering in which Zac could remember seeing them.

But none of those things touched the core of what caused Zac to be more aware of her than of anyone else in the room. None of these were the source of the radiance that seemed to reach out and encompass everyone around her. There was something more, some essential quality he had missed.

With a shiver of horror, Zac realized that quality was innocence, purity, something he'd never really known anything about. Nor prized very much. He had even considered it a hindrance. It usually made people narrow-minded and judgmental.

But not Lily.

He couldn't help but wonder why she was dancing, why she seemed so taken with the saloon, with his way of life. With him. All this should have offended a woman of her background. Some things did—like his cussing—but not enough to cause her to turn her back on him. She seemed determined not to reject the whole because she disapproved of some parts. Zac found that attitude totally unexpected.

And charming.

Good God! They were showing her how to do the high kick. A few minutes more and she'd have her skirts over her head. That wasn't something she could practice of evenings in Bella Holt's parlor.

He hurried toward the stage.

"That's enough for one morning," he said, dismissing the girls. "If you don't get back to your beds, you'll be so tired by midnight you'll be spilling whiskey on the floor instead of down the customers' throats."

As the girls trundled toward the stairs, he turned to Lily. "You'll be too tired to go job hunting."

"Nonsense," Lily said, her cheeks pink with exertion and pleasure. "Back home I'd have been working since six o'clock, milking, helping with breakfast, clearing away, washing—"

"Stop before you make me so tired I have to go back to bed," Zac said as he staggered over to a chair and gratefully accepted the cup of coffee Dodie handed him. "You sound like Rose when she first came to the ranch. I never could get over all the work she expected me to do."

"I like being busy," Lily said, coming toward him. "Papa says I'm tiny, but I'm full of energy."

Zac winced dramatically. "See if you can harness it long enough for me to drink this coffee. I'll never do it with you bouncing about on the stage making more noise than a Chinese procession."

"Do you have a headache?"

Dodie chuckled.

Zac threw her an evil look. "Nothing that couldn't be cured by seven more hours of sleep."

Lily came closer and peered at Zac as though she were checking for spots. "Did you imbibe too freely of spirits?"

Dodie's crack of laughter earned her a fiercely growled, "Don't you have work to do?"

"Nothing that won't keep. I wouldn't miss this for the world."

"Miss what?" Lily asked.

"Zac drinking coffee before ten-thirty."

"Go to hell," Zac snapped.

"I'm waiting for you," Dodie said. "I figure your invitation is edged in gold."

"One isn't invited to hell," Lily said. "You're sent there."

"Then Zac will be bound in golden chains and carried away in a flaming chariot."

"Have you been drinking spirits, too?" Lily asked Dodie.

Now it was Zac's turn to laugh. "Don't pay any attention to her," he said. "She's just trying to needle me."

"Papa says spirits make you dull. He says—"

"It's not spirits," Zac snapped. "It's lack of sleep. And don't peer at me like that," he rapped out when she started to inspect him again. "I don't drink."

"I thought all gamblers got drunk on a regular basis."

Dodie chuckled again.

Zac threw Dodie a smoldering glance and took a gulp of coffee. "I have to keep a clear head if I'm to make a living. If I sat around drinking all evening, I'd be as muddle-headed as the poor fools who come in here hoping to get rich."

She looked dubious.

"I run a clean house. Nobody cheats; nobody goes upstairs with the girls. Likewise, nobody drinks but the customers. I'm not against it on principle. I just don't think it mixes with business."

"Oh."

She looked surprised, but she appeared to believe him.

Her innocence intrigued him. She'd obviously been taught that everything connected with gambling was evil, most particularly the gambler, yet she was ready to believe anything he told her. That was a nice change. The rest of the world was only too ready to distrust anything he said.

"Close your mouth," Zac said. "Somebody will think you're a fish and drop a hook in it."

Lily closed her mouth.

"Now sit."

She sat.

"Would you like some coffee?"

"I already had my coffee."

"Sorry, I forgot you got up to milk the cow. How is she?"

"Who?"

"The cow. Did she sleep well or did you wake her after only three hours' sleep?"

Lily smiled. "I know milk comes in bottles in San Francisco. I saw it."

"Must be very little cows. Not much room in a bottle."

"Is he always like this?" Lily asked Dodie.

"I don't know. I've never seen him up this early."

"And you're never going to again," Zac said as he got to his feet. He grabbed Lily by her wrist and pulled her to her feet. "Come on. We have to catch those jobs before somebody else gets them."

"But you haven't had your breakfast."

"I just did. You weren't paying attention. You were dancing and talking about cows."

"You had coffee."

"That's all I ever have."

"You can't keep your strength up that way."

"I haven't needed to until now. Tell the cook to serve something with meat for dinner," he told Dodie. "I feel a weak spell coming on."

Lily jerked her wrist from Zac's grip. She glared at him angrily. "I will not be made fun of. I don't know a lot, but I'm not stupid."

"Nobody ever said you were stupid."

"You're treating me like I am."

Zac could tell she was truly upset. He hadn't meant to distress her. He was just talking foolishness the way he always did. It was part of his patter. Everybody expected it of him. The customers loved it. Nobody took his sarcasm personally, not even drunks who were losing more than they could afford. Why did this innocent from the Virginia hills have to be different?

"Here," Dodie said, shoving another cup of coffee into

his hand, "have some more. While you're at it, ask her what kind of work she can do."

Zac didn't want any more coffee. He didn't want to get to know Lily. He didn't care what kind of job she took as long as she let him sleep.

But he reined in his temper, his impatience, his desire to pretend this last hour had been just a dream. It wasn't her fault that he extended invitations he didn't mean or that her view of the world was practically the opposite of his. He had to help her find a job so she could begin to take care of herself. Then he could get some sleep.

"I didn't mean to hurt your feelings," Zac said. "Ignore a lot of what I say. It's not worth listening to anyway."

"Papa says you shouldn't say anything unless it's worth saying."

"I was sure your papa would have something to say on the subject," Zac said, the edge back in his voice. "He seems to have something to say about everything."

Lily looked abashed. "I guess I shouldn't always be telling you what Papa says."

"Maybe not so early in the morning," Dodie said.

"Not at all," Zac said. "Now stop looking like you're about to cry and tell me about yourself. Sit down. You might as well begin by telling me why you decided to come all the way to California, and why you don't want to go back."

"Are you sure you wouldn't like some coffee, too?" Dodie asked Lily.

"No. Papa says . . . no."

"You probably wanted to get away from all those *Papa says*," Zac said, seating himself again. "The man must talk nonstop to get all this mumbo-jumbo said, even if he does get a head start by getting up at six o'clock. Okay, start explaining," Zac said when she seemed reluctant to begin.

"I didn't want to marry a minister," Lily said.

Zac thought she ought to be married. It would be the safest thing for her, but it would be a shame to waste her on a mountain minister. He'd probably keep her in black bonnets and prayer meetings for the rest of her life and fail to appreciate her intelligence or her wonderfully open, accepting nature. He'd probably insist she stay at home, away from anyone who might be a bad influence on her. It would never occur to him that her influence for good might be even stronger.

Aloud, Zac said, "Is that all you're afraid of?"

"It seems like enough to me," Dodie threw in.

"It is quite enough," Lily agreed. "Would you like to be a rancher like George and the twins?"

"God forbid!" Zac said. "I hate cows. Not to mention the dirt, smell, and aches and pains from riding a horse all day and sleeping on the ground all night."

"Being married to Hezekiah wouldn't be that bad," Lily conceded.

"Hezekiah!" Zac exclaimed. "Why would any rational woman name her baby Hezekiah?"

Lily smiled. "Hezekiah quite likes his name. He thinks it suits him."

"Does it?"

"Unfortunately, it does, which is another reason I don't wish to marry him. He's not terribly nice looking—"

"Couldn't be and be named Hezekiah," Zac interpolated.

"—but he's very good and absolutely honest."

"Sounds like a dead bore," Zac concluded.

Lily sighed. "I admire him a lot, but he would never let me learn to dance. Do you think I could try that kick tomorrow?"

Zac was forced to admit Hezekiah might know a thing or two when it came to Lily. One thing very often led to another until you found yourself in a pickle and wondering just how you got there.

"There must have been somebody else who wanted to marry you," Zac said, hoping to get her mind off the high kick. "I can't imagine a girl like you not having a gaggle of swains panting after her."

Zac didn't know why he was talking so much or pretending to be interested in Lily's private life. It wasn't the least bit like him. It must be the lack of sleep. He was so muddled he didn't know what he was doing.

"Papa would never allow it."

"Didn't that man have anything to do besides watch over you? Surely, even in Salem, there must have been some stray sheep that needed rounding up."

Lily sighed. "He didn't have to watch me. On my fifteenth birthday, he announced in church that it was the Lord's will I be Hezekiah's wife. He said terrible things would happen to anybody who tried to interfere with this divine plan."

"Did anybody try?"

"I'm afraid not. Would you?"

"Probably not. I imagine it would be terribly hard to be romantic and sweep a girl off her feet when you're worried about bolts of lightning, plagues of frogs, and those bugs that eat everything up."

"Locusts."

"That's it. Did you tell your Papa you didn't want to marry this dull Hezekiah?"

"I told him over and over, but Papa never listens to females. He says women should be seen and not heard."

Since he had been known to utter the same sentiment, Zac moved on. "What did your mother have to say?"

"She likes Hezekiah. She thinks I would be perfectly happy."

Zac leaned back in his chair and put his feet on the table. "Why wouldn't you? You're always quoting the Bible and rattling off everything your papa says."

"Papa thinks I'm a sinner in the making."

"You!" Zac yelped. He sat up so quickly that he jostled the table. Coffee sloshed out of his cup. He ignored it. Dodie cleaned it up. "What did you ever do that you couldn't shout from the rooftops?"

"I like to laugh and go to parties. I like to have people tell me I'm pretty. I want to dance."

"My, what an evil child you are," Zac said. "And to think I never suspected."

Lily grinned happily. "Did you know I'd never danced before today? Papa forbids it. Hezekiah agrees. He says his wife must be above reproach, a model for the community. He says I would have to wear my hair under a bonnet. He thinks it's self-indulgent to want people to see it."

"He's probably looking forward to having you all to himself and doesn't want anybody getting ideas," Zac said. That hair would do more than give a man ideas. It had given him a few already, and he wasn't the least bit interested in the only kind of relationship that was suitable with a woman like Lily.

"Hezekiah isn't like that," Lily said. "He says ministers must inure themselves to the lures of the flesh."

Zac nearly choked. "Sounds like you got out of Salem in the nick of time. I don't know that the hell I'm going to do with you, but I couldn't send you back to a place like that. Sounds like everybody's a little bit crazy."

"I think the word's *holy*," Dodie said.

"Any man who can look at Lily and say he's beyond the lure of the flesh is either crazy or missing some important parts."

"Do you think I'm pretty?" Lily asked.

"Of course I do," Zac said. "Any man would."

Zac saw the gleam in Lily's eyes and immediately started to feel uneasy. He'd been around enough women to know what that meant. Lily would want him to spend the next hour telling her how pretty she was, discussing each part of her as if she could be pulled apart and put back together again. He never could see how a man could get excited about a pair of eyelashes. They were nothing but a bunch of little hairs.

"Tell you what," Zac said, before Lily could ask the question she had opened her mouth to ask. "I think you ought to visit Rose. With the twins away at school, she'd love the company. It's dull as ditch water in South Texas."

"I'm not going to any ranch in Texas," Lily said. "That would be worse than living in Salem."

"It would," Zac agreed. "I've lived on the Circle Seven. Even the cows are glad to leave. How about Madison? He's got five boys. He'd never even know you were there."

"I'm tired of being surrounded by men. They think the entire world has to revolve around what they want."

"That's Madison to the life," Zac agreed. "Well, there's no help for it. You'll have to go stay with Tyler and Daisy at the hotel."

"What hotel?" Lily asked.

"She can't stay at the Palace," Dodie said.

"Why not?" Zac demanded. "It the best hotel in San Francisco. Hell, it's the best hotel in the West."

"That's what everybody thinks who's lucky enough to end up with a few hundred dollars in their pocket," Dodie informed him. "Is that the kind of people you want hanging around your cousin?"

Zac thought of the last time he had been in the Palace bar. Might as well throw Lily into a den of lions. She'd be devoured before the night was over.

"I guess you're stuck with Bella Holt." Zac got to his feet. "Time to see about finding you a job, one that starts bright and early and won't give you a minute to yourself until six o'clock."

"So I can't possibly wake you up again."

"Exactly," Zac replied, not the least abashed. "My head's still not working right. I doubt I'll be able to remember half of what I've said."

"I'll remind you," Lily offered. "My head is quite clear. I think morning is a wonderful time of day."

Zac groaned. "It's a good thing we aren't going to see much of each other."

"We aren't?" Lily asked, dismayed.

"How could we? You'll be working all day. By the time I get my eyes open, you'll be ready for a quick supper and a topple into bed so you'll be ready to go the next day."

"Maybe I could come here when I finish work," Lily said. "I could talk to Dodie, if she doesn't mind, or some of the other girls. I won't bother you."

"I don't think that's such a good idea," Zac said. He could just hear what Rose would say about leading young girls astray. He might be twenty-six, but to Rose he would always be a six-year-old in need of her guidance.

"I don't know anybody else," Lily said. "I'll get rather lonely. I promise not to cause trouble."

Lily sent him a look that would have melted a heart of stone. It almost caused him to change his mind, but he didn't because he knew it was the worst thing he could do for Lily. She had no business knowing anything about the life he led. She was so naive, so trusting, she couldn't see anything but the excitement, the glittering surface. Still, she'd never stray very far from her father's teachings. It wouldn't be long before she'd start disapproving of him even more than his family did.

He knew he wouldn't like that.

"You don't understand. You can't—"

"If Mr. Big Britches is too busy, I'll be happy to visit with you," Dodie said. "So will the girls. They like you."

Lily smiled so brightly, seemed so relieved, that Zac suffered a twinge of conscience. He wasn't used to that and didn't like it a bit.

"Come on," Zac said. "Let's go see what we can find in the way of a job."

Lily jumped up and hurried after him.

"What kind of things can you do?" he asked when she caught up with him at the door.

"Oh, just about anything," Lily told him. "I can cook, sew, milk, and clean house. Mama says nobody's better at churning butter than I am."

"I can see this is going to be a snap," Zac muttered. "All I have to do is find a farm in the middle of San Francisco."

"If you don't mind, I'd rather not do any of those things."

"Nonsense," Zac said, turning to face her. "Cooking's the natural choice. I know the perfect place."

The sun was much too strong. He had to shade his eyes. Even then he could only make out Lily's shape. "Come on. Don't drag your feet. You wanted a job. I'm going to get you one."

Charlie Drayton owed him a favor. Besides, he always needed a cook. Zac practically dragged Lily down a narrow alley and through the back door of Charlie's Homestyle Restaurant. They stepped into a kitchen, already filled with the smell of food being prepared for the midday meal.

Charlie was cutting up a piece of beef. His apron was covered with blood stains and bits of meat. So were his arms up to his elbows. His two assistants were equally soiled. Everything in sight—pots and pans, stoves, ovens, walls, floor, curtains, the cooks—seemed to be covered with a layer of grease. The smell of burning oil, cooking lamb, and garlic caused Zac's nose to quiver in distaste. Heat from the ovens made the kitchen miserably hot.

Zac had never realized a kitchen could be so unpleasant.

Charlie paused in his work. "What are you doing in here?" he asked, never taking his eyes off Lily.

"I want you to give my cousin a job," Zac said, his certainty that this was the perfect solution for Lily fading. "She says she can cook."

"Great. I can always use more help. What's your specialty?"

"Opossum," Lily answered promptly.

"What?" Charlie asked, stunned.

"Opossum," she repeated.

"She's just kidding," Zac said, nearly as shocked as Charlie. "Tell him what you really cook."

"I'm also good with coon and squirrel. I can do rabbit, but not as well."

"I might as well ask my customers to eat rats."

75

"I've never tried rats, but I don't imagine they're very different from squirrels."

"Pork," Zac said, revolted by the images that filled his mind. "You can cook pork."

"I can cook hog bellies at least five different ways," Lily said as though one could actually take pride in such a questionable talent. "Everybody says I make the best pickled pig's feet in Salem. Of course, it takes a while for them to set up before you can serve them."

"Do they ever eat beef where you come from?" Charlie asked.

"Sure. Mama makes this blood sausage—"

Charlie turned back to the piece of beef he was working on. He hit it a good whack with the cleaver. It fell into two pieces of equal size. "I don't think I need a cook right now. Why don't you take her over to Chinatown? Maybe they eat some of that stuff she cooks."

Chapter Six

"You did that on purpose," Zac said when they were once more on the boardwalk.

"Did what?" Lily asked, her gaze wide and innocent.

"Told him you could only cook those ghastly things. Does anybody in Salem actually eat that stuff?"

Lily laughed. Zac didn't hear the least bit of guilt in the sound.

"I really can cook rabbit and squirrel. I've never eaten pickled pig's feet, but I know a lot of people who like them. As for hog belly and blood sausage—"

"Forget I asked!" Zac interrupted, truly horrified anyone would eat such things. "I don't think being a cook is a suitable job for you. I never realized a kitchen was such a dirty place. I can't understand why Tyler likes them so much."

"I imagine his are much cleaner," Lily said. "How about cleaning and sewing?"

"Not those either," Zac said, eliminating the easy

choices. "You need something more suitable for a young lady."

He didn't know why he hadn't thought of that before. It was stupid to think Lily would be comfortable working with Charlie. Besides, it wasn't proper. She was a relation, even if a very distant one. He couldn't have her doing menial labor.

"What do you want to do?" he asked. The sun was in his eyes again. He gave up trying to see her expression and concentrated on getting her as far away from the Barbary Coast as possible.

"I'm not certain. I could work in your saloon. You could teach me."

Zac stopped and stared at her from under his hand once more. "If this is the kind of thinking people do when they get up early, it's a good thing I don't. My saloon's the last place you can work."

"Why?"

"Because everybody would take you for a saloon girl."

"But I would be a saloon girl."

"But you aren't, not inside. A saloon girl likes rough men. At least, she doesn't mind them and knows how to deal with them. A lot of the girls drink and gamble and take men to their rooms. My girls don't, but others do, and the reputation would rub off.

"You could never be like that, so don't argue with me. The sun's making my eyes ache, and that's making my head ache. Purse your lips, try to look as sour as a lemon, and let's see if we can talk old Mrs. Ripple into giving you a job in her dry goods shop."

They couldn't. Mrs. Ripple said she had two sons and a nephew working in the shop and she had no intention of turning them into gaping fools. The proprietors of the next two shops said they didn't need any help at the moment. Zac doubted they'd have hired Lily if they did.

The first one, a butcher shop, was owned by a jolly fat man with a thin wife. The looks she gave Lily were not welcoming. The other shop was owned by a hatchet-faced harridan with a French accent who tried to sell bread to her customers while glaring at them as though she would have preferred to cut their throats. He wasn't surprised when they were shown the door with what he assumed were Gallic curses. His schoolboy French didn't reach that far.

"This isn't going to be easy, is it?" Lily asked.

"I'm not asking in the right places," Zac confessed.

He was awake enough now to have gotten over feeling aggrieved over his loss of sleep. His brain had also begun to function well enough for him to realize there were no suitable places of employment for Lily anywhere near his saloon. If he hadn't been in such a hurry to get rid of her, he would have realized that and not wasted his time. Besides, the farther away from the saloon she worked, the less likely she would be to drop in on him.

But even looking in the right part of town didn't help. It seemed no one needed extra help.

"Nobody will hire her," Zac told Bella Holt when he had escorted Lily back to the rooming house. "If she can't get a job, she'll have to go back to Virginia."

"She won't," Bella said. "We had a long talk last night, and she's dead set against it."

"I know," Zac said gloomily. "She even asked me to let her work in the saloon."

"What did you tell her?"

"I refused. What did you think I'd do?"

"I never know with you."

"Do you think I'm crazy?"

"No, just selfish. I figured you might think she'd bring extra customers into the place."

"She probably would," Zac said, "but they'd be more interested in staring at her than gambling."

"Always thinking of yourself, aren't you?" Bella said.

"Dammit, Bella! I've been thinking of Lily all day. I even decided not to let her take a job cooking or cleaning."

Bella exhaled in disgust. "I know why she hasn't gotten a job."

"Why?"

"Because you're with her."

"What's wrong with me?"

"Look at you. Black coat, mustache, top hat, spotless white shirt and tie, and looking so handsome it's sinful."

"What's wrong with that?" Zac asked, finding nothing to object to in Bella's description.

"Nobody is going to think a woman hanging on your arm is innocent. They'll take one look and be certain she's—"

"You needn't say it," Zac said, hoping this explanation hadn't occurred to Lily. "I'd rather you turn your mind to figuring out how to talk somebody respectable into hiring her."

"What would I get in return?"

Zac had been asked that question too many times not to know how to answer it. Most women he knew were happy to accept money and gifts, maybe even his undivided attention for a short while. But ever since Bella had turned respectable, he never knew what to expect of her.

"I'm not cutting the interest on your loan," he said.

"I didn't ask you to."

Zac could tell from the tightness of her expression and the slight rigidity of her posture that that was exactly what she had meant to ask. "Now stop trying to look like a Mormon and tell me how I'm going to find Lily a suitable job."

"You aren't," Bella said. "I am. For a fee."

"How much?"

"A week's room and board for each day it takes."

Damned steep, but cheap if it allowed him to sleep. "Done. Can you start before nine o'clock tomorrow?"

"Why? Nobody opens until after ten."

"Then you've got to do something to keep her busy. Make her change clothes half a dozen times, or fix her hair a dozen different ways."

"Why?"

"If you don't keep her here, she'll come wake me up again."

"Wake you up?"

"She broke into my bedroom before ten o'clock. I got less than three hours' sleep. I'm so groggy I tried to get that fish-faced bread woman to give her a job."

"Mrs. Boulanger?"

"That's the one."

Bella went off in a peal of laughter. For a moment she sounded like the Bella of old. Zac liked the old Bella better, but she needed respectability, and he needed her to be respectable for Lily.

"I wish I could have seen that," Bella said.

"I'd have been happy to give you my place," Zac said. "Now before Lily comes back downstairs and conjures up something else for me to do, I'm off. If I don't get a few hours' sleep, I'm liable to lose my shirt before dawn."

"You could always give up gambling."

"You're beginning to sound like Rose."

"Smart woman."

"That's why I stay as far away from her as I can. Let me know how you get along with Lily tomorrow."

Zac made his escape.

"Where's Zac?" Lily asked when she came downstairs. She had hoped to talk him into taking her back to the saloon for the afternoon. She liked the girls. She liked their bright smiles and good spirits. Most of all she liked their sense of freedom, the feeling they could do what they wanted and not worry what anybody else thought about it. She'd never felt that way in her entire life. It seemed like a wonderful way to feel.

"He had to catch a few hours' sleep," Bella said. "You wouldn't want him so sleepy he'd lose his saloon, would you?"

"No, nothing like that. I was just hoping . . ."

"I know. That's what every woman hopes who meets

81

Zac. But hope is as far as it gets.''

"Oh, I don't mean like that. I—''

"I know exactly what you mean, but we're not going to sit around the house all afternoon. I'm going to take you to meet my minister. Don't worry,'' she said when Lily frowned. "He's not nearly so strict as your father.''

Lily didn't feel comfortable in the severe parlor of the Right Reverend Harold Thoragood. She realized this must be how other people felt when they came to call on her father, but that didn't make it any better.

"Lily is new to San Francisco,'' Bella was explaining to Mr. Thoragood.

"Do you have family here?'' Mr. Thoragood asked.

"Yes. I have two cousins.''

"Would I know them?'' Mr. Thoragood asked.

Bella frowned, but Lily plunged ahead. "I'm sure you do,'' she said smiling brightly. "One is named Tyler Randolph. He owns the Palace Hotel. The other is Zac Randolph, his brother. He owns the Little Corner of Heaven on Pacific Street.''

Mr. Thoragood grew stiffer than a starched shirt drying in the wind.

"I strongly encourage you to have nothing to do with him,'' Mr. Thoragood said. "I'm certain your father wouldn't want you even to know such a man.''

Lily decided it probably wasn't a good idea to tell Mr. Thoragood she was running away from her father, but she wasn't about to let a stranger talk about Zac like that, not and think she agreed with him.

"I don't know what you've been told about Zac, but if it's to his disadvantage, you've been misinformed. He took me to Mrs. Holt as soon as I arrived. Then he offered to provide me with anything I might need until I could find employment.''

"I'm sure he did, but you can't—''

"He's been so kind and helpful. I won't have you speaking against him."

"He's only telling you this for your own good," Bella assured her. "I would have told you myself, but I thought it would be better coming from Mr. Thoragood."

"He may be quite sincere in his desire to help you," Mr. Thoragood conceded, "but he's a gambler and a womanizer. If you wish to have any reputation at all, you will stay away from him and his place of business."

"My father has always preached against gambling," Lily said, "but now I wonder if he knows very much about it. He said saloons were pits of vice, nests of sin, and sinks of degradation."

"He was right," Mr. Thoragood said.

"But everybody there was very kind to me." She directed a look at Mr. Thoragood. "I don't plan to depend on my cousin or anyone else for my support, but I can't let you malign Zac without meeting him. Even my father wouldn't do that."

"Lily's father is a minister," Bella interjected in a manner that indicated she was anxious to calm waters that seemed to be growing troubled.

Mr. Thoragood positively beamed. "Is his congregation close by? I believe I know most of the ministers from here to Sacramento."

"He's in Salem," Lily said.

"I don't know a town by that name."

"It's in Virginia."

For a moment he looked blank. "Do you mean the Virginia all the way across the country?"

Lily nodded.

"I wonder he should have let you come so far."

At those sharply spoken words, the three people in the parlor looked up to see a woman who Lily assumed was Mrs. Thoragood.

"As long as she's in Mrs. Holt's care, we can feel perfectly comfortable about her," Mr. Thoragood assured his wife, his smile not quite as broad now. "Shall I see you in our congregation this Sunday?" Mr. Thoragood asked Lily.

"I've barely had time to think about it," Lily said. "I've been so worried about getting a job."

"One should think of the church first," Mrs. Thoragood intoned. "If one does that first, all else will follow."

She sounded exactly like Papa.

"I'm sure she does think of the church, my dear, but you must admit it's very worrying to be without employment."

"I've undertaken to find her a job," Bella said in a manner that was positively fawning.

Lily decided she liked Bella better when she wasn't around Mrs. Thoragood.

"In that case, I shall have no worry," Mrs. Thoragood said with a tight smile. "Now I'm afraid you'll have to excuse us. Harold has an appointment."

Lily jumped to her feet before Bella could prolong their visit. "I shall look forward to hearing you speak," she said, extending her hand first to Mrs. Thoragood and then to her husband.

"You are in for a treat," Bella said. "Mr. Thoragood could cause the Devil himself to quake."

"He would," Sarah Thoragood said, her expression growing positively sour, "if we could ever get him inside the church. What's the good of all those words when the men who need to hear them are lying drunk in an alley or in a bed not their own?"

Lily wondered why she felt so certain Mrs. Thoragood was referring to Zac. She also wondered why she resented it so much.

"Then he should go out and find them," Lily said.

"That's impossible," Bella replied.

"Papa would find them." He would find Zac and preach the devil right out of him. Once again Lily started to wonder why that should disturb her, unless it was that she liked Zac just the way he was, devil and all. She knew that was wrong, but somehow it didn't change the way she felt.

"What are you smiling about?" Mrs. Thoragood asked, suspicion in her voice.

"I was just thinking about San Francisco and being glad I'm here. It's such a beautiful city."

Lily wasn't used to telling lies, not even little ones, but no one would understand if she told the truth. She was thinking about Mr. Thoragood storming into Zac's bedroom, shaking him awake, only to find himself staring at a sinner lying stark naked in the bed.

A giggle escaped her.

"You're laughing at my husband, aren't you?" Mrs. Thoragood accused her.

"I don't find him the least bit funny," Lily assured her.

"Good. Trying to save the souls of these sinners"—she waved her hand to indicate most of the inhabitants of San Francisco—"is a mighty serious business. We can use all the help we can get."

"I'll be happy to do anything I can."

Mrs. Thoragood considered Lily for a moment. "I'm not sure you're exactly what we need. You look more like an invitation to sin than an agent of retribution."

Lily decided that was quite the nicest thing anybody had said to her all day.

Zac didn't come down until nearly eight o'clock that evening. The saloon was filled with men laughing, shouting, and cursing their luck. The players at his favorite poker table were into their fourth game.

"I was beginning to think we weren't going to see you again today," Dodie said. "Did your little cousin wear you out?"

"Stop trying to get a rise out of me," Zac said, his sunny mood completely restored by his long sleep. "I couldn't get anybody to hire her, so I turned her over to Bella. She's under strict orders to get her a job that starts before nine o'clock and doesn't end until at least six."

Dodie laughed. "Are there any such jobs?"

"Apparently there are lots of them. I had no idea people kept such ridiculous hours."

"It's a natural thing to rise with the sun," Dodie said.

"Not for me. Now stop picking at me and direct me to the richest game on for tonight. I'm feeling particularly lucky."

He didn't feel that way when he trudged up to bed at about five-thirty. He had suffered through the worst run of bad luck he could remember ever having. He'd been lucky to end the night with the shirt still on his back.

He told himself it was the natural swing of the pendulum, that after drawing a royal flush, he could expect bad luck to balance things out. But he hadn't won a single hand. At least a dozen times his hands had been so bad he'd thrown down his cards without even making a bet.

He hoped that this run of bad luck had nothing to do with Lily, that it wasn't the result of a curse her father had put on him for enticing his daughter away from the safety of her home.

No, he was being foolish. Tomorrow things would be different. Tomorrow he wouldn't be awakened at nine o'clock.

He wasn't all wrong. He was awakened at eight o'clock by Lily shaking him and chirping in a disgustingly cheerful voice, "Wake up! Wake up. I got a job."

"Wonderful," Zac muttered then buried his head under the pillow.

"Don't you want to hear about it?"

"No."

"You've got to. I have nobody else to tell."

"Tell Dodie."

"She's busy."

The merciless shaking continued. Next thing he knew, the pillow was jerked out of his grasp, and he was staring directly into a beautiful face that dazzled him quite as much

86

as the sunlight that streamed through the windows with appalling intensity.

Zac slammed his eyelids shut, but he was too late. The brilliant rays had pierced his eyeballs and slammed into the center of his brain with explosive force. He probably wouldn't have felt any worse if he had had a hangover.

"You're not going to go away, are you?" he asked, peering at her out of one eye.

"I ought to, but you've got to get up."

"If you leave, I won't get up."

Zac didn't know what perverse desire to inflict torture on himself had caused him to utter those words. He had actually asked her to stay, to ruin his rest, to make him miserable.

He must be insane.

True, there was this tiny part of him that wasn't entirely sure it wanted her to go away, but it was a very tiny part. He was generally able to ignore impulses that had insanity written all over them. Besides, she was a flower woman. He knew he was walking on thin ice already. Inviting her into his bedroom was the same as racing headlong toward the thinnest patch of all.

No woman had ever had this effect on him. He didn't know what caused it, but it was making him feel decidedly odd.

Maybe it wasn't Lily at all. Maybe it was something he'd eaten. He'd have to ask the chef about the mussels. If the seafood caused customers to feel like this, they'd start eating elsewhere.

"Dodie says I'm to bring you downstairs directly," Lily said. "She says I'm to tell you Josie is ruined and the enforcers have gone to bring in the gull. I have no idea what she's talking about, but she says you'll understand."

Zac groaned louder. "I told that silly girl what would happen if she kept hanging around that useless layabout. She ought to know you can never trust a gambler."

Zac sat up and started to throw back the covers, but his

hand paused in mid-air. "You'd better go back downstairs while I get dressed."

"I'll wait," she said. "Dodie said it would move you faster."

"I'm naked, and you don't like that."

"I'll keep my eyes closed until you reach the bathroom. If you leave the door slightly ajar, we can talk while you dress."

Zac knew he ought to insist that she leave, but he didn't have the energy. "Turn around."

When she did, he grabbed his sheet and made off to the bathroom at a very undignified trot. He made haste to run his bathwater. He was in and out in five minutes. If he was lucky, she'd be through talking without his having heard a single word.

But when he got out of the tub, the suite was silent. He dried himself, put on his underclothes and his pants, and sat down to shave.

"Now that you're through with your bath, I'll tell you about my job."

Zac looked up to see one blue eye peering through the open door. He jumped. Fortunately he was working up his lather. He most certainly would have cut himself if he'd been shaving.

"I'm sure your papa would be horrified if he knew what you were doing."

"I used to bring him his shaving water and take it away again when he was done."

"Well, mine will disappear down this drain."

"Where does it go?" Lily asked.

"I don't know. Probably into the bay."

"How does it get there?"

"Through pipes."

"Do all houses have them?"

"I guess so."

"Bella's doesn't. Where does the hot water come from?"

"This pipe." Zac turned a knob and steaming water came out.

"Papa and the boys would love this," Lily said. "Papa's always complaining the water's too hot or too cold, and the boys hate chopping and carrying wood. Does the bath work the same?"

"Yes." It was strange to see Lily marvel at things he had come to take for granted.

"Can I take a bath in it sometime?"

"I don't think so. You'll have to be satisfied with Bella's."

For once Lily didn't ask why. Zac was relieved.

"What's this?" she asked.

"It's a commode," Zac said, wondering how to explain it. "Water takes everything away when you're done."

Lily looked at it in amazement.

"Mama and Papa would never believe half of this. I'm not sure I do."

"You'll get used to it," Zac said. "Now before it gets any later, I'd better get shaved. Bring in a chair and tell me about your job."

Lily brought a chair in from the bedroom and sat. Zac's lather had gotten dry. He had to wash it off and make some more.

"It was the most unexpected thing," Lily began. "Last night Bella took me to visit one of her friends, a perfectly charming old lady. It turns out she had just the job for me—working in a women's clothing store. You know, where they sell all the garments men aren't supposed to see."

"I probably know more about them than you." Zac smiled wickedly into the mirror.

"I'm to start at twelve o'clock today," Lily said, apparently considering his remark too dangerous to pursue. "I had to come tell you. I knew you'd want to know. Bella was rather put out that she wasn't going to earn any commission, but I assured her you'd pay her anyway."

"You're mighty generous with my money," Zac said,

then immediately regretted it. Lily looked conscience-stricken. "Forget it. I was only kidding. You know gamblers, always happier to spend somebody else's money than their own."

"I know nothing about gamblers except what Papa used to say, but you're not as bad as that."

Zac had an annoying urge to ask her why she didn't believe the worst about him, but he fought it down. Once a man started wondering what a woman thought, there was no end to the foolish questions he might ask.

"Why don't you go tell Dodie all about it." He wanted her downstairs. He wasn't comfortable with her sitting with him while he got dressed. The situation felt positively domestic. Anything of that nature sent chills up and down his spine.

"I tried to tell her," Lily said, "but she was too upset about Josie. She said you'd want to know immediately. I guess you should hurry. I cut my story quite short so I wouldn't make you late."

Zac had to give her credit. It was obviously possible for her to talk less and say more. Since he had a notion he was going to see a lot of her, that thought cheered him considerably.

Zac had always liked women—but he liked them on his terms. That meant he thought of them when he was with them but could hardly remember what they looked like when they weren't standing in front of him. He didn't think of himself as using women or being unkind to them. The enjoyment was mutual, any warm feelings transitory.

Zac finished shaving. He opened his closet to choose something to wear. His gaze landed on a coat with maroon velvet lapels and cuffs. Then he remembered he was going to a wedding today. He reached for a plain black suit.

He wasn't exactly having warm feelings for Lily—how could he when she'd caused him nothing but trouble?—but thoughts of her kept filling his mind. Haunting him, more like. He kept feeling he was a sinner, she the angel sent to save him. Because he was such an unregenerate sinner, they'd sent him the most beautiful, helpless angel they had.

It wasn't fair to send him a seemingly defenseless female. Everybody knew that Southern chivalry was deeply embedded in his family. He'd worked hard to dig it out, root and branch, but it only needed Lily's appearance to show him he still had a lot of it left.

He struggled with the starched collar. The damned thing was well nigh impossible to button. He wished inventors would stop messing around with light bulbs and horseless carriages and come up with a shirt with an attached collar. He cursed when the collar button spurted out of his grasp and rolled behind the clothes hamper. He got down on his hands and knees to look for it, but Lily was ahead of him. She found it with no trouble. With nimble fingers, she pushed it through his collar.

"I used to fix Papa's collar all the time. Give me the others."

Zac handed her the other buttons. For a sanctimonious old puritan, Isaac Sterling had given his daughter license to do a number of things that made Zac uncomfortable.

Zac didn't know why such a simple thing as the feel of Lily's fingers on his neck should agitate him, but it did. Her touch was light, gentle, almost feathery, but it stirred something quite remarkable in him, a liking for this nearness, this kind of companionable intimacy.

He heard a knock at the door. "Answer it," he told Lily, anxious to get a little more space between them until he could understand what was happening to him.

"It's Dodie," Lily said, coming back almost immediately. "She says the gull is here and willing. She says you're to hurry before he changes his mind. I thought a gull was a bird."

It wasn't safe to let Lily loose in a town like San Francisco, Zac thought, not for the first time. No telling what kind of trouble she would get into. Moreover, knowing her, she'd bring it all to him.

Zac slipped into his coat, checked his image in the mirror, and gave his hair a few brushes. "A gull is a man you talk into doing something he doesn't want to do."

"Like what?" Lily asked.

"Marrying Josie."

Chapter Seven

"Is that the gull?" Lily whispered to Dodie when Zac went straight to a man who looked far too angry to be on the verge of getting married.

"That's the miserable bastard!" Dodie said. "Sorry, I forgot you don't like cussing."

"I didn't know any cuss words until I met Zac," Lily confessed.

"You're kidding me," Dodie said.

"Men never cuss in front of women back home. Not Mama and me, anyway. Papa disapproved of it. He said it was the result of a small mind and a limited vocabulary."

"Not in this case," Dodie said, indicating the man who was arguing with Zac.

"If he's so bad, why do you want Josie to marry him?"

"I don't. I think she ought to shoot him, give her baby up for adoption, and forget the whole thing. But Saint Zac won't allow it. He says any gal who gets pregnant has to marry the father of her baby. He says there's nothing worse for a kid than growing up without parents."

Lily wondered what Zac's parents could have done to make him feel like that. She'd heard stories about his father all her life. Her father used him as an example. According to him, if the Devil had ever walked on earth, it had been in the person of William Henry Randolph. She thought Zac was better off not having known his father.

"Does Zac miss having parents?"

"He must," Dodie said, keeping a close eye on the progress of the discussion, which was threatening to get violent. "Although he has so many brothers, I don't see how he could have noticed they weren't there."

Lily knew all about Zac's brothers. She also knew they had spoiled him, but that wasn't the same as having parents.

"Where's Josie?" she asked Dodie.

"I sent her upstairs. I didn't want her to see the object of her dreams having to be forced to do the decent thing."

"She wants to marry him?"

"Can't wait. She wouldn't give any man the time of day until this one came along." Dodie snorted. "Just look at him. I've seen better specimens washed out of the gutter after a heavy rain. Can you figure?"

Actually Lily could. If she loved a man enough to have his baby, she'd want to marry him. Even if he did have faults.

"What's his name?" Lily asked.

"Cat Bemis," Dodie said, disgust heavy in her voice. "Would you want to marry that man?"

Lily hadn't the slightest desire to marry Mr. Bemis, but she could see his attraction. He was tall, well-muscled, and young. He was in a temper just now, but he seemed more angry than mean. He probably didn't like being forced into things, even something he might want to do. She had discovered that most men didn't.

"Uh-oh," Dodie said. "They're going into the office. That means Zac is about to apply the clincher."

"What's that?" Lily asked, expecting to hear it was some kind of special gun.

"He'll offer to lend them enough cash to get set up somewhere."

"Why would he do a thing like that?" Lily asked, stunned. "Why should he care that much?"

"I don't know. Why don't you ask him? If you get an answer, it'll be more than the rest of us have ever gotten."

"Oh, I'd never do that."

"Why?"

"Men hate to be asked questions, especially about themselves."

"It would serve him right. I told him not to bring her here, that she was going to be trouble, but he insisted I give her a job."

"Zac brought her here!"

"Lord, yes. He picks up every helpless stray he finds. Half the girls upstairs are here because he found them down on their luck. He brings them here, gives them a job, and expects me to train them. All he asks is that they walk the straight and narrow."

"What straight and narrow?"

"I could never tell," Dodie said. "It seems to be different with each girl. If I didn't know he spent his nights gambling with every kind of two-bit crook who washes into a place like this, I'd swear there was something of the preacher in him."

Lily couldn't help but laugh. If Dodie thought there was anything about Zac that even remotely resembled a preacher, she hadn't seen any real preachers. He was too good looking, too charming, too happy. He gambled and stayed up late. According to Papa, he also did a lot of other things, but Papa had never told her what they were, just that they were sure to lead him straight to the Devil.

Lily thought it would be a shame for such an attractive man to be swallowed up by the Devil. There was a great deal more to Zac than either Dodie or her father knew. Any man who took so much trouble to look after women in distress couldn't be all bad, even if he did sleep during the day and do she hadn't the slightest idea what all night. He not only cared about what happened to Josie and her baby. He was prepared to do something about it. Wouldn't her father be surprised to find a gambler playing the good Samaritan?

No, he wouldn't believe it.

But Lily did. She couldn't forget what he'd done for her. He hadn't wanted her on his hands, but since she had told him about her father's plans to marry her to Hezekiah, he hadn't said a word about sending her back to Virginia.

No matter how close Zac had trod to the gates of hell, Lily was convinced he'd never stepped inside.

In that moment, Lily decided she had been sent to San Francisco to save Zac Randolph. She accepted her charge as solemnly as if it had been delivered by the archangel Gabriel himself.

Zac got up from the table in disgust. He hadn't won enough money in the last five nights to pay for his dinner. He could hardly have had worse cards if his worst enemy had chosen them for him.

"Your luck finally desert you?" Chet Lee asked. He hated Zac and made no attempt to disguise the pleasure in his voice.

"Seems that way," Zac said. He looked at the chips piled in front of Lee. "Yours seems to be almost as good as mine is bad."

"Yeah," Chet said. "It almost makes me think you run a clean house. Almost," Chet added with a sarcastic edge to his voice.

The expressions on the faces ringing the table grew rigid.

"You always say that when you're losing," Zac said. "I'm sure you'll be saying it again soon enough." He didn't smile at Chet because he didn't feel like it.

"I won't have to until you start playing again."

Zac did smile then, but it was a dangerous smile. "I know your kind, Chet. You can't stand to think you're not the

best. You come here only because you know you can beat
me.''

"Sure, like that time in—"

"This table's closed for tonight, fellas. Chet's going to
cash in his winnings and go home."

"I'm not through!" Furious, Chet jumped to his feet so
quickly that he upset the table. Chips and cards spilled onto
the floor and rolled in all directions.

Play came to a halt at neighboring tables as the gamblers
stopped to stare at the thousands of dollars worth of chips
rolling around the floor. Only Zac's presence kept the men
from diving after them. That and the two huge bouncers who
seemed to materialize out of nowhere to take hold of Chet
Lee, one on each side.

"You sorry son of a bitch!" Chet shouted. "You're too
much of a coward to fight your own battles."

"I pay to have my garbage hauled away," Zac said.

Zac never considered banning Chet permanently. Better
the devil he knew than one he didn't.

Chet struggled to break away. One of the bouncers, easily
half again as big as Chet, twisted Chet's arm behind him
until Chet finally went still.

"He's packing a gun," the man said to Zac. "I can feel
it."

Zac felt his blood turn cold. The rest of the saloon faded
from his vision until he could see only Chet and the men
around him. Zac didn't allow guns. No saloon owner could
afford to, not with the dangerous mixture of gambling and
whiskey.

"Seems you just can't follow any rules, Chet," Zac said
as he threw Chet's coat open. Chet struggled, but the men
had no trouble holding him.

"It's strapped to his back," the bouncer said.

They stripped Chet of his coat. He wore an ingenious
holster, invisible from the front, that held a small pistol. Zac
took the pistol. It held just two bullets, but that was enough
to kill two men.

And ruin Zac's business.

"Give him his chips, boys," Zac said, tossing Chet his coat, "and help him to the front door."

"They're all on the floor," one of the gamblers said. "How're we going to make out who gets how much?"

Zac glanced down at the floor and a broad grin spread slowly over his face. "Now look what you've done," he said to Chet. "You've mixed everything up so nobody can tell what belongs to whom. Divide the chips equally, boys."

"Most of that's my money!" Chet Lee roared.

"I know, but no one knows how much," Zac said, his voice deceptively pleasant. "The only thing I can see to do is divide the chips among all the players except me. I already lost mine."

Chet struggled to break loose, but he was no match for the two bouncers.

"Escort him outside, boys," Zac said. "I'll get one of the cashiers to take his money to him."

Zac turned his back on Chet Lee and walked away.

"I'll kill you for this!" Chet roared. "You've cheated me for the last time."

As he was dragged away, he continued to call Zac by every filthy name he could think of while promising to kill him.

"I can't take that money," one of the gamblers said. "I didn't have more than a hundred left."

"Keep it. Give it to charity or light your cigars with it," Zac said, no longer interested.

"What are you going to do about Chet?" one of the men asked.

"Forget him as quickly as possible."

"But he said he was going to kill you."

"Lots of men get drunk and make threats. Then they sober up and forget all about it. Chet's been threatening to kill me ever since Virginia City."

"What happened there?"

"I won his shares in a gold mine. They turned out to be

worth about a million dollars."

"Damnation! I'd want to kill you myself," one man said.

"He'd just won them off some poor fool with a wife and seven kids. I gave them back."

"You gave them back!" several stunned men said almost in unison.

"Well, some of them," Zac said, grinning despite his irritation at a situation which could have been quite dangerous. "It doesn't pay to be too greedy."

Bella Holt was standing on the steps, her hands on her hips, a forbidding scowl on her face, as Lily came up the sidewalk. Lily turned to the three men who had accompanied her from work to the rooming house.

"I'm certain I would have been perfectly safe walking by myself," she said, "but it was most kind of you to see me home."

"No trouble."

"Glad to do it."

"I'll be delighted to see you home every day."

"Go on about your business," Bella ordered as she came halfway down the steps.

"They were only trying to help," Lily said, as she started to climb the twenty steps from the street.

"I know what they were trying to do," Bella said, "and I'll not have them doing it around here."

Lily waved to the men before going inside. They waved back, not one of them moving as long as she was in sight.

"You can't be walking the streets trailing men like ribbons from a hat. People will talk. No telling what Mrs. Thoragood will say."

"I only let them accompany me because you said it was unsafe for a woman to walk the streets alone. Zac said the same, so I figured it must be true. I didn't think it would be a good idea for me to be seen walking home with just one man."

"Quite right," Bella said.

"So I let all three accompany me," Lily said, quite pleased with her foresight. "That way nobody can accuse me of behaving imprudently with any one."

Bella groaned. "My dear, three men are not better than one."

"I don't see why not."

"No men are better than one or three or a dozen."

"I'd never let a dozen escort me home," Lily said. "There wouldn't be room for them on the sidewalk."

Zac had just won his third big pot of the evening when Lily walked into the saloon. The oddest wash of feelings swept through him. He felt pleased, irritated, relieved, and apprehensive, all at the same time. He had never been prey to such contradictory emotions.

He looked at his cards. Another winning hand. He needed it. He'd hardly won anything since the night Lily arrived. Why couldn't she have waited until tomorrow night?

But then Lily looked at him with those robin's-egg-blue eyes, and resentment died. With a barely audible sigh, he laid his hand down on the table and got up.

When he did, he realized every man within fifty feet was staring at Lily as if there were no other females in the saloon. All around him wheels spun unheeded, counters paused in mid-air, and sentences remained unfinished.

All the protective and possessive instincts that had been bred into male Randolphs for generations came rearing and snorting out of their long confinement. He had to get her out of the saloon as quickly as possible. In the meantime, if any man so much as touched her, he'd pitch him out into the street.

He took Lily by the arm and hurried her toward the room he and Dodie used for an office. "I told you not to come here again."

"I had to," Lily said, almost stumbling to keep up with him. "I wrote to you twice. I waited, but you didn't come."

Zac thought of the two notes crumpled in a coat pocket

somewhere in his closet. He had read them but decided it would be better if he didn't go. It was nothing Bella couldn't handle.

"I've been busy," he said.

"You just didn't want to bother. You probably thought I was going to cause you more trouble," she said as he ushered her into his office. "And you're right."

"What have you done this time?"

"I haven't *done* anything."

He could see she was agitated. He hoped the problem wasn't too serious. He was eager to get back to his game.

"Then why did you say you were about to cause me trouble?"

"Because I've lost my job," she said, on the verge of tears.

Zac found himself reaching out and putting his arm around her. "What did you do wrong?" He had expected to feel like a big brother comforting his sister, but there was nothing brotherly about the feelings that jolted him. He guided her to a chair. Once she was seated, he backed away. He didn't trust himself.

"Nothing," Lily said. "At least I don't think I did anything wrong."

"Didn't they tell you why they fired you?" Zac backed up until he could sit on the corner of his desk.

"Mrs. Wellborn said I brought too many new customers into the store."

"That's crazy. She should have been jumping for joy."

"That's what I thought. Well, not exactly jumping—Mrs. Wellborn is nearly seventy—but I did think she'd be pleased. Instead she said I was driving off her other customers."

Lily dabbed her eyes with a handkerchief. Zac started to get up, then thought better of it. He folded his arms across his chest and told himself to sit still.

"It was the men, you see."

"No, I don't see." He should have though. Anything to do with Lily was bound to involve men sooner or later.

101

"Well, all these men kept coming in to buy things for their wives or daughters or mothers. Mrs. Wellborn said she didn't think they had any daughters or mothers, certainly not any who needed as many underclothes as they were buying. She said normally she wouldn't mind the extra business, but she didn't think I'd stay with her long. Then the men would disappear."

Lily paused and looked up at him as if she expected him to say something. Zac got up, went behind his desk, and sat down. "Go on."

"She said all these men were driving her regular customers away. She said they didn't like to see big, rough men putting their hands all over garments they intended to wear next to their skin. I said I thought they looked quite presentable, but she said it was the principle of the thing. She agreed to let me finish out the day, but said I wasn't to come back."

Zac had an unexpected desire to visit Mrs. Wellborn and have a few well-chosen words with her. He rejected the idea for two reasons. First, he'd never had the desire to protect a female in quite the same way he wanted to protect Lily. It confused him and made him uneasy. It wasn't the same thing he felt about Josie and the others. He'd always hated to see women mistreated, but this went beyond that. He wanted to do harm to a little old woman just because she'd hurt Lily's feelings.

In the second place, he wouldn't go because he wasn't in the habit of making a fool of himself. Verbally assaulting an old woman because she'd fired Lily for being too pretty would make him look like a fool, and a lovesick one at that.

Despite the oddness of his feelings at this very moment, Zac knew he wasn't in love. In lust, definitely. In love, no. He might not be very experienced in warm emotions, but he did know the things he wanted to say to Lily, to do to her, were not the things you said and did to a woman you wanted to be your wife.

"You should have asked Bella to help you."

"Mrs. Wellborn is Bella's friend. I expect she feels she did her a disservice by talking her into hiring me."

"That's nonsense," Zac said. "We're going to see Bella right now. It shouldn't take more than a few minutes to get this all cleared up."

It took a little more than that.

"I haven't refused to help her find another job," Bella explained. "But we need to wait a few days until things have time to die down."

"What things?" Zac demanded. "She worked only a few days."

Bella pursed her face in an I-told-you-so expression. "She's been entertaining men."

"You're full of . . . oh, come off it," Zac said, stumbling over his choice of words. "Lily wouldn't know how to entertain men."

"Ask her if she doesn't lend a sympathetic ear to their stories. Ask her if she wasn't seen publicly in their company."

"I couldn't very well tell them not to talk to me," Lily said, "especially when they're making a purchase. As for being seen in public with them, one young man spotted me when I was eating lunch. He's going through a particularly dreadful time. I couldn't turn my back on him when all he asked was that I listen."

"It'll ruin your reputation," Bella said.

Zac decided that respectability didn't agree with Bella. It had turned her into a sanctimonious prude.

"Papa would say a person shouldn't worry about her reputation as long as she's working for the good of mankind."

"That may be fine in Salem," Zac said, "but there are not a lot of good men in San Francisco. You can take it for gospel that if your friend approached you in the street, he's not one of the few.

"Now that that's taken care of," Zac said, turning to

103

Bella, "I don't see why you can't start looking for a job immediately."

"Because of Mrs. Wellborn," Bella said. "She's been talking to everyone who'll listen. In a few days they'll have forgotten. Then we can try again."

"But I must have a job," Lily said. "I can't keep letting Zac pay for everything."

"Don't worry. I'll wait until you can pay me," Bella said.

"I can't do that," Lily objected.

"Then you'll have to go back to Virginia," Zac said. He realized with some surprise that his words didn't sound very convincing, even to himself.

"I'm not going back," Lily said with some asperity. "I've already told you why. I wish you wouldn't refer to it again. You're getting to be tiresome on the subject."

"Me, tiresome!" Zac had been called many things, quite a few of them unflattering, but no one had ever called him tiresome and turned away as if he were a little boy whining about something he couldn't have.

"Close your mouth, Zac," Bella said, not trying very hard to cover a smile.

"I suppose I have no choice but to ask you to let me postpone payment of what I owe you," Lily said reluctantly, "but you've got to let me pay you interest."

Chapter Eight

Lily jumped down from the California Street cable car and picked her way across the cobblestones to the boardwalk. She had turned her ankle once before, and she was taking care it didn't happen again.

She never tired of the view of the bay, the mountains in the distance, the city flowing down the hill to meet the shore. Yet she needed only to turn her head slightly to come face-to-face with the Barbary Coast, the ugly side of San Francisco.

Lily was quite near the young woman before she noticed her. She appeared to be arguing with a man. She looked badly frightened. The man wasn't hurting her, but it was obvious that he wanted her to do something she didn't want to do. She kept shaking her head, trying to draw away from him. He kept reaching out to her, trying to caress her cheek, touch her arm. She appeared to recoil from his touch as much from revulsion as fear.

Lily didn't know where she got the courage to intervene. Actually, she didn't think about it. She just acted.

"There you are, Susan," she said to the stunned girl. "Mama wondered where you'd got to. It's time to start dinner. Papa and the boys will be home from the docks soon."

The man stared at Lily, the poor girl momentarily forgotten. Lily was a little frightened by what she saw in his eyes.

"Why don't you forget your family and come along with me," he said. "They can't be much fun if they keep you dressed in black."

Lily took the girl's hand and started walking away from the man as quickly as she could. The girl looked confused and frightened, but she followed.

So did the man.

"I'll take you both," he offered, running to get in front of them. "I got a friend who'll pay plenty for a bird like you."

"I'm not a bird," Lily told him. "As you can see, I'm completely without feathers. Nor do I squawk, fly, or scratch for worms." She didn't slow her steps.

When the man showed no sign of leaving them alone, she looked around for refuge.

"Aw, come on, let's have a bit of fun. A gal like you could have just about anything she wanted."

"I've got what I want," Lily said. "At least I will when you leave off pestering us."

An ugly expression came over the man's face. Lily didn't think he would assault them in broad daylight on Kearny Street, but she wasn't sure. For the dozenth time, she wished Zac wasn't in the habit of sleeping all day. She would give anything to see his tall frame advancing down the street.

But there was no hope of Zac. He'd be just getting out of bed about now. It was up to her to get this girl safely to Mr. Thoragood's. Once there, she was confident the minister could handle the situation.

The man blocked their path.

"Let me by."

Lily tried to go around, but he moved in front of her.

She'd never had to deal with anyone like this in Salem. She had no idea what to do except run away. But she couldn't with the man blocking her path.

"If you don't move, we're going to be late," she said. "If we don't reach home soon, father and the boys will come looking for us. They're always angry when they have to wait for their supper."

The threat made the man pause long enough for Lily to slip past, but it wasn't long before he was blocking their path again.

"I'll bet you don't have a father. I'll also bet you're not sisters. You're just hoping to catch a bigger fish. Well, not tonight, gals. Tonight the two of you are going to have to settle for me."

Lily might have come from the mountains, but she knew men wanted the same things from women in San Francisco as they did anywhere else. She spied the butcher shop where Zac had tried to get her a job. She didn't know the butcher's name, but she remembered he was a big man and had a wonderful collection of very sharp knives. Taking firm hold on the girl's hand, she darted inside the shop.

The man followed.

The butcher was busy serving a customer, but Lily didn't feel she could wait.

"I'm back. I found Susan strolling along as if she hadn't a worry in the world."

The butcher froze, his knife raised in the act of cutting. He stared slack-jawed at Lily. Lily didn't wait for him to gather his wits. Pulling the girl behind her, she hurried behind the counter and disappeared through a door leading to the back of the butcher shop.

Lily felt as if she'd stumbled into an oversized smoke house. Partially dismembered carcasses of chickens, rabbits, turkeys, ducks, and geese lay on tables, piled in tubs, or hung from racks or nails in the ceiling beams. Larger animals—a beef and a sheep, Lily guessed—hung in what looked like a cold locker. Yards and yards of sausages rested in sacks hung from the ceiling. Livers, gizzards, and parts Lily didn't want to identify lay in piles along a counter.

A very surprised woman looked up from her work.

"I apologize for barging in here," Lily said, "but this young woman and I are being followed by a man who insisted we go with him for purposes I'd rather not have to explain."

"No need," the woman said, immediate understanding and sympathy in her expression. "Where is he now?"

"Out front."

"Don't worry. My husband will take care of him. You can wait here until he's gone."

But Lily didn't want to wait. She was used to helping her mother prepare fresh meat, but this overwhelmed her. Everything seemed raw, red, and bloody. She was certain she'd be unwell if she had to stay here very long. The girl looked as if she felt the same.

"Can we use your back door?" Lily asked.

"Sure. If you go up the alley, you'll come out on Grant Street."

"Thank you," Lily said.

"Where were you going?" she asked the girl once she was certain no one was following.

"I was looking for a job when that man started to follow me."

"How long have you been in town?"

"Three days. I've been to dozens of places, but no one will give me a job."

"What can you do?"

"Anything."

Lily knew what that meant—nothing. She sounded just like herself. "I'm going to take you to see Reverend Thoragood. He'll help you."

She intended to followed Grant to Washington Street and the church just off Portsmouth Square. All went as planned until they reached Washington Street and started to turn east.

"There she is!" they heard someone shout. Lily looked

up to see a man she'd never seen before heading toward them. The man she'd hoped she'd eluded emerged from an alley more than a block away. They were blocked off from the church.

"Follow me," Lily said. "Hurry."

"Where are we going?" the girl asked.

"To my cousin's saloon," Lily said.

"But I don't want to go to a saloon," the girl said, pulling back.

"Would you prefer they catch up with you?"

There were three of them now. Lily realized they were in serious danger.

"No."

"Then follow me." Lily turned up Jackson Street and ducked down an alley. Working her way between buildings, she came out on Pacific about two blocks from Zac's saloon.

"Hurry," Lily urged. "They're bound to figure out what we did soon."

"I don't want to go to a saloon," the girl repeated. "That's the kind of place I've been trying to avoid."

"This is different," Lily assured her as she looked over her shoulder. "Zac will take care of you. He's doesn't like it when men take advantage of women."

"What's wrong with him?"

"I don't think he's above taking advantage himself, but he won't let anybody else do it."

"But won't he—"

"You'll be safer than any place in town. Zac's a Southern gentleman. He can't help but—"

Just then the men rounded a corner, spotted the women, and started toward them at a trot.

Lily grabbed the girl's hand. "Run like your life depended on it."

They darted around startled men, across busy streets, causing drivers to pull up their horses, and around and behind carts and wagons. Still the men gained rapidly.

"They're going to catch us," the girl wailed.

"Just another half block," Lily said. When the girl showed signs of lagging behind, Lily grabbed her hand and pulled her along. They were within yards of the alley next to the Little Corner of Heaven when the girl clutched her side and cried that she couldn't go another step.

"Would you prefer to die running these last few steps or from being assaulted by those men?"

Put that way, her words compelled the girl to follow Lily the last few yards. They darted down the alley and disappeared through the back door just as the men reached the head of the alley.

Lily locked the door behind her and staggered into the saloon. She collapsed at the first table.

The saloon was a beehive of activity. Young women in colorful outfits that showed lots of leg and bosom hurried about setting up tables. Other women with longer skirts but deeper bosoms were getting their gambling stations ready for action. A couple of women in high heels and net stockings were running though a dance routine with a bored piano player. The several bartenders were polishing glasses and making a last-minute check on their supplies.

"We got here just in time," Lily said. "They open in about ten minutes." She dragged the protesting girl through the saloon until she found Dodie consulting with a cashier on the amount of cash available for the night.

"I thought Zac told you never to come here again," Dodie said, clearly less than pleased to see Lily.

"I didn't mean to, but I had no place else to go," Lily said. "I found this man bothering—oh dear, I forgot to ask your name."

"It's Julie," the girl said. "Julie Peterson."

"You brought someone here and you don't even know who she is?" Dodie asked, amazed.

"I didn't know where else to take her. Some men are following us."

"Three of them," Julie added.

"You told me Zac was most particular about men who mistreated women."

"What am I supposed to do with her?" Dodie demanded. "This place opens in less than five minutes."

"You took care of Josie. I thought you could take care of Julie."

Dodie rolled her eyes. "This is not a home for wayward girls."

"She's not a wayward girl," Lily stated, "and she doesn't want to be one."

"I can't deal with this now," Dodie said. "Sit in a corner, hide in a closet or under a table. Just clear out. I've got a saloon to open."

Julie cringed before Dodie's rough impatience. She looked ready to make a dash for the door, but Lily had no intention of letting Julie run away or letting Dodie ignore them. She was about to tell Dodie this when Zac appeared at the head of the stairs.

"Zac," Lily said with a sigh of relief. "He'll take care of everything," she said to Julie. "You'll see."

Dodie spun around to face the stairs, a light of unholy amusement glowing in her eyes. "Zac, honey, get your butt over here," she said, her voice dripping with honey. "Little Bo Peep has just brought you a lovely lost sheep."

At that moment, they heard a loud banging on the front door.

"And unless I miss my guess," Dodie added, "that's the wolf at the door."

Zac took one look at Lily and knew she was in trouble again. It wasn't a difficult conclusion to reach. Since she had a girl with her who looked scared half to death, he had no reason to think this time was going to be any different from the others. He was strongly tempted to turn around and let Dodie deal with it, but there was something about the way Lily looked up at him that made him descend the stairs a bit faster.

Somewhere in the back of his head a voice warned him

he was sinking deeper and deeper into a bottomless pit. But Zac had made a lifelong habit of ignoring warning voices. Besides, Lily was looking particularly lovely today. He felt himself smiling foolishly as he descended the last steps and crossed toward her.

He was going to have to do something about this reaction to her presence. The smile was okay, but the queer feeling in his chest wasn't. It felt as though there was an air bubble somewhere under his heart. Or maybe it was his left lung. He didn't think it could be his stomach. Hell, he didn't know. He'd never been any good at anatomy.

She was always wanting him to do something he didn't want to do. But she was so charmingly apologetic when she asked, it was virtually impossible for him to refuse.

He ignored the banging at the front door.

"You're looking mighty nice this evening," Lily said. "You trying to dazzle your customers into losing their money?"

Her unexpected compliment caught him off guard. He was wearing a white shirt, white tie, and white waistcoat tonight with a black coat of formal design. He dressed this way one or two nights a week. It lent an extra touch of class to the Little Corner of Heaven. His customers seemed to appreciate it, but he had hardly expected a compliment from Lily.

He shouldn't have cared. Every extravagant phrase known to womankind had been used to describe his looks. *Mighty nice* shouldn't have caused a ripple in the pool of his self-esteem. It had set off a sizeable wave. Zac decided he must be coming down with something. This lightheaded feeling wasn't normal.

"You didn't come here to talk about my looks," Zac said, gathering his thoughts. "What is it this time? Dodie, go see what fool keeps banging on the door."

Lily cast an uneasy glance toward the front doors. "This is Julie Peterson," she said, introducing the young woman, who stared at him as if she'd never seen a man before. "She

112

needs a job and a place to stay.''

''Why did you bring her here?''

''I was going to take her to Mr. Thoragood, but they got in our way.''

''Who got in your way?''

''They did,'' Lily said, pointing at the three men Dodie had let in and who were advancing purposefully toward them.

All around them, the saloon staff continued with their preparations for opening time.

''You got my bird,'' one man bawled belligerently to Zac. ''Hand her over.''

A few of the girls stopped to watch.

Zac hated men like this. It almost made him ashamed to be male. The man reached out to grab Lily, but she darted behind Zac, pulling Julie along with her.

Great. He'd always wanted to be a human shield.

''I don't keep birds,'' Zac said. ''I find they're impossible to house train.''

''Don't get smart with me,'' the man growled. ''I know your type.''

''I doubt you know anything about my type,'' Zac said at his most urbane. ''Or about decent women, if you think you can pick them up willy-nilly off the street.''

More people stopped to listen, some drawing closer so they could see better. Zac hated that. He felt as if he were in the middle of a circus.

''Cut the gaff,'' the man said. ''Just get out of my way.''

''I advise you to leave before I throw you out.''

''And mess up your pretty clothes!'' The man's laugh was full of scorn. ''You couldn't throw the cat out. Hand over the birds, or I'll take'm.''

Zac heaved a sigh. This part of being a saloon owner was worse than having to put up with cheaters. ''I'm not handing them over to you or anybody else, so I guess you'll have to try to take them. Is this a one-man operation, or do you always need help to overwhelm a woman?''

The man flushed red. "I'll make you eat those words."

"I'm not hungry," Zac practically purred in response.

By now they were surrounded by a circle of onlookers, all watching in eager anticipation. One of the bouncers pushed his way through. "You want us to throw them out?"

The man's companions looked as if they'd be only too happy to leave on their own.

"Why don't you have a chat with his friends while I take care of a little business."

"You, take care of me!" The man appeared to be insulted.

"Dodie, get me a cup of coffee. This won't take long."

The man was so angry, he charged blindly. Zac skipped easily out of his way.

"Why don't you stand still and fight, you damned pimp?" the man shouted.

"My pretty clothes, remember?" Zac replied.

"I'll ruin more than your clothes," the man hollered as he charged again.

Zac skipped out of his way a second time but managed to land a blow to the temple that staggered the man. Turning unsteadily, the man charged again. Zac's fist shot out. A single blow to the throat had the man down and gasping for breath.

It was over so quickly, it almost seemed like an anticlimax.

"Now before I get really angry," Zac said to the other two men, "take your friend and get out. If I hear of him trying to force himself on a woman again, I won't be so easy on him. The rest of you get back to work," Zac said to his staff. "It's practically time to open the doors."

The bouncers lifted the man to his feet and helped him to the door. His friends followed without protest.

"Here's your coffee," Dodie said to Zac.

"Forget the coffee," Zac said with a grimace. "I think my hand's broken. That guy has a head as hard as iron."

Lily stood like a statue, apparently stunned by the swift, brutal confrontation.

"Let me see," she said, as though coming out of a trance. She took Zac's hand and carefully spread his fingers, moving each to insure it wasn't broken. "I think they're just bruised," she said. "That's to be expected. You hit him very hard." She still sounded dazed.

"I didn't think he'd go away without some encouragement," Zac said. He had an uneasy feeling that Lily held him responsible for the fight, brief as it was.

"No. You had no choice."

Damn! She really was upset with him. If she hadn't wanted a fight, why had she led them here? They might back down before a preacher, but not a gambler. Surely she knew that.

No, she wouldn't. That wasn't the kind of thing people learned in Salem, Virginia. They learned to eat hog belly, to cook opossum, and to marry their daughters off to men with names like Hezekiah. What could he expect from a woman who'd probably never seen anything more violent than a pillow fight?

"What do you want me to do for your friend?" Zac asked, indicating Julie Peterson. It didn't do any good to go on worrying about what Lily thought of him. It only reinforced his conviction that she was completely unsuited for life in San Francisco.

"Let her stay here. Give her a job."

"Why should I do that?"

"You don't have to pretend to be so hard-hearted," Lily said, her manner toward him softening a little. "Dodie told me how you take care of young women in trouble."

"Dodie talks too much."

"Then you ought to get up early enough to keep an eye on me," Dodie said, arching one eyebrow.

Zac threw her an evil look. He turned to Julie. "What can you do?" he demanded more sharply than he intended.

The girl was too tongue-tied to answer.

"Don't be afraid of him," Lily said. "He just growls like that for show."

Dodie nearly exploded with laughter.

"I growl when I think I'm about to be taken advantage of," Zac said. "You and Dodie go find something to do," he said to Lily. "Make coffee, make beds, make Indian whiskey. Just leave me to talk with Miss Peterson."

"Come on," Dodie said to Lily. "He really does work better alone. His kind always does."

Lily looked back and forth between the two of them, but she let Dodie drag her off.

"Come over here and sit down," Zac said to Julie. He led her to a table far enough away to offer privacy but close enough so she could see everyone as they came and went. He didn't want her to feel threatened. "I want you to tell me exactly what happened from the time you left home until you walked through my door. Don't leave anything out. Would you like something to drink?"

She shook her head.

"Okay, start talking."

It wasn't anything new. Zac had heard it all before. Parents dead, uncle wanting a demonstration of more than ordinary affection. Young suitor just as bad. She was determined to get out of her small town while her looks still offered her the chance for something better in life.

He wondered how many girls out there had failed and sunk from sight. He didn't want to know. He had more than he could handle right now. But with Josie gone, there was space for one more.

"Okay, you're not to think about that anymore. It's over. Now let's see if we can figure out something for you to do."

Zac could see the uncertainty in her eyes. She wasn't sure about working in a saloon. He guessed she was nearly as prim as Lily. She'd probably faint if he asked her to wear a dress that didn't come up to her chin. Oh well, he'd find something.

Lily had looked at him as if he were the answer to a maiden's prayer. Even though he knew he'd regret it in the end, he couldn't resist trying to live up to her expectations. This was a new role for him, but he sort of liked it.

Chapter Nine

"What's he doing out there?" Lily asked Dodie. "They've been talking for the longest time."

"They tell him their life story, every sad little detail of it, then he makes it all better," Dodie said. "They end up worshiping him for the rest of their lives."

"You feel that way about him, too, don't you?"

Dodie looked startled. She started to speak, then simply nodded.

"Did he help you?"

She paused for a long moment. "If I'm going to tell you about it, I need something stronger than coffee." She opened a cabinet and took out a heavy bottle made of dark glass. The label was bordered in gold.

"What's that?" Lily asked.

"Zac's best brandy."

"You said he didn't drink."

"He doesn't. He keeps this for special customers. And me."

"You!"

118

"Surely you know women drink."

"No, actually, I didn't."

"Zac disapproves of it, but he never says anything. I think that's why we all love him. No matter what we've done, when he says it's over and forgotten, he means it. Sometimes I think he wipes it out of his mind so he can see us the way he would like for us to be." Dodie poured several ounces of the dark amber liquid into a glass. "The way we'd like to see ourselves," she added.

"You don't have to tell me," Lily said.

"Yes, I do. Zac's never going to change, not the good or the bad. If you take him, you'll have to accept him the way he is. That out there is just about the best of him, but it might be the hardest for you to take."

"I don't mean to *take* him, nor he me."

"Not yet, but you will soon enough."

Dodie took a swallow of the dark liquid. Her entire body shivered. "God, I love this stuff."

"Why, if it makes you quiver all over?"

"A lot of good things make you quiver all over."

"That doesn't make sense."

"It will."

Lily wanted an explanation of that statement, but Dodie was staring into her glass, her mind apparently drifting back to some tragic event. The weight of that memory caused her to age right before Lily's eyes.

"It was in a small mining town in the California hills. The name isn't important. I was eighteen. I had run away from home when I was fifteen. There was nothing I hadn't seen. There wasn't much I hadn't done. I was living with an ugly brute who beat me when he was drunk. I didn't care. I was drunker than he was."

She took a sip of the brandy.

"I noticed Zac when he came into town. Every woman did, but I never thought he'd notice me. To this day, I don't know why he did."

Dodie stopped. She was turned away from Lily, but Lily

119

could tell she was close to being overcome with emotion.

"One day when Bill Setter wasn't around—that's the man I lived with—Zac came over and asked me if I'd like a job in his saloon. I couldn't believe he was serious. I told him to go to hell and got drunker than usual. That night Bill beat me, then threw me into the street."

She took another sip.

"Zac found me and took me to his room. He took care of me, fed me, gave me just enough liquor so I didn't go crazy. For five days I didn't see anybody else. I knew I couldn't stay. When I told him, he didn't say anything. He just got a mirror and made me look at myself.

"I didn't recognize the woman I saw. The bruises, the cuts, the swollen features, one eye barely open. He asked me how old I was. He said I wouldn't live to see twenty if I went back to Setter. He said he'd give me a job, help me get on my feet, help me do anything I wanted as long as I didn't go back.

"I thought about it for a long time. I think I was more scared of failing Zac than I was of Setter beating me. It took me two days to decide. It took me another day to work up the courage to tell Setter I was leaving him."

She walked several paces but kept her back to Lily.

"I wouldn't let Zac tell Setter because I was afraid of what Setter would do to him. I should have worried more about myself. He nearly beat me to death. Then he want after Zac. I don't know how I did it, but I followed him.

"Setter busted into the saloon Zac was running back then, shouting he was going to kill him. Zac simply stood up and invited him to try. I wouldn't have believed it if I hadn't seen it myself. Setter pulled a knife on him, but somehow Zac got it away. Then Zac beat him until he couldn't stand up. For a while I was afraid Zac was going to kill him, but he just threw him into the street and said if he ever came near me again, he'd kill him."

Dodie took another sip of brandy, but this time she turned to face Lily.

"I warned him Setter would come back with a gun, but Zac told me not to worry. It was almost a month before it happened. Setter came busting through the door with a double-barreled shotgun screaming he was going to blow Zac into a million tiny pieces. What he said he would do to me gives me chills even today.

"Men dived through windows, doorways, behind anything they could find. Women screamed all around me. Setter told Zac he was going to blow the place to smithereens, then he was going to kill Zac."

Dodie took another sip of brandy.

"He shot mirrors, tables, and chairs into splinters. Zac just stood there and watched him. That made Setter furious. He waved the shotgun at me. I couldn't move, I was so scared. Zac told him if he even thought about pulling that trigger, he'd kill him. Setter just laughed. He swung the shotgun to the side and unloaded two barrels into the wall. Some of the buckshot ricocheted off the wall and buried itself in my back. Setter laughed even louder when he saw the blood. Then he aimed the shotgun straight at me. Zac calmly pulled a small gun from his inside pocket and shot him dead."

Dodie finished the rest of the brandy in one swallow. "Now you know why I'll do anything I can for him as long as I live."

Unable to move, even to nod her head, Lily stared at Dodie in wide-eyed disbelief.

"Don't go out there right now expecting to see him in his suit of shining armor," Dodie said, "because you won't. It's like he's two people. Most of the time he's exactly what you see, a selfish, lazy, lucky gambler, not interested in anything but having a good time. But when there's real trouble, he turns into somebody else."

"I don't like it when he's so violent," Lily said.

Dodie set the empty glass down. "Zac's too lazy to like violence, but he's not afraid of it." Dodie studied Lily. "That goes against your beliefs, doesn't it?"

Lily nodded.

"Then you'd better do like Zac told you and go home."

"I'm not going home. How many times do I have to say that?"

"Then get used to an occasional bit of savagery. It's men like Zac who keep those three men, and others like them, from taking any woman they want.

"Now enough lecturing for one day. I'd better go see how things are going with your little friend. Zac will be the one to win her heart and undying loyalty, but I'm the one who'll have to figure out what the hell to do with her."

Lily remained in the office after Dodie left. It was difficult for her to digest what she had just heard. She could believe Zac would defend a woman, even if it put him in danger. But to kill a man, even a man who was about to kill someone else! That jarred Lily to the very foundation of her soul. She'd always been taught to do everything possible to save life, no matter how degraded it had become. It seemed incredible that someone like Zac would take it away.

She told herself that he had done it to save Dodie's life, probably his own life as well. She could understand that. She was honest enough to admit that she would probably have done the same thing, if she'd had a gun, and if she'd known how to fire it and hit what she was aiming for.

But that didn't lessen the shock. Zac had killed a man. She wondered if Setter was the only one.

Lily had been fired again. She didn't dare tell Zac. It would add more fuel to his argument that she ought to go straight back home to Virginia.

"I could beat him up for you," offered one of the men accompanying Lily back to Bella's rooming house.

"I don't think that would be the answer."

"It would teach him not to fire a beautiful woman like you," said another.

"Who else could attract so many people into his shop?" asked a third.

"That was the problem," Lily said. "He was trying to sell books. How many books have you read?"

"One," the first man said. The other dozen men apparently hadn't read any.

"But we bought a lot," one man said. "I think we ought to burn down his shop."

"No! It's not his fault."

"It's certainly not yours. You're the prettiest bookseller in San Francisco."

Zac was waiting on the porch with Bella when Lily got home. She didn't know whether she was more pleased that Zac had come to see her or mortified that he should see the men trailing along behind.

"The crowd gets bigger every day," Bella commented. "Go on with you," she shouted at the men as though she were shooing away livestock. "You've seen her home."

"How long has this been going on?" Zac demanded, annoyed, as Lily came up the steps. "You look like you're leading a parade."

Lily didn't know whether she thought he had any right to be pleased or displeased. Until now he'd never bothered to worry about how she got home.

"They were feeling sorry for me. Mr. Hornaday dismissed me right in front of everybody. If I hadn't let them escort me home, they might have done him some harm."

"You got fired again?" Zac asked, following her into the parlor.

"I really did try this time. I didn't smile at the men or encourage them to stand around talking. I told them if they didn't leave, I would get in trouble. That only seemed to make them more determined to stay."

"I'm not surprised," Zac said.

"What are you going to do now?" Bella asked.

"Look for another job. What else can I do?"

"You can go back to Virginia," Bella suggested.

"Can't you help me find another job?"

123

"I've helped you find two already, and you've lost them both."

"Maybe you should look for one where they aren't any men," Zac suggested.

Bella laughed. "There's no such place for women like Lily."

"I never had this trouble in Salem," Lily said.

"I imagine your father's position in the community protected you in a manner you've been unable to appreciate until now."

Lily had been hearing a lot of home truths lately that she'd just as soon not have to face. This was another one of them.

"You don't think I'm going to make it in San Francisco, do you?" Lily asked Bella.

"No, I don't. First, you know nothing about people. You trust everyone when you should trust no one, especially men. Second, you have no skills. How can you possibly support yourself? Third, you are exactly the kind of woman men will pursue until they get what they want."

"They won't get anything from me," Lily snapped. She couldn't remember when she'd been so angry. She knew she had a lot to learn. She also knew she tended to be very trusting and think the best of everybody. But to be written off as a total failure after a week was too much.

"I will make it," Lily said, her chin jutting, her lips compressed with determination. "Nobody in my family has ever been a failure. Papa says people only fail because they're too lazy to work hard. Well I'm not lazy. I'll find a job, by myself if I must, and I'll find one I can keep for more than two days. I'm going to stay in San Francisco. I'm going to make it."

"Well, you can worry about that tomorrow," Zac said. "Tyler invited us to the hotel for dinner tonight."

Lily felt a little rush of happiness. She had expected a lecture. She had expected Zac to try to convince her to go back to Virginia. Instead, he was taking her to dinner. He'd never taken her anywhere before. The day didn't seem quite such a terrible failure anymore.

"Actually, Daisy ordered me to bring you over," Zac confessed. "I think she's worried I'm not taking proper care of you."

"You're not," Bella stated flatly. "Now leave. Lily's got to hurry if she's going to get bathed and dressed by the time you pick her up."

"You don't have to do anything special," Zac said. "We're just going to dinner."

"Leave it to a man," Bella said, "to say that an invitation to the Palace Hotel is *just going to dinner*."

Lily was absolutely certain the Palace Hotel was the most enormous building in the whole world. Towering over everything in the city, it rose seven stories and covered an entire block. Her eyes grew wider as the cab drove through a huge archway in the middle of the building. She found herself in a circular inner court with a paved carriage drive. A giant palm tree stood in the center. When Zac handed her down, she looked up in amazement. All around her, arching balconies rose one above the other until she had to crane her neck to see the top. The whole court was covered by a glass roof that allowed the sunlight to filter through in soft rays.

"Tyler had to have the biggest hotel in the world," Zac said. "He spent every cent he had on this place. It cost him more than five million dollars."

Lily had never known there was that much money in the world.

"George was afraid he'd go broke, but I told him it was outrageous enough to become the rage. It did. Tyler's got eight hundred rooms, but the place stays full."

Lily was speechless. She allowed Zac to lead her into the main lobby. Marble columns supported a painted ceiling twenty feet above her head. The lobby was so big that if it had been a field, it could have grown enough corn to feed all the cows in Salem for a year.

125

Lily was relieved when Daisy emerged from one of the small offices.

"I wasn't sure you'd come," Daisy said to Zac, a disarming smile on her lips.

"I respond very well to orders from the family."

"When it suits you."

"Well, yes," Zac admitted with a grin.

Lily was feeling quite nervous. Daisy had seemed so ordinary, so human, when she was in Virginia. But seeing her now as the owner of this incredibly grand hotel—well, she seemed like someone else altogether.

"Introduce me, Zac," Daisy prompted.

"You already know Lily. You met four years ago."

"She's changed a lot since then. I wouldn't have recognized her."

"This is Lily Sterling. She's some sort of cousin. My sister-in-law, Daisy Randolph."

"I'm delighted to see you again," Daisy said. "I hope you'll come to visit me often. It can be lonely in San Francisco."

"For your own safety," Zac said to Lily, "you ought to know that Daisy has two little monsters she calls children hidden somewhere around here. I hope they're tied, gagged, and stowed in a tunnel under the hotel for the evening."

"They've already had their dinner and have been put to bed," Daisy said, her gaze never leaving Lily. "I hope that won't deter you."

"Oh, no," Lily assured her. "I love children."

Just then the door opened, and Tyler entered.

"Gaston told me you had another dazzling woman on your arm," he said to Zac. "I don't know how you keep finding them. I certainly don't know how you're going to top this one. She's a stunner."

"I apologize for my husband's lateness and his crassness," Daisy said to Lily. "If you'd been a plate of chicken Bolognese, he'd have been more suitably appreciative."

Tyler grinned sheepishly.

"I think it's time we went in to dinner," Daisy said. "I had intended to use one of the private dinning rooms, but we've had a last minute reservation."

"And waste showing her off," Tyler said with a mischievous grin. "Bring her here every evening. We'll double our business."

"I'm continually apologizing for my husband," Daisy said. "He only thinks of food and money. I'm not sure which comes first."

"You do, my dear."

"Only if someone made a perfume that smelled like roast beef."

Zac didn't know why he hadn't brought Lily to the hotel before. He was a fool not to have done so the night she showed up. Daisy would have taken care of her, and he wouldn't have had to worry about a thing. They were getting along famously.

"You'll have to come back soon," Daisy said.

"For a dinner like this, I'll be here every night," Lily said.

"Tyler is a good cook," Daisy said modestly. Tyler had disappeared into the kitchen the minute dessert was finished, leaving them to enjoy their coffee.

"He's wonderful. Everything was delicious."

"What would you think about moving into the hotel?" Zac asked Lily on the way back to Bella's.

"What for?" she asked, surprised.

"It's a nicer place, Daisy would make good company, and you could enjoy Tyler's food every day."

"And be plagued by all those young men?"

Zac couldn't figure out why Lily's attitude didn't upset him, since it threatened to ruin his whole plan. "They're from some of the best families."

"I can find a dozen more like them in Salem," Lily said,

blithely dismissing several of San Francisco's most eligible bachelors.

"You might find you liked one of them, or one of their friends."

"I'm not out to marry a rich man," Lily said. "I want to learn to take care of myself."

"But what will you do after that?" Zac asked, alternately disappointed that his idea was sinking so quickly yet relieved that Lily wasn't overly impressed by those wealthy young men.

"I'm not certain. Ask me that when I've held a job for at least a month."

Lying in her bed a week later, Lily wasn't certain she'd ever manage to keep a job for a month. She'd been fired again. Zac's friends had further swelled the ranks of her admirers. Her latest employer, a restaurant owner, hadn't cared at first. The men might sit for twice as long as they should, but they also ate twice as much. But when two of them got into a fight over who should sit at her table and who had to sit elsewhere and just watch, he drew the line. He gave her a week's wages and told her to leave immediately.

She had walked half the streets in San Francisco since then, but no one would hire her. In a way she couldn't blame them. No matter what she did, things just wouldn't work out. Still, she was determined to try. She refused to return home defeated, begging to be taken back.

She wondered what her family thought of her now. There probably hadn't been enough time for her letter to reach Salem. There certainly hadn't been enough for an answer to reach her. She wanted to hear from them, but she was afraid of what they would say. Especially her father.

She still doubted he would come after her. She had dared to defy him. He was more likely to declare her dead to the family, even if he thought she was still innocent, which he probably didn't. Hardly anybody in San Francisco thought so. She'd gotten plenty of offers for employment she couldn't accept.

She was determined not to ask Zac for help again. She didn't want him to frown or groan or roll his eyes when she entered the saloon. She would have given just about anything to see him act as if he were glad to see her.

Zac was never downhearted. Even when he was fussing at her, he made her smile. He talked nonsense, but it always made her feel better. She guessed that was why she had been crazy enough to take the gamble of following him to California. He made her feel better than she'd ever felt around anyone else.

Lily sighed. She'd try again tomorrow. There had to be something in this city she could do. And if not, she'd head into the country. Somebody had to have some cows that needed milking. She couldn't imagine that a gaggle of young men would be anxious to stand around in the muck at dawn to watch her. Maybe she could keep that job.

Zac's luck was still swinging wildly from one extreme to another. He'd spent the last week trying to keep from losing his shirt. Yet in three hands tonight, he'd won more than he'd lost in three nights.

This wild careening back and forth was beginning to get on his nerves. He'd never been a nervous gambler, not when he first moved to New Orleans, not when he worked the Mississippi riverboats, not even when he was running a saloon in the wildest of the mining towns. His luck had never deserted him. He'd always been a steady winner.

Those days seemed to be past.

"You're hot tonight," Dodie said when he got up to stretch his legs. "I guess that means Lily is coming by."

Zac started like a man holding five aces when he hears the hammer of a gun click.

"What? Where?" he said looking around.

Dodie laughed. "She's not here now. I just said she's

bound to show up. She does every time you have a run of luck these days.''

"She does, doesn't she? Like a bad penny.''

But that wasn't the way he really felt about her, not anymore. He realized he'd been thinking about Lily every day, wondering what was happening with her job, wondering how she was getting along, wondering if his friends were still following her around. There were so many ways she could get into trouble, even with Bella Holt watching over her.

"I think I'll get a breath of fresh air,'' Zac said.

Dodie looked at him questioningly. "When did you start wanting fresh air? I've known you to go weeks without once stepping out of doors.''

Zac was starting to get irritated with Dodie. She was too much like a conscience.

"Maybe it goes back to growing up in Texas where there wasn't anything but fresh air,'' he replied somewhat irritably. "Maybe it comes from these wild swings, one night losing every hand, winning them all the next. It makes me doubt my skill, and I've never done that. It's the one thing I could always depend on.''

"Skill, yes, luck, no,'' Dodie replied. "And you've had an awful lot of luck.''

"Maybe,'' Zac said as he moved away.

The Barbary Coast was always busy at night. Saloons, theaters, and dives of every description lined both sides of the street. Men entered and left in a constant stream of humanity. The noise of music, the jangle and whistle of gambling machines, the cacophony of human voices raised to every level of pitch and volume, the light that poured from street lamps and through windows, all created a miasma of human excess that inhibited most people's ability to think or reason.

It used to heighten Zac's excitement, used to make him feel he had everything he'd ever wanted. Yet now he felt restless, unsatisfied, as though there were something essential he'd overlooked. Only he couldn't figure out what it was.

He didn't understand why it disturbed him to look into the future and see himself as the aging owner of a chain of successful gambling saloons across the country, or why it should trouble him to see himself surrounded by a multitude of faceless women singing and dancing their lives away.

Zac took out a cigar, cut off the end, and lighted it. Rose said it was a filthy habit, but he didn't listen to Rose. He didn't want any female telling him what to do, when to come home, what to think, what to feel. He threw off the feeling of confinement that had begun to envelop him. He pushed back the doubts that only moments ago had made him question the last eight years of his life.

He was the man he wanted to be, living the life he wanted. Even his brothers suffered from moments of self-doubt. That was all this was.

Relieved the moment of doubt had passed, he drew on his cigar and blew the smoke into the foggy night. Only then did he notice the cab that had drawn up in front of the saloon, and the woman with the halo of hair like moonlight who stepped out.

"Lily!" he exclaimed, choking on a mouthful of smoke. "What the hell are you doing here?"

"I've thrown her out," announced Bella Holt as she climbed down from the cab. "I'm bringing her to you."

Chapter Ten

Lily looked demoralized. Zac had never seen her so wilted, so totally lacking in self-confidence and determination. She looked as if she'd been punished at school and knew she was going to get worse when she got home.

Zac got angry. And for one of the few times in his life, he wasn't thinking of himself.

"What the hell do you mean by doing this? I paid you plenty."

Bella didn't answer immediately. She was too busy directing the driver to unload Lily's trunk and suitcases.

"It was my fault," Lily said.

"What on earth could you do to cause Bella to throw you out into the street?"

"I'm not throwing her into the street," Bella said, turning her attention from the luggage to Zac. "I'm handing her over to you."

"I got fired from my job," Lily said.

"Not again."

"It was the fourth time," Bella told him. "Now nobody will hire her."

"I don't have enough money for my rent," Lily said.

"If that's all—" Zac began.

"That's not all," Bella interrupted. "Do you think I'd throw her out just because she couldn't pay her rent, especially when she has a cousin with far more money than he knows what to do with?"

"Then why are you doing it?"

"For giving my place a bad name."

"I thought she gave your dreary mausoleum a touch a class for a change," Zac said.

"Do you consider it a touch of class to have a dozen men hanging about the steps morning, noon, and night?" Bella demanded angrily, her temper flaring in defense of her reputation. "How about fights to see who gets to escort her home, or down the street, or hire a cab for her? Not to mention scaring poor Mr. Hornaday within an inch of his life."

"Who the hell is Mr. Hornaday?" Zac demanded, annoyed that the conversation should be making so little sense.

"He's the unfortunate man who was kind enough to give her employment in his bookstore," Bella said. "That was her second job. They came close to beating him up for dismissing her."

Zac sniggered.

"You should have been there when they stormed into Mrs. Chickalee's store. That was after she'd been fired for the fourth time," Bella said, incensed that Zac wasn't taking this in the right spirit. "The poor woman was so unnerved, she collapsed and hasn't been able to raise her head off the pillow since."

Zac exploded with laughter.

"You can laugh if you want," Bella said, obviously furious, "but I won't have it any longer. I had more men hanging about the place than—than—" She turned around, looking for inspiration. "—than Salem House," she said, pointing to the elegant house halfway up the next block.

"Maybe you should change your line of business."

That suggestion didn't please Bella in the least.

"I should have expected scorn from you. Considering what you do day in and day out, I'm not surprised that—"

Bella broke off, but not because Zac was no longer laughing. Lily had taken hold of Bella's arm and jerked her almost off her feet.

"Don't you dare say one more word about Zac," Lily said. "After all he's done for you, it's really quite unforgivable for you to even think such things."

Bella stared at Lily with open-mouthed shock.

"Ellen told me what you were before Zac found you. She also told me he lent you money to buy your rooming house, how you had the nerve to charge him extra for my room, as well as charging him to help find me a job—yes, I know all about that, too. Well, I never would have thought it of you. Your taste in home furnishings may be quite deplorable, but I had thought you were an honest, fair woman."

Zac stared at Lily, stunned by her outburst. A real fire-eater was hidden inside this seemingly mild angel. He could practically see the Reverend Isaac Sterling calling down fire and brimstone to consume poor Bella, and all because she'd said what everybody thought.

While Bella stood speechless, Lily turned back to Zac. The fire-eater seemed to disappear as if she had never been there.

"It really isn't her fault. I tried to stop the men from threatening Mrs. Chickalee, but they wouldn't listen. I was truly afraid they were going to hurt Mr. Hornaday."

Zac had difficulty focusing on what Lily was saying to him. He still couldn't get over her being ready to attack Bella because she dared to slander his name. Hell, worse things than that were said about him every hour.

He felt a pang of conscience that he hadn't been equally zealous on her behalf. He should have made it his job to check on her, to see that things were going right. Whether he wanted to admit it or not, Lily was his responsibility. If he hadn't opened his mouth, she would never have thought of running away from home.

Still, the thought of a clutch of young dandies threatening to assault a little old lady tickled his funnybone. "I'd like to have seen the woman's face when her shop was invaded by a dozen infuriated swains."

"If you think it's so funny, you deal with the hordes of men who hang about her. And that includes some of your friends," Bella shouted as she got back into the cab. "But don't ask me to help her further."

"We won't," Dodie called out as the cab started to move away. She had come out in time to hear most of Lily's attack on Bella. "And good riddance to you. Taking her to your place was a mistake from the start."

"Where should I have taken her?" Zac asked.

"You should have put her on the first train and escorted her back to Virginia yourself," Dodie said.

"She wouldn't go," Zac said.

"You didn't try hard enough," Dodie said. "But that's water over the dam. Things are different now. The question is what are you going to do next?" She pointed to the luggage sitting on the boardwalk. "You'd better make up your mind. That's going to attract a lot of attention."

"I can go to another rooming house," Lily offered. "There must be someone who's never heard of me. It doesn't have to be as nice. I—"

"You'll do no such thing," Zac said. "I'll take you to Tyler's hotel."

"Please don't send me there," Lily begged. "I like Daisy very much, but I'd be petrified in such a grand place. Everyone looked down their noses at me there."

She tried not to show it, but it was impossible not to notice the fear in her eyes.

"I think she ought to stay here," Dodie said, "at least for the night."

"Yes, please," Lily said. "I won't be any trouble."

The relief in Lily's expression was evident, but Zac felt an equivalent increase of tension within himself. "There's no place for you to sleep. Every room is full."

But that wasn't the real problem. A woman like Lily had no business in a place like the Little Corner of Heaven. Even though he tried to protect the virtue of his employees, women who worked in saloons had bad reputations just for that fact. Some of it was bound to rub off on Lily.

"The hotel's the perfect place," Zac insisted. "Daisy will take good care of you."

"I'm sure she would," Lily said, "but I'd feel a lot more comfortable here. I won't be a bother. I don't need anything more than a place to sleep. I promise I—"

"But we don't have any extra beds," Zac said.

Lily's face fell.

"You'll like the Palace," Zac assured her. "You've only seen the dining room. Wait until you see the rest. There's nothing like it in the world. It'll take you days just to stop staring at everything."

"She can do that some other time," Dodie said as she picked up one suitcase and handed a smaller one to Lily. "Right now she needs to be with friends." Taking Lily by the arm, she turned toward the saloon.

"But there's no place for her to sleep," Zac repeated.

"I know the perfect place," Dodie said. "Now stop scowling and get somebody to bring up that trunk."

Zac muttered to himself as he set about getting the trunk taken inside. It seemed he had spent his life doing the bidding of one female after another. First his mother, then Rose. Now, when he was a grown man and ought to be having things his way at last, he was dancing to strings pulled first by Lily, then by Dodie. There was something wrong here. He was the boss; he was the one who held the purse strings. But if that was so, why was he seeing to the luggage?

And where the hell was Dodie going to put Lily? There wasn't an empty bed in the place. There was nothing left except his closet.

"Dammit to hell!" Zac exclaimed, suddenly knowing exactly what Dodie intended. "I'll break her neck!"

He crashed through the doors and bulldozed his way through the saloon shouting curses at Dodie every step of the way.

Customers looked up, glanced at their neighbors, shrugged, and went back to their gambling.

"I can't!" Lily protested, drawing back from the door as though it were the doorway to the abyss her father had warned her about so often. "Zac would kill me."

"No, he won't. Besides, it's the only place we've got."

"Where's he going to sleep?"

"Let him sleep in his brother's grand hotel. Believe me, he won't have nightmares because the place looks more like the palace of one of them awful sheiks, sultans, or whatever they call those men who run about wrapped up in a bedsheet and have their wives watched over by men who've had parts I won't mention cut off, than it does a hotel for decent folks."

"But it's not right for me to take his bedroom. I wouldn't get a wink of sleep." She pointed to the bed. "Zac sleeps naked in that bed."

"I don't know why you should care. It's the best bed in the house."

"But it's Zac's bed. I'd be thinking about my body touching the same place his body touched all night long."

"I can't help it if you have naughty dreams," Dodie teased. "Though if you're going to have them, this is a good place for it."

"Dodie! I never!" Lily exclaimed, her face burning hot.

"Then it's about time you did," Dodie said, pushing Lily into the bedroom before her. "A woman who's behaved as well as you deserves a decent dream once in a while."

"Do you have dreams like that?" Lily asked, so curious she forgot her shock. She'd been so ashamed of her one such dream, she'd never said a word to anyone. But if Dodie had them, too, they couldn't be all bad.

"I have dreams that would singe your papa's eyebrows," Dodie said.

Lily grinned.

"One of these days, when you've got a little more experience, I'll tell you about them."

"I'm more experienced already," Lily said. "Tell me now." No one had ever offered to explain anything to her about the physical nature of a woman. She wasn't about to let this chance slip away.

They heard the thump of footsteps on the stairs echoing down the hall.

"Later," Dodie said, pushing her across the room until she flopped down on the bed. "Right now we've got to defend your territory."

Lily started to sit up. "But I don't—"

"I do." Dodie pushed her back down just as Zac burst through his bedroom door.

"Get off my bed!" he shouted.

Lily tried to stand up. Dodie pushed her back down. "No."

"That's my bed, Dodie Mitchell. If you want her to have somewhere to sleep, give her yours."

"That's what I was going to do at first, but then I realized it wouldn't work. You can't stay here no matter where she sleeps. So she may as well have your bed. You can sleep in the hotel."

"Why can't I stay here?"

"Because you'll ruin her reputation."

"Don't be absurd. I've always slept here, and this place is full of women."

"Do you want her to have the same reputation we do?"

Zac felt as though he'd been stopped in his tracks by a steam locomotive. He knew immediately that he didn't want to do anything to damage Lily's reputation, but neither did he want Dodie and the other girls to think he didn't value their reputations just as much. They were just different, that was all. Only he didn't know how to say that. George was the only one in the family who was good at saying things. The rest of them just waded in and dealt with the consequences later.

"I don't want to do anything to ruin anybody's reputation," Zac said, "but I don't see why that should involve giving up my bed."

"Because you can stay in that hotel without starting speculation. Lily can't. Cora Mae will be leaving at the end of the week. Lily can have her room. Then you can have yours back."

Zac realized that moving to the hotel for a few days would mean he would be able to get a full night's sleep. Lily wasn't likely to go that far to wake him up. At least he didn't think so.

Still, he wasn't satisfied. He didn't like the idea of being away from the saloon all day while Lily was up and doing things that would most likely cause no end of trouble. And he couldn't depend on Dodie to stop her. Dodie wasn't acting like herself these days. She'd always been willing to do anything he wanted. Now she didn't seem to hesitate to go against him at every turn.

"Okay," he said, "she can stay here, but just for the night," he said, turning to Lily. "If I thought his wife wouldn't throw you out, I'd take you to stay with Mr. Thoragood."

Lily was relieved. She had no doubt the Thoragoods would take her in, but she knew Mrs. Thoragood wouldn't be happy about it. Lily had discovered she didn't like not being wanted.

That had never happened to her before. People had always been kind to her, always done things for her. She'd never taken advantage of it—Papa wouldn't have allowed it—but she'd come to expect that people would be kind to her. San Francisco had changed all that. She never would have thought she'd be thankful merely for a bed that wasn't begrudged her.

"I'm sorry," she told Zac. "I never meant for this to happen. I never thought—"

"Don't worry about it. Everything's set for now. You don't have to worry about any of those men bothering you. I'll make sure nobody gets by me."

"Go see what's keeping her trunk," Dodie said. "I'm going to put her to bed. She's worn out."

Zac looked as if he didn't understand how anybody could be ready to go to bed at nine o'clock in the evening, but Lily *was* tired. She'd had a long, disappointing, and worrisome day. She had to figure out what to do next. She couldn't keep causing Zac so much trouble. It wasn't fair.

"You hungry?" Dodie asked as she closed the door behind Zac.

"No. Bella fed me."

"That's a kindness I didn't expect. Oh well, I guess she's not so terrible, but I just hate it when a woman won't use a little gumption. I could have gotten rid of those men. If nothing else, I could have threatened to hug and kiss every one of them."

"That wouldn't have done any good," Lily said. "You're pretty."

"Where'd they go? Maybe I can catch myself one before they disappear. I could use a good man."

"You'll find one," Lily said, "and not one with nothing better to do than follow me about the streets."

She pulled herself up on the bed and leaned against the mound of pillows. She was so tired she could hardly keep her eyes open. If she was ever going to see anything of Zac and Dodie, she had to stop getting up at five-thirty. There was no point in it. There was nothing to do for hours and hours.

"Sure I will," Dodie said, "but in the meantime I'm going to help you get undressed and in bed before you go to sleep with your clothes on."

"Mama wouldn't like that," Lily said, half asleep already.

"First time I ever heard you mention your ma," Dodie said. "I was beginning to think your pa had done away with her."

"Mama doesn't talk much," Lily said. "She says men don't like women's talk. She says I'm going to have a hard time finding a man to put up with me."

"Well, that's where your mama's wrong. I should think you would have figured that out already."

"Men do like me, don't they?" Lily said smiling sleepily.

"Yes, they do. You're very nice, and you don't go about thinking a lot of yourself."

"Papa says——"

"And you're not to think of another thing your papa says. You'll sleep a lot better for it. You sure the noise downstairs won't bother you?"

"What noise?"

"I guess not. I wish I could drop off like that. I guess it's the sleep of the innocent."

"I wish I weren't so innocent," Lily mumbled. "It's tiresome to go about forever being pure. Don't you agree?"

"Maybe I would if I could remember what it was like," Dodie muttered. "You go to sleep and stop worrying about being pure. That'll change one day. Then you'll have plenty of time to decide which you like better."

"My clothes are inside," Zac said. "You can't expect me to wear the same thing tomorrow."

"She's asleep."

"You should have thought of that before you pushed me out of my room."

"Can't you make do for one night?"

"No," Zac said. The thought of having to put on wrinkled and soiled clothes caused his skin to crawl.

"Then go in through the closet."

"I can't. After you so kindly showed Lily how to sneak in, I had it nailed shut. This is the only way in or out. Now, out of my way. I'm going in whether you like it or not."

141

"I'm not leaving until you come out again."

Zac gave her a sharp look, then smiled. "You don't trust me, do you?"

"Hell, no!"

"Damnation, woman, she's a preacher's daughter. What do you take me for?"

"A man, much like any other. Lily's a beautiful woman. I've seen you—"

"You've never seen me ravage an innocent female," Zac snapped, his irritation turning to something a little warmer.

"No, but you never had one sleeping in your bed. Go on, get your clothes."

"You sure you're not jealous?"

Dodie paused for a moment. "Yeah, some. Part of me wishes I could be like her. Not just her beauty, but her innocence. I couldn't go to sleep in a man's bed in a place like this without locking the door and keeping a loaded shotgun on the pillow beside me. She went right off without a moment's worry. I'm a little jealous of that. How about you?"

"Are you kidding? If I were that innocent, I'd have lost this place months ago. Where would you and the rest of the girls be then?"

"I said it was just a part of me. I know what losing this place would mean to us, but you're rich anyway. You could go home to your family."

"You haven't met my family. I'd rather be on the street than locked up with them. Now stop keeping me chatting away in the hall and let me get my clothes."

"I'm coming in with you," Dodie said.

"You going to hold my hand so the spooks won't get me?"

"Not even a spook would want you."

They tiptoed in and through the bedroom to the closet like children trying to sneak into the house without waking their parents. Zac closed the door to the bedroom and lighted a lamp. It didn't take him more than a few minutes to collect the clothes he wanted. Figuring out how to get them into a suitcase without their ending up in a crumpled ball was something else.

"Here, let me pack those things for you," Dodie whispered. "I never did see a man as helpless as you. Wait outside."

But Zac didn't make it to the door. He was still miffed that he'd had to give up his bed. He didn't begrudge Lily a place to sleep. He just didn't see why it had to be his bed. He walked over to the bed, not making any particular effort to be quiet. He didn't know what he wanted to do—pull the covers off, tie her hair in knots, anything to get her back for turning him out of his own room.

It was childish, and he knew it, but it didn't stop him from feeling that way. Nor did it make him feel ashamed. More like regretful. He'd given up long ago expecting himself to be anything like George. He was spoiled, selfish, and determined to have his way in everything. Odd that a poor innocent like Lily should have enough faith in him to put her fate in his hands. He didn't want it, thank you very much. Nonetheless, it seemed he had it, at least as long as she was sleeping in his bed.

He drew closer. She looked so young and innocent. She was too lovely for her own good. Of course he wasn't drawn to her particular type of looks. He preferred a riper kind of beauty, a more sophisticated woman, one who was interested in enjoying herself without making plans for the future. He was like the bee who sampled all the flowers in the garden. He saw no reason to limit himself to one.

Not that he couldn't appreciate her beauty. And her innocence. It had a kind of appeal, even to a jaded man of the world like himself. He supposed every man liked to indulge in the fantasy of finding that one beautiful, guileless woman who could love no one but him, who would adore him, cling to him no matter what, believe in him regardless. It sounded good. For a few moments it made you feel like you were king of the mountain. But there was a price to pay for such loving adoration, and Zac had long ago decided that the disadvantages outweighed the advantages.

Still, maybe it wouldn't be as bad as he'd imagined. Lily wasn't the clinging kind of female. She certainly wasn't going to wait for a man to do everything for her. Any female who could cross the country by herself had a lot of gumption, more than he'd given her credit for. She might be ignorant now, but he would bet she'd know more about San Francisco in six months than most of the people who'd lived here for years.

It was a shame she kept getting fired. He didn't know what she was going to do about a job, but he'd have to figure out something. Maybe she ought to hide her hair under a black hat instead of letting it fall over her shoulders. It was a problem that men kept following her around, though hardly surprising.

The covers had slipped a little. Next thing you know they'd be off the bed. He didn't want her to get pneumonia. But as he moved forward, a wave of desire hit him with the impact of a fist. For the first time he looked at Lily as he looked at other women. What he saw threw his body into a state of raging need.

It was a warm night. An arm and a leg were uncovered. A long, slender leg that tapered from a very shapely ankle to a dimpled knee to a thigh mostly hidden by the sheet. Zac had never seen a limb so white, so perfectly formed. The temptation to caress her thigh, to move the sheet aside, was nearly irresistible.

Zac shifted his attention before his imagination could enflame his body.

Her arm was nearly as enticing. It lay outstretched toward him, palm up, her hand dangling over the edge of the bed, the inside of her arm exposed to his gaze. It looked so soft, so warm, he had to press his hand to his side to keep from touching her.

But it wasn't her arm or leg that sent him over the edge. She wore a thin nightgown. At times the angle of the light made it virtually transparent. Zac could see the side of her breast, the edge of the dusky circle that surrounded her nipple.

The tip of his tongue slowly moistened his dry lips; his body turned rigid with desire. He could almost feel the warm softness of her skin. He could hear the soft moans as he gently teased her breast, as he bathed it in moist heat with his tongue. He could imagine the feel of her nipple as it firmed under his touch.

He realized with a slight shock that he hadn't been with a woman since Lily arrived. Her presence had driven all thoughts of other females from his head. But not the need from his body. That was greater than ever.

He groaned. He had to leave before he did something he'd regret. He reached over to pull the blanket up around her.

"What do you think you're doing?" an irate voice demanded.

Zac jumped nearly a foot.

"I told you to wait outside," Dodie said, "not molest the girl in her bed."

"I was just going to pull the covers back over her."

"You men are all alike."

Zac started to protest, then gave up. Dodie wouldn't believe him. Once you got a reputation for liking women, people seemed to think you couldn't pass a female without going crazy. It didn't matter what you said. Black you were and black you'd stay.

Oh well, it didn't matter. Lily would soon be out of his saloon and he could get his bed back.

He turned away. He denied himself the chance to touch her, the right to look at her. He drove all thoughts of pleasure he could find in her arms from his mind. It was madness, it was torture, and he didn't need either one.

"Fix the sheets," he told Dodie. "They're coming off the bed."

Chapter Eleven

Zac had returned to his own bed three days later, but Lily was still in the saloon. Cora Mae had left sooner than expected, and Lily had taken her room. From all Zac could tell, she didn't mean to give it up.

"You've got to let me do something," Lily insisted. "I can't just sit around doing nothing."

They were sitting in Zac's office. He was on his second cup of coffee.

"Helping Dodie isn't nothing," Zac said.

"I don't mean it like that. I sometimes feel I get in her way, that she doesn't need me."

"She's just not used to having help. Give her time. It won't be long before she's shoving so many things your way, she'll be sleeping later than I do."

"Did I hear my name being taken in vain?" Dodie said, entering the office.

"I was just trying to convince Lily that helping you is important."

"Of course it is," Dodie agreed, "but she wants to do

146

something else, and I think you ought to let her.''

Zac wondered why Dodie enjoyed stabbing him in the back. ''What does she want to do, run a roulette table?''

''Some day,'' Dodie said, ''but first she wants to sing.''

''No!'' The word exploded from Zac like a Chinese fire-cracker.

''You don't have to shout,'' Lily said. ''We've both got very good hearing.''

''No. Never. Absolutely not. Out of the question. I can't believe you would make such a suggestion.''

''See, I told you he wouldn't be hard to convince,'' Dodie said to Lily.

''I don't want to sing a lot of songs,'' Lily said. ''Just one or two.''

''No!'' Why couldn't she understand it would cheapen her? He kept telling her, but she acted as if that was un-important.

''The girls look like they're having so much fun.''

''Your father would turn over in his grave.''

''He's not dead.''

''Then *my* father would turn over in *his* grave. He's prob-ably burned on one side anyway.''

''Don't be sacrilegious,'' Lily said, ''and stop making senseless objections.''

''You want to sing in a saloon, and you say I'm making senseless objections?''

''Yes. You'll be here. What can go wrong?''

''That's right,'' Dodie chimed in, ''tell us what can go wrong.''

It was just like the women to gang up on him. ''She'll lose her reputation,'' Zac said.

''According to Bella, I don't have one.''

''I don't want you up there being stared at by hundreds of men you don't know.''

He hadn't admitted it to himself before, but he'd been uneasy ever since he saw those men outside Bella's. He couldn't explain it, but he somehow felt Lily was safe as

147

long as she was his alone. Once he gave her up to everybody else, he couldn't control what happened to her.

He didn't like that feeling.

"I'm stared at by hundreds of men I don't know every time I walk down the street," Lily pointed out.

"You ought to be in bed that time of night."

"I never go to bed before nine o'clock. The first show is over by then."

"Your father would cut my heart out and make a pin cushion of it if he knew."

"He won't. He hasn't even answered my letter."

"You'll endanger your immortal soul."

"Not by singing a few songs."

This argument went on until Zac thought he would go crazy from the constant nagging. "All right, dammit!" he finally shouted two days later. "You can sing!"

Lily and Dodie had tackled him in his room before he'd finished dressing. He'd tried to hold out, but Lily appeared more anxious every time she brought up the subject. She seemed to think it was terribly important. He didn't know what she hoped to prove by it, but he knew it wouldn't work. He'd tried to protect her, but she wouldn't let him.

Okay, she could sing. But she would fail. Maybe then she'd be content to work with Dodie. Maybe she'd even lose her fascination with the saloon and agree to move into the hotel. Tyler and Daisy were willing to take her.

"You may sing only one song," Zac said. He sat at a table in front of the small stage in the empty saloon. Lily was alone on the stage. She looked nervous. "The rest of the girls have got to be on stage with you, and you've got to be in bed fast asleep by nine o'clock."

"But I can't—"

"Don't start with objections. That's the deal. Take it or leave it."

"Take it for now," Dodie said. "We can talk some sense into him later."

That remark didn't make Zac feel very confident. Neither did the song Lily wanted to sing.

"You can't sing a love song to these people," Zac said. "They want something snappy. What else have you got?"

Lily's fifth choice proved acceptable. It was lively and had amusing lyrics.

"Okay, you stand right at the back of the stage in the middle. We'll put a dozen girls all around you. We'll let them dance a bit, then do a few kicks at the end. That ought to liven things up."

"If you do that, nobody will even know she's on stage," Dodie said.

"Okay, let's run through it the way I outlined it," Zac called out. "That's exactly what I'm after," he said to Dodie while Lily and the girls rehearsed the number. "Then maybe she'll stop wanting to parade about."

"She wants to be useful. She wants you to pay her some attention."

"Damnation, woman, I pay attention to her all the time."

"That's a lot of rot. You sleep all day and then run her off to bed before she's had time to settle her dinner. What do you plan to do about her? She can't spend the rest of her life helping me run this place."

"I don't know," Zac said, his eyes on Lily. Even wearing black and positioned at the back of the stage, standing still while the other girls moved around her, she drew his eye. She was simply too lovely to be outshone.

"She needs a hat to cover up all that hair," Zac said as soon as there was a pause on stage. "It's too bright in all that light. It's liable to blind somebody."

"Why don't you put her in the corner, or behind the curtain?" Dodie said.

"I wouldn't have to worry about putting her anywhere if you'd given me a little support," Zac snapped in return.

"It'll never work," Dodie predicted. "People will notice her no matter what you do."

* * *

"I shouldn't be doing this," Lily kept repeating as Julie Peterson helped her make the final adjustments to her hat before she went on stage. "Zac didn't want me to. My father thinks it's sinful. It was stupid of me to keep insisting."

"You're going to do fine," Julie assured her. "You've got a nice song, you sing it well, and you're beautiful. That's all that counts."

Julie had ventured out of the kitchen tonight, something she never did when the saloon was open, to help Lily get ready. Lily knew Julie was thankful for the safety and security the saloon offered, but even though Lily had become comfortable with her surroundings, Julie still felt out of place.

"They won't see me with all those other girls up there," Lily said. "I really should have worn a different dress. Nobody will notice me in black."

She felt like a crow among bluebirds. She didn't know why she hadn't thought of it before. But it was too late to change now. Besides, she didn't own anything that wasn't black.

"They'll notice you," Julie said.

Lily wasn't sure she wanted the men to notice. That was where all the trouble started. She had finally admitted to herself that she was doing this to attract Zac's attention. But as the time to go on stage grew closer, she started to question whether she couldn't have found a better way.

But little as it was, singing was her only talent. She could wash his clothes, iron his shirts, or cook his food, but somebody already did those things. She wanted to stand out, to be someone special. She felt ordinary, easily ignored, taken for granted.

She'd never tried to attract a man's attention before. She didn't really know how to go about it. She also had qualms about it being the right thing to do. She knew what her father would say, but this was her first experience of being ignored as a woman. Her father couldn't know anything about that, or he'd know singing in a saloon was only the beginning of what she'd do.

"My throat's dry," Lily said. "I won't be able to sing a note."

"It's natural to be nervous," Julie said. "You'll feel perfectly fine once you start singing."

But as she stepped on stage, Lily decided she'd never felt less perfectly fine in her whole life.

Zac watched from his position near the bar. Dodie was right. The men did notice Lily. Maybe if he put the girls in shorter skirts and moved them around a little more, it would do the trick. Of course he could always turn down the lights on Lily and turn them up on the girls. In all that black, she'd practically disappear.

But not her face. Only a complete blackout could dim her inner radiance.

Zac smiled to himself. She was scared to death. She was smiling, and she was singing with every bit of nerve she could muster, but if anybody said boo, she'd probably faint on the spot. He had to give it to her. She had guts.

Her voice was rather good. Maybe even a little too good. More of the men had stopped to listen. A few even drew close to the stage to get a better look. Zac didn't like that. He wanted them to keep their distance, to show only a marginal interest.

At the same time, he was proud of what she'd managed to do in spite of her stage fright. The volume of the applause caught him by surprise. They did more than notice her. They liked her very much.

"You ought to get rid of those other girls and feature Lily," Dodie said. "She's got a pretty good voice. Once she gets over her stage fright, she won't be half bad."

"I'll do nothing of the kind," Zac said, aware that he was speaking more forcefully than necessary.

"Why not? The men like her. Look around. Half the games in the room have stopped."

Leigh Greenwood

"I don't want the games to stop. I can't make money that way."

Dodie leveled a penetrating glance at Zac. "You don't want her to succeed," she said. "Why?"

"It's not suitable for a girl like Lily. Look at her. Is she what you'd expect to find in a gambling hall?"

"No, and that's exactly why featuring her would bring in twice as many people. All men can appreciate a woman like Lily."

"I didn't want her up there in the first place. I'm not going to compound my error by turning her into a byword along the Barbary Coast."

Even now he wanted to pull her off the stage, send her upstairs, and tell everybody she'd gone back to Virginia. He wanted to shield her from their prying eyes and protect her from the thoughts he could see behind their hungry, glistening eyes.

Who were these men? What could they offer her? Nothing. The most decent ones were married, but even they wasted their time and money on whiskey and gambling. They stared openly at women's bodies, made crude and suggestive remarks, and went home so drunk they couldn't find their way without help.

That wasn't the kind of man for Lily. She deserved a nice, respectable, faithful, attentive husband who would give her the love she deserved and the home she wanted. She wasn't cut out for the kind of existence Zac found so appealing.

Zac didn't know how she was going to find the right kind of husband singing to a bunch of drunken gamblers in the Little Corner of Heaven.

Lily wasn't mistaken. Somebody was crying. She never would have known if she hadn't returned to her room in the middle of the day. It was her time of the month, and she wasn't feeling her best.

It didn't take her long to locate the room. The name on the pasteboard was Kitty Draper. Lily knocked softly. The crying stopped abruptly. Lily knocked again.

"Who is it?" a voice asked.

"Lily Sterling."

"What do you what?"

"I heard you crying. Is there anything I can do to help?"

"No."

"Are you sure?"

A pause. "Yes."

"Can I come in?"

A longer pause. The door opened about two inches. A brunette Lily couldn't remember seeing peeped through the crack.

"You don't have to. I'm all right."

"I know. I just thought you might like me to sit with you for a minute. It gets awfully lonely around here sometimes."

Kitty burst into tears. Lily pushed her way into the room, sat them both down on the edge of the bed, and held Kitty in her arms until she stopped crying.

"I'm sorry," Kitty said. "It's just when you said . . ."
She started to cry again.

"What's wrong?" Lily asked.

Kitty reached inside the pocket of her robe and handed Lily a letter.

Dear Kitty,

The baby is sick with the croup again. The poor little mite makes such terrible noises, it scares me half to death.

Old Mrs. McCutchen and her daughter are moving, so I'll have to be on the lookout for another wet nurse. He does hate the bottle so. It breaks my heart to see him not eat when I know he's hungry.

I didn't mean to send such bad news, but I thought you ought to know."

Love, Ma

"He's only three months old," Kitty said when Lily returned the letter. "It broke my heart to leave him."

"Why did you?"

"I came looking for his father, but he's disappeared."

"Why didn't you go back?"

"There's no work back home. Besides, I had no milk. I thought I could earn enough here so Ma could take care of him. I could also keep looking for his father. But I didn't know I'd miss my baby so much."

"Why don't you have your mother come to San Francisco?"

"I can't afford it."

"What do you do?"

"I run one of the roulette wheels. I'd make more money with a faro bank, but Dodie says I can't move up until I have more experience."

"I have no objection to moving Kitty to a faro bank," Dodie said. "It's Zac's rule. Six weeks is the absolute minimum."

"But she's been here almost five weeks."

"Then she's only got ten days to wait."

"She's missing her baby," Lily said. "The other girls say she cries herself to sleep every night."

"Don't take it out on me. Talk to Zac. But not until he gets up," Dodie hastily added when Lily immediately got to her feet.

Lily was waiting at the bottom of the stairs when Zac came down.

"Don't say a word until I have my coffee," he said, his eyes only half open. "I can see you're going to be after me for something."

Lily couldn't help smiling as she watched him make his way to his office. He was so adorable when he was half asleep. He was like a big baby. She almost wanted to give him a cuddle.

She didn't think he'd appreciate it.

She waited a moment before she followed him. He studied her over his coffee cup, wary, distrustful.

"You want me to do something," he said. "I can see it in your eyes. You're just like Rose."

"She must be a wonderful woman."

"An absolute queen among women, but she's the most unrestful human being I know, unless it's Iris."

"I think Rose and Iris are both charming."

Zac took a hasty swallow of coffee and burned his tongue. "Okay, out with it."

"I want you to bring Kitty's mother and baby to San Francisco."

"Who the hell is Kitty? Why should I give a damn about her mother and baby?"

"You're never this cross when you get up. What's wrong?"

"I had another go-around with that damned fool Chet Lee. I spent half the night at the police station."

Lily let him get down a few more swallows of coffee. She knew he'd give in. He was too soft-hearted not to. She just had to let him growl and snarl for a bit to show he was the master. Just like her father. He would balk if he thought he was being managed. She suspected Zac would do the same.

The thought stunned her. It seemed incredible that they should have anything in common, that Zac could be as much like her father as he was his opposite. It made her more wary of Zac. At the same time, she began to wonder if her father was as far wrong as she had thought.

"Now tell me why I'm supposed to care about this woman's baby," Zac asked. He looked up suddenly. "You don't have her outside the door, do you, or hiding in the closet?"

"She's getting ready to go to work, but I told her I'd tell her what you decided."

"You women are all the same. You gang up and back a man into a corner. Then you tell him you'll be happy with whatever he decides."

155

"But I won't," Lily said. "I'll be very upset if you don't help Kitty bring her baby to town."

"Kitty," Zac said half to himself. "Brunette. Runs a roulette wheel. Does very well."

"Exactly. Only she needs to move up to a faro bank to make enough money to support her baby."

"She hasn't been here long enough. She's got a little more than a week to go."

Lily decided Zac was pulling the wool over Dodie's eyes. He pretended he didn't know what was going on in the saloon, but he obviously knew more than either of them thought.

"Dodie says she's good enough already. She has no objection if you—"

"Can't do it. It wouldn't be fair to the other girls."

Zac was clearly getting his feet under him. He was also becoming unexpectedly businesslike.

"But you don't understand her situation."

"Okay, make me understand."

Lily was feeling decidedly uncomfortable with this side of Zac. While she explained, she looked in vain for some sign of softening. Maybe this was the other person Dodie had said was hiding inside Zac. But why had he decided to come out now?

"It's cruel for her to be separated from her baby," Lily finished up. "It's only until she finds its father."

"I doubt she'll find him," Zac said. "I won't move her up until she's been here a full six weeks, but I will lend her the money. She can pay me back when she gets promoted."

"I was thinking you might give it to her."

Lily didn't like the hard glitter in Zac's eyes. It made him look very unfriendly. Cold and hard.

"I never give anybody anything," Zac said. "It only encourages them to expect more. I run a business. I expect to make a healthy profit. If I don't, half those girls out there will be in the street."

Lily didn't know quite what to say. She didn't like this

side of Zac, but she couldn't argue with it. It was exactly what her father would have said.

Zac's gaze turned even harder. "Did she put you up to this?"

"No," Lily hastened to assure him. "I heard her crying. She didn't want to tell me. It was my idea to talk to you."

"Next time, I'd appreciate it if you'd talk to me before you go making promises. You might make one I can't keep. None of us would like that."

"No," Lily agreed, feeling she had been justly chastised.

"Go find Kitty. We might as well put her out of her misery."

Lily was on the verge of fleeing, but Zac's expression changed. Suddenly he was smiling, looking like the Zac she was used to. She held her breath, waiting.

"You've got a soft heart," he said. "Maybe too soft."

She made no reply.

"I have to be careful. I can't help everybody. If I stretch myself too thin, I might fail the ones I've promised. You understand, don't you?"

She did. She was a fool not to have seen it earlier. She felt an overwhelming desire to cry.

"I can't keep going on stage looking like I'm going to a funeral," Lily said to Dodie.

"Talk to Zac. He's the one who doesn't want anybody to notice you."

"I have, and he won't listen. Those black eyes start to go hard, like some of that black rock I saw in Utah. He glares at me as if he wants to send me to my room. Then he tells me he's only doing it for my protection."

"You don't believe him?"

"Of course I believe him. Zac wouldn't lie to me. Don't arch your eyebrows. I can't imagine Zac lying to anyone. It's too much trouble. Besides, since he doesn't care what anyone thinks, why bother?"

Dodie burst out laughing. "You don't have a great opinion of the man, do you?"

Lily grinned. "I like him too much for my own good, but I'm not blind. Papa may be hardheaded and stubborn, but he taught me never to make a fool of myself by seeing in people only what I want to see."

"I'm glad your pa said something useful, but that doesn't solve the problem of a dress, or why you want one."

"I'm tired of Zac looking through me as if I'm not there," Lily confessed. "Maybe if the customers really liked me, he'd stop treating me like a nuisance he hopes will go away."

"You're not getting sweet on him, are you?" Dodie asked.

Lily had asked herself that question a dozen times without getting a satisfactory answer. She hadn't given up on her goal to save Zac from himself, but the more she was around him, the more she believed he really didn't need saving, that he only needed a reason to stop throwing his life away on a gambling hall.

When she thought of the women he had helped, she wondered if she wasn't the one with the limited perspective. In his own way, Zac was doing far more good than she ever had.

"I don't know," Lily answered truthfully. "Despite what he says about himself, he's a good man. He has very strong principles and holds firmly to them. Then, of course, there's his looks."

"Yes, every woman gets around to his looks sooner or later. Mostly sooner."

"How could you not swoon over a man who looks like Zac?"

"I can't help you there. I certainly did."

"And you still care for him, don't you?"

Dodie took a moment to light one of her thin cigars. "If I have to be totally honest, I guess I have to admit I'll always love Zac. He gave me my life back again, and he wouldn't take anything in return. I used to think he was incapable of feeling real emotion. Then you showed up.''

"Me? He hardly knows I'm alive. If I disappeared tomorrow, he'd breathe a sigh of relief and forget my existence within a week.''

"No, you've shaken him. I'd never have dared put him out of his bed for anyone else. If anybody else had been doing your number, he'd have had her front and center, dress hemmed high and cut low, enough paint on her face to be seen coming through a fog.''

"Are you sure? He doesn't seem interested to me.''

"You're in love with him, aren't you?''

"I don't think so, but it's terribly hard to decide with him ignoring me. I can't tell if I truly like him, or if I'm only interested because he's hurt my vanity.''

Dodie let out a crack of laughter. "At least you're honest.''

"Papa said—''

"Don't tell me. I feel like I know the man, and I've never set eyes on him. Do you really want to find out what Zac feels?''

"Yes, even though it frightens me a little. I'm petrified I could never live up to his expectations.''

"If Zac ever truly falls in love, he'll be so busy trying to live up to his own expectations, he won't notice if you slip a little once in a while.''

"I think it's time we find out,'' Lily said. "Let's talk to the other girls. I want to change the whole routine.''

Chapter Twelve

"If you don't hold still," Dodie admonished, "you'll have lipstick smeared from one side of your face to the other."

Lily couldn't sit still. She'd never worn face paint. Her father said it was a sin to alter what Mother Nature had given you. But Dodie said Lily would wash out under the strong lights. If she wanted to make an impression on Zac, there was no point in half measures.

Lily had changed her hair, too. Instead of letting it fall over her shoulders, she had put it up in a French twist. Then she had pinned a spray of blue forget-me-nots in her hair.

"Ready for your eyes?" Dodie asked.

"Just outline them," Lily said. "I don't want them to get lost in my face. My eyebrows either. I'm too fair. I wish I had been born a brunette." She thought of Zac's ebony eyebrows and lashes with envy.

Lily was not sure about the dress Julie had chosen for her. Julie might be reluctant to appear in the saloon herself, but she was only too happy to make a dress for Lily of a clear blue material that glistened in the light. It was nearly off her shoulders and cut so low that Lily felt she was in a constant draft. The hem was so high, people could see her ankles.

Papa would have apoplexy if he saw her in anything like this. She just hoped Zac didn't have a similar reaction.

"There," Dodie said. "All done. Now you're ready to go out and face the world."

"Let me see," Lily said.

"You're not going to look like yourself," Dodie warned.

"After all this, I hope not."

Lily took the mirror and held it up. A brazenly painted face stared back at her.

"Do you like it?" Dodie asked.

"Of course she does," Julie said. "Can't you see she's speechless?"

Lily could hardly believe she was looking at herself. The entire character of her face had changed.

"Do I really belong to that face?" she asked Dodie.

"Not yet," Dodie replied, understanding instantly what she meant, "but if you're going to undertake the capture and taming of one Zac Randolph, you'll have to."

But Lily wasn't sure she wanted to capture and tame Zac enough to go around looking like this all the time. She felt like Delilah on the prowl for Samson.

Julie took the mirror from her. "You don't have time to admire yourself. I hear your music starting. You'll be going on stage in about two minutes."

Lily stood. She felt awkward in such high heels. It was even harder to dance in them, but she knew it was necessary. No half measures. She wasn't certain she agreed with her own philosophy, but once she had talked everyone into helping her, she couldn't back down.

She was so nervous, she worried she wouldn't be able to sing a note. She had worked on the number for a week. The other girls had gotten up an hour early each day so they could rehearse without fear of Zac coming downstairs and finding out what they were doing. She couldn't fail them now.

They were playing her introduction. Lily felt a moment of panic. Had Hezekiah appeared before her at that instant, she might have thrown herself into his arms and begged him to do with her as he wished.

But Hezekiah wasn't there, and this change was all her idea. There was no point in getting weak in the knees now. All she had to do was sing a little song in front of a few men. There was nothing to it. She'd done it for a week already.

Lily put a smile on her face, offered a prayer to the angel in charge of fools and drunks—she hadn't bothered him lately—and stepped out onto the stage.

Zac had taken his coffee to his office while he looked at the returns for the week. The saloon had never made so much money. If things kept up like this, he was either going to have to buy a second saloon or start putting his money into some legitimate investments. He smiled to himself. Wouldn't Madison and Jeff love that. They'd been investing his share of the family income for years, but Zac had never let them touch his gambling money.

The noise from the saloon intruded on his thoughts. It was hard to concentrate. He ought be out there now, but he'd stayed up later than usual last night. The cards had gone his way. He couldn't seem to lose. Chet Lee had had to be hauled away shouting curses at his head. Zac knew he was a fool not to ban the man from the saloon, but he couldn't resist taking his money. Chet seemed to have a genius for locating newly rich investors and cheating them out of their mine stocks. It kept Zac busy winning Chet's ill-gotten gains away from him.

Damn, maybe he'd better go see what was going on. The noise was getting louder. As he got up, he wondered where Dodie was. She usually liked to be at his side when he looked over the figures for the week. She probably couldn't because of the noise. It sounded as if they were having a riot. If Chet Lee was responsible, he was going to have to break his head.

But once Zac entered the saloon, it was clear there was no riot. They were going crazy over some singer he'd never seen before. And rightly so. The woman was stunning. She sounded a lot like Lily, but she didn't look or act like her. Zac saw Dodie leaning against one of the abandoned hazard tables and walked over to her.

"Why didn't you tell me you had a new singer? Was Lily upset when you replaced her?"

"Not a bit," Dodie said without turning around. "It was her idea."

Zac looked a little closer. "She looks familiar. Who is she?"

"Somebody."

"Where did you find her?"

"Around."

"Don't get coy with me." Zac could hear the amusement in Dodie's voice. "A woman like that is never just around. She'd have crowds of men following her down the street."

"She did. It made it impossible for her to keep a job."

Zac felt as if he'd been hit over the head with a rifle butt. It couldn't be! It was impossible! But it had to be.

That woman was Lily!

He didn't know which staggered him more—her looks, the way she was acting, or the fact that at least a hundred men were staring at her in rapt wonder. Some even reached out trying to touch the hem of her dress when she passed close to the edge of the stage. He was, however, sure of one thing. He had to get Lily off that stage, and he had to get her off now.

Zac wasn't quite sure how he got there, but the next thing he knew, he'd pushed his way through the crowd and was mounting the stage. He reached Lily in half a dozen strides. Around him the girls forgot their steps in the surprise of seeing him, thunderously angry, in their midst. Lily gazed at him in shock, the last note of her song dying on her lips.

"Sorry, fellas, but she can't stay. There's been a death in her family." Taking Lily by the arm, he hurried her off stage and out of the main room before the shocked audience realized what was happening.

In the background, the piano started up once again.

Lily stumbled along, nearly falling in the unfamiliar high heels.

"Was this your idea?" Zac demanded of Dodie as he charged past.

"It was mine," Lily told him. "And I would very much appreciate it if you would release my arm."

"Not until I've had a few words with both of you in my office."

Those black-rock eyes were back again. Lily felt something quiver in the pit of her stomach. Dodie merely smiled and headed toward the office without making the slightest objection.

"Now," Zac said when he had slammed the door behind them, "what in hell were you doing out there looking like a strumpet?"

"Lily wanted you to notice her," Dodie announced. "She said she was tired of being treated like a piece of furniture."

Zac gaped at Lily. Lily stared right back.

"Glad to see you're on the same wavelength," Dodie said. "Now I think I'd better take a look outside. Your walking off with the star of the new number is bound to cause a flap."

"What the hell is she talking about?" Zac demanded. "I think she's gone queer in the head lately."

"It's not her fault," Lily said. "It was my idea."

"So Dodie said, but what's this about me noticing you? You've been underfoot for weeks."

"That's just it," Lily said, a little of her courage coming back at his terrible choice of words. "I'm something under foot, in the way, a bother, a responsibility you'd rather be without."

"I never said that," Zac protested. "I—"

"You just said I was underfoot. If you never said the rest, you thought it."

"A bad choice of words," Zac admitted. "You got me a little rattled."

"Good."

"What do you mean *good?*"

"It's better than being ignored."

"I haven't ignored you. You've been more trouble than any dozen females I know."

"See, that's exactly what I meant. Now I'm trouble."

"Dammit to hell, you're twisting my words."

"Don't curse."

"I'll curse as much as I damned well please, and don't tell me it's a sign of a limited vocabulary. When I say dammit to hell, I *mean* dammit to hell!"

"Papa says—"

"Don't you ever think for yourself?"

"Of course I do."

"Then stop prefacing every word by *Papa says.* I don't give a damn about your old man. As far as I'm concerned, he's a jackass and a fool or he'd never have let you run away from home. As for all those wise things he says, he probably got them out of some book. The man's clearly not smart enough to know he's got a beautiful, intelligent, courageous daughter. If you were mine, I'd be here right now dragging you back to Virginia. And I'd shoot any gambler who so much as thought about laying a hand on you."

Lily didn't say a word. She just stared at him.

"Don't look at me like that," Zac said. "It makes me nervous."

"I can't help it," Lily finally managed to say. "I was sure you thought I was a country simpleton who would get gobbled up in five minutes if you weren't there to watch over me all the time."

"I do. Well, not the simpleton part. But you don't know what to do in a city. You're too damn trusting. You nearly had those men out there worked into a frenzy."

"Yes. Wasn't it wonderful?"

"Wonderful! I was ready to shoot the eyes out of the lot of them. I don't know how I'm going to explain to them that you won't be appearing again."

"But I will."

"No, you won't. This is my saloon. I say who appears in it."

"I can ask for a job next door. Or across the street. After tonight, they'll hire me."

"No, they won't. I'll shoot them if they try."

Lily laughed. A happy, delighted laugh. "You can't go around shooting everybody."

"Yes, I can."

"Now you're the one who's acting like a simpleton. I'm just going to do one number. Twice."

"Twice!" Zac had never known his voice could rise so high. It sounded like a squawk.

"Dodie says it's always slow for the first two hours. She thinks my number is just what you need to get things started earlier. Then you can make more money and not have to stay up so late."

"No!"

"You keep this up, and you're going to lose your looks before you're thirty. Papa says"—Lily paused to clear her throat—"*I* say you need more rest, better food, and more regular hours."

Zac began to wonder if he might not be the one turning simpleminded. Why was it that Lily could turn everything upside down until it came out the way she wanted? Always before, he'd been the clever one, the one to manage people, to get them to do what he wanted, to have the answers before they thought of the questions. Now he seemed to have the thinking capacity of a longhorn bull that had been grazing on locoweed.

"I want to sing twice," Lily said. "That way I'll feel like I'm earning my money."

"I'm paying you to help Dodie."

"But she doesn't need help, at least not enough for what you pay me. But if I bring in extra customers, I'll be worth it."

How could he convince her his objections had nothing to do with money? She was obsessed with paying her way. He didn't care if she never earned a cent if it meant she had to display herself in front of all those leering gazes.

"It has nothing to do with the money."

"Yes, it does. I've been a drag on you ever since I got here. Now I've found something I can do, a way I can help. That's important to me. You ought to understand that. You said that's how you felt when you ran away to start your own saloon."

Zac nodded.

"I can't tell my father I think he's wrong about me when I can't take care of myself. That would make me a failure— a stupid, selfish failure—and I refuse to be that. Do you understand?"

Of course he did. She sounded so much like himself eight years ago, it was uncanny. But it wasn't the same for a woman as it was for a man. She couldn't just go out and take the world by the tail. It was liable to turn on her.

But she wouldn't understand that, not while she was basking in the glow of success. He'd have to wait, pick his time, choose his words carefully, but he was going to have to convince her she was wrong.

"Now you stay here until I'm done," Lily said, her smile restored to its full power. "I don't think you ought to come out if it's going to upset you. Why don't you have some of that brandy you keep for Dodie? She says it's a wonderful pick-me-up. You look like you could use one."

Zac sat staring at the door that closed behind Lily, trying to figure how he'd gotten here from where he was just an hour ago. It was as though a flash flood had washed away all the trails, carrying him along with it. Now he was high and dry on the rocks and couldn't figure what the hell he was going to do next.

He got to his feet. He would have a drink. That was the best idea Lily had had all evening. Then he was going to go out there and punch the daylights out of the first man who forgot to treat her like a lady.

"I can't imagine what any decent woman would do with this," Mrs. Wellborn said, holding up an undergarment made of nearly sheer material and decorated with knots of ribbon and embroidered with rosebuds.

The women were sorting through clothes in Mrs. Thoragood's parlor, a curiously overdecorated room in stark contrast to Mrs. Thoragood's severity of dress and character.

"Maybe it can be altered," Bella said.

"I should think it would have to be cut up and used for something altogether different," Mrs. Thoragood said. She looked at the pile of garments they were sorting. "It's a disgrace that most of the clothes we have to distribute came from dance hall girls and saloon doxies."

"I think we should be thankful for the clothes no matter where they came from," Lily said. "They're very colorful, and the material is in good condition."

"But how can a decent woman make use of this?" Mrs. Thoragood demanded, jerking up a gown made of material so thin it was nearly transparent.

"It'll make a nice shift for the summer," Lily said.

"Maybe in Sacramento where it gets boiling hot," Mrs. Thoragood said. "But not for San Francisco with its fog and damp. A woman could catch pneumonia in something like this."

"We could refuse to accept them," Mrs. Chickalee said.

"I've considered that," Mrs. Thoragood said. "I've even talked to Harold. He says it might be better to have nothing to distribute to the poor than to give them something which might further undermine morals already dangerously loose."

"I don't agree," Lily said.

The four women turned in unison. "Why not?" Mrs. Thoragood demanded.

"I don't think we should ever refuse a gift. I believe giving does far more for the giver than for the receiver. Besides, it's un-Christian to ask people to donate their discarded clothing and then tell them what they've given isn't good enough."

"Are you daring to place your opinion in opposition to my husband's?" Mrs. Thoragood demanded, her color dangerously heightened, her speech unnaturally deliberate.

"But they're dance hall girls," Bella interposed, in an apparent effort to head off an explosion.

"We don't want people to think we approve of what those women do," Mrs. Wellborn said.

"What do they do that's so bad?" Lily asked.

Her companions were at a loss for words.

"Have you ever been to a saloon?"

"How dare you ask such a question?" Mrs. Thoragood said.

"Then how do you know?"

"My dear, we all know that coming from a small town in the Virginia mountains as you do, you aren't aware of what goes on in San Francisco."

"I expect I'm a good deal more aware than any of you," Lily snapped, her patience gone. "I live in a saloon."

Bella turned red. The other women gasped in shock.

"I thought you were staying with Bella," Mrs. Thoragood said.

"Didn't she tell you?" Lily said, unable to deny the tiny bit of malicious pleasure in her soul. "Bella threw me out because she thought I was giving her place a bad name. She took me to the Little Corner of Heaven. Since I had no money, my cousin had no choice but to let me stay there."

"But Bella said you had a job."

"I did, several of them, but Mrs. Wellborn and Mrs. Chickalee both fired me. They said I was giving their places a bad name, too."

Clearly none of the ladies had had the courage to tell Mrs. Thoragood what they had done. Lily was honest enough to admit she enjoyed seeing the three women squirm under the ominous glare of their minister's wife.

"Would you refuse any clothes I might give?" Lily said, hoping to draw the discussion back to the original point.

"Of course not," Mrs. Thoragood said, reluctant to have her attention drawn from such interesting shortcomings in her flock.

"Even if I sang there?"

"Don't be absurd," Mrs. Thoragood said. "It's ridiculous even to attempt to imagine such a thing. You wouldn't—"

"I do," Lily announced. "I wear a blue dress and put flowers in my hair. I even dance a little bit. I don't do it very well, but the customers seem to like it. The other girls are much better."

"Other girls," Mrs. Thoragood echoed in a faint voice.

"Twelve of them. Zac said everybody had to be on stage with me."

The four women gaped at her as though she were Salome lacking only her seven veils before she would go into a dance so scandalous, it would echo down through twenty centuries.

"You can't continue to do such a thing," Mrs. Thoragood said, suddenly finding her voice. "You've got to stop immediately."

"It's my job," Lily said.

"We'll find you another job," Mrs. Thoragood said, her voice throbbing with outrage.

"I'm finally able to pay for my room and board and I still have something left over."

"We'll find a place for you to stay as well," Mrs. Thoragood said, casting a glance full of foreboding at Bella. "It's inconceivable that a woman of your nature should be dancing in a saloon. Think of the danger, the nearness of so many men barely better than animals."

"Don't worry," Lily said, forced to smile at Mrs. Thoragood's lurid idea of what went on inside a saloon. "I'm perfectly safe. Zac never leaves the room when I'm performing. He has two huge men—he keeps them to throw out people who cause trouble—stand between me and the customers. The worst thing that has happened is some men got into a fight over who got to keep a handkerchief I dropped. Another time they started to throw dice to see who got to buy my supper, but Zac stopped them."

"Fights, dice throwing, singing and dancing," Mrs. Wellborn said in a voice that grew weaker with each word.

"Something will have to be done," Mrs. Thoragood announced. "A member of our congregation shall not be forced to work in such a place."

"It's not that bad," Lily assured her. "I think it's fun."

"See, I told you sin could ravage even the most righteous soul," Mrs. Thoragood intoned. "There's not a moment to waste."

Chapter Thirteen

"Oh my stars and garters!" Dodie exclaimed. "If I'm not seeing what I think I'm seeing, I'll never touch brandy again."

"What the devil are you talking about?" Zac barked.

He'd woken up at three-thirty from a dream about Lily being kidnapped by Barbary pirates and carried off to Turkey in a boat that looked like a cross between a Chinese sampan and a twelve-masted clipper ship. The fact that his dream was far-fetched and nonsensical only served to blacken his mood.

"It's the preacher's wife and what looks like a temperance committee."

Zac looked up to see Sarah Thoragood leading her little band as though through a room full of serpents. They kept to the middle of a narrow aisle, their arms held close to their sides.

"On second thought, it looks like a vigilante committee," Dodie said. "I wonder where they're hiding the rope."

"You can be sure Lily's at the bottom of this somehow. Where is she?"

"Gone with Kitty to spend the afternoon with her mother and baby."

"So I get to deal with the vigilantes without interference."

Dodie gave Zac a sharp look. "Be careful what you say. Lily will be the one to suffer the consequences."

"Damnation!" Zac cursed. He was feeling ripe for murder, just the right mood for Mrs. Reverend Thoragood. "What is Bella doing trailing along with her?"

"I don't know," Dodie answered, "but she doesn't seem to be happy about it."

As Bella draw nearer, Zac thought she looked willing to give up a month's income to be able to escape. This situation got more interesting all the time.

The delegation came to a halt before Zac. Two women he didn't know flanked Sarah Thoragood. Bella stood in the back—so she wouldn't have to look him in the eye, Zac guessed.

"Are you Mr. Zachary Taylor Randolph?" Mrs. Thoragood asked.

Zac winced at the name. Luckily, Dodie kept a straight face.

"I'm Zac Randolph. Did you ladies lose your way? Or did you forget to check your watches? We don't open for another two hours. But if you don't want people to know you're taking a flyer, Dodie can open a table early for you. Only you've got to promise you won't use any money you *borrowed* from the offering plate."

Zac thought Sarah Thoragood was going to explode.

"I'm not going to dignify those remarks by a reply," she said, even more pompously than Zac expected. "I've come on a matter of utmost urgency. I only heard about it this morning, but it has upset me so, I couldn't put it off a single day. All of us feel the same way."

The flanking ladies nodded their agreement. Bella remained in the back.

"What's so urgent?" Zac asked. "Has the Devil come to town? I would have thought he'd stop in here before going to the church."

"Mr. Randolph!" Mrs. Thoragood thundered in a style she must have copied from her husband. "Do you dare make light of this serious issue?"

"I don't know what the issue is. I'm just making light for the fun of it."

He could tell Dodie was trying not to laugh, but she was also shaking her head. He'd gone far enough. It would only be harder on Lily if he kept this up.

"It has come to my attention that Lily Sterling is at present living in your saloon."

"True," Zac said moving to the side until he could catch Bella's eye. "She was living in a rooming house, but the landlady evicted her."

"I've also been told she's singing and dancing on your stage."

"After everybody fired her, it was the only way she could earn a living," Zac said. "You seem to have dragged most of the guilty parties along with you. Are you going to hang them or crucify them? I vote for the latter, but I don't know where you can find three crosses."

"Mr. Randolph, if you are going to persist in uttering blasphemy, I will be unable to continue this conversation."

"You promise? I've got lots more."

"You'll have to excuse Zac," Dodie said, unable to remain quiet any longer. "A bad dream woke him early, and he's not himself yet."

"A dream of your own descent into hell, no doubt," Mrs. Thoragood said.

"No, Lily's," Zac said, suddenly tired of baiting this foolish woman.

"Then you agree we must do everything we can to keep her from that terrible fate."

He didn't know what the harridan had in mind, but he did agree with her sentiment. He nodded.

"Then you will also agree the very best thing would be for her to return to her parents' home in Virginia."

"I told her that the evening she arrived."

"Then I'm compelled to ask you to attempt to persuade her again. I've tried, but she seems to think she would be deserting you. I hesitate to tell you this—you may put the wrong interpretation on my words—but I think she believes she's been sent to save your soul."

Zac's bark of laughter caused all four ladies to jump. "Not even Lily could believe that's possible."

"Anything is possible; however . . ."

"However, you don't believe so in this case. Don't bother to answer. I'll talk with Lily, but I doubt she'll go back to Virginia."

"I know she won't," Dodie said. "It's a waste of time to ask her."

"Nevertheless, you will try?" Mrs. Thoragood asked Zac.

"Yes. What's your fall-back strategy if she refuses?"

"In that eventuality," Mrs. Thoragood said, clearly displeased with Zac's attitude, "you will agree we must find her a suitable place to live and a position of employment that is above reproach."

"I agree," Zac said, just wanting to get the visit over. If he had to have much more to do with this woman, he might have to resort to brandy to preserve his sanity. He didn't know why Mr. Thoragood wasn't a habitual drunk.

"These ladies have accompanied me because they have reconsidered their positions," Mrs. Thoragood said.

From the expressions on their faces, Zac decided that Mrs. Thoragood had done most of the reconsidering.

"Miss Sterling can return to her room at Bella's," Mrs. Thoragood said. "Mrs. Wellborn and Mrs. Chickalee will each hire her for half a day. Perhaps that will prevent so many young men from gathering at either shop."

Zac's respect for Mrs. Thoragood rose considerably. He

didn't know the two older women, but he did know it took a powerful lot of persuading to get Bella Holt to change her mind about anything. Clearly Mrs. Thoragood was a woman not to be taken lightly.

"You'll have to talk to Lily about that," Zac said.

"Of course."

"She's not here at the moment."

"When can we have her call on you?" Dodie asked.

"The sooner the better," Mrs. Thoragood said.

"I'll tell her you want to see her the minute she comes in," Dodie promised.

As Mrs. Thoragood turned to go, her gaze fell on the stage. "Is that where she performs?" she asked.

Zac nodded.

Mrs. Thoragood's gaze surveyed the cavernous space of the saloon. "You must have more people in here every night than my husband has in church." It was clear she considered the imbalance unfair and undeserved.

"Ask Lily to do a little song for you," Zac suggested. "I bet it'll do wonders for Sunday attendance."

Mrs. Thoragood swept from the saloon followed closely by her supporters.

"What are you going to do now?" Dodie asked when the doors had closed behind the women.

"I don't know."

"She won't go."

"I know, but you have to admit it would be the best thing for her."

"Would it be the best thing for you?"

Zac snapped out of his abstraction. "It sure would. It would be a burden off my mind."

He got up and wandered over to the stage. It *would* be best if Lily went home. He could stop worrying about her. He could stop hating the men for staring at her. It was getting in the way of his gambling. He'd always gambled for fun and because he was good at it. Now he found himself searching out men who seemed to be overly interested in

Lily, drawing them into a game, trying to empty their pockets as fast as possible so they'd leave. It was a compulsion that pushed him relentlessly.

It would be a load off his mind, but he would miss her. She caused more trouble than any female was worth, but somehow he didn't mind as much as he'd expected.

Sarah Thoragood entered her husband's study without knocking. "We've been overwhelmed by donations this past week," she told him. "I would never have believed your appeal from the pulpit could have had such results."

Mr. Thoragood appeared more than normally pleased with himself. "I put a lot into that sermon," he said. "I guess those sinners finally got the message. If they don't shape up while they're down here, they needn't bother when Gabriel blows his trumpet."

"Yes, you made that abundantly clear, my dear. But you've done so before without such spectacular results."

"Spirits shouldn't be the only things that get better with age. Why not preachers?"

"Why not?" said Mrs. Thoragood. "I've posted the names of half a dozen men as the largest contributors. I can't understand it. Before it's always been their wives who donated."

That night a fist fight broke out over a card game. That in itself wasn't unusual. The reason for the game, however, was not in the least bit ordinary. Lily had let it be known that she would have dinner with the man who could raise the most money for the church benevolent fund. When Mrs. Thoragood posted six names as the top donors, the six men agreed to a card game to determine the winner.

Several mines, a ranch, two saloons, and a freight company had changed hands before the fight broke out. One of the losers objected to the winner holding four aces when he already held two. Zac told them he would give more money than any of them, so they could all take their property back.

He wasn't going to have Lily's name bandied around town because they were such fools.

"I told you Zac wasn't the wicked man you thought," Lily said when Mrs. Thoragood told her about the check. Lily had gone to the Thoragoods' home to drop off some more clothes donated by the girls at the saloon.

"But I don't understand why he should give money to us," Mrs. Thoragood said. "He's not a member of the church. He's never even been inside its doors."

"I don't think you can expect him to attend," Lily said.

"I'd be a very odd minister's wife if I wished for gamblers to make up part of a Christian congregation."

"You should count yourself fortunate if you did," Lily shot back. "He does more good for this community without telling anybody about it than anybody else I know."

"Are you comparing his work to my husband's?" Mrs. Thoragood asked, her bosom beginning to swell.

"No, but I venture to suggest that if Zac wanted something done, he'd get more people offering to help than Mr. Thoragood."

Mrs. Thoragood couldn't argue with that, though she desperately wanted to. She had often bemoaned the unpleasant reality that evil had more power to move men than good. She had no doubt Zac had a direct access to an unlimited supply of wickedness.

Mrs. Thoragood was further displeased to learn that Zac hadn't yet had his promised talk with Lily. She would have been more than willing to do it herself, but Lily had shown a pronounced aversion to having anyone criticize her behavior or tell her what to do. She absolutely refused to allow anyone to disparage Zac Randolph within her hearing. Mrs. Thoragood was not a coward, but she was a sensible woman. She knew when to trim her sails and wait for more favorable winds.

* * *

Two pistol shots in the street broke Zac's concentration like a snapped thread. He slammed his cards face down on the table and sprinted across the saloon. He opened the door and came to an abrupt halt.

Two men were down and bleeding. One lay on the sidewalk, the other sprawled half in the street. A quick inspection showed the wounds to be serious but not fatal.

"What the hell are you bleeding all over my doorstep for?" Zac demanded.

"The damned bastard shot me," the offending bleeder said. "He didn't even bother to give me a warning. He just followed me out the door and shot me."

"What for?"

"I called him a yellow-bellied, low-down skunk of a liar."

"That'll usually get a man's dander up," Zac observed wryly.

"He shouldn't have said anything about Miss Lily."

Zac's body stiffened. "What did he say? And don't shout it all over the street for everybody to hear."

"I wouldn't let them words pass my lips," the man said between labored breaths. "I told him if he repeated them to a soul, I'd kill him."

"Looks like he tried to shoot you in the back."

"What else could you expect of a man who'd defame the reputation of an angel like Miss Lily?"

At first Lily had been furious when Zac told her she couldn't perform that evening. Not even her feeling of guilt when he said it would be nice to pass an evening without riots, fist fights, or gun battles could make her accept being banned from the stage.

She had finally realized there was a little of the wanton in her. She liked singing, dancing, the glitter of the spotlight, the feeling of power over men, and the knowledge that the big, brutal rulers of the world would do virtually anything to please her. She supposed this was the hidden seed of sin her father had seen deep inside her years ago. It must have been the reason he'd watched her so carefully and pledged her to Hezekiah so early.

It had worried her at first, but as the days went by and nothing terrible happened, she had begun to relax and enjoy her success. She'd never experienced anything like it before. It was hard not to want still more.

Which was why she was so angry with Zac.

He said he wanted to talk about her future. That was ominous. He hadn't mentioned her future for days, but she could tell he had been burning to. It was like a huge lake building up behind a high dam. Apparently the dam was going to break tonight. She was determined it wouldn't wash her away.

She didn't plan to spend the rest of her life singing in the Little Corner of Heaven, but neither was she about to give it up until she had something better to do.

On top of everything else, Zac wasn't acting like himself. It was almost as if he was trying to placate her, trying to coax her into a good humor. She didn't trust him when he was like that. She knew something serious was in the air when she headed past his office and he called her in.

"We can't talk here," Zac said. "Get something to wrap up in. It's always cold on the water at night."

Dodie handed her a thick shawl.

"On the water?"

"I'm taking you to dinner on a yacht on the bay."

Lily was prey to several emotions. Like all mountain people, she had an innate distrust of large bodies of deep, wave-crested water. Neither was she thrilled with the idea of bobbing around on it in a small boat. The ferry boat had been bad enough. That anyone should be able to enjoy eating dinner on a moving vessel was beyond her comprehension.

However, she didn't say anything. She would attempt to swim the bay at its widest point before she would let Zac think she was a coward. She didn't know why that mattered so much, but it did.

It wasn't very far to the pier, but Lily was glad Zac had chosen to take her in a cab. It gave her less time to worry about what he was going to say. She became uneasy when the cab hit the boards of the wharf. The horse's hooves rang loud on the planks, but it was the sound of the boards rattling as the cab passed over them that completely unsettled her. The waves of the bay lapped noisily under the wharf at the pilings that held them above water.

Lily was almost relieved to reach the yacht.

"I don't see any masts," she said. "Who's going to row us?"

Zac laughed. "You stayed in your mountain valley too long. The yacht is powered by a steam engine. It's noisy, so we'll bank the boiler while we eat."

If it was anything like the train, Lily thought, it would be deafening. But she didn't have time to worry about the noise. As the yacht began to make its way slowly into the bay, the city took on a whole different appearance. Lily found herself moving under the cloak of night, staring back at the lights of the coast as it moved farther and farther away.

"Everything looks so small," she said to Zac. "The lights look like the fireflies I used to catch when I was a little girl."

It wasn't long before they had moved far enough out into the bay to be hit by the ocean winds that came whistling through the Golden Gate. Lily shivered and reached for the shawl Dodie had given her.

"It's beautiful," she said, thankful for the shawl and the shelter of Zac's body. "But I can see why more people aren't enjoying the view."

"Why?" Zac asked.

"Because they're afraid of freezing, being blown overboard, or getting lost in this endless darkness."

"Do you want to go back?"

"No." She did, but she'd never let him know.

Lily was relieved to discover they were to eat below deck.

"It's not nearly so enjoyable down here," Zac apologized, "but on deck the wind practically blows the food from in front of you."

"It's fine," Lily said, trying not to sound relieved.

Dinner was wonderful. She was used to the delicious things the chef at the saloon created, but tonight she had her first taste of lobster and crab.

Her enjoyment of the evening, however, was blunted by the knowledge that Zac had brought her out here for a purpose. She didn't know what it was, but she didn't think she was going to like it. It didn't look as though he was either. He kept up a steady stream of harmless chatter throughout the meal, but without his usual sense of fun. It seemed forced, as if he was making himself entertain her.

Nonetheless, she liked being below deck. They were anchored in a cove. The waves were so gentle, she soon forgot about them. She couldn't see the bay if she didn't look out the windows. The food was cooked right in front of them on several braziers. The heat from the coals warmed the cabin until the effect of the food and the heat were so relaxing that she could hardly keep her eyes open.

Then Zac asked her the question he'd obviously been meaning to ask from the beginning. "What about your future?"

Lily jerked out of her daze. "What about it?"

"What do you intend to do with yourself? You've seen just about all there is to see in San Francisco. It's about time you start thinking about going back home."

"I'm not going back home," Lily said. "I thought you understood that by now."

"I thought you were running away so you wouldn't have to marry that preacher fellow. Surely you've made your point by now."

"You've missed the point. That's not why I really left home," Lily said, irked that men seemed to see a woman's life only in terms of marriage to one man or another. They didn't seem to understand that even if she did want to be a wife and mother, a woman wanted to feel she had an identity of her own as well.

"Maybe it's not all your fault," she conceded. "I admit when I came out here, all I was thinking about was getting away from Papa and not marrying Hezekiah. But I see things differently now. I realize I could never spend the rest of my life in Salem, especially as Papa's daughter. I have too many ideas that would make people uncomfortable, Papa most of all."

"Such as?"

"I like having my own job. I like being free to do what I like with my time. Mama is forty-six years old, and she's never had a minute when some man wasn't telling her what to do. I don't mean I won't want to please my husband, but I also like pleasing myself. I love singing a new song, changing the dance routine, or deciding on a new dress. I know they're tiny things, but I never felt I accomplished anything before. Everything I did was planned for me by someone else."

"So you do want to get married, have a family, do all those wife-and-mother things?"

"Not right away, but someday. But I don't want to go into marriage with my husband thinking he owns me and I'll do everything he says without question. I don't want him to think he's the only one with any requirements. I'm not going to marry just any man. If he doesn't come up my standards, he can go peddle himself somewhere else."

Zac laughed. "You sound dangerously radical. That's not considered a popular trait in a woman. Were you always this feisty?"

"Yes, but nobody paid me any attention. Papa said I was just talking to make him mad. Mama thought I wanted to shock people. My brothers through I was crazy. I had no choice but to run away."

"That may well be, but you're not going to get where you want to go from here," Zac said.

"I don't understand."

"You need to get away from me."

"I still don't understand."

But she did. She had known for a long time that Zac didn't think he was worth very much. She realized it was part of the reason he talked so much, was always making people laugh. He didn't want anybody to get to know him, to get close. With the girls, he kept things on a very businesslike basis. Only Dodie could occasionally step inside his defenses, and then not very far.

"You're not going to find the kind of husband you want hanging around me. The Little Corner of Heaven is on the edge of the Barbary Coast, the most lawless part of any city outside of the Tenderloin District in New Orleans. I located it there on purpose. You know why? Because I wanted to attract men who were gamblers, who were willing to risk losing their last dollar for the sake of a game."

"But Dodie says you get men from some of the best families in San Francisco."

"I get the worst men from some of the best families, the ones who can't hold a job, who see more of their mistresses than they do of their wives, who probably wouldn't recognize their children. The dregs of society come to my saloon. Not only are you not going to meet anyone suitable there, if you don't get out soon, you'll get a reputation that will keep you out of society."

"I don't care about that."

"You just think you don't. You're having fun now. It's all new and exciting, but it won't last. It doesn't for any of the girls. Haven't you seen how fast they leave?"

"Yes, but—"

"Most of them are like you. They come in all starry-eyed and expecting something wonderful. It doesn't take them long to realize there's nothing behind the glitter and the excitement. They soon figure out the people who come to the Little Corner of Heaven are trying to escape the very kind of life they want. So as soon as they get a chance, they get married and get out.''

''What about you?''

''I crave the excitement. Cards are like a living thing for me. The game, the gamble, the excitement are better than any woman. I don't have to worry what anybody thinks about what I do, say, or think. I don't have to worry about ruining my wife's reputation, driving her friends away, or giving my children a name unfit to take into society.

''Fortunately for you, my family has excellent connections. I just got a letter from Madison. He'll be moving here in a month or so. Between him and Tyler, they can introduce you to just about everybody who counts. Even George and Jeff visit from time to time. Anybody they don't know isn't worth knowing.''

''I don't want to be introduced to a bunch a strangers just because they're rich,'' Lily said.

''I didn't say anything about being rich,'' Zac said. ''But if they are, it's all the better. I'm talking about the kind of people Mrs. Thoragood would approve of. Your father isn't the only person who disapproves of me. Most people do. They disapprove of Dodie and everybody else who works here. You've got to leave the saloon and forget about us. We'll only bring you down.''

''Why do you think so little of yourself?'' Lily asked.

Chapter Fourteen

He did. And he didn't. But that was going to be hard to explain. He wasn't even sure he understood it himself, not to put into words. It was just a feeling that had been there as long as he could remember.

"We're not talking about what I think," he answered, aware that he was avoiding her question, "but what people who really matter think. They don't have anything to do with gamblers, not even one who tries to run a straight house. They especially don't approve of the women who work for us. There's no use saying it's unfair. It is, but there's nothing you or I can do to change it."

She was quiet. He knew she was mulling over what he'd said. He could tell from her expression that she was finding it hard to digest.

"I'm not going to try to talk you into returning to Virginia, even though I told Mrs. Thoragood I would. It would be the best thing for you, but I understand why you won't. I ran away from my family for much the same reasons."

"Then you understand—"

"Of course I understand. Why do you think I didn't send you back right away? I knew it was wrong not to, but I also knew it would have killed me to live with George and Rose for the rest of my life. I love them dearly, but I couldn't do it."

"Then why are you sending me away now?"

She knew he meant it. She'd gotten around him before, but she wouldn't this time. This whole evening—the yacht, the dinner, the seriousness of his expression—had the appearance of finality. She might refuse to do what he asked, but that wouldn't enable her to keep on performing at the Little Corner of Heaven. She could go home, go back to Bella, or go stay with Tyler, but she wouldn't be part of life at the saloon any longer.

"Because you're not like Dodie and me. You're not really different from your family. You believe in most of the same things. You want the same kind of life. The only real difference is you want to be treated as a person, not a thing.

"You'll want your husband home every night in bed beside you. You'll be broken-hearted if he even thinks about being anywhere else. You'll expect him to go to church and be active in the community."

"What's wrong with that?"

"Nothing, but you won't find that kind of man in the Little Corner of Heaven."

"You're there."

Zac laughed, a harsh sound. "Stop fighting it, Lily. You belong to one world; I belong to another. Nothing is ever going to bring the two together."

"What about all the good things you do for the girls?"

"That doesn't count. I do it for the wrong kind of women. But that's not all. Have you looked down the street? Have you seen who my neighbors are? Saloons, gambling halls, grog shops, places like Salem House, dives where men are doped and wake up to find themselves on a ship heading to China. That's where I work, that's the kind of people I meet every day. Apparently I'm like my father, minus a few of his most objectionable traits. I'm not the kind of person a decent woman ought to know.''

"That's ridiculous. You're as good as anybody I know, and that includes the Thoragoods.''

Zac didn't know what it was going to take before she would see him for what he was. She'd made up her mind and wasn't about to change it. At least she'd made it up in his favor. It was rather nice to know at least one person who saw only good in him. It didn't change anything, but it sure made him feel better.

However, his feeling good wasn't going to help Lily.

"It's nice of you to feel that way," Zac said. "I'll see about moving you to the Palace Hotel first thing in the morning. Zac and Daisy will look after you.''

"I couldn't possibly afford to stay there, not even if I kept working at the saloon.''

"Don't worry. You'll be treated like one of the family. Besides, they'll find you a job as a nanny or a lady's companion in no time.''

"What if I don't go?''

"You don't have any choice. Mrs. Thoragood came to see me, flanked by her ladies' auxiliary. Don't you understand what that means?''

Lily shook her head.

"It means they're giving you one last chance to save yourself. You turn this one down, and they'll turn their backs on you.''

"They haven't been any help to me.''

"Mrs. Thoragood has persuaded Bella to let you have your room back. Mrs. Wellborn and Mrs. Chickalee will each hire you for half a day. I think you ought to tell them to go to hell and march yourself straight off to the Palace, but it's up to you.''

"I'd rather keep doing what I'm doing now.''

Why didn't she give up? Didn't she realize that this was as hard on him as it was on her? If she'd just yield to the inevitable, it would be a whole lot easier on both of them.

"Damnation, Lily. Use your head. Men are gambling over you. They're shooting each other in the street. Before you know it, your name will be a byword throughout the Coast. It won't matter what you're really like. It'll only matter what people say about you. I know you've brought in hundreds of extra customers, but I'd have to be more selfish than I am not to fire you. I know I'll make less money, but to keep on would ruin you."

Lily got a very stubborn look about her mouth. Even in the dim light, Zac could tell she was angry and having trouble controlling her temper. "I know you don't like it, and I don't blame you, but there's no other choice."

She didn't answer. She just kept looking at him, the hurt big in her eyes. He thought she was going to cry. If she did, he might as well jump overboard and start swimming for shore. He couldn't stand that. He'd promise her anything she wanted, and then they'd be in a worse situation than they were now.

"I think you ought to move to the Palace as soon as we get back. But whatever you decide needs to be done by tomorrow. No point in putting it off."

She didn't answer, just sat there staring at her hands in her lap. It made him feel like a villain. He could cheerfully have strangled Mrs. Thoragood. She had gotten him into this.

No, he had gotten himself into it when he hadn't taken better care of Lily from the start. Maybe he couldn't have forced her to return to Virginia, but he could have done better than Bella Holt. He could have made sure she got a decent job.

Yet he couldn't blame himself for everything. It wasn't wicked or immoral to want to keep Lily around because he liked her, because he enjoyed her company or wanted to be near her innocence.

Maybe that was it. He'd never known anybody as guileless as Lily, anyone so unable to see anything but good in others. It amazed him; it appalled him; it scared him to death. So far she'd managed to survive, but it was a miracle.

He couldn't fool himself into thinking he was keeping her around to protect her. He'd let her go off with Bella. He'd let her start dancing. He'd let her move into the saloon. Some protector he was.

Then how the hell did he feel about her? Damned if he knew, and that bothered him more than anything.

"Can we go up on deck?" Lily asked.

"I thought you were cold."

"Not anymore."

Zac helped her up the narrow stairs. After sitting so long, it felt odd to be walking, especially with the movement of the yacht as it rode the waves.

The night was surprisingly clear. A ferryboat left the waterfront. Bright lights sparkled along the many piers, some of them red and green, throwing splashes of soft, wavering color on the water. The city streets up the steep hills twinkled like stars. Across the bay, the lights of Berkeley winked at them from the upper slopes. The dark, dim land masses and the blackness of the sky above left a solemn and mysterious sense of vastness and loneliness.

Lily carried the shawl, but she didn't wrap it around herself. She walked directly to the rail. "So much water. It's hard to imagine this much." She turned to look out over the bay toward the ocean. "Have you ever wondered what's out there, beyond where you can see, across the ocean?"

"I've seen enough Chinese here in San Francisco to guess what it's like."

"There's more to the world than China. Or India. Or the Ottoman Empire. So much more, and I've never seen any of it."

"You wouldn't like most of it," Zac said.

"How do you know?"

"They don't like women to have any freedom. Some places they won't even let females go outside."

She turned to face him. "Are you trying to make me think my father isn't so bad after all?"

"No, but he isn't. He might be bossy, but he does love you."

"How do you know all this?" she asked without turning around.

Zac laughed. People were always surprised when a gambler seemed to know anything beyond cards. "George saw to it that I got the best education money could buy. He even sent me to Harvard before I ran away to New Mexico and got stuck in a blizzard with Tyler. Besides, ships come here from all over the world. You can learn a lot just by listening."

He joined her at the rail. The wind was getting stronger, but she made no move to put on her shawl. She turned to face him, her back resting against the rail. "Why did you bring me here? You could have told me this at the saloon."

"I told you. I wanted a quiet night."

"Then we could have gone upstairs, down the street, to Mr. Thoragood. Thousands of other places. Why a yacht? It's normally considered a romantic gesture, and I'm not sure you even like me. You certainly consider me a headache. Don't deny it. There's no point in trying to spare my feelings. I know I've been a bother to you from the moment I got into town.

"I never wanted to be. I had good intentions, but things didn't work out the way I expected. All those men kept following me and then everybody got so skittish. I never could understand why."

"Don't you, really?"

"No. They weren't doing anything wrong. If anyone should have been annoyed, I was the one. Oh, I know it's not considered proper to talk to strange men, but nothing happened. For that matter, it's probably worse for me to be on this boat with you."

"I'm your cousin. Besides, there's the crew."

She turned back to face the water. "I guess there's no point. You're getting rid of me at last. Is that why you brought me here—to fill me with good food, to show me this wonderful view? Was it to soften the blow so I wouldn't feel so rejected?''

''I never meant that.''

''Because if it was, you failed. I've never felt more rejected in my whole life. You don't even think I'm pretty.''

Zac took her by the arms and turned her until she faced him. ''You're crazy. Everybody thinks you're beautiful. Stunning. And terribly nice. What do you think the fighting is all about? Nobody does this for other women. Surely you can see that.''

''You don't think I'm stunning.''

''Of course I do.''

''You can't. You have never once tried to seduce me. You haven't even wanted to kiss me.''

Zac didn't say anything. He just stared at her, wondering what she was going to say next.

''Surely you didn't think I was so naive I didn't know what all the fuss was about. Even in Salem, women get seduced and have to get married because they're going to have a baby. People kiss, too. Not Papa. He says— Never mind what he says. But I've seen it. It looks very nice. I once asked Mary Beth—she's one of my friends back home—and she said it was one of the most wonderful things in the world.''

''Hasn't anybody kissed you?''

''No.''

''Not even your precious Hezekiah?''

''He agrees with Papa. He thinks a minister should—''

''I know what he thinks. Didn't that damned cold fish ever hold your hand?''

''No.''

Zac held out his hands. Lily put her hands in his. They felt big and strong and warm. She felt the pressure as his fingers closed over hers. It was a nice feeling, being touched. She realized that her father had never touched her, at least not in the way of kindness. No young man had dared touch her at all.

"Don't let go," she said when she felt the pressure grow slack. "I like it. Do people normally touch each other a lot?" She'd never thought about it until now, but she didn't remember seeing many people touch.

"Some people touch all the time. Others not so much. It depends on what they like."

"I think I would like being touched a lot," Lily said. "Does that make me bad?"

"Not in my book. Of course, I don't think Mrs. Thoragood would approve of it."

"I don't care about Mrs. Thoragood."

She didn't. She never had. She didn't know why Zac worried about her so much.

"This may sound awful," Lily said, not daring to look at Zac, "but would you put your arm around me? I saw Mary Beth and Sam doing it, and she seemed to like it a lot."

Zac looked at her strangely.

"You don't have to if you don't want to. I just thought it might be nice, and since I didn't know anybody else I could ask . . ."

She didn't have the courage to look Zac in the eye. She didn't know how she found the nerve to make such a request.

"I'd be happy to," Zac said, with a softness in his voice she'd never heard before. "But you'd better wrap that shawl around yourself. It's getting cold."

Lily didn't feel the cold. Excitement, combined with the heat of embarrassment, warmed her from head to toe.

Zac's hold on her was tentative. She wondered if he didn't want to hold her. She wondered if she was doing something wrong.

"You have to relax and lean a little toward me," Zac said, his voice gentle on the breeze.

Lily hadn't realized she was so stiff. And scared. What if Zac was only doing this because she'd asked him? She realized now that she wanted him to *want* to hold her. Not just because she'd never been held before, but because she'd been wanting Zac to do exactly that from the moment she'd first set eyes on him.

It was about time she faced up to the fact that she'd had a crush on him from the moment she saw him. She hadn't realized it until just now, but it would have been impossible for her to fall in love with Hezekiah or anyone else. She had come to California because she knew unconsciously that she had to answer the question about Zac before she could do anything else.

Only she hadn't recognized the answer when she found it. She only understood now because he was telling her she had to go away. She was in love with Zac Randolph, and she couldn't go away without some evidence, however slight, that he at least liked her.

People didn't love because it was sensible. If so, she'd have loved Hezekiah. Neither did they love because somebody wanted them to. Otherwise Zac would have loved Dodie. It was a chance thing when it happened. Only in their case, it didn't seem to work both ways.

She'd fallen in love with Zac, but he hadn't fallen in love with her. Very bad planning on somebody's part.

She leaned against him. She liked the warmth. She liked the strength of him. She liked his size. She didn't mind in the least being ten inches shorter than he. Looking up at him might give her a crick in her neck, but she'd gladly put up with it to feel his arms around her, to feel safe and protected.

She had to remind herself that she wasn't safe and protected. He only had his arms around her because she'd asked. Tomorrow he was going to force her to go away.

"Would you kiss me?"

Lily couldn't believe her own ears. She couldn't have really asked Zac to kiss her! She was surprised the night sky didn't glow with the reflection of her embarrassment.

"Why would you ask something like that of me?"

"I've never been kissed before. If I'm going to have to marry somebody rich and proper, he might also think it's a good thing to be immune to the lures of the flesh. Then I'd never know what it's like."

"No man could marry you and be immune to anything."

"Hezekiah could."

"Then he's already dead and doesn't know it."

He didn't want to kiss her. That was why he was stalling. Well, it ought not to surprise her. Nobody else had either. Maybe all those boys hadn't been scared off by her father. Maybe they simply didn't want to kiss her in the first place.

"I'm not the kind of man who ought to give you your first kiss," Zac said. "You ought to share that with some boy who's as innocent as you, someone so swept away by your loveliness, he wouldn't even think about what he's doing."

"Can't you do that? I'd rather be kissed by someone with experience."

No. It was obvious from his expression he couldn't. But he did look sorry.

"Experience can never take the place of true feeling."

"I know you don't like me, but—"

"That's not true. I like you very much, much more than I should."

"Then why is it so hard to kiss me?"

"It's only hard *not* to kiss you."

"But I want you to. I—"

"I might like it so much, I wouldn't want to stop."

Lily didn't know why Zac thought she would feel cold. She felt almost too warm. "Then you do like me. You do think I'm pretty?"

"I've always thought you were beautiful. Everybody does. You ought to hear Dodie."

"I don't care what Dodie says. Only you."

"You shouldn't. Wasn't there a boy back in Salem you liked more than all the rest? Maybe if you—"

"Don't you think if I had found anybody in Salem I could love, I'd be married already?" Lily asked. "Stop making excuses and kiss me."

Zac was looking at her in the most peculiar manner. For a moment, she thought she might have been too frank. Men liked to make the first move. Even the slightest suspicion that they were being pursued, and they were off like a deer. But she must not have shocked Zac too much, for he took her in his arms and kissed her.

Not on her lips as she expected. He kissed her on the end of her nose. It felt funny, but she liked it. Then he kissed her eyes. That was something Sam had never done to Mary Beth. Lily wondered what her friend would have thought of it. But Lily had fewer and fewer thoughts to give to anything other than what was happening to her.

She liked being kissed with her eyes shut. Zac had his arms around her in the most satisfactory fashion. He felt wonderfully strong, and she felt wonderfully secure. She slipped her arms around his neck. For a moment, she was afraid she was being much too bold, but she'd been shameless already. It didn't much matter what she did now. He couldn't think much worse of her.

Then she reminded herself that Zac was used to abandoned women. He probably preferred them. Most likely the kind of female he was *least* familiar with was a bashful, blushing, nervous virgin. She was certain Zac's usual females could think of something much more stimulating to do than putting their arms around his neck.

He was kissing her ears now. Shivers raced up and down Lily's spine. She didn't think Sam had done this, either. She was certain Mary Beth would have told her of anything this absolutely delicious. She felt Zac's breath on her ear, on the fine hairs on the side of her neck, and her body turned to jelly. She'd thought kissing was a couple of smacks on the lips and that was that. Wait until she told Mary Beth what she'd been missing.

Then Zac kissed her on the lips, and it didn't in the least resemble a couple of smacks.

He merely brushed her lips at first, toying with the side of her mouth, nibbling at her lower lip. Then he moistened her lips with the tip of his tongue. Slowly, thoroughly. His lips were warm and soft, gentle and insistent, firm and moist. Lily had never known her lips could be so sensitive. For such an innocent part of her body, they held a hidden treasure of feeling.

If Zac hadn't been holding her, she was certain she would have melted into a quivering heap. Tiny electric shocks exploded in every part of her body, turning her into a pincushion of achingly sensitive nerve endings. She was hot and cold at the same time, tense and limp, petrified of what was happening yet eager for more.

She was aware of his hands on her back, supporting her, cradling her, holding her close to him. It was impossible not to be aware of her breasts pushed firmly against his chest. Not only had Lily never been kissed, but her body had never touched a man's body. Her breasts had never been pushed up against the firmness of a man's chest.

Feelings, sensations, desires that Lily had never experienced before woke from their long hibernation and rushed to the surface of her consciousness. Her entire being was flooded with feelings not only new, but tremendously exciting. A kind of liquid heat seemed to flow outward from her core until it reached every part of her body.

Then Zac took her mouth, and Lily felt jolted all the way down to her toes. The intimacy of it was shocking, exhilarating. In that moment, Zac seemed to belong to her, and she to him. She found herself kissing him back with a hunger made voracious by so many years of starvation.

Then his tongue invaded her mouth, and Lily was certain the firestorm that blazed up within her would surely consume her, leaving nothing but ashes and wisps of smoke. She gasped in shock.

They broke apart.

Their parting was abrupt and jarring. She felt as though she'd suddenly been cut off from her life source. Her heart beat too fast; she couldn't breathe. She felt light-headed. She was thankful for the cold wind off the ocean. It helped return her to normal.

Lily was surprised that Zac appeared to be as shaken as she. His breathing was quick and raspy. Even in the dark, she could sense the tension that gripped his body; she could see it in the light that flashed from his black eyes.

After a long pause, during which his breathing gradually slowed, his body became less tense. "Now you can't say you've never been kissed."

She was thoroughly shattered. Zac sounded only a little less so.

"Thank you." Her voice was little more than a hoarse whisper.

They seemed such stupid words to say after what had just happened to her. Not only were they inadequate, they didn't even begin to reflect what she was feeling. But then, it was probably best she kept that to herself. This was the end, not a beginning.

That made all the difference in the world.

"It's about time we headed back," Zac said.

He still sounded unsteady, but he was recovering faster than she was.

"Can't we stay out here a little longer? It's such a lovely night, and the city looks so beautiful."

"It's getting cold."

"I'll wrap up. Just let's not go yet."

"Okay. But let's sit down. That way I can throw a blanket over you."

Lily allowed herself to be ushered to a seat built into the back of the boat. Zac started to wrap her in the biggest blanket she'd ever seen.

"Sit with me," she said, holding out her hand to him. "It won't be any fun alone."

He wrapped the blanket around them both. Lily snuggled up next to him, and Zac put his arm around her. She figured it was probably a very brotherly snuggle, but since she'd never been snuggled before, it was quite satisfactory.

"Everything looks so big," she said. She was looking toward the sea and the mountains of granite that formed the gates to the bay. Beyond that the ocean stretched endless miles to distant and exotic lands she'd only vaguely imagined. Overhead the canopy of stars seemed endless. The moon, huge and low on the horizon, cast its reflection on the restless waves of the bay.

Lily felt tiny and insignificant. Yet the evening was the most momentous in her life. She had reached a decision. Some way, someday, somehow, she was going to marry Zac Randolph.

You poor fool! What the hell do you think you're doing sitting here in the middle of the bay with a sleeping woman in your arms? An innocent, naive, trusting woman at that. You ought to have your head examined. You ought to get her home, get her into her bed, get her out of your life. You ought to do just about anything but sit here like a love-struck fool prolonging a moment you knew had to end even before it began.

You're too smart for this, Zac Randolph. You've never wasted your time on the impossible.

But he couldn't move, not yet. This night hadn't turned out as he had planned. He had expected Lily to put up more of a fight. Yet she seemed to know from the first that it was no use. He hadn't expected to feel so bereft at the thought of her leaving. She'd disrupted his life from the minute she walked into his saloon. He should have been relieved she was going.

In a way, he was. She was an enormous responsibility, but he would be sorry to see her go. She seemed to have been able to touch everyone, to make them all seem a little more like a family. Not that he was big on the idea of family, but it was nice to have people thinking of the saloon as home more than a place to pause before passing on to something more permanent.

Somehow she'd made it all seem respectable.

Zac felt like kicking himself. He hated it when he got hung up on respectability. He didn't care what people thought. He had no intention of conforming to any rules but his own, but he hated it when people looked down on his girls.

Usually he was able to put that out of his mind, but Lily had brought it all to the fore. Now he was going to have to put it all out of his head again. It was never easy. He guessed there was just enough of his mother in him to keep him from being entirely comfortable ostracized from society.

But there was too much of his father in him to let him be broken to the bridle of respectability. He was an outsider, a maverick. He always would be. There was no point in fighting a battle that had already been decided.

"Let's head back to shore," he said when the captain came on deck. "It'll be morning in a couple of hours."

As the yacht began its slow journey to the shore, Zac realized that for the first evening in nearly eight years, he hadn't held a card, thrown a pair of dice, or spun a roulette wheel.

And he hadn't missed it.

Chapter Fifteen

The streets were empty. Or as close to empty as they ever got on the Coast. The cab wheels bounced over hardened ruts, and Zac thought wistfully of the cobblestone streets in the better parts of town. Lily didn't wake. She'd probably sleep until noon. He was certain she'd never been up half the night before.

When the cab stopped and he got out, the sun was just beginning to lighten the sky in the east. Zac was feeling a little sleepy himself. Rather than wake Lily, he picked her up and carried her into the saloon. The cab driver held the door for him.

The interior was dark, but Zac knew every inch of it more intimately than he knew any woman's body. He could have walked every aisle, gone unerringly to any table or wheel.

He was acutely aware of the woman he held in his arms. Thoughts he wouldn't have admitted to any man flashed through his brain. He hadn't completely recovered from the effects of their kiss. Desire still smoldered within him, waiting only for the breath of passion to turn it into a conflagration. Zac knew that might happen at any moment.

He walked faster. He had to get Lily to her bed and himself to his own room as quickly as possible. He was usually pretty good at curbing his sexual energy when necessary, but his self-control had been stretched to the limit tonight.

Carrying Lily up the stairs wasn't as easy as he had anticipated. He hadn't lifted anything heavier than a deck of cards in months. Maybe he ought to pay heed to Jeff's suggestion that he begin a course of exercise to keep himself in shape. After all, he was twenty-six. He wasn't going to be in the prime of his life forever.

The halls were narrow, and the floorboards squeaked. Zac had never realized how difficult it was to sneak into the saloon. He guessed that was one reason the girls rarely tried it.

There was a piece of paper tacked to the door of Lily's room.

Cora Mae came back. Put Lily in your room. You'll have to go to the Palace.

Dodie

Damnation. He'd told Cora Mae she was making a mistake going off with that drifter. Men like him were never dependable. They didn't like to stay in one place long. They hated to feel responsibility for another person weighing on them all the time. Nobody knew that better than he did, but Cora Mae wouldn't listen.

He wished she could have waited one more night to come back. He didn't want to be traipsing off to the Palace at this hour. Tyler was bound to ask questions. He always did.

Zac didn't want to put Lily in his room. It had been inconvenient before. After what had passed between them tonight, it was difficult in a different way now. It made him think of impossible things, of things that might have been if . . .

If was such an underrated word. If people only had the

power implied in that word, whole lives could be turned around, changed into something people could be proud of.

Zac didn't know what was getting into him. He was turning philosophical, and that wasn't like him. It was a waste of time. Things were the way they were. The sooner he accepted that, the happier he would be. The sooner he got Lily to bed, the sooner he could go to sleep and put this odd, unaccountable mood behind him.

Zac made his way back through the halls to his suite. He managed to get the door open without dropping Lily. But by the time he laid her down on the bed, he was perilously close to the end of his strength. He was going to have to do something about this. Clearly an occasional session with the boxing gloves wasn't enough.

He looked down at Lily. She lay on her back, her head to one side, her legs slightly bent, her arms akimbo. Zac moved her limbs so she looked more comfortable. She sighed and rolled up on her side. He started to put a blanket over her, but decided he couldn't put her to bed with her clothes on.

There was nobody to undress her but himself.

Not that he hadn't undressed women before. But none of them had been Lily. If she woke up, he hoped she wouldn't scream until he'd had time to explain what he was doing.

Zac licked his lips uneasily. The buttons of her dress ran down the front. There seemed to be hundreds of them. He took a deep breath and started at her collar. He tried not to notice the white skin of her throat when the dress fell open. He tried not to think about the softness of her breasts as he undid the buttons in the valley between these tempting mounds. He ignored the gentle rise and fall of her belly. He closed his mind against all thought of the flare of her hips and the secret places of her body. Instead he forced himself to concentrate on getting the dress off her shoulders and her arms out of the sleeves.

He had to sit Lily up and lean her against him. Her softness, the feel of her head on his shoulder, nearly destroyed his concentration. He struggled to get the dress off before she woke up or he lost control.

Lily's body was limp. She mumbled and made sounds in her sleep, but she didn't wake up.

Zac finally undid the last sleeve button and was able to get her arms out. He laid her down and breathed a sigh of relief. After that it was a simple matter to slip the dress from under her. He laid it across the wing chair nearest the door. He unlaced her corset, slipped that from under her, and then covered her with a sheet.

He backed away, breathing like a man who'd just performed a strenuous task. Nothing had ever strained his self-control like the events of this night. But that was his fault. He'd made a serious miscalculation. He'd begun this evening thinking he could control his feelings for Lily, that they were no different from what he felt for other attractive women. He ended by realizing that he hadn't been able to forget her even when she wasn't around. When she was, he couldn't think of anyone else.

It was a good thing she was moving to the Palace in a few hours. This situation was fraught with all kinds of danger.

He started to gather some things to take with him to the hotel but changed his mind. Dodie would be getting up soon. Lily could move to her bed, and Zac could crawl back into his own. He wouldn't have to go anywhere or make awkward explanations.

He would sleep on the couch. It would only be for three hours at most.

Zac undressed, carefully hung his clothes in the closet—he hated rumpled clothes—and put on a bathrobe. There were blankets in the closet and extra pillows on the bed.

The minute Zac's head hit the pillow, he realized that he wasn't sleepy. His mind wanted to replay the whole evening over and over again. He knew that was useless. It would only make him more restless, more awake.

Making use of the concentration that had made him such

a successful gambler, he pushed everything out of his mind. He dropped off right away.

Zac woke to find blinding sunlight streaming in through the windows. He groaned. He had forgotten to close the curtains. He shut his eyes, but the sense of light was still there. It was amazing how bright the sun could be at nine o'clock in the morning. Why couldn't it be rainy or foggy? It was, most mornings.

Unable even to consider going back to sleep with the sunlight searing his eyeballs, Zac got up from the sofa. Only then did he remember where he'd been sleeping. And why.

He glanced over at the bed. Lily was still sound asleep. Good thing there were no cows waiting for her. They'd be miserable by now.

He walked over to the bed, cows and sunlight forgotten.

He didn't know how it was possible, but she seemed even more innocent and vulnerable lying there, the sheet kicked off, her arms and legs flung every which way. She also looked more alluring than ever. Her chemise was pulled up to reveal one leg halfway up her thigh.

Lily was an absolutely voluptuous creature. Even wakened out of a deep sleep at an early hour, he felt himself growing uncomfortably rigid. Clearly the sensible thing to do was pull the sheet over Lily and yell for Dodie to hustle her off to some other bedroom.

Instead he sank down on the side of the bed and put an extended index finger into Lily's open palm.

It was a tiny, insignificant action, but his response was momentous. His entire being seemed to be covered with pins and needles. He had a powerful urge to reach out and consume this woman, to make love to her until his body no longer hardened at the thought of her tenderness or her purity.

He pulled his hand back. That was exactly the reason he was forcing her to leave the Little Corner of Heaven. Men like him would look at her and think only of satisfying their physical needs. Zac was certain Lily would be a wonderfully satisfying lover, but she needed much more than that, more than he or any man of his ilk could give her.

He heard footsteps in the corridor. It would be Dodie. Good. It was time Lily moved. He was feeling terribly vulnerable. He wasn't sure just how long he could be responsible for himself.

He was vaguely aware of the steps growing louder, more hurried. He smiled to himself. He bet Dodie didn't trust him either. He reached over to pull Lily's chemise down over her leg when the door flew open and Sarah Thoragood burst into the room followed by Mr. Thoragood, Bella Holt, Dodie, and several of the girls.

Zac had never had occasion to wonder what an avenging fury looked like, but if he had, he wouldn't have wondered any longer. Sarah Thoragood's face was so red and misshapen with fury, he could hardly recognize her.

"Lecher! Carnal beast! We have caught you in your foul nest with the broken body of your innocent prey!"

For once in his life, Zac was speechless.

"Satan will devour your soul in hell! He shall rip your body with his talons, and you shall spend eternity in everlasting torment!"

Zac managed to find his tongue at last. "What the hell are you screeching about?"

"I always knew you were a depraved libertine, but I never thought you would sink so low as to ruin this innocent, who trusted you with her life and her body."

"You're crazy!" Zac said. He turned to Dodie. "Do you know what she's carrying on about?"

"They think you slept with Lily," Dodie said, her eyes as hard as agate. "Did you?"

Zac's gaze went from Dodie to Lily to the rumpled sofa and back to Lily and the invading furies. "You think . . ." He glanced back at Lily. She was asleep in his bed in nothing but her chemise. Here he was standing over her half undressed.

"No, I didn't sleep with her. I know what it looks like, but nothing happened."

"You expect me to believe that you, a debauched, immoral, depraved, lecherous despoiler of women, would—"

"What she's trying to say," Dodie interrupted, "is that the circumstantial evidence is against you."

"You fornicator! You vile seducer—"

"I don't care what it looks like," Zac interrupted, trying to ignore Mrs. Thoragood, "I didn't touch her. If I'd wanted to do anything like that, I could have done it long before now."

"Aha!" Sarah Thoragood screeched, "You're proud of your powers to seduce, to despoil, to de—"

"I didn't want to go to a hotel," Zac said. "I thought it would only be a couple of hours before you came and took her off to your room."

"I was coming when they burst in on me."

"Just in time to catch you in your heinous crime," Sarah shouted.

Lily stirred. Zac didn't know how she'd managed to remain asleep this long.

"Remove yourself from her sight before she wakes," Sarah intoned. "The poor fallen angel will be stricken with enough remorse without having to face the instrument of her downfall."

"Zac?" Lily called, her eyes half open, trying to focus on the scene before her, her mind obviously finding no logical reason why all these people should be in Zac's bedroom. "What are all these people doing here?"

Dodie hurried forward to cover Lily.

"We've come to rescue you from this reprobate," Sarah Thoragood announced. "We understand your shame, we share your pain, but we shall not forsake you. This man shall be made to pay for what he has done. He shall—"

Zac practically hurled himself across the room. He clamped his hand over Sarah Thoragood's mouth before she could say any more. Sarah's wide-eyed, horrified gaze indicated that she feared Zac meant to despoil her on the spot.

"If you don't want me to do violence to your wife," Zac hissed to Harold Thoragood, "you'll shut her up before Lily figures out what she's saying. I don't care what you think of me," he hissed at the terrified Sarah, "but if you say one more word in front of Lily, I'll pitch you out that window."

Dodie was helping Lily into a robe offered by one of the girls.

"They've come to make sure I don't keep you here any longer," Zac said. "Apparently Bella can't wait to get you back to her rooming house."

"It's all very fine for you to want to spare her feelings," Mr. Thoragood said at his most pompous, "but I will not be party to a lie."

"I can pitch you out right behind your wife," Zac threatened.

"Nobody is going to pitch anybody anywhere," Dodie said. "Things are in a mess, and they've got to be sorted out before anybody leaves this room."

She walked over to the door and closed it. "Everybody sit down, and don't you open your mouth," she said, pointing at Sarah Thoragood, "until we get a chance to hear what happened last night."

"Nothing happened," Zac said.

"That's not true," Lily said. "A great deal happened."

Everyone stared at Lily, expressions ranging from horror to fury.

"I told you—" Sarah Thoragood began.

"Shut up!" Dodie commanded. Zac turned on the woman. Sarah retreated behind her husband.

"Now tell us what happened," Dodie said to Lily.

"Zac took me for a wonderful ride on a yacht. We had a beautiful dinner. I asked him why. He said it was to show me a good time, but it wasn't true. That wasn't what he wanted at all."

"See, I told you!" Sarah started again. "I—"

Zac flung back the curtains and opened the window to

the alley below. Sarah's eyes grew huge, and the words died in her throat.

"He wanted to tell me he wasn't going to let me perform in the saloon anymore. He also said I ought to marry some sober and boring millionaire."

"Is that all?" Mr. Thoragood asked.

"Why didn't you come back earlier?" Dodie asked.

"Zac wanted to, but I asked him to stay awhile longer. It was such a beautiful night. I didn't want it to end. Besides, if I was going to have to live in a hotel and become a lady's companion, I wasn't going to rush to do it."

Dodie cast Zac a glance that contained tightly controlled amusement.

"But what are you doing in Mr. Randolph's bed?" Mrs. Thoragood demanded, being careful to keep her husband between herself and Zac.

"I don't know," Lily confessed. "I fell asleep. I woke up when you were yelling at Zac."

"What's your explanation?" Mr. Thoragood asked Zac.

"I had no place to put her," Zac said. "She's been sleeping in Cora Mae's room, but the silly girl came back. Dodie wanted me to give Lily my bed and go to a hotel. I started to, but Tyler doesn't like being awakened at dawn. He invariably wants to know more than I want to tell him. I figured Dodie would be up in a couple of hours. Lily could then move to her room."

"Where do you say you slept?" Mr. Thoragood asked.

"On the sofa."

"Did he?" Mr. Thoragood asked Lily.

"Are you deaf?" Zac demanded. "She just told you she was asleep the whole time."

"If Zac said he slept on the sofa," Lily said, "then that's where he slept."

"I'm afraid that's not good enough," Mrs. Thoragood said.

"I don't think so either," Dodie said.

"What!" Zac said, rounding on his friend.

"I don't think it's enough," Dodie repeated. "You've compromised Lily's reputation. Nobody will believe she's innocent after what you did."

"I fully agree with Miss—with this person," Mr. Thoragood finished, embarrassment making his face pink.

"My name is Dodie Mitchell, and despite the fact that I live in a saloon, I do have a sense of what's right and wrong. That goes for the rest of the girls. Isn't that true, girls?"

A chorus of assent greeted Zac's stunned ears.

"I don't think anybody here is looking for a testimonial to your sense of morality," Zac snapped. "It seems what's needed is a little bit of faith in mine."

"That's the crux of the problem," Dodie said. "It seems no one has any."

"Now just a minute."

"What Miss—Mrs.—"

"Miss," Dodie supplied.

"—Miss Mitchell is trying to say is that your poor reputation has compromised Miss Sterling."

"He's ruined her!" Sarah shouted.

"I don't think that's a problem," Dodie said. "Zac has always insisted that any man who ruined one of his girls must marry her. Haven't you, Zac?"

"Always. I never let—"

Zac broke off. He saw the strange light dancing in Dodie's eyes. "Damn you, Dodie. If you think for one minute I'm going to—"

"You don't have any choice," Bella said. "When I was here, you said time and time again it was one rule you would never break."

"You were here?" Mrs. Thoragood gasped.

"You said there could be no exceptions," Bella continued, ignoring Sarah Thoragood's stunned question.

"Just a few weeks ago, you made sure Josie got married," Dodie reminded him.

"Yeah, I remember that," Leadville Lizzie said.

"But I didn't ruin Lily," Zac said. "I didn't even touch her."

"Nobody's going to believe that," Mr. Thoragood said. "As much as I regret to say it, I agree with Miss Mitchell. You must marry Lily."

"He can't do that," Lily said, her attention rapt. "Zac doesn't want to get married."

"It's about time you struck a blow for the home team," Zac said, relieved. "I thought you were going to leave me to get out of this all by myself."

"I couldn't keep quiet. They're talking about my marriage, too."

"Glad you noticed that."

"Zac doesn't love me," Lily said. "He doesn't even really like me. I do nothing but cause him trouble."

"That's not true," Zac replied, feeling every foolish complaint he'd ever uttered coming back to haunt him like cackling demons. "I like you a lot," he said, even though he knew hostile ears were hanging on his every word. "I told you that last night."

"What else did he tell you last night?" Dodie asked.

"He said he wouldn't kiss me because he might like it too much. But then he did. And he did—like it, I mean."

Zac wondered what it was about women that made them divulge the very things they should have taken to the grave with them.

"That's not exactly how—"

"Did you press your attentions on Miss Sterling?" Mr. Thoragood demanded. He seemed to be working up to his hellfire-and-damnation voice. His words echoed around the room.

"I damned well did not," Zac replied, incensed. "She asked me to kiss her."

Bella gasped. The girls giggled. Mrs. Thoragood seemed incapable of words. Dodie was trying her best to smother a laugh. That was the only reason Lily was able to get a word in.

"That's true. I'd never been kissed, and I asked him to show me what it was like. I asked him to hold me as well. I liked both very much. Zac does it very well. But then, I imagine he's had a lot of practice."

Sarah Thoragood turned purple with indignation. Dodie lost her battle with the laugh.

"You actually asked him to do these things?" Mr. Thoragood said, not quite as shocked as his wife.

"He said I would have to marry someone very proper," Lily explained. "The only proper people I know don't like kissing and holding hands."

"I should think not!" Mrs. Thoragood said.

"I'm afraid this shows a great want of delicacy on your part," Mr. Thoragood said.

"Now just a damned minute," Zac said. "I won't have anybody talking about Lily that way."

"I don't see any solution except for him to marry her," Dodie said.

"I regret to say I agree with you," Mr. Thoragood said.

"Marry him!" Sarah Thoragood practically screeched. "He's a lecher, a seducer, a—"

"Woman," Zac thundered, "you call me a lecher and a seducer one more time, and they'll be the last words that pass your lips!"

"Don't you threaten me!" Sarah Thoragood exclaimed. "I have God on my side."

"He'd better be *at* your side if you don't shut your mouth. This is all nonsense about me marrying Lily," he said, whipping around on Dodie. "Do you actually think I violated her?"

"It doesn't matter if you did or didn't," Dodie said. "You've ruined her."

"I think it matters a hell of a lot."

"So do I," Lily said. Unfortunately, Zac thought she sounded more wistful than scandalized. That wasn't going to help their case a bit.

"Miss Mitchell is right," Mr. Thoragood said. "At this

point, the truth doesn't matter. Only what people will believe happened."

"You can say that and still call yourself a minister?" Zac exclaimed.

"I'm a realist, and I say you must marry Miss Sterling without delay."

"No!"

"You can't refuse. It's your own policy," Dodie said.

"I said ruined girls must marry. I didn't ruin Lily."

"You might as well have."

Zac was beginning to wonder if this wasn't all a bad dream and he'd wake up later with a tremendous headache. "Why don't you all wait outside," he said angrily. "Lily and I will engage to ruin each other as thoroughly as we can. Then we'll have something to talk about."

"Mr. Randolph!" Mr. Thoragood thundered. He had achieved full hellfire-and-brimstone pitch. "Are there no depths to which you will not sink!"

"I don't know. You got any depths I don't know about?"

"Don't pay him any attention," Dodie said to Mr. Thoragood. "He's just trying to be obnoxious to distract us." She turned back to Zac. "The important thing is to protect Lily. You know that. You've ruined her, so you can't do anything but marry her."

"Don't be absurd."

"Do you think any of your proper young men will marry her when they hear about this?"

"Who's going to tell?"

"There are ten people in this room right now. Then there are the crew of the yacht, the cab driver, and anybody else who might have seen you. Then there's Lily herself."

"What do you mean?"

"She's so innocent, she'll tell on herself like she just did a minute ago."

"I'll talk to her, teach her what to say."

"And make her like the rest of us," Dodie said, "sifting through the truth looking for the parts it's safe to tell, to

213

color, to ignore. Is that the kind of person you want her to become, the kind of person you want to make her? I thought her innocence was what you liked best about her.''

Maybe it wasn't what he liked best, but it was the quality that had first drawn him to her. That and her ability to see the best in others, to want to help them whether they deserved it or not. That and her silver mantel of hair, her ridiculous habit of quoting her father, her . . .

"Lily doesn't want to marry me," Zac said. "She came out here looking for her freedom, not a husband."

"What about it?" Dodie asked Lily. "Could you marry this rogue in gilt wrapping?"

"I'm sure any woman could marry Zac," Lily said. "He's very nice and really sweet when he wants to be."

"The girl is bewitched," Sarah Thoragood exclaimed. "You must have doped her."

"I did not," Zac exclaimed. "I don't want her to marry me, remember!"

"Would it be so bad to be married to me?" Lily asked.

"It would be terrible," Zac said. "You'd expect me to get up early and learn to milk some damned cows you're bound to come up with sooner or later. You'd sing and dance until every man in the place was ready to shoot, knife, or bite his neighbor just to get a smile from you. You'd have whole armies of men following you down the street wherever you went. You'd have this blood-sucking preacher and his passel of furies yapping at my heels, invading my bedroom, accusing me of things I've tried my damnedest not to even think about doing. You'd have me going crazy trying to fight the lot of them to keep you to myself."

"It sounds like love to me," Dodie said. "I say we call for a preacher and do the deed."

Chapter Sixteen

"I must agree that despite the deplorable way he chose to state it," Mr. Thoragood said, "it does sound as though Mr. Randolph cherishes an affection for Miss Sterling. That relieves my mind considerably. I would also remind you that I'm a preacher, and I'm already present."

Zac could see the jaws of hell closing around him. Every word he uttered seemed to bring him closer and closer to sounding the death knell on the only kind of life he'd ever wanted.

"Lily doesn't want to marry me," he said, not caring that his desperation sounded in his voice. "She wants her freedom. I'll be a tyrant of respectability. I'll keep her locked away in this room. I'll never let her downstairs while there's a single man in the place. I won't let her have anything to do with those females over there."

The girls giggled.

"I won't even let her set eyes on Dodie. She'll be forbidden to work. The only people who can visit will be Mrs. Thoragood and her carefully chosen friends."

215

"I hope I shall be one of those friends," Bella said.

"Probably. You're getting to be more of a self-righteous bitch than I ever thought possible."

"There's no call for vulgarity," Mr. Thoragood said.

"You charge in here and accuse me of violating the one woman I wouldn't touch if my life depended on it and you call me vulgar! If I were you, I'd take another look at that Bible you've been reading. I don't think you got a good translation."

"He sounds more like a lover by the minute," Dodie said.

"You shut up!" Zac snapped. "By the way, you're fired. Get your things and be out of here by noon."

"You can't fire Dodie," Lily protested. "Who's going to run this place while you sleep?"

Dodie laughed easily, not the sound of a woman fearful of her future.

"This whole conversation is absurd," Zac said. "I'm not going to marry Lily, and that's that. Besides, you know as well as I do, she shouldn't be allowed to marry anybody like me. Her father would probably shoot me."

"We know you're not worthy of her," Dodie said. "No one will argue that."

"I will," Lily interjected, but no one heeded her.

"What would you do about her dilemma?" Mr. Thoragood asked.

"Take her to my brother Tyler," Zac said. "He and Daisy can handle it from there."

"Do you plan to tell him what you've done?" Dodie demanded.

"I haven't done anything!" Zac nearly shouted.

"How do you plan to explain it all to George when he finds out?" Dodie asked.

"He won't."

"If Tyler doesn't tell him, I will."

Tyler would tell him. He probably wouldn't agree to help Lily unless Zac told him the whole story. Tyler was like that. And if George thought Zac had ruined a young woman, no matter whether he'd actually done anything or not, he'd be furious. Nobody took this Southern chivalry thing more seriously than George, not even Jeff.

Someone would tell Monty and Hen—they found out everything sooner or later—and they'd come after him. They might shoot him or beat him to a pulp first, Zac didn't know. He'd never understood the twins, but he did know they'd bring him to the altar, tied hand and foot if necessary.

"You can't force Lily to marry this monster," Mrs. Thoragood said. "I'd rather find some decent young man for her."

"I bet you would," Zac snapped. "And keep her tied to a cold, loveless marriage the rest of her life. Lily is warm and generous and loving. She needs a husband who is as kind and giving as she is. Otherwise, you may as well marry her to that Hezekiah fella."

"Would you mind marrying Zac?" Dodie asked Lily.

"That's not what you're supposed to ask," Zac cut in. "You're supposed to ask if she loves me, and you know she doesn't. How could she? I'm not a bit like her."

Lily blushed charmingly, and Zac cringed inwardly. Few things could be more dangerous than a female who blushed at the wrong time. When they blushed like Lily, you might as well give up and put your head on the chopping block.

"I like you quite a lot," Lily said. "You're kind and warm and generous. All of the girls here say the same thing. I don't think I'd mind being married to you at all."

Zac could hear the rattle of the chains, feel the irons being placed around his wrists and ankles.

"Think of all the things you don't like about me," he pleaded. "I gamble and stay up all night. I cuss. I sleep naked. You told me you hated that."

"You've seen him in his natural state!" Sarah Thoragood squawked, her face turning beet red.

Zac cursed his panic. He was putting as many nails in his own coffin as Lily was.

"There's just as many things about you I do like," Lily

said. "You've taken care of me from the beginning. You take all these girls in and find them husbands when they get in trouble."

"Everybody knows Zac's a Good Samaritan when it comes to girls in trouble," Dodie said. "We also know you're the only one who can't see anything but good in him."

"It sounds to me as though they're admirably suited," Mr. Thoragood said. "I'll be happy to perform the ceremony. Shall we say at the church in an hour?"

Zac heard the iron door slam and the key turn in the lock. He was trapped. There was no escape. No way out. Unless . . . There was one desperate chance. It was a means he'd rather not use, but a drowning man will grab for any lifeline.

"Okay, I'll do it," Zac said. "But we'll be married right here in the saloon and by my own man."

"I don't think—" Mr. Thoragood began.

"I don't give a damn what you think," Zac snapped. "You've come in here, throwing your weight around, shouting about morals and goodness and ruined females. Okay, I've agreed to what you want, but we'll do it my way. You can stay if you want and make sure the knot is tied to your satisfaction, but once it's done, I want you out of here. And don't ever set foot in my place again, or I'll have you thrown out."

"I should think your wife will have something to say about that," Mrs. Thoragood said, a smirk on her face.

"My wife can go where she wants, visit who she pleases, do what she wants, but this saloon is mine," Zac declared, "and what I say goes."

Both Thoragoods glared at him, but neither was willing to push him any harder.

"Are you sure you want to do this?" Zac asked Lily. There was a tenderness in his voice that hadn't been there before.

She nodded.

"Dodie, take her off and get her ready. You girls can help. The rest of you get out of my bedroom."

"It's not too late to change your mind," Dodie said to Lily. "You could find yourself a small town back east and pretend you never heard of Zac Randolph."

They were alone in Dodie's room. Lily was wearing her best dress, but she found it very difficult to keep her spirits up. That half hour in Zac's room was the most earth-shaking of her entire life. Everything had happened too fast, had been too unexpected. She hadn't had time to think properly. She still wasn't sure she was doing the right thing.

"I want to marry Zac," Lily said. "I have for some time, but I didn't realize he would be so angry at having to marry me."

She had told herself that marrying Zac was the best way to save him. Up until now she hadn't been able to do anything for him. As his wife, things would be different.

But she wasn't kidding herself. She was in love with Zac. She wanted to marry him for that reason alone. Yet she wouldn't have agreed to the marriage if she hadn't believed that somewhere, deep down in the bottom of his heart, he loved her. At least a little.

"When you kept smiling, kept telling him his only choice was to marry me, I was sure I was doing the right thing," Lily said. "But he was so angry. It wasn't fair for you to mention George."

"Sure it was," Dodie said. She was brushing Lily's hair, experimenting with several different ways of coiling it atop her head. "Zac doesn't know what's best for him. He never has. Half the time he doesn't even know what he wants. The other half he's certain he doesn't deserve it. The only way he was going to get married was to trap him into it."

"I can't do that," Lily said. She jumped so quickly, she pulled the blond coil from Dodie's hands before she had secured the end. Dodie pushed Lily back down in the seat and began to coil her hair all over again.

"Better you than some hussy who doesn't love him."

Lily twisted around in her chair, but Dodie was ready for her this time. "Yes, every female in the place knows you're head over heels in love with Zac. Every female except you, that is."

"I know I love Zac, but I'm beginning to wonder if he loves me. I thought he did. Last night, on the boat, I was certain he couldn't kiss me like that, hold me that way, and not love me at least a little. But after this morning, I don't know."

"Zac Randolph is the most selfish man God ever created. He thinks the world ought to revolve around his wants, but I'm sure he loves you. True, he doesn't know it yet. He thinks he has no right to love anybody like you. He's just as certain a woman like you can't love him."

"Why? He's such a wonderful person."

"Zac likes himself very much—he has to, he's all he thinks about—but he doesn't admire himself."

"I don't understand."

"I'm not sure I do. I just know it's true. He'll do anything to ensure his creature comforts, to make certain he gets his way when it comes to the saloon, but he doesn't think he deserves the best of life. He's even talked himself into thinking he doesn't want it."

"But Zac deserves all the best. Everybody knows that."

"Not everybody, but I guess it's only important that you do."

"You do, too."

"Yes, fool that I am, I think the man is a prince. To be perfectly honest—and if you ever breathe a word of this, I'll deny it and sell you into white slavery—I'd marry him in a minute if I thought it had even the remotest chance of working out. But Zac has been dead set against marriage from the day I first saw him. He thinks he still is. The moment I knew you loved him, I was determined he would marry you. That's why I helped you with that dance routine.

That's why I pushed so hard this morning. You're going to save Zac Randolph from himself.''

Lily smiled broadly. "I decided to do that some time ago."

But a sliver of doubt remained. Lily had no idea how she was going to save Zac. He didn't seem to be a man who was particularly easy to guide. She could ask Dodie, but she couldn't depend on somebody else for something like this. A relationship between two people who loved each other couldn't involve a third party, no matter how interested.

She wondered if her innocence, the very quality that had attracted Zac in the first place, would be the reason for her failure.

She must not fail. She couldn't. Otherwise she owed it to Zac to back out now. There were plenty of other women willing to try.

But Lily couldn't bring herself to give up the chance of having Zac for herself. For days she'd thought of little else. A young girl's fantasy might have brought her to California, but a woman's dreams were born that night she walked in and saw him at the gambling table. She knew right then that she'd made the right choice. She just hadn't known what she was going to do about it.

She did now.

"It's about time," Dodie said. "And remember, if you need any help, I'll be around."

"Thank you, but this is something I'm going to have to figure out for myself."

"Don't look at me like that, you slimy old reprobate," Zac said to the man who sat at his ease in a wing chair in his office, smoking one of Zac's best cigars and enjoying what was left of a very large glass of brandy. "And don't pretend you haven't done things like this before."

"Sure. I ain't denying it. But I thought you were a

straight shooter, not one who'd pull such a rotten trick on a sweet girl like Lily."

"What do you know about Lily?" Zac demanded, suddenly wondering if every piece of vermin that crept and crawled about the Barbary Coast knew about Lily.

"I've heard about her," the Reverend Ambrose Winston Dumbarton III said. "Everybody on the Coast has. Hell, she's been passing out clothes to half the women on the streets."

Damn! Something else she'd been doing when he should have been watching her instead of sleeping. "Well, if you know that much about her, you know she's too good for the likes of me. But this damned preacher and his crowd have got me backed into a corner. I've got to marry her, but there's no point in ruining the poor girl's life. If you don't register the marriage, it won't be legal and binding. If everybody keeps his mouth shut, nobody even has to know she's married. Then a few months from now, after things have quieted down and she's had time to realize she's made a mistake, she can disappear. She can tell people she was never in California. I'll make sure she has enough money to start life over someplace else."

"And what are planning to do in the meantime?" Windy asked. "Sleep on the sofa?"

That was exactly what Zac planned to do, but he could see Windy wouldn't believe him. No one would.

"I'm taking her to stay with Bella. With that dragon guarding her, everything will work out as long as I stay here. If not, she could always say her husband died. A rich widow has some advantages over an unmarried girl."

"I'm sure you know all about that," Windy said, "but that's not getting us any forwarder."

"We don't have to get *forwarder*," Zac snapped. "I want you to perform a sham marriage so Lily can get out of it whenever she chooses. It's that simple. All you have to do is say yes or no."

"And if she doesn't?"

"She will."

Lily could hardly believe she was married. Everything had happened so quickly, it seemed unreal. As the minutes rolled by, she became less and less certain she'd done the right thing. Zac had been irritable during the wedding ceremony. He'd practically run Mr. Thoragood and his wife out the minute the service was over.

Now, as their cab rolled toward Bella's rooming house, he sat next to her sunk deep in thought. She didn't want to go back to Bella's. She was more frightened than when she'd left Salem. At least she had been going toward something then. Now Zac seemed to be putting as much space between them as possible.

"I still don't understand why I can't stay at the saloon with you," Lily said.

"It's not a proper place for you," Zac said, his expression unchanged. "It never was."

"But I don't want to go to Bella's."

"That's something else. I've let you make too many decisions."

"It's my life."

"But you made me responsible for it the minute you left home. If I hadn't been such a lazy, selfish, good-for-nothing slouch, I would have seen that from the first."

"But you did. You've been looking after me all along."

"I don't mean that. I mean I should have put you on a train and taken you back to Virginia, kicking and screaming if necessary. I couldn't take my nose out of the cards long enough to see what was happening. I kept pretending things would get better, hoping you would go away. Now look what's happened. You're married to me."

"Is it so awful?"

"I don't know, and neither do you. But you're not going to find out from me."

"What do you mean? You're not going to send me back to Virginia now, are you?"

"No, it's too late for that, but from now on you're going to stay at Bella's. If you don't like that, we can find you a different rooming house. I'd take you to the hotel, but I don't want to have to deal with Tyler just yet."

"I still don't see why I shouldn't stay with you. It'll just take longer to get to the saloon."

"Don't you understand?" Zac said, turning on her with anger born of frustration. "You're not to set foot in that saloon, ever again."

Lily didn't know what to say, but she couldn't let him toss her into a rooming house and close the door and forget her.

"How am I going to help Dodie?"

"Dodie's gotten along by herself for years. She'll manage."

Lily wasn't about to let things stay like that, but she didn't know what she could do about it yet. "What am I supposed to do all day long?"

"You don't have to do anything."

"If I don't, I'll go crazy."

"Maybe you could help Mrs. Thoragood. At least you won't have to cook, clean, or milk cows."

She looked hopefully for a gleam of humor in his eyes but found none.

Lily opened her mouth to argue, but closed it again. There was no point. He wasn't listening to her. He'd made up his mind and nothing she could say would make any difference. She didn't understand. He'd never been this close-minded before. It was as if he'd been driven into a corner and was clinging to his only solution.

But it wasn't a solution for her. She didn't think it was for Zac, either, but she would have to wait until she figured out what to do and until he was willing to listen.

"What are you doing back here?" Bella asked. She sounded petulant.

"I'm bringing Lily to stay with you," Zac said.

"You can't do that," Bella said. "I don't have men in my house."

"Lily's staying here," Zac said. "I'm staying at the saloon."

Lily had been afraid he was going to say something like that, but it was even worse when she heard the words.

Bella made no attempt to hide her surprise. "But you just got married."

"I know that," Zac said, "but it's not right for her to live at the saloon. You and Mrs. Thoragood made that very clear."

"Yes, but—"

"It'll have to do until I figure something out. In the meantime, don't say anything to anybody. It won't do Lily any good to have tongues wagging."

"They won't stay quiet for long," Bella said.

"I'd say that depends on you and Mrs. Thoragood."

It was a clear challenge.

"I would appreciate it," Lily said. She didn't think she could bear to have everyone speculating about the relationship between her and Zac. And they would if anyone discovered they were married and not living in the same place, even if that place was a saloon.

"All right," Bella said, "but you'd better figure something out in a hurry."

"Thanks. I'll leave you to help Lily settle in. I've got to get back to the saloon."

Lily's hand almost reached out to pull him back. She longed to ask him to stay, but she knew he wouldn't. Maybe it was best to let him go. He'd suffered more of a shock than she had. She wanted to be married. He didn't.

"I'll come back as soon as I can," Zac promised Lily, "but no matter what, you're not to come near the saloon. Do you understand?"

Lily nodded.

225

"Good. Now don't worry. Things will sort themselves out before you know it."

"What did he mean by that?" Bella asked after Zac left.

Lily had no idea, but she wasn't about to let Bella know that. "Zac has me and the saloon in his life, but he thinks we don't go together. He's got to figure out what to do with us."

"Be careful he doesn't decide he likes that saloon more than you," Bella warned.

Lily was afraid of the same thing. She was only now beginning to realize how much she'd hoped Zac would fall in love with her. She'd denied her feelings for so long, she hadn't seen them growing all the time she'd been in San Francisco.

Then last night and today her blinders had fallen away. She'd not only realized she'd been desperately in love with him, she'd realized she was looking forward to being his wife. But even after he'd agreed to marry her, she had known it wasn't going to be easy.

Zac's decision to leave her in Bella's while he stayed in the saloon tore at the heart of everything. He seemed determined to cut her off, separate her as much from his life as possible. She was tempted to refuse point blank, but the black mood that had descended on him was unfamiliar to her. She'd heard about the Randolph temper. If she made him angry enough, she wouldn't put it past him to put her back on the train yet.

Worse than that, she was afraid it would make him fight against her so hard he would never let himself see he loved her. Zac was afraid of love, afraid he couldn't have it, afraid he didn't deserve it. She had to find some way to help him see what he was doing to himself, or his fear could keep him from ever being truly happy.

And her, too.

Chapter Seventeen

Zac had spent the last fifteen minutes cussing himself, Harold and Sarah Thoragood, Bella, Dodie, Windy, the saloon, his family, his customers, San Francisco, his idea to take Lily to dinner on the yacht, just about everything that came to mind.

Everything except Lily.

No matter how angry he got at everyone else, he didn't get angry at Lily. That made him angrier than ever. It also cast him into black despair. He had no business feeling the way he did about Lily. It seemed nothing he did made any difference. Every day seemed to find him a little more under her spell.

He could have withstood sheer beauty. He could have survived an all-consuming physical passion. He thought he could have ignored her charm and kindness. But it was her damned innocence that was his downfall. He only had to look into those shining eyes to feel himself drowning.

Damn flower women! What was it about them that made it impossible for Randolph men to forget them? This would teach him to pity his brothers for being so weak. He had boasted he could remain invulnerable to the blandishments of any female. He'd survived dozens of well-orchestrated campaigns. Yet when a wide-eyed innocent came wandering in from Virginia, he'd fallen like a roped steer.

He had to make sure she stayed at Bella's. That was the only way he might break this fascination she held for him. It was also the only way he was going to keep his hands to himself. If he was tempted before, he was doubly tempted now that the world thought she was his wife.

He couldn't tell her the real reason he had sent her to Bella's. He couldn't tell anybody. How could he explain that he didn't trust himself to keep his hands off his wife? Everybody expected them to sleep together. That was all most newlyweds thought about for the first few months.

But he couldn't afford to do that, not when he was certain Lily wouldn't want to remain his wife. He might be many things, but he was neither so selfish nor so thoughtless that he would father a child who would come into this world without a full set of parents. He hadn't let it happen to Josie's baby or dozens of babies before. He certainly wasn't going to let it happen to his own child.

Zac couldn't remember his father. He'd left before Zac was two. He couldn't really remember his mother, though she'd lived two more years. Rose and George had tried to fill the gap, but he'd always felt disconnected from the family. His brothers had memories and experiences he couldn't share, memories that excluded him from a very important part of their lives.

He'd never understand their drive to prove themselves. He'd seen their struggles and counted himself lucky to have escaped that burden. Yet he felt deprived, unattached, rudderless. He had no goal in life other than to please himself.

It wouldn't be any better if Lily decided she did want to stay married to him. What kind of father would he make, a man who didn't want to be married, didn't want children, didn't love the woman the world thought was his wife?

He groaned. The night he opened the Little Corner of Heaven had been one of the proudest and happiest moments of his life. It had given him a purpose, a sense of direction. He'd finally achieved the kind of operation he'd envisioned for years. He had arranged everything to suit himself, and it had worked. Each time he turned the corner and saw the elegant facade of his building, he experienced a feeling of enormous pride, of happiness, of homecoming.

Until tonight. Now he felt as if he were being sent into exile.

Worse than that, he didn't even know what his feelings for Lily were. He could have understood it if he'd been in love with her. He'd seen his brothers fall all over themselves to please their wives. He'd have been mortified to act that way, but he'd have understood at least.

It was the fascination, infatuation, or whatever it was that he didn't understand. He felt bewitched, obsessed, tormented. It wasn't love, but what was it?

Agony. He felt betwixt and between, powerless to go either way. If he didn't decide something soon, it was going to drive him crazy. If Lily decided she didn't want to be married to him, that would solve everything.

Of course he would be sorry to see her leave. He liked having her around. But he wasn't at all what she wanted in a husband. It wouldn't take her long to figure that out. He hoped he'd be over this fascination or whatever it was by the time she decided to leave. It was nearly impossible for him to concentrate on his gambling.

"You can't come in here," Dodie said when she saw Lily enter the front door of the saloon. "Zac gave strict orders you weren't to come near the place."

Lily avoided Dodie by darting around the far side of a table. She still hadn't made up her mind how best to attack the problem of getting close to Zac, but she had to be able to enter the saloon. Zac had made it clear that he wasn't coming to her. She had to prove to her dense husband that he would be much happier with her than without.

"I'm the wife of the owner of this saloon," Lily said, walking rapidly to stay ahead of Dodie. "You're an employee. If he wants me out of here, let him get out of bed and put me out."

Dodie stopped in her tracks, a smile slowly appearing on her lips. "That wouldn't be wise of me, would it? Suppose Zac changed his mind? I would have made an enemy of you. You would probably have him fire me."

"P-probably." Lily couldn't imagine herself doing such a thing, or Zac listening to her if she tried.

"So having defied your husband and put me in my place, what do you intend to do?" Dodie asked.

"Help you the way I did before."

"No more?"

"Not yet." Lily saw the gleam of amusement in Dodie's eyes and knew she'd judged correctly. "I'm still working on a plan."

"Are you going to let me know what you decide?"

"I don't know. I don't want Zac to get angry at you, too."

"Don't worry. With you around, he doesn't have time."

"Can you show me how to gamble?" Lily asked Dodie.

Lily had a gift for figures. So did Dodie. Between the two of them, they had cleared away the morning's work in a few hours.

"Are you crazy! Zac would cut my liver out."

"I don't want to actually do it. I just want to know how it works. I can't imagine what Zac and all these men find so exciting about it. It looks boring to me."

"Bite your tongue. If everybody felt like that, we'd be out of business."

"I'm serious. Why do they do it?"

"For the chance to win."

"But they lose most of the time."

"I know, but the true gambler is an eternal optimist. He's

certain his luck is going to change on the next hand, that he'll win more than enough to make up for what he's lost.''

"But Zac doesn't lose."

"Zac plays the odds. Besides, he's the best judge of people I've ever known. It's like he can look inside people's heads and tell if they're bluffing."

"How do you play the odds?" Lily asked. "I thought you just put your money down and took your chances."

"That's what most of our customers do. That's how we make money. Here, let me show you how it works in poker."

Lily found the game fascinating. She could see why her father didn't want her to know anything about it. She could spend hours dealing the cards to see the kinds of hands she could get. Even more fascinating was trying to figure the odds of getting any particular card or of improving her hand.

"You sure you haven't played this game before?" Dodie asked.

"No. Papa would die if he could see me now. He'd be sure I was headed straight to hell."

Dodie laughed. "That wouldn't be as bad as what'll happen if Zac catches us. You'd better put them up."

"I will in a little while."

That little while turned into the whole afternoon. She asked Dodie questions from time to time, but she mostly dealt hands, tried to improve them by discarding, then saw which hand won. She had just put the pack in her pocket when Zac came down the stairs.

Lily felt panic flood through her. She'd meant to be ready for him when he came down. She'd let herself get caught up with the cards, and he'd caught her by surprise. One more reason why gambling was dangerous.

She was heartened to see him smile the moment he set eyes on her. He turned it into an angry scowl almost immediately, but she hadn't been mistaken. He *was* glad to see her. The problem now was how to force him to admit it. He was coming toward her. She was quick to wipe the smile of satisfaction from her face.

"What are you doing here?" he demanded while he was still several yards away.

He spoke so loudly that nearly everyone in the room turned. Usually Zac didn't care that people overheard his conversations, but tonight he seemed acutely aware that he had an audience.

"Come into my office," he said. "There are a few things we've got to get straight."

Zac didn't know why he had thought Lily would stay at Bella's. She hadn't stayed anywhere else he'd put her. Yet it was a shock to come down the stairs and see her sitting at one of the tables, as beautiful as an angel, just as if they hadn't gotten married the day before.

He realized he had no right to complain about that. He'd been the first one to try to impress on Lily that their marriage wouldn't make any difference in their lives.

"I told you not to come here again," he said as soon as he closed the door.

He didn't know why he should continually be surprised by her loveliness. He'd seen her every day for weeks, yet each day he discovered something he hadn't seen before. She was wearing a dark blue dress today. It made her eyes more vivid than usual. She was also wearing her hair up in an elegant knot atop her head, a small bunch of blue flowers nestled in the knot. She looked very grown up and remarkably elegant.

"I couldn't stay in my room all day with nothing to do."

"Why didn't you go see Sarah Thoragood?"

"I didn't think that was wise. After the way she treated you yesterday, I'd be bound to say something quite unpleasant."

Zac had to smile at Lily's determined defense of his reputation.

''I thought of visiting Daisy, but decided you wouldn't want me to.''

''You'd be bound to say something you shouldn't, but you can't keep coming here.''

''Why? It's where my husband lives and works. What more suitable place for his wife? That's what we have to discuss. Bella tells me rich men don't sleep in the same room with their wives. I know we don't always do things the fashionable way in Salem, but I've always expected a man and his wife to at least sleep under the same roof.''

Zac had known this was coming, and he dreaded it. He should have told her yesterday, but he had foolishly hoped she'd figure it out for herself. He should have known that even if she had, she would have wanted to talk about it.

''If you keep coming here, it'll ruin your reputation and cause all kinds of talk.''

''Not if people knew we were married. I would think it would cause even more damage to my reputation if we're never together.''

She might be innocent, but she had figured a few things out. He might as well level with her and stop dancing around the issue.

''Setting aside all the other reasons for our not living in the same place—and there are many—I couldn't stay in the same room with you and not touch you.''

''But I *want* you to touch me,'' Lily said. ''I liked it very much. I've been hoping you would do it again soon.''

Zac had always chosen his clothes with great care so the lines would never be affected by his posture, but he hadn't counted on the effect Lily had on him.

He wished Rose were present. He'd have been willing to endure one of her blistering scolds just to have her spare him this part of the explanation.

''That's not all I'm talking about,'' Zac said. ''When men and women sleep in the same bed they . . . It's considered normal for a married man and woman to . . . A man is only able to control himself so much," he finished up in desperation.

"Are you trying to say a man is anxious to make a baby?"

"Yes," Zac said, grasping at that straw of understanding, though a baby was the farthest thing from his mind.

"I know all about that."

"You know how . . ." He couldn't think of a way to finish his question.

She smiled. "You can't grow up on a farm and not know."

He breathed a sigh of relief. The worst was over. "Then you understand. If we had a baby and you decided you didn't want to be a gambler's wife any longer, you'd be stuck. This way, when you get tired of me, you can go away and pretend it never happened. I'll give you enough money to live comfortably until you find someone you do want to marry."

"But I don't mind being a gambler's wife," Lily said, her distress at his lack of understanding clear in her expression.

"Maybe not now, but you will soon enough. You'd hate it if you had to tell everyone the father of your children was a gambler."

"No, I wouldn't," Lily insisted. "I'd be proud. Besides, you're nice to look at."

Zac couldn't help but smile. But his thoughts were bittersweet. All his life he'd been told he was handsome, charming, amusing. Most people said it as if it was something he should be ashamed of, or something he didn't deserve. Many times he'd been told his looks couldn't compensate for the serious defects in his character. He'd just as soon Lily not get the chance to come to the same conclusion. She was the only person in the world who didn't see anything wrong with him, and quite frankly, he liked it that way.

"I know you don't understand, but I'm doing this for you.

You can't come here again. I'm going to tell the men at the door not to let you in."

"But—"

"No. You've got to do as I say. You don't think so now, but you'll come to hate being married to me. Then you'll thank me for what I've done. Now I'm going to take you back to Bella's."

Lily didn't move.

"Are you going to get up, or do you want me to pick you up and carry you?"

He hoped not. If he so much as touched her, he wasn't sure he could keep from carrying her upstairs.

"I was just thinking," Lily said, getting her to feet. "I thought Papa was the most stubborn, pigheaded man in the world. But you are. And I had to be dumb enough to come all the way to California to fall in love with you."

"You don't love me. You only think—"

"Don't tell me what I think. Papa did that for nineteen years, and I'm quite tired of it."

Zac was startled at her tone. Lily had never come so close to being angry with him.

"At least I hope it's only pigheadedness," Lily added as she allowed Zac to open the door for her. "Whatever it is, I plan to show you you're wrong. I may be a mere woman, and I may have grown up milking cows and churning butter, but I do know my own mind. And whether you like it or not, Zac Randolph, I love you. Don't look so astonished. It may not be the thing for a proper wife to say, but it certainly isn't against the law."

Lily was relieved to find Bella alone in her parlor. "I need your help," she said without preamble.

Bella put aside the ledger she was studying. "How?"

"I need to buy a dress—red, I think. I want it to be quite striking, but I don't want it to be shocking."

Bella's eyes widened. "Could I ask where you mean to wear this dress?"

"In Zac's saloon."

"You can't. He's forbidden you to go there again."

"I'm not interested in what Zac does and does not forbid. He's got some stupid notion that I don't love him, that in a few days I'll be sorry I married him and ashamed to admit I ever married a gambler."

"And you won't?"

"I want to be married to him for the rest of my life."

Bella took a minute to digest this information. "So what do you want this red dress for?"

"To wear at the saloon. I intend to personally greet every man who comes through the doors. I mean to make the Little Corner of Heaven the most popular saloon in San Francisco."

Chapter Eighteen

Lily avoided the saloon all the next day. Zac had miserable luck at the gambling tables. To make matters worse, Chet Lee was on another winning streak. At the rate he was going, Chet would own the saloon before the month was out.

Quite a few men came in, saw Lily wasn't around, and left for their usual haunts. Since Zac didn't offer drugs or sex, he had limited himself in clientele from the beginning. He had banked on there being enough men in San Francisco who wanted a straight game in a nice place with good food served by attractive women.

There were. He had the most successful gambling house in the city, but the fun seemed to have gone out of it. His luck was so bad, he didn't dare enter a game. He quickly discovered that most of his enjoyment in owning the saloon had come from being able to gamble anytime he wanted for as long as he wanted. Now that he couldn't, the bloom was off the rose.

Actually the bloom was on the lily, and Lily was all he

could think about. It didn't help to have Dodie follow him into his office just to needle him.

"How's your bride today?" she asked, knowing full well that Zac hadn't set eyes on Lily.

"She's all right. Bella is taking care of her."

"How do you know? I wouldn't be surprised if Lily were gone for half the day without Bella knowing a thing about it."

"I trust Bella." He didn't want to talk about it. He was irritable and wanted to be left alone.

"I never thought you'd make a good husband, but I thought you'd at least take better care of your wife than you do the girls who work in your saloon."

"Is that why you were so anxious to help Mr. Thoragood and his wife force me to marry Lily?"

"I shouldn't have done that. Lily could do better on her own. With her looks and innocence, she could catch a dozen husbands better than you."

"Then why didn't you help her?"

"I couldn't. Who do I know but gamblers and scalawags?"

Zac's eyes narrowed. He felt the cold anger he had learned to avoid. "Watch what you say, Dodie. You may be a favored employee, but I can do without you."

"Are you threatening to fire me? Gracious, let me see if I'm trembling yet."

Zac spat out a curse.

"I can find a dozen jobs in this town, but you'll never find anybody else you can trust to run this place for you so you can go on being the little boy you've been for twenty-six years, avoiding your responsibilities, playing at being the big, important gambler."

Zac rarely got angry, certainly not with Dodie, but he was coldly angry now. "If you've got something to say, spit it out. Just be aware that I may throw you out when you're done."

Dodie looked him squarely in the face. "That threat might have scared me into silence a short time ago, but that's when

I thought you were a man I could admire. You've stumbled since then, Zac Randolph. You've stumbled badly, and you don't even know how to get on your feet again.''

"Stop talking in riddles. Say what you have to say.''

"I wanted you to marry Lily because she loves you. It was a dirty trick to play on such a nice girl, but I have to admit I was thinking of you instead of her. I thought she just might be the one who could make something out of you. Lord knows, I've failed. Instead you've given her over to Bella to take care of while you go on as usual. You don't even go over to see if she's happy, if she needs anything.''

"I told Bella to buy her anything she wanted.''

"I wasn't speaking of money. There are other things in life. I used to think you knew that, but now I wonder. I don't like you, Zac Randolph, and I don't like myself for helping you to do what you're doing to that poor woman. She's your wife. She adores you.''

"Don't you think I know that? Why do you think I'm trying to stay away from her?''

"Tell me, Zac. I've been wondering about that.''

"I don't want to compromise her.''

Dodie's snort was crude and comprehensive.

"She'll get tired of being married to me. This way, when she wants to leave, she can go, and I won't have taken anything from her.'' Or from their child, he thought.

"She can't go, you fool. She's married to you.''

Zac was reluctant to tell anyone what he'd done. He was ashamed of it, but Dodie was his friend. It was important that she understand. "No, she's not.''

"I saw it. I was there.''

"Windy performed the service, but he didn't register the marriage. She's still legally unmarried.''

For a couple of seconds, Dodie gaped at him in stunned silence. Then she exploded in fury. "Why, you selfish, stupid son of a bitch!''

Dodie slapped him as hard as she could. Zac grabbed her hand in an iron grip.

"Go ahead, break it," she said through clenched teeth. "It may make you feel better, but it won't change what you are."

Zac let go.

Dodie stepped back, massaging her wrist. "I'm quitting, as of right now. I'll clear out my things and be gone by tomorrow. I don't want to work for you any longer, but I will say one last thing. If there is any decency in you at all, you'll go to that woman on your hands and knees, beg her forgiveness for what you've done, and try your damnedest to be the best husband you can be. If you don't, you're no better than people think you are."

Dodie turned and stalked out, leaving a stunned Zac in her wake. The entire quarrel was unexpected. The outcome was appalling. Dodie was his best friend in the world. He could hardly believe she would say such things about him. But to quit, to turn her back and walk out on him, it was incomprehensible.

He had thought that she of all people would understand.

Zac couldn't sleep. It was nearly noon, and he hadn't slept a wink. He'd had a perfectly miserable night. Without Dodie, nothing had gone right. It was enough to make him wonder how he'd survived before he found her.

He had never wanted Dodie to leave. He hadn't even meant to threaten her. If she just hadn't started in on him about Lily . . . That was the one thing he couldn't stand. He missed Dodie. He'd come to think of her as part of his world. She was always there.

He missed Lily even more, and she was responsible for his world falling apart. He kept telling himself that bringing her to the saloon would only make things worse. Still, the idea wouldn't leave his mind. He knew she wanted to be with him. Just the thought of sharing his bed with her made his body stiff with desire. He was sweating, and it wasn't even hot.

Dodie had been wrong about him. True, in years past he'd

been everything she said. But he was determined he wouldn't ruin Lily.

He ought to feel good. For years Rose had told him that doing things for others would give him a sense of satisfaction, pleasure, even joy. Well, he must have done something wrong because he felt rotten.

He punched his pillow, arranged his body so his hardness didn't make him so acutely uncomfortable, and tried to go to sleep.

He was going to have to hire someone to replace Dodie. He couldn't stay up all night and be up half the day making sure everything was ready for opening. He thought immediately of Lily. She'd been helping Dodie. He told himself to put her out of his mind. He must avoid having Lily become an integral part of the saloon at all costs. If that ever happened, his resolution would fade away as though it never were.

Lily stood on the boardwalk, trying to decide the best way to get inside the saloon. She knew Zac had ordered the doors locked against her. She'd already tried them to no avail, but she was determined to get in.

She was feeling in a melancholy mood. She'd spent the last hour with Kitty and her baby. Kitty was still searching for the baby's father, but she was less hopeful with each passing day.

"They've shanghaied him," she kept saying. "I just know they have."

Lily found it hard to believe men could be kidnapped off the streets or from bars and whisked off to ships headed for distant ports. It hardly seemed such a thing would be allowed in the United States.

While she was mulling this over, she saw Dodie emerge from an alley. Coming out of her abstraction, Lily waved and hurried to catch up. "Just what I was looking for, an unlocked door," Lily said before she noticed that Dodie carried a suitcase. "Is something wrong?" Lily could tell Dodie had been crying.

"You may as well know, I've quit the saloon."

"Why? What happened? Does Zac know?"

"Of course the big idiot knows. It's all his fault, just like everything else. He threatened to throw me out if I said something he didn't want to hear. So I said it anyway and quit."

"Did it have anything to do with me?"

Dodie took a big breath. "I told him he was a fool to stick you off with Bella and never go near you. He thinks you'll get over him and go off and marry someone else."

"I won't."

"I know that. Everybody else knows that. Even the doorposts know it, but not idiot Zac."

"He's not an idiot."

"He is where you're concerned. He's in love with you and doesn't even know it."

"He doesn't want to be in love."

"You know that, and you still married him?"

"What else could I do? I couldn't help him if I was married to some proper stuffed shirt living miles away."

"You can't help him from Bella's either."

"But I don't intend to stay there."

"What are you going to do?"

Lily told her. Dodie's eyes grew bright with merriment. "I wish I could see it."

"Why don't you come back? You know Zac didn't want you to leave."

"It's time. I've been kidding myself for years. I'm not over him. I won't be as long as I keep seeing his handsome face every evening, smiling at me like the world's his oyster and he's going to share it with me. Maybe for five minutes."

"I'm going to miss you."

"I'll miss you, too, but I'll be pulling for you. Give him the devil."

"I'll be trying to get rid of it instead. He's got too much

of that already." They both laughed. "Now tell me how to get inside without anyone knowing."

Zac awoke late with a throbbing headache. He looked at the clock and started cussing Dodie for not waking him. Then he remembered that Dodie had quit, and he cussed that much harder.

As he hurried to the bathroom and started his preparations, he wondered why she'd gotten so angry with him. He was terribly angry at the time, but she ought to have known he'd get over it. He always did.

He paused to listen. Things seemed to be going okay downstairs. From the noise, there seemed to be a bigger crowd than usual. Good. He could use it to make up for some of his losses.

But he became uneasy as time went by. The buzz of activity seemed to be steady, not subject to wild bursts followed by moments of relative quiet. He hurried to get dressed and go downstairs.

He knew something was wrong when the first girl to see him blanched under her grease paint and made a point of getting out of his way. A quick glance around showed nothing unusual. He had just started forward when he saw her.

Dodie was back. He was surprised at how relieved he felt. She was all the way across the room with her back to him, talking to some customers. They were huddled around her like cows at a desert water hole.

She was dressed differently. She was wearing something red and very tight. It must have taken a cast-iron corset to get Dodie in that dress. She'd done her hair differently, too. It was up on her head with a couple of long red feathers stuck in it. She was even wearing long, red gloves.

It was an unusual getup for Dodie, but maybe she was still mad at him and wanted to show him he couldn't get along without her. Okay, he'd play along. He'd just wait for her to come over. Zac had hardly leaned his lanky frame against the bar when Dodie turned to great another customer who'd just entered.

It wasn't Dodie.

An uneasy tremor ran through Zac. Then it turned to an electric shock that burned a path all through his body. That outrageous female was Lily.

He started for her with what he knew was a thunderous expression on his face. It sent people scurrying out of his path.

From the moment she decided what to do, Lily had known this moment was going to come. She had thought she was prepared for it. One look at Zac's face, and she knew she wasn't. Well, she wasn't going to face his cannon fire alone.

"I want you to meet my husband," she said to the two men who'd just come in. "He seems to be a little out of sorts with me. I guess I forgot to wake him on time."

She hooked a man on each arm and started forward.

"No man in his right mind could be mad at you," the taller man said. "I'm surprised he could get any sleep at all."

Lily decided that it was a good thing Zac was too far away to hear that remark.

"I see you've finally gotten up, my dear," she said before Zac could speak. "Mr. Hawkins and Mr. White are new to town. This is my husband, Zac Randolph."

Lily had intended to make her escape while Zac exchanged greetings with the two men, but he reached out and grabbed her wrist before she could move out of reach.

"You're going to have to excuse me, gentlemen. My wife and I have a few things we need to talk about right away."

"Sure," the tall man said with a wink. "Take as long as you like."

Lily wished Mr. White hadn't winked. That only made Zac madder. He practically dragged her into his office at a run.

"What do you mean turning up here, looking like a strumpet, acting like you were brought up in a saloon?"

"I was just trying to help my *husband* with his business," Lily answered. But it was not her usual, mild response. She was almost as mad as Zac. "Of course it's hard to remember he is my husband. I have to come here every so often to remember what he looks like."

"Don't get smart with me, Lily Sterling."

"My name in Lily Randolph, or don't you want to remember that?"

"I can't forget it. You're driving me crazy."

Lily was of two minds as to whether that statement represented progress or not.

"What do you mean by painting your face? You want those men to take you for a saloon girl? Come here and let me wipe it off."

No, not any progress yet. He took out his handkerchief, but Lily darted behind his desk.

"I didn't paint my face. I just used a little color on my lips and something to outline my eyes and lashes. I need some color in my face, or I become invisible in all this light."

"If Bella talked you into this, I'll throttle her."

"I did it myself. Now stop shouting at me and try to talk sensibly."

"How can I when you go about behaving in a manner calculated to drive me out of my mind?"

He made a grab for her, but she jerked her arms out of his reach.

"Do you like the way I look? I tried very hard to decide what you would like."

"Let me get my hands on you, and I'll rip off every last thread. I ought to beat you and lock you in your room."

"Stop threatening me. You dare beat me, and I'll write to every one of your brothers before the night's out."

"I'll rip the letters up."

"Then I'll go straight to the hotel and tell Daisy. She just might be able to handle you herself.''

''I knew Daisy when she had singed hair and a scar down the middle of her head, so don't think you're going to sic her on me.''

He came at Lily across the top of a chair. She uttered a tiny scream and fled, but he caught her.

''Now, we're going to talk.''

''No, you're going to yell at me and pretend you've been saying something intelligent.''

''I'm not yelling. I'm just trying to get your attention. You never seem to hear anything I say. Stop that.''

Huge tears had welled up in each of her eyes.

''I'm not hurting you.''

''You're scaring me.''

''You've never been afraid of anything in your life.''

Tears rolled down each cheek, leaving trails of moisture. Her eyes glistened with more tears.

''Oh, dammit to hell!'' he cursed, letting go of her wrist. ''I can't stand it when women cry. Here, wipe your eyes and be careful not to smear that black stuff all over your face. You'll look like an urchin coming out of a coal bin.''

''Remind me never to come to you for sympathy,'' Lily said.

''When you've got reason for real tears, you might get it.''

''How do you know they're not real?''

''I've got two nieces who're twice as good at that as you. Besides, you're dealing with a master at deceiving people.''

''Okay, let's talk,'' Lily said, carefully dabbing her eyes. ''I may as well begin. It'll save a lot of time.''

''I ought to go first. I'm bigger and stronger and meaner than you. I can lock you in a room upstairs any time I want, and no one will dare let you out.''

''I know that.''

''I can put you on a train and force you to go back to Virginia.''

''I know that, too.''

"I can bury you on a ranch in the country, hire body-guards to make sure you never set foot in San Francisco."

"Then why don't you do it?"

She had him there. Zac knew it, and he knew she knew it. That had been the nub of his trouble all along. From the very first, he'd never been able to force her to do anything against her will. He might as well have been made of jelly. He was as bad as his brothers, and all because she was named after a flower. If he could change her name to Priscilla, maybe he'd have a chance.

"You know you won't do any of those things," Lily said. "You try to deny it, but you like to have me around, which is the way it should be since I'm your wife."

"I don't want you here."

"I won't come to any harm as long as you're here."

"That's not what I mean."

"I know what you mean, and I don't care. If I could fall in love with a gambler, do you think I mind being known as a gambler's wife?"

"You don't love me. You just think—"

"Don't tell me that I think," Lily snapped, her eyes blazing. "Now that Dodie's gone, you need someone to help you. I can do most of her work. You can teach me the rest. That way you can go back to your old schedule."

"And you will go to bed when I say?"

"When is that?"

"Eight o'clock."

"Eleven."

"Eight."

"Could you go to sleep that early?"

"No."

"Neither can I. If I'm going to be up, I may as well be doing something useful."

"Okay, but you leave the saloon at nine."

"It's nearly nine already. Make it ten. I think it would be best if you went around with me to make certain everyone

247

knows I'm your wife now. It will make things go more smoothly.''

She had backed him into a corner again. If he acknowledged that she was his wife, she would have the run of the place. She could do as she damned well pleased, especially since he wouldn't be awake to prevent it.

But if he didn't acknowledge her, she'd come anyway. She'd already shown him that her innocent appearance was just a cover for the most stubborn will he'd ever encountered. He guessed he was stupid not to have realized from the very beginning that any woman willing to travel across the country by herself, unsure of where she was going or of her reception when she got there, wasn't going to balk at entering a saloon.

He did have a couple of options. He could take her back to Virginia and let her father keep an eye on her. But that wasn't any good. She'd already gotten away from him once.

He could change his habits—get up in the morning, sleep at night, ask his brothers for a respectable job. He threw out that alternative without even thinking about it. He couldn't work with his brothers, and he couldn't think with sunlight streaming down all over the place.

That left him with her suggestion. If he told everybody she was his wife, they'd know to treat her with respect. If they didn't, he'd break their heads. That way she could go places without him having to be at her side every moment. And she was going to go places. He'd never seen a more energetic female in his life.

But that would force him to acknowledge what he had been trying to keep a secret. That would make it virtually impossible to later pretend they'd never been married. Especially with old prudes like Mr. Thoragood and his wife constantly looking over his shoulder. Oh well, he could find Windy and have him register the marriage. At least this way, she'd have the protection of his name.

She would have to divorce him, but maybe that wouldn't

be too bad. If she went back East, she could always say she was a widow.

"All right, but you can't wear that dress. You look like an invitation to start a riot."

Chapter Nineteen

Zac's nerves were on edge every minute Lily was in the Little Corner of Heaven. This was the third night she had spent welcoming the customers. She had obediently followed every one of his orders. Well, almost. She had worn a less sensational dress, but she had continued to use makeup to give her face color. Zac had to admit that it made her look even more lovely.

It also made him absolutely crazy to have hundreds of men staring at her, lusting after her, fantasizing about her. It had turned him into a madman. He couldn't sleep. He couldn't eat, and he prowled the aisles of the saloon, growling and snapping at anyone who spoke to him.

He was dressed and downstairs every night before she arrived. He subjected every aspect of her appearance to intense scrutiny. He argued with her, shouted on occasion, threatened to lock her in his office if she didn't change the latest thing that had aroused his anger. She listened calmly to everything he said, dropped some things, changed others, ignored him on a few, and entered the saloon on the dot of seven o'clock.

He followed, cursing women—especially those named after flowers—and himself.

The place was packed every night. Word had gotten around, and men lined up at the door before they opened. Zac wasn't sure they gambled more—at least not until Lily left—but they sure drank more. The girls had to practically run to keep up with the orders. Once he'd even pressed Julie into service. But she'd looked so uncomfortable at the attention she attracted despite the modest dress she wore, he'd sent her back to the kitchen.

"She's very beautiful. You don't deserve her."

Zac whipped around at the sound of Dodie's voice.

"I didn't see you come in." He could tell right away that she'd been drinking. She held an empty whiskey glass in her hand. "What are you doing drinking whiskey?"

That hadn't come out the way he'd intended. He was glad to see Dodie back in the saloon. He hoped she'd come back permanently, but he was so frazzled over Lily, he hardly knew what he was saying. Now she was talking to some guy who looked as though he was straight in from the mines. He hadn't even stopped to take a bath, judging by his aroma.

"Don't worry. I'm not going to stay," Dodie said, following the direction of Zac's gaze. "I heard Lily was doing wonders for this place, and I wanted to see for myself. She's much better than I ever was."

Zac could hear the note of jealousy, of regret, of resignation, and his heart went out to Dodie. She'd served him faithfully for years. It must be terrible to believe she could be replaced so easily. He wondered if that was why she had gone back to drinking the hard stuff. Instinctively, he put his arm around her and drew her to him in a friendly hug.

"Nobody can ever replace you, not even Lily. I have to watch over her every minute. You could hold this place together by yourself from dusk until midnight and still be up next morning checking the books."

251

"I was a faithful hound dog," Dodie said, "but you've got something very special now. I hope you realize it."

"I realize she shouldn't be here."

"Then do something about it."

"What? She won't stay at Bella's unless I tie her down."

"Bring me another whiskey, honey," Dodie said to one of the girls hurrying past; then she turned back to Zac. "I guess you'll figure it out when you're ready."

"Don't you think you've had enough?" Zac said.

"I know when to stop," Dodie assured him. "Don't worry about me. I'll take my drink and sit in the corner. When I'm done, I'll leave."

"What are you doing these days?"

"Taking it easy. I decided I needed a little time off."

"I wish you'd come back."

"We both have things we need to work out. You have to do it your way. I have to do it mine." Dodie gestured with her empty glass.

"You know you can always come back, don't you?"

"Sure. I knew that when I left." She took the whiskey the girl handed her. "Now I'm going to find myself a guy who won't be watching his wife the whole time he's talking to me."

Zac turned to face her. "Sorry. I didn't realize."

"I know. You never do when she's around."

Dodie moved away, leaving Zac to digest that remark. He didn't like what it said about him, but he supposed it was true. As long as Lily was out there, he couldn't think of anything else. Half an hour later, Lily looked his way. Zac nodded. It was time for her to go. She obediently brought her conversation to an end and worked her way across the room. She followed him to his office.

"Your cab's waiting," he said as he picked up her cape with the large hood. He never let her leave the saloon without being covered from head to foot.

"I'm not leaving until I get my good-night kiss," Lily said, a trace of pink coloring her cheeks. "It's the least a wife can expect after slaving all day for her husband.''

Zac couldn't decide whether this was his most dreaded or most anticipated moment of the evening. Either way, he decided Lily was using the good-night kiss as a means of torture. It worked. From the time he came downstairs, he could think of nothing else. Yet when it was time for her to leave, it was the last thing he wanted to do.

To have to kiss her and pretend he didn't want to rip off her clothes and make love to her in the middle of the floor was more than he could do without a violent struggle.

He didn't try to give her a quick brush on the lips. He'd tried that the first night. By the time she'd made him do it over three times, he felt about to burst into flame from spontaneous combustion.

The second night, he'd started with what he hoped was a middle-of-the-road kiss—long, sensual, but not so long and sensual that his condition became painful. That hadn't worked. She'd liked it so well, she wanted a second one.

The third night, he'd begun with a hot, searing kiss, invading her mouth with his tongue, letting their bodies touch from knee to breast. That had worked. It had left her so shocked, she'd let him put her in a cab and send her off before she recovered. The fact that it had taken him hours to regain his own equilibrium was something he preferred to keep to himself.

But one look at Lily told him that tonight wasn't going to be so simple.

"You confused me last night, then sent me away before I recovered. Why?"

"It was safer."

"What's so dangerous about a kiss? Even Bella says it's all right for married people to kiss."

"You tell Bella what goes on between us?"

"No, but I did tell her Papa disapproved of kissing. She said it was okay. If that's true, why are you always trying to get rid of me?"

"I don't like to leave the saloon while it's open," he

prevaricated. "You never know what people are going to do when there's nobody watching."

"It's time you hired somebody to help you. I hardly ever see you. We have no time together."

"I warned you about that when you first came to San Francisco," Zac said, feeling more like a heel all the time. "You get up when I go to bed. You're always going to church, and I won't set foot in the place. Everything about our lives is exactly opposite."

"It doesn't have to be. We could change things. All we have to do it sit down together long enough to talk about it. I'm sure we could work something out. I miss you."

Now she was pulling out the long knives. She was cutting deep, to the only part of him he hadn't been able to seal over.

"We can't do it now," he said, anxious to go before guilt made him agree to something he'd regret. "I've got to get back on the floor. Chet Lee is out there, and I don't trust him."

"You're not leaving until you kiss me," Lily said.

Zac pulled her to him and gave her a quick kiss. She smiled up at him, a dazzling, seductive smile that completely rattled him.

"You're not leaving me with that pitiful peck and a promise. After last night, I know you can do much better. I intend to see that you come up to the mark."

It wasn't hard to take Lily in his arms. He loved kissing her, be it a brushing of the lips, a nibbling at her ear, or a passionate, open-mouthed kiss. It was all so easy. Her sigh of contentment, the tiny gasp of excitement, the sudden increase in her rate of breathing, were all subtly flattering signs that encouraged him to ignore what he knew to be right and fair and give in to the instincts that shouted at him to make her his own right then and there.

He forgot she was the daughter of a preacher who would consign him to the fiery furnace of hell for what he was doing. He forgot she was young and trusting and free from guile. He remembered only that she was the most beautiful woman he'd ever seen, that she was in his arms, that he was nearly exploding with desire.

The feel of her, slender and fragile, the smell of her perfume, the warmth of her body as it pressed against his own, acted on him like an aphrodisiac. He planted kiss after kiss on her nose, eyelids, and mouth, heedless of what it might do to his self-control.

She clung to him, her need as great as his own. Her body answered the pressure of his own, its muscles strung just as tightly. Her mouth opened to meet his. Her tongue hungrily explored his mouth, dueled with his tongue, retreated, and attacked again.

They broke apart, each panting for breath.

"You'd better be going," he said, sounding as if he'd run five miles.

"Why? I have nothing to do but go to bed."

"You have to go, or I won't be responsible for myself."

"What are you afraid of? We're husband and wife."

She looked at him, pleading for more, her mind begging for answers, her body knowing exactly what it wanted. He knew he was on the verge of breaking down.

"This isn't the time or the place to discuss it." He grabbed her cape and threw it around her shoulders. He regained some measure of control when she pulled the hood over her head.

"But you promise we will discuss it."

"Yes. Soon. Now you've got to go, and I've got to get back."

She walked to the door, then turned back. "Do you love me?"

She'd never asked him that before. He'd thought they had a tacit agreement not to speak of it. He should have known better. Sooner of later he must answer, for her and for himself.

"I don't know."

"Are you sure you're not saying this just to get rid of me?"

"Would it be that easy?"

She smiled at him, and a little of the humor returned to her eyes. "No. Papa says I'm as determined as a mule and stick like a leech."

"For once I'm in agreement with your papa."

"I want you to love me."

"Does it mean so much?"

"It means everything. Doesn't it to you?"

He didn't know. For him love had always been a tepid emotion. Even his affection for Rose and George was formed mainly by self-interest. He'd taken the loyalty of his family, of the women who worked for him, as his due, thinking all the while that he was equally loyal to them.

Now he wondered.

Did he know what love was? Maybe he was just bewitched. Maybe his sexual needs had overpowered everything mental and emotional.

"I've never understood love, not the way other people mean it," he said. "Daisy says I'm cold and callous. But I do know I can't get you out of my mind. You're like an obsession."

"I don't want to be an obsession. That's unhealthy," Lily said. "I want to become a part of you. I want you to feel incomplete without me."

"Is that how you feel about me?"

"Almost from the first. Why do you think I was always coming here, always waking you up? It didn't matter that anybody else knew or cared what I was doing, only that you cared. I had to tell you even though you threatened to do terrible things to me."

"I wouldn't have hurt you."

"I knew that."

Zac jerked himself out of the daze into which he was rapidly sinking. "You've got to go. There'll be riots on the floor, shootings, and screaming women, if I don't get out there soon."

"Why are you always making jokes to hide what you really feel, to keep people from getting close to you?"

That stopped him in his tracks. No one except Rose and George had ever understood him so clearly.

"Because I'm afraid," he said in that one shattered moment of honesty. "I know what I look like, how that affects people, but I'm afraid that's all there is. I'm afraid to love, to give myself, for fear I'll be rejected. I couldn't deal with that."

He stopped. Somewhere inside him a door slammed shut. He put on the dazzling smile that had protected him his whole life.

"Now you've really got to go. No more questions. Any more and you'll find out I'm just as boring as the next person."

He hustled her outside, into the cab, and sent her off with a stream of chatter that didn't allow her any chance to reply. But as he reentered the salon and closed the door behind him, he realized she'd forced him to open that door to himself. She'd forced him to look inside and see the truth.

Having done so, he didn't like what he saw. He had finally admitted the truth to himself, had actually put it into words. He couldn't ignore it any longer. If he did, he might lose himself forever. He would surely lose Lily.

Sarah Thoragood entered the saloon with all the caution and trepidation of someone approaching the portals of hell. Lily noticed her immediately. The banging of the front door behind Sarah echoed through the empty hall. Lily rose to her feet.

"I didn't expect to see you here," Lily said.

"Nor I," Sarah Thoragood replied, looking around at the gambling machines as though they were instruments of the Devil.

"Have a seat. Would you like some coffee?"

"I can't stay," Sarah Thoragood said. "I only came because I felt compelled to speak to you. I haven't seen you in more than a week."

"I'm sorry, but I've been so busy here, I haven't had time. Is there anything I can help you with?"

"I have heard a rumor that you've been appearing at the saloon again."

"No. Zac made me stop singing when we got married."

Sarah Thoragood looked vastly relieved, though no less disapproving. "I can't imagine why people persist in spreading malicious lies," she said. "They seem to delight in trying to besmirch the reputations of others."

"Zac said singing would ruin my reputation. It was all I could do to get him to let me act as hostess."

"Hostess!" Sarah repeated on a faint voice. "That's even worse."

"Oh, no," Lily assured her. "Zac makes me dress ever so soberly."

"I see you've given up your black dresses."

Lily was wearing a lemon-yellow gown the saleswoman had assured her was quite proper yet eye-catching. Lily had given away every black dress she owned.

"Zac said he didn't want me wearing black. He said it wasn't suitable for a new bride, that it would make people think I was in mourning. He said it would have all kinds of unsavory people hanging about hoping I had inherited his money."

Clearly Sarah hadn't considered it from that angle.

"Zac never takes his eyes off me when I'm down here," Lily continued. "And he sends me off promptly at ten o'clock."

"That's something else I wanted to talk with you about."

Lily had been expecting this, but not so soon. However, she didn't intend to let Sarah Thoragood get the upper hand.

"I imagine some people have been wondering about that," Lily said, "but it really isn't their business."

Sarah Thoragood blinked in surprise.

"I'll explain it to you because I want to put your mind at rest."

Lily wasn't used to lying. It went against her nature. However, since coming to San Francisco, she'd learned that the entire truth was not always a good thing. Sometimes even a little bit could cause an enormous amount of trouble. She had virtually no experience at mixing truth and falsehood. She hoped she didn't get it wrong.

"Living in two places is a little awkward, but Zac refuses to let me live in the saloon. He says it's not proper."

"Quite right, but—"

"He's really very protective."

At least that was the truth. She had seen the way he looked at the men as they crowded around her, and she cherished every scowl and muttered curse.

"You ought to live somewhere else entirely, and you shouldn't work here at all."

"It hardly makes sense to live elsewhere when Zac has to be here all night and I all day."

"He ought to change his line of business. It's not at all suitable for a minister's daughter."

"I ceased to be a minister's daughter when I became a gambler's wife." Lily's patience was getting short. She was tired of people criticizing Zac, acting as though he were some terrible person just because he liked to gamble.

"You will never cease to be a minister's daughter," Sarah Thoragood said.

"Then let's say I feel greater allegiance to my husband than to my father."

Sarah opened her mouth to speak.

"The Bible does say a woman should leave her family and cleave only to her husband."

"But it doesn't say she should marry a gambler."

"All of life is a gamble. Zac just does a little more of it than most people."

"If you persist in thinking your husband can do no wrong—"

"I'm sure he could do quite a lot of wrong if he wanted," Lily said, "but Zac is kind, generous, thoughtful, and wonderfully protective. I couldn't have found a better husband in the whole world."

"You're besotted!"

"Yes, I'm afraid I am."

"You're not going to quote the Bible to excuse that, are you?"

"No, but Papa says if you're going to believe a thing, you ought to believe it with your whole heart."

"It's too bad you didn't learn all your father's lessons so thoroughly," Sarah Thoragood scolded. "Don't think you've heard the last of this. I'll be back."

And with that, she turned and marched out of the saloon.

The rain was a torrential downpour. No one was going to bring a horse out in this weather. It would either sink in the mud or fall and break a leg on the slippery cobblestones. Zac couldn't even find a ricksha from Chinatown.

"Nobody's going to move until the rain slacks off," Zac said. "You'll have to wait awhile."

"I don't mind."

"I do. I don't like you being here any longer than necessary."

Lily yawned. She was tired. She hadn't said anything to Zac, but being at the saloon for more than twelve hours a day was beginning to wear her down.

"I think I'll go up to your room and put my feet up." She was thinking more of lying down.

"It shouldn't be too long," Zac called up the stairs after her. "You want me to have someone bring up some coffee?"

"No. Just let me know when you can get a cab."

In the meantime, she meant to figure out what to do next. Zac had been more jumpy than usual since the night he'd admitted to being afraid of love. She'd decided to give him a little time to work things out in his own mind. But if he was too slow, she had every intention of pushing the issue along. She was tired of being a wife in name only. She might have come from the country, but she knew a wife was supposed to share her husband's life, home, and bed.

Chapter Twenty

Zac climbed the stairs, his footsteps making brushing sounds as his shoes grazed the carpet. The noise from the saloon faded as he turned a corner and mounted the last few steps. His customers hadn't minded the rain. They'd simply ordered more to drink and gambled a little harder. It would turn out to be a very profitable night.

He had never known it to rain so hard for so long. It was past eleven o'clock. Lily would be exhausted. He was surprised she hadn't come downstairs earlier. She might complain about returning to Bella's at ten o'clock each night, but he knew she was always tired. She might say she came to the saloon only because she was lonely, but Zac knew she worked very hard. Only one week had passed since Dodie had left, and already Lily was beginning to put her stamp on some phases of the saloon's operation. The girls had begun to dress more modestly. Much to Zac's surprise, nobody complained.

He opened the door to his bedroom, words on his lips. They died there. The room shimmered in soft gaslight. Lily lay sound asleep on his bed. His first impulse was to close the door and let her sleep, but he knew he couldn't. He drew closer to wake her, but didn't. The strangest feeling came over him. He couldn't describe it. He'd never felt it before. It was almost one of reverent disbelief.

It was hard to believe there was another woman in the entire world as lovely and innocent as Lily. That she trusted him was hard to believe. That she saw only good in him was incredible. That he only had to reach out and she would gladly become his was something he didn't even allow himself to think about.

He felt he was gazing down on the most precious human being in the entire universe. Nowhere could there be a woman more worthy of a devotion so single-minded that it superseded all other loyalties. It made him feel almost desperate to keep her safe from unhappiness as well as from physical harm. It terrified him that he might lose her. He knew now that if he lost her, he would lose the best part of himself as well.

The intensity, the magnitude of it, startled and frightened Zac. He'd never felt anything so powerful, so profound, in all his life, and he didn't know how to react. To be honest, it scared him silly. It scared him so much, he didn't even hear the steps in the hall or the knock on the door.

"You going to want this cab any time soon?"

The voice caused him to jump and turn.

"I can't stand around waiting," the cabby complained. "I could get a dozen fares right now."

"I'm coming," Zac said, pulling himself together. "She's fallen asleep. I was just trying to figure out how to get her to Bella's without waking her."

"I guess you'll have to carry her."

"I can't leave the saloon."

"Then I guess you'll have to wake her. You can't be in two places at once."

Zac looked down at Lily sleeping and knew he didn't have the heart to disturb her sleep.

"What the hell!" Zac said. "The worst that can happen if I'm not here is they burn the place down. That would give me a chance to build a bigger and better saloon."

"That's the spirit," the cabby said with a grin. "Look on the bright side of things."

All day Lily walked on air. Zac had left the saloon to take her home last night. She hadn't considered it important until one of the girls pointed out that it was the first time anybody had come between Zac and his saloon while it was open. They were staggered when he actually left the premises for an hour.

It was flattering. It was exciting. It was wonderful.

Lily sailed through her work with only half her mind on what she was doing. The girls assumed something quite different had happened. They greeted Lily with sly smiles, winks, leading questions, each one an invitation to share with them the secrets of the evening.

But that was something Lily wouldn't do, even if she had had something to share. She went about her work, humming, smiling to herself for no reason, and generally throwing every female in the place into feverish curiosity and speculation. It was a welcome relief when Kitty came in carrying her baby.

Only Kitty was crying.

"What's wrong?" Lily asked, her own happiness put aside.

"Mama's after me to forget about Jack. She says he's run off and I'll never see him again. She wants me to marry this man who lives up the street from us. He says he'll take good care of me and the baby."

"Do you like him?"

"Yes, but he's not Jack. I know he didn't run off. I know in my heart he was shanghaied and is chained up in the bottom of some awful ship."

They had had this conversation before. There was nothing new to be said.

"Why did you bring the baby? It's nearly time for you to get dressed."

"Mama had to go see a doctor. This fog is bad for her lungs. She'll be back soon."

"Here, let me hold baby while you dress."

"You sure you don't mind?"

"Of course not. I've visited you at least a dozen times already just so I could hold him."

"You're so good to me."

"Nonsense. It's just selfishness," Lily said holding out her arms for the baby.

"Okay. I'll be back down in a jiffy," Kitty said. "If Zac was to find you holding a baby, it'd probably give him a heart attack."

Both women laughed, but it set up a train of thought in Lily's mind that had been just below the surface ever since she got married. She tried not to let herself think about it, but Kitty was right. It would scare Zac to death.

The baby started to cry. "I didn't mean to ignore you, darling," Lily said in a crooning voice. "I promise to give you all my attention until your mama comes back."

She stood up and started to walk slowly about the room, singing softly as she went. The baby stopped crying and looked up at her with big blue eyes. He was such a beautiful baby. He had a head of fuzzy brown hair, a pug nose, and a tiny mouth that turned enormous when he yawned. He was nearly four months old, but he was still small. Lily hoped he wasn't going to be short. It was so important to a man's self-esteem to be tall. Like her father and brothers.

Like Zac.

Zac's son would have black eyes and hair, just like his father. He'd be big and noisy, demanding what he wanted with loud yells, not soft whimpering cries. He'd be strong. He'd reach out and grab what he wanted. His mouth would be stubborn, his chin jutting when he got angry, which he would do whenever he was hungry or wet or tired or just plain ornery.

But he'd be gorgeous. When he was happy, he'd have a smile that would melt any heart in the world. Even her papa's. Then maybe he would forgive her for running away.

It would be so nice to see Mama again. Lily had missed her mother. She'd often been angry at her for not standing up for her against her father, but that didn't change the fact that she loved her mother and missed her and the boys. They were rough, noisy, and almost as convinced as Papa that they were superior to every female in the world, but they spoiled her, watched out for her, and were proud of her.

And of course she wanted to see Papa. They were too much alike ever to be able to live comfortably in the same house, but it was this very similarity that made them mean so much to each other. She missed his strength, his comforting presence, knowing he cared enough to argue with her.

She chuckled.

She'd miss them most at Christmas. That was the time when they managed to put aside all their differences and enjoy the best in each other.

They always let her go with them to choose the Christmas tree. They swore every year they wouldn't, but they always did. She wouldn't let them cut any but the very best tree. Papa said it was a pagan custom, but he always put the star on the top. He made them wait until January 6th to open their presents, reminding them that the Wise Men didn't have trains. They had to cross the desert by camel.

She could almost taste Mama's Christmas goose served with pork sausage and cornbread dressing. There was always so much food—venison, baked apples with walnuts, corn, beans, the last of the turnips, and plates of steaming biscuits to slather with fresh butter. For desert there were sweet potato and pecan pies served with thick whipped cream. And later, while they sat around the fire before going to bed, they would devour mounds of oatmeal cookies along with a bowl of hot mulled apple cider.

It would be nice to go home for Christmas.

Lily

* * *

Zac found her walking the baby and singing Christmas carols, tears streaming down her face. A cowardly inner voice counseled him to turn around, go back to his room, and not come out again for at least an hour. It sounded exactly like the kind of advice he would have taken only a few weeks ago. With a fatalistic sigh, he ignored it.

He couldn't stand to see Lily cry. He had no idea what had caused it, but he had to try to fix it. He doubted he could—he usually made things worse—but he had to try.

"Do you always cry when you sing Christmas carols?" he asked. It wasn't the right thing to say, but he couldn't think of anything else.

She turned to him quickly, a smile brightening her face.

"I was just being sentimental, singing the baby to sleep and thinking about going home for Christmas. That combination is guaranteed to make any woman cry."

Zac decided he'd never understand women. That combination was enough to give him the shakes. If he were a drinking man, he'd head straight for the bar and order a double something.

"Of course you'll go home for Christmas," he said. "It won't take more than a few days on the train."

"I was just thinking about the way it used it be, when I was little. It'll never be the same."

"Nothing ever is. Growing up changes everything."

"Maybe I don't want to grow up."

"Are you already tired of being independent? What happened to that determined rebel?"

She laughed. That made him feel a little better, but he still hadn't gotten at whatever was hidden behind her sadness.

"I still feel like that most of the time, but sometimes I just want to cozy up in a corner for a while."

"Feeling homesick?"

"A little. Papa never did write. Did you feel homesick when you ran away?"

267

"I never got a chance. George peppered me with so many letters—all containing bitingly personal contributions from Rose—I was glad I wasn't anywhere near Texas."

"I wouldn't mind what Papa said. I just wish he'd write."

"He will. He's probably just trying to figure out what he wants to say."

"Papa's never in doubt about what he wants to say."

Zac could believe that. The infernal man apparently never stopped talking.

Zac felt himself growing a little sentimental just watching Lily. She was holding the baby close and singing again. The little brat didn't look too frightful. At least he was quiet. Having a baby wouldn't be so bad if they were all like this one.

Vivid memories of Rose's twins, Adam and Jordy, and Jeff's pair caused Zac to shudder. Maybe other people's babies were all right, but Randolph offspring ought to be branded and turned out on the range to fight it out with the wild beasts until they were at least sixteen.

If Lily wanted a letter from her father, she'd get one. He'd light a fire under the old cuss if he had to write a letter himself. It wasn't a bit of good going around preaching about Christian duty if you couldn't remember your own.

Kitty came hurrying down the stairs, interrupting Lily's singing and Zac's rambling thoughts. She looked embarrassed and a trifle nervous that he should have found Lily holding her baby. He knew she was aware that it was strictly against the rules to bring children into the Little Corner of Heaven.

"I'll take him," she said reaching for her child, even though Lily didn't seem ready to give him up. "You must have a hundred things to do."

"I don't mind. Really."

But Kitty insisted, so Lily gave him up.

"Come on," Zac said. "Let's go to my office."

Lily hesitated, her wistful gaze following Kitty and the baby.

Touched by the longing in her eyes, Zac put his arm around Lily. "You'll have babies of your own one of these days, and Christmas trees, and so many visitors you'll wish half of them had stayed home."

"I know I'm being silly," she said, shaking off her melancholy mood. "But you must know women are terribly sentimental."

Actually, he'd never thought about it. He'd always considered himself an expert on women, but Lily was rapidly showing him that that was a mistaken assumption.

"You've probably just been working too hard," he said, guiding her to his office. He put his hand under her chin and lifted her face to his. "You look a little tired."

Lily broke away and entered the office ahead of him. "Are you hinting I'm losing my looks?"

"No, just that I've been too selfish to notice you've been working too hard."

Lily's eyes glistened with moisture. "I think I'll last a few more days."

"I hope so. I'd miss you if you weren't here." He closed the door. "Now tell me, why were you really crying?"

Lily looked him straight in the eye and said, "I want a baby."

Every bit of concern and worry for Lily vanished from Zac's thoughts to be replaced by pure panic. He dropped into his chair with what he was certain was a stupidly stunned look on his face. He should have taken the coward's way out and hidden in his room, but it was too late now. He didn't think he had the strength to get out of the chair, even if he had had the nerve.

"You can't just go out and order one," Zac managed to say. "You have to . . . we would need to . . . but you wouldn't want to . . ."

Oh, hell! This was the one conversation he'd hoped to avoid, and he'd walked right smack into it.

Damnation! Where was Rose when he needed her?

"I don't know if I would or not," Lily said. She obviously felt much more comfortable with this discussion than Zac. "Papa says it's a woman's duty to her husband. Mama says a woman must suffer for the sake of children."

"Good lord!" Zac exclaimed. "If that's the way they talk in Salem, I'm surprised the place hasn't dried up and blown away."

"I decided it can't be too terrible," Lily said. "Everybody has babies. Except Mary Ellen Warren. Mama says she wants one awful bad."

Zac decided this conversation was a perfect reason why he made it a rule to avoid the company of married women. All this talk of babies was enough to make a man start looking around for a means of escape.

It also made him as hot as a Chinese firecracker. What it took to make babies had been on his mind almost without interruption from the moment they had finished that fake marriage ceremony. Of course he hadn't put much emphasis on the baby part.

Well, actually, none.

But here was Lily talking about it as if it was the one desire of her life. He tried to tell himself he couldn't make love to Lily unless he loved her, certainly not until the marriage was official. Neither would it be right to risk giving her a baby when the thought of conventional married life gave him the shakes.

But he wanted her badly. The battle going on inside him had resulted in more than one sleepless night. His head hadn't been clear enough for gambling all week.

"Do you think we could have a baby?" Lily asked.

Zac swallowed. "It wouldn't get here in time for Christmas."

Lily giggled. "It'll save until next Christmas."

That was what worried him. It would save for Christmas after Christmas after Christmas. If things went the way this sort of thing usually did, it would soon have company. Before long there'd be a mob of selfish little monsters demanding all of Lily's time and attention. Zac didn't like that at all.

But he was almost willing to chance it. The thought of making love to Lily was just about to torch his body.

"This isn't something to be taken lightly," he said, trying to grab hold of the last shred of his sanity before it went up in flames. "You've got to think about this."

"I have."

"*We've* got to think about it," he said. "Everybody knows I'd make a terrible father. Maybe you don't want—"

"Who dared say such a thing?" Lily demanded, martial light flaring in her eyes. "If Sarah Thoragood had the nerve to come into your own saloon and say something like that, I'll—"

"No, not Mrs. Thoragood. Everybody says it," Zac said. He cringed at the thought of Lily attacking the preacher's wife because she'd spoken out against her gambler husband.

"It's time to open," Zac said, grabbing for straws. "We can't discuss it now."

"When?"

She wasn't going to let this go.

"Tomorrow, if you're still of the same mind. Now you'd better hurry up. I don't want all those early birds beating down the doors wanting to know where I've hidden you."

"I wouldn't care what they did if you'd just hide me in the same room with you."

Zac could feel the flame encircling him. Another few seconds and he'd be nothing but a pile of ashes.

"Tomorrow," he said, virtually pushing her out the door. "We'll talk about nothing but babies."

"Promise?"

Hell, how did he get himself into these things! Talking about babies was just about as cheerful as talking about arming cuckolded husbands with shotguns. But he couldn't refuse. It was obviously important to Lily. And anything important to her was also important to him, even if it did make him as nervous as a cat.

271

"I promise," he said, brushing his finger along her jaw. She took his hand and pressed it to her cheek. When she dropped a kiss in the middle of his palm, his resistance nearly collapsed. She looked up and smiled, and he felt himself sliding helplessly.

"I'd better go," she said, standing on tiptoe to give him a quick kiss. "I think I hear them already."

She disappeared through the door just in time. One more minute, and he'd have started the baby-making process right there on his office carpet.

He collapsed in his chair. Well, so much for gambling tonight. Instead of kings and queens, he'd be seeing pink and blue babies. He wouldn't be able to beat Lily at cards tonight.

Chapter Twenty-one

Zac trudged up the stairs. He had had some miserable nights lately, but this had been the king of them all. His life was going to hell in a handbasket, and he couldn't seem to do a damned thing about it.

He'd been thinking of Lily all night. He might as well have stayed in his office. People spoke to him, and he didn't hear them. His staff asked him questions, and he didn't answer. He had wandered through the saloon as if he had no idea where he was going or why he was there. It was a good thing Dodie wasn't there. She'd have laughed herself sick.

All because Lily wanted a baby.

No, because he wanted to give Lily a baby.

He couldn't believe it himself, but after an evening when he'd thought of virtually nothing else, he realized it was true. He wanted to give Lily babies.

Damnation, hellfire, and forked-tongued devils! He didn't even like children, and here he was thinking about them in the plural. He ought to check himself into an asylum. No, what he needed was a good night's sleep. He was run down and exhausted. He was hallucinating. A solid eight hours in bed and he'd see things in a whole new light.

He walked down the narrow hall, his footsteps muffled by the runner. It was an unnecessary precaution. Most of the girls were so tired, a freight train wouldn't have awakened them.

He entered his room, lighted the lamp on the table by the door, and walked through the bathroom to his closet. As he took off his clothes, he kept telling himself he couldn't make love to Lily until he found Windy and got the marriage registered.

Zac's body didn't have any such reservations. Just the thought of making love to Lily caused him to come stiffly erect. He had to smile. It was probably the only time he'd ever been practically ready to jump out of his skin with rampant lust, and he was preparing to go to bed alone.

He thought of Lily sleeping soundly in her own bed. It wouldn't take long to reach Bella's. He could put his clothes back on in a matter of minutes. There was nothing wrong with his showing up at his wife's bedroom. True, she really wasn't his wife, but nobody knew that, and he intended to see about fixing that first thing in the morning. Or afternoon. It didn't matter what order you got things in as long as it all worked out in the end.

Zac actually reached out to take his pants off the rack again. Instead he muttered a string of curses, took off his underwear, picked up his lamp, and headed for the bedroom. He had to get into bed and fall asleep before he did something crazy. He was halfway across the room before he realized that Lily was sleeping in his bed.

Instantly his body was at full attention.

He didn't know how she had gotten in without anyone noticing. He looked at her dress folded neatly on the chair. It wasn't the same one she'd worn earlier in the evening. She must have gone back to Bella's and then changed her mind.

She'd been thinking about babies as much as he had.

He had to wake her and get her back to her own room.

He stopped in his tracks. He couldn't wake Lily and give her hell for sleeping in his bed while he was buck naked. He hurried back to the closet and put on some underclothes and a robe. He sat down on the edge of the bed to make his bulge less apparent. He shook Lily awake.

She came awake gradually. She smiled when she saw him. "I came back."

"So I see, but you can't stay here. You've got to leave before anybody notices."

"But I don't want to leave." She yawned. "I came to tell you I've been thinking about what you said about the baby."

"I said we'd discuss it in the morning."

"But we don't need to. I've already decided. That's why I came back. I want to start right now. Tonight."

The bulge got harder than ever. Zac shifted uncomfortably. He was feeling terribly hot.

"It's almost morning," Zac said. His protest lacked conviction even to his own ears. "I've been up all night."

"Jacob said that doesn't make any difference to men."

"What?" Zac said, utterly confused.

"My brother. I heard him talking to Joseph, my other brother. He said men can make a baby any time of the day or night."

Zac was feeling hotter still. He couldn't tell if it was anticipation or the long underwear he had on.

"I really don't think—"

"Don't you like me?"

"Of course I do."

"Jacob said it was the women who always hung back. He said men didn't need any encouragement."

Zac's temperature went up another five degrees. He decided that all the Sterling men talked too much, especially when they were within Lily's hearing

"I like you very much," Zac said. "I can hardly control myself as it is, but I want you be sure you—"

"I am sure." Lily threw back the covers. "See, I'm naked."

She was right about that. The young, firm breasts he'd dreamed of for weeks were right there for him to see. All he had to do was reach out and touch them.

Zac thought he would explode. He'd never actually heard of it happening, but he was certain this kind of sexual temptation could cause a man to go crazy. He could almost feel himself beginning to melt into a mindless puddle.

Perspiration rolled down his nose. He had to get out of the long underwear or die.

Zac pulled the sheet up. "Cover yourself," he said, his voice tight with emotion. "A sight like that could cause a man to die from shock."

"I don't want you to die. I want you to—"

"I know what you want, but you've got to be sure. You can't decide tomorrow you'd like to change your mind."

Her delighted chuckle stopped him.

"You don't have to be afraid I'm going to change my mind. And you can stop hiding your feelings behind silly remarks. I know exactly what I'm doing."

"I'm not trying to hide anything. Well, that's not exactly true, but it's not what you think."

Zac jumped to his feet, turned his back to Lily, reached inside the robe, and jerked the long underwear down to his ankles. He sighed with relief. Keeping his back to Lily and his robe well bunched, he sat back down on the bed. When he turned around, she had the covers down again.

"Won't you come to bed with me?"

"I . . . you . . . for pete's sake, stop pulling the covers down!"

"Jacob said a man couldn't resist the sight of a woman's naked breasts."

"Your brothers talk too damned much."

Lily didn't move. Her invitation was impossible for him to refuse any longer. "Let it be recorded somewhere that I tried. But flesh and blood can only stand so much."

He stood up, undid his robe, and jumped under the covers.

"Oh!" Lily said.

"You weren't supposed to look."

"But you didn't look like that before."

"You hadn't teased and tortured me before."

"Oh!"

"Stop saying *Oh!* like a scared virgin, or I'm going to start feeling guilty again."

"Do you often feel guilty?"

"This is the first time."

"Then I'm glad."

"I'm not. It sets up a confusing set of crosscurrents."

"Can we start now?" Lily asked.

"Wait a minute," Zac said. "I need to get mentally adjusted. The baby won't come any slower if we take a few minutes to work into this properly."

"Is there a proper way to work into it?"

"Well, maybe not a proper way. Everybody goes about it a little differently."

"I should have asked Dodie about your special way. Then I'd be ready."

Zac blushed from hairline to toenail. He reached out and took Lily's hand. He kissed her fingers. "You don't need to ask anybody anything. It could never be the same as with you."

Lily felt like a queen as Zac kissed her fingers, lingering over each one as though it required individual attention. He moved from knuckle to knuckle. She wouldn't have believed he had such patience. She wasn't certain she did. She wanted him to get to the kissing and holding part. She knew about that, and she knew she liked it.

Now he was kissing the palm of her hand. Quite a delicious feeling radiated along her limbs. But it was barely a prelude to the sensations that assaulted her when he kissed her wrist and then her inner arm. She nearly melted.

He started with the fingers of her other hand, and Lily decided that this was quite a pleasant way to go about having a baby. She wondered if all men used this method. She couldn't see how any woman could consider it suffering. She wouldn't mind trying to have a baby just about every day.

When Zac's lips reached her upper arm, the crescendo of sensations took Lily's mind off everything except what was happening to her. She had feared she was being too brazen when she climbed into his bed without any clothes on. Now she was glad she had. Her nakedness against the sheets made her skin all the more sensitive to Zac's lips.

She wondered if she could stand any more. He was kissing her shoulder, the side of her neck, the tops of her breasts, sending arcs of hot desire racing through her body. She'd never known she could feel anything remotely like this. It made her want to reach out, grab Zac, and pull him to her. But she didn't. Everything he had done was quite wonderful. If there was a proper way to go about doing this, she didn't want him to miss a single step. So far she'd liked every one of them.

Zac touched her nipple with the tip of his warm, moist tongue, and Lily nearly lifted off the bed, as if a bolt of lightning had raced to every part of her body and back again to her nipple. Then Zac took the nipple gently into his mouth, and Lily thought she would die of pleasure. She grasped his hair but immediately relaxed her grip for fear she'd pull it out.

She moved her hands down his neck, across his shoulders, and down his back. She felt like a wanton, luxuriating in the feel of a man's body, wallowing in the pleasure of what he was doing to hers. She knew she wasn't supposed to be enjoying this so much, but she couldn't see how she could do anything else.

The suffering part must come later.

Zac's lips deserted her nipple. Leaving a trail of kisses across her bosom, neck, and jaw, he kissed her firmly on the lips. Lily lost all reserve. She flung her arms around Zac, pulled his body down on top of hers, and kissed him with all the happiness and excitement in her heart.

She was relieved to see that Zac wasn't offended by her show of aggressiveness. In fact, he seemed quite heartened by it. He slipped his arms under and around Lily and squeezed her until she thought she wasn't going to be able to breathe.

She was relieved to see another myth debunked. A nice girl didn't have to wait for the man to make all the advances. Lily decided that she liked not waiting for Zac to think of everything. She put her arms around him, pressed her body firmly against his, and kissed him with all her might.

There was something decidedly hard and hot pressed against her abdomen, something that distracted her thoughts from Zac's kiss. She knew what it was.

Maybe that was the part she wouldn't like.

She planned to get as much pleasure beforehand as she could. She kissed Zac all over his face. His mustache tickled, but nothing slowed her down until Zac's rumbling laugh.

"You don't have to go so fast. We've got all night."

She didn't want to tell him she was trying to get so drunk on his kisses that she wouldn't feel the suffering.

"It's getting light already," she said between kisses. "It'll be time to get up in a hour."

"Not this morning," Zac said taking her face in his hands and planting a kiss on the end of her nose. "You can spend this morning in bed."

"Does it take all morning to make a baby?"

"It can if you want it to."

She wasn't going to make up her mind until she knew about the suffering part. In the meantime, she loved being next to Zac, being held in his arms, having him kiss her eyelids. She felt positively decadent. She was certain the Queen of Sheba had behaved something like this. Surely it wasn't right for her to like the same things as a pagan queen.

But Lily forgot all about queens, pagan or otherwise. Zac

was alternately nibbling and blowing gently in her ear. She could hardly stand it.

"Is this how you make a baby?" she murmured.

"Not precisely," Zac whispered against her neck, "but it makes it more fun."

Lily had to admit it was electrifying, but she was growing nervous about the bad part. It must be truly awful to make a woman want to give up what Zac was doing to her now.

She was tempted to forget about the bad part and the baby and just enjoy herself while she could. When he started kissing her breasts again, she was certain nothing could be more wonderful than this. But then his fingertips began a delicate meandering over her body, along her side, over and around her breasts, and down her belly. When they didn't stop at her navel, Lily's body grew rigid.

Zac's fingers made a quick detour over her hip, down her leg, and behind her knee. It set her entire body on fire.

"Don't be frightened," Zac said. "I'll tell you when it's going to be uncomfortable."

So it *was* going to hurt. Her mother was right. She would have to suffer. Okay, but she was going to garner every bit of pleasure she could beforehand. She threw her leg across Zac. It gave her a delicious sense of being as worldly and provocative as he was. She was his equal. She could meet him advance for advance.

Until he slipped his hand between her thighs.

She lost every bit of her desire to be bold and seductive. She tensed in expectation of the pain.

"This won't hurt," Zac said.

She wanted to believe him, but she was frightened. She couldn't help tensing when his finger entered her. She was almost painfully sensitive.

She held her breath, but she felt no pain, only the exciting sensation of something moving within her. Then he touched a nub, and she nearly rose off the bed. With pleasure.

Instinctively, she had clamped her knees together. Gradually, she relaxed. Once more, Zac found the ultra-sensitive spot, and a wave of pleasure washed over her body. Not just one. Zac continued to move inside her until the waves began to come closer and closer together. They were almost like a pulse now, each one stronger than the last, each one forcing a moan of pleasure from her lips.

Suddenly they started coming like an avalanche, one after the other, each bigger and more fierce than the last, until she thought she couldn't stand it any more. She heard herself moaning Zac's name as she bucked against his hand. When she thought she could stand no more, the waves washed over her, and she felt her entire body shudder with release.

Even as she felt her body floating down from the heights, Zac moved above her. She felt him withdraw his finger and replace it almost immediately by a larger pressure. Despite herself, she felt her body tense.

"This will hurt," Zac warned. "But only a little. Then I will never hurt you again."

He was trying to make her feel better. This was the part no woman liked; this was the part she had to endure. Well, she would if she must. She wanted a baby more than anything in the world.

The pain as Zac thrust into her was sharp. But it was brief. It was gone almost before she was aware of it.

Now Zac was moving within her just as he had before, only this time she felt stretched to the limits, filled with him. He lifted her hips so he could penetrate more deeply. She helped as much as she could. She knew the baby had to grow deep in her body, sheltered from all possible harm.

But it wasn't long before she forgot all about babies or of more pain to endure. The waves of pleasure started coming again, only they were more intense this time. Lily didn't understand how that was possible, but it was rapidly being proved to her there was more to baby-making than she guessed.

This time, however, it seemed to be affecting Zac the same way it was affecting her. He was no longer the calm master in control of her body. His escalating passion seemed to be keeping pace with hers. His breath was more labored, his movements more excited.

Gradually his thrusts became quicker, penetrated more deeply, came closer to reaching the very core of her. She felt herself gradually losing control. She was conscious only of herself and Zac, their bodies inextricably joined, as they floated higher and higher on a mounting crest of sensation that threatened to overwhelm all conscious thought.

She clung desperately to Zac. He was her lifeline, her anchor, her magnetic north. Without him she felt certain she would fly off into space and disintegrate into a million tiny pieces. She clung to him, strove to absorb him, to become one with him, until she felt their bodies begin to melt into a single mass of heated passion.

Then, just as she was flung to the very edge of consciousness, she felt herself begin to float down once more, born earthward by waves of release too exquisitely sweet for words to describe.

She felt Zac tense, heard him gasp, felt his body spasm as it released its seed deep within her.

She finally felt married.

"Is that all there is to making a baby?" she asked a few minutes later.

Zac didn't know how to take that. He didn't know whether she was hoping for more, or if she'd been disappointed in his performance. No one ever had been.

"Sometimes you have to do it again. Do you think you could endure that?"

"Right now?"

Zac began to be even more concerned. "Well, maybe not this very minute."

"How long are you supposed to wait?"

Zac rolled up on his elbow. "You don't have to do it again. If it was that unpleasant—"

"No, I don't mean that at all." Lily blushed. "I liked it

quite a lot. I was hoping we didn't have to wait very long before we could try it again.''

Zac kissed her on the nose and pulled her close. ''We won't have to wait very long at all.''

''Did you leave any steps out?''

Zac sat up, self-doubt plaguing him again. ''Why?''

''I just thought if there was anything you left out, I'd like to try it the next time. Now that I'm not afraid anymore, I'm sure I would enjoy everything.''

''I'll see what I can do,'' Zac said, nuzzling her neck, ''but I'm not made of iron, you know. I have to rest now and then.''

''But not for too long?''

''No. In fact, I'm feeling remarkably rested right now. Just in case we didn't make a baby the first time, we might have to do this a lot more,'' he warned. ''Monty and Iris didn't have their first baby for six years.''

''I hope we won't have to wait that long.''

Zac thought such a period of repeated trials seemed a perfectly wonderful way to spend a large part of the next six years.

He was just about to embark on what he hoped would be a long period of trying to get the proper procedure just right when the bedroom door burst open with a shattering crash. He looked up to see a tall, thin man with a long black beard standing in the doorway, glaring at him like a fiend from hell.

Oh, God! He knew he shouldn't have made love to Lily before making certain the marriage was legally recorded. Now the Devil himself stood on his threshold, ready to drag him down into hell.

Chapter Twenty-two

"Who the hell are you?" Zac demanded, sitting straight up in the bed.

"I'll ask the questions, thou debaucher of innocent women, thou archfiend among fiends!"

This was beginning to sound like a reenactment of Sarah Thoragood's sermon. Zac thought the Devil considered himself the archfiend. Besides, now that he got a better look, this fella didn't look all that devilish. Just ugly.

"Oh, for goodness' sakes, Hezekiah," Lily said as she scrambled to cover her nakedness and her embarrassment, "stop carrying on like a great fool. Zac and I are married. Do you think I would be in the same bed with him if we weren't?"

"You mean this skinny windbag is the man your father picked out for you to marry?" Zac asked.

"Yes. This is Hezekiah Jones."

"Hezekiah *Jones!*" Zac repeated, nearly choking on the name.

"Yes. His name is a great mortification to him, so I'd

prefer you not make a point of it. Hezekiah, this man," she said, pointing to Zac, "is my husband, Zachary Taylor Randolph."

"Zac will do."

"Hezekiah believes in being formal."

"Then let him get the hell out of my bedroom until we get some clothes on. I bet he never popped in on your ma and pa at a time like this."

Lily found it difficult to believe her mother and father had ever experienced a time like this.

"Don't think you can escape punishment for violating this poor, innocent woman by cursing and blaspheming," Hezekiah thundered. "The gates of hell yawn at your feet. You shall be swallowed whole. You shall—"

"You shall suffer a bullet in the head if I'm forced to get out of this bed."

"Please, Hezekiah, leave," Lily implored. "Go downstairs and have somebody make you a cup of coffee. I'll be down as soon as I can get dressed."

"I find it difficult to believe the evidence of my own eyes," Hezekiah declared, abandoning bombast for honest bewilderment. "But I'm not leaving you, even though you've compromised yourself. I couldn't look your father in the face if I left you with that—that libertine one minute longer."

"That's enough," Zac growled as he threw back the covers, his patience completely gone.

Hezekiah gaped in horror. "Sir, I feel compelled to point out that you're not wearing any clothes."

"Then you know you're about to be beaten senseless by a naked man, probably a first for you. But given your propensity for opening doors that should have remained closed and uttering the first ill-considered thought that springs to your very narrow mind, maybe not."

"You really married this man?" Hezekiah asked Lily, backing up in the face of Zac's advance.

"Yes, she did," Zac said, suffering only a twinge of guilt

at the lie. They *would* be married before Hezekiah found out the details.

Hezekiah backed through the door.

"Wait downstairs," Zac barked. "There's a full bar. Help yourself."

He slammed the door in Hezekiah's stunned face.

"Your father should be roasted on a spit in hell for even thinking about marrying you to that man," Zac shouted.

"I guess this means we won't get to try making a baby again," Lily said.

Zac shouted with laughter. "You're the perfect wife for me."

Much to his surprise, he meant every word of it.

"Why didn't Papa come if he was so worried about me?" Lily asked Hezekiah when she'd dressed and gone down to the saloon. "He never wrote. Nobody did. I thought nobody cared."

"He didn't trust himself not to murder the man who enticed you away. He thought I, as your fiancé, would be a more suitable choice."

"You're not my fiancé," Lily said. "You never were. I told you that over and over."

"But your father—"

"Papa never listened to anything he didn't want to hear," Lily snapped. "Furthermore, I didn't run away because of a man."

"Then you're not married to that naked man upstairs."

"Yes, I am, but I didn't come out here to marry him. I came to get away from you and Papa. I knew Zac would help me, but I never expected to marry him."

"But he's a gambler! How could you marry such a sinner?"

"Let me remind you that you're talking about my husband. If you continue to say unkind things about him, I shall do something quite awful to you."

"What could you do to me?" Hezekiah asked with all

the natural arrogance of a man who had been born certain he was superior to any woman created.

"If you hold his mouth open, I'll pour a bottle of whiskey down him," Zac said. "Being found dead drunk on the steps of a gambling saloon ought to do wonders for his character. It might even turn him into a human being."

Lily looked up to see Zac coming toward them. Just seeing him caused her to nearly burst with pride. He was wearing nothing but a bathrobe—his bare feet and legs showed plainly—but she was certain there couldn't be a taller, more handsome husband in the entire world. That he should be her husband was a surprise that still took her breath away.

"Even if you hadn't already sold your soul to the Devil, you wouldn't be a suitable husband for a woman of Lily's purity," Hezekiah announced.

"But your dried-up, hide-bound, sanctimonious little soul would be a perfect match for her sweetness and innocence, right?"

"Her father chose me to be—"

"Her father didn't have to marry you. He might have changed his mind if he had."

"Your soul is already damned," Hezekiah announced. "Why must you drag Lily into hell after you?"

"Actually, I'm counting on her to keep me out of its fiery jaws," Zac said. "Now, I've heard all I'm going to listen to from you. I don't care what you think of me, but Lily happens to think better of me than you or I do. I won't have her being subjected to your diatribe."

Hezekiah opened his mouth, but Zac interrupted him.

"If you feel you must continue rebuking me, look up the local preacher and his wife, Mr. and Mrs. Thoragood. I have no doubt they'll hang on your every word. I've been up all night, so I'm going to bed. If you feel you must see my wife again, come back after we open."

"I would never enter this place when it was doing the work of the Devil."

"Fine. Tell Lily good-bye, and get the hell out."

Hezekiah tried not to look apprehensive, but Lily knew he wasn't used to being challenged. Besides, he was five or six inches shorter than Zac, and Zac really did look a little devilish just now. She supposed it was those black eyebrows and black eyes. Hezekiah gave ground. "I'll be back," he announced as Zac sent him stumbling through the door with a push. Zac slammed the door behind him.

"If you ever considered for so much as one second being the wife of that man, you're not worthy of being a Randolph," Zac said.

"I never did," Lily said. "Do you really think I'll make a good Randolph?"

"The best," Zac assured her. "You know, I'm not as sleepy as I thought. Do you think we might have another go at baby making?

Lily giggled. "I guess Jacob was right. A man really can make a baby any time day or night."

"Baggage!" Zac cried. "Wait until I get my hands on you."

Lily would have beaten him upstairs if she hadn't stumbled over the hem of her dress.

Zac couldn't find Windy Dumbarton anywhere. Nobody had seen him. Nobody knew when to expect him back.

"He never goes far from whiskey and a faro game," Zac said to the bartender at one of Windy's favorite haunts.

"Sure, but he can find that in just about any town west of the Mississippi."

Which Zac had to admit was true. Some cities and towns had begun to settle, to put down roots and put up churches and schools. But most were made up of men wandering from one place to the next, looking for excitement, gold, or a chance to avoid the humdrum lives they had led back East.

"Tell him I need to see him the minute he gets back" Zac told the man. "Tell him I'll give him a hundred dollars if he finds me within an hour of returning to town."

"You must want him real bad," the bartender said.

"Usually people are only too glad to get shut of Windy."

"Once I talk to him, I will be, too," Zac said. "He's been the cause of the worst nightmare of my life."

Zac didn't know where to look next. He'd covered all Windy's known haunts and every place he might wander into by accident. Yet he couldn't stop looking. He had made love to Lily for the last four nights.

Guilt was eating at him like acid. No matter what she said, no matter how much she pleaded, he should never have touched her.

He tried to stay away. Each night he spent hours fabricating plans to keep from going to bed with her. Each morning her smile, her nearness, the sight of her welcoming body caused them to blow away like dried grass.

They were married now in every sense of the word. Not even the black cloud of Hezekiah's presence had the power to change that, but the lack of a properly registered marriage could. Zac lived in fear of Hezekiah's trying to confirm their marriage and finding nothing on record.

He was certain that if Lily ever discovered what he had done, she would leave him. If his brothers discovered what he had done, they'd kill him. It wouldn't matter that he had regretted his actions almost from the first. It wouldn't matter that he'd wasted four days trying to find Windy and set things right. It would only matter that, as usual, he'd done the most comfortable thing for himself despite the consequences to others.

He'd also failed to do the one thing that could possibly have made his behavior seem less awful. He'd not kept his promise to himself to leave Lily untouched. He'd taken her virtue and left her a woman living in sin.

For a woman of Lily's background and beliefs, he couldn't imagine how he could have done anything worse. He'd done many things in his life, but he'd never dishonored any woman. Now he had, and it was something he couldn't live with.

Of course he could always marry her again. He would

have done that in an instant, but it would require explaining why he wanted a second marriage ceremony when he had been so opposed to the first one.

He couldn't do it, not until he'd exhausted every possible alternative. He couldn't bear to think of the look that would come into her eyes. One of the things he liked best about Lily was her belief in him, in his innate goodness. After a lifetime of having everyone, including his family, assume the worst, it was wonderful to have someone who believed the best. It made him want to live up to her expectations. Honesty compelled him to admit that his family was closer to an accurate understanding of his character than Lily, but still it made him want to try.

It seemed awfully perverse of Fate to make off with Windy Dumbarton so Zac couldn't do the right thing just when he'd finally made up his mind to do it. But questions of right and wrong didn't really bother him. It was the loss of Lily's trust that scared him more than anything. He didn't care what his family or the Thoragoods thought of him as long as Lily still believed in him.

Sunlight struggling to enter through stained-glass windows illuminated the interior of the church. Walls of brick and floors of stone kept the interior as cold as the frown on Mr. Thoragood's face.

Lily, however, felt the heat rise from under her collar until it caused her cheeks to flame. She wasn't certain whether it was from embarrassment or anger. But at this point, it hardly mattered. The longer she listened, the angrier she got. Hezekiah had talked Mr. Thoragood into letting him deliver the Sunday sermon. Lily felt certain he'd written it specifically for her.

She was sure everyone in the congregation knew it.

He was preaching on the Woman at the Well, the one who was living in sin. When he couldn't quite bend that around to fit Lily, he moved on to something about gambling saloons being the equivalent of the modern day Sodom and Gomorrah. Apparently feeling himself on more fertile ground, he had launched into a full-scale attack on the girls who worked in such places, equating them to women only too happy to cast aside the morals their parents had tried to instill in them for the pleasures of the flesh.

Lily saw people in the congregation nodding their heads in agreement. She knew most of them wouldn't know one of Zac's girls if they saw them. She also knew most of them wished she wouldn't come to their church.

Suddenly she could stand no more. She got to her feet to leave, but instantly changed her mind.

"I've heard a lot of talk from you and Mr. Thoragood about the sinful women who work in saloons," she said in a very loud voice when Hezekiah paused for breath, "but I have yet to see either of you try to help them."

The gasp of shock was audible even over the rustle of people turning to stare at this woman who had done the unthinkable, interrupt a preacher in the midst of his sermon. Hezekiah stood speechless. Mr. Thoragood looked stunned. Mrs. Thoragood was as red as a tomato.

"Many of these women are just as decent and honest as anyone here. They came to San Francisco hoping to better themselves. Because they're unmarried, the only jobs they can get are in saloons. I know because the same thing happened to me."

"We found you a job," Sarah Thoragood spoke up, finally regaining possession of her voice and senses. "Several of them."

"And I was fired because I attracted too many men. Everyone seemed to feel that if the men's intentions weren't honorable, mine couldn't be either. That's exactly what you've decided about these young women."

"You can't deny that many of them are sunk in a sinful way of life," Mr. Thoragood stated.

"I can only speak for the women who work at the Little Corner of Heaven."

"The very name is a sacrilege," someone muttered.

"I also know this congregation has never done anything to try to improve their lives."

"We've invited them to church."

"Have you gone to the saloon, spoken with them, issued the invitation in person?"

"It wouldn't be suitable—"

"Neither have you tried to get to know them, to help them find other jobs, to help them meet young men who might marry them. Instead you've stayed in your homes, safe from the sin you're so afraid of, yet complaining it's all around you."

"You can't defend these women or the men who hire them."

"I have more right to defend them than you have to call yourselves good, caring Christians."

A roar of angry protests greeted that remark.

Hezekiah raised his hands for silence. Gradually the noise subsided. Lily decided to speak first.

"I challenge you to come to the saloon and meet the girls where they work." She included the congregation in her dare. "I challenge all of you to learn who they really are, where they come from, what they are looking for in San Francisco. I think you're afraid to find they're not very different from you or me."

The congregation buzzed like a hive of angry wasps. Protests came from every corner of the church, but Lily kept her eyes on Hezekiah. She knew he prided himself on being fair as well as right. She hoped he couldn't resist the opportunity to prove her wrong. She watched him struggle with himself. Lily knew what his answer would be by the grimness with which he faced her.

"I will come," he announced.

The congregation emitted a sharp murmur of protest. Mrs. Thoragood looked stunned.

"I think today would be the best time," Lily said.

"But it's Sunday!" Mr. Thoragood protested.

Once again Lily watched Hezekiah struggle with himself,

but she knew he wouldn't back down.

"What better day," Hezekiah said. "Now let us bow our heads and pray for our souls as well as those of the unfortunate women."

Lily would have preferred he not refer to the girls as "unfortunate women," but she wasn't about to quibble. He had agreed to do far more than Mr. Thoragood would.

"I still don't like his being here," Zac said. "If he gets the girls stirred up, I'm throwing him out."

Zac hadn't liked the idea when Lily explained it to him while he dressed. He liked it even less when he came downstairs to find Hezekiah talking with Julie Peterson and several of the saloon girls. He looked ill at ease, even a little unfriendly, but Lily noticed a slight relaxation from when he'd arrived. Maybe he was finally loosening up enough to really listen.

"I don't trust people who act like a lion one day and a coyote the next," Zac said. "If he does what he wants, I'll be looking for girls to take their places. These girls are good at what they do. I don't want them leaving to become cooks, parlor maids, or companions to little old ladies."

"He only wants to help them meet nice men. Besides, there are always more girls. Why, just yesterday—"

"I know. I saw her, too. She came in last night. I told her to sleep as long as she liked. She's to see you when she wakes up."

Lily stood on her tiptoes, pulled Zac's face down, and gave him a big kiss.

"Hey, watch that," he said in mock consternation. "You'll give the place a bad name."

"It already has a bad name."

"In that case . . ." Zac took her in his arms and kissed her quite thoroughly. "I always hate it when places don't live up their reputations," he said when he finally came up for air.

Hezekiah detached himself from a group of young women

and came over to them. Lily wished he could have waited at least a few minutes longer.

"Well?" Zac said, a slightly hostile ring to his voice.

Hezekiah looked as stiff as a ramrod. Lily knew it was very difficult for him to admit to her and Zac that he'd been wrong.

"I would like to come back," he said to Zac. "It appears I may have misjudged you. The young women have been most insistent that without your help, several of them would have been forced into a life of shame just to survive. Miss Peterson was most vocal in her praise of you and Lily—uh, Miss Sterling—I mean, your wife."

Hezekiah obviously found it difficult to accept Lily's marriage, but he was willing to admit when he was wrong. She'd always liked that about him, though it hadn't been enough to make her love him.

"Now that you're satisfied I'm not running a brothel, what do you intend to do?" Zac asked. "This is still a gambling saloon."

Zac wasn't taking this well. Lily guessed he wouldn't be happy until Hezekiah went back to Virginia.

"Miss Peterson and I think it would be a good idea for everybody to get together at a social of some kind."

Zac frowned.

"It would be best if we had it here," Hezekiah said.

"Are you crazy!" Zac said. "Those people would die before they'd set foot in this place. They'd be sure something would rub off on them."

"That's why we think they ought to come here," Julie said.

"It would have to be sometime in the afternoon. The girls don't get up until late," Zac said.

"It can't be before seven. The men have to get off work and have time to eat their supper."

"The place is full of gamblers by then."

"You'd have to close for the night," Hezekiah said.

Zac exploded. "You're crazy if you think I'm losing a

night's income so a bunch of close-minded old bats can come poking their noses into everything I do!''

"It won't work if we go anywhere else," Hezekiah said. "The congregation has got to see where the girls work and live. They've got to know they're helping nice girls."

"Oh, so you believe they're nice as well, do you?"

"Miss Peterson has convinced me I might have let my predisposition to believe the worst blind me to the best in these women," Hezekiah said.

Something in Hezekiah's voice made Lily look at him more closely. What was it—confusion, uncertainty? He was looking at Julie in a peculiar way. Julie was looking just as odd. Lily almost burst out laughing when she realized that Hezekiah and Julie were attracted to each other. That must have come as quite a shock to him. Poor man, it was a shame nothing could come of it, but at least it had helped Hezekiah change his mind about the girls. Lily had every confidence that he would convince the Thoragoods to fall into line with his plans.

Now if she could just convince Zac.

They lay in the bed, sated with lovemaking, Zac too aroused to sleep, Lily too languid to want to get up. It was one of the too-brief times during the day when their lives intersected. Lily found them much too short. She feared Zac found them exactly to his liking.

She was beginning to wonder if he would ever turn into a conventional husband, someone who was home for dinner at six o'clock, not just getting up. The more she learned about him, the more she admired him. It must have taken a lot of courage to set up an honest saloon when everybody swore you had to cheat to make a living. It must have been even more difficult to assume the responsibility for so many women. The Little Corner of Heaven was the only place in town where men were not allowed to go upstairs.

But all of this had nothing to do with being a husband, at least the kind of husband Lily wanted. Zac seemed to want a bed mate and a partner, someone with whom he could satisfy his desire and share his pleasure in the saloon. He seemed perfectly content with that. He still talked about making a baby, but Lily knew he rarely thought of a real, live, breathing child. That didn't fit into his plans.

There was so much she wanted that didn't fit into his plans. Children, a house of her own, regular hours so she could have time to be with him, a feeling they shared the same world, a commitment to their life together. And real love, deep and abiding.

But she couldn't expect that, at least not yet. She'd dragged him kicking and screaming into this marriage. She didn't know how much more he could absorb. Papa always said tigers didn't change their stripes. Maybe people weren't any different from tigers.

"You really think I ought to close the saloon for a night?" Zac asked.

It took Lily a moment to figure out what he was talking about.

"Yes. Hezekiah is right. It won't be the same if they don't come here."

Zac was silent for a minute. "Okay, but only for two hours. They'll have to go out the back. It'll drive my regulars away to see that bunch leaving when they're trying to come in. They might confuse it with a prayer meeting."

"I doubt that," Lily said. "I don't think they'll mind going out the back door. You might have to lock it to keep some of them from sneaking out early."

Lily was proud of Zac. Closing the saloon was a difficult thing for him to do, but he had managed it. Her coming into his life had made a great many demands on him, but he'd managed to rise to the challenge each time.

Then why did she feel so unhappy?

She'd realized while she was standing there watching Hezekiah and Julie try to pretend they weren't attracted to each other that Zac had no trouble keeping his attention on the girls, or the saloon, or any other problem that happened to be occupying his mind at the moment. True, he was showing a definite fondness for her. And he was certainly enthusiastic about their lovemaking, but he'd never once said he loved her.

Lily realized with a kind of sickening shock that she'd been so upset about their living apart, so excited about working for him in the saloon, so utterly amazed by their lovemaking, that she'd forgotten the most important part of all.

Zac didn't love her. Well, maybe a little. He might like her, need her, want her, but he didn't love her passionately, fervently, madly.

And she loved him so desperately.

She didn't know what she was going to do. Never in her life had she expected to be married to a man who didn't love her as much as she loved him. That was why she'd run away from Salem. For one brief, horrible moment, she wondered if Hezekiah had felt as she did now. Then she realized he hadn't. His pride might have been hurt, but his heart had never been touched.

Hers had, and it ached miserably now.

What could she do? She couldn't make Zac love her. She'd learned that much. She couldn't honestly say he was any closer to loving her the way she needed to be loved than he had been the day they got married. She had conveniently fitted into his life. She added something without costing him anything. Naturally he would like her for that.

But that wasn't enough for Lily. She wondered if he would ever love her. She was sure that if he did, she could do without everything else. But as long as love was missing, nothing else counted.

Chapter Twenty-three

They finally decided to have the social in the church after all.

"The wives have asked me to speak for them," Mrs. Thoragood said to Hezekiah. "They won't enter a saloon."

"But it would show a wonderfully forgiving and understanding spirit if they would meet the girls on their own ground," Hezekiah said. "The girls are more likely to believe in the genuineness of our effort."

"They won't enter a saloon," Sarah Thoragood repeated. "And don't call it *our* effort," she added. "You let Lily Randolph talk you into this. Nobody asked us what we thought."

"You must see it would be a good show of faith."

"It would be a good show of stupidity to expose our husbands to the kind of women we'd rather they know nothing about," Mrs. Thoragood said with asperity. "Everybody knows men have little resistance to the lure of evil. It's a foolish woman who knowingly puts her husband in the way of temptation."

"I think you're taking too harsh a view of the character of these young women," Hezekiah said. "I was most favorably impressed by several, especially Miss Julie Peterson."

"I'm sure you were. Men usually are impressed by that kind of woman, even good men. But the fact remains, the women will not enter a saloon. And I support them in this decision."

"Then we shall have the social at the church," Hezekiah said, conceding defeat. "I fear we won't have such good attendance."

Sarah Thoragood had seen to it that the parish hall was decorated for the social, but it wasn't working.

When Zac found they planned to use the church, he refused to close the Little Corner of Heaven. "I don't see why I should lose revenue for no reason at all," he'd told Lily.

"It would show you support Hezekiah."

"But I don't support him. I'll be there to back you, but as far as I'm concerned, trying to be respectable has ruined Bella. I won't keep any of my girls from going, but I won't force them either."

Lily had been ready to argue for hours, but Zac had made his decision, and he refused to discuss it. Lily didn't like it, but she had no choice but to accept his stand.

Some girls weren't the least bit interested in the social. Others said they'd prefer to wait and see what came of it. Still others wanted to go but didn't want to miss work. In the end, only seven girls went.

The congregation wasn't any better represented. A few of the ladies turned out, but they left their husbands at home. And their sons. And nephews. And grandsons.

"The whole purpose was for them to meet a different kind of young man," Lily said, despairing.

"They obviously don't intend for it to be one of their men," Zac said. He was watching Hezekiah talk to Julie Peterson, a faint smile on his lips. "You and Hezekiah will

299

have to work that out if you plan to do this again."

"If we don't do something soon, there won't be a next time," Lily said. "They won't come back again to be stared at and kept at a distance."

"What do you suggest?" Zac asked.

"We've got to find something they have in common."

"They have nothing in common."

"Yes, they do. They're all women. They all have family, homes, clothes, this town, dozens of things. We just have to find one we can use to get them talking to each other."

Just then Kitty Lofton came hurrying in with her baby.

"That's it!" Lily said, excited. "Babies. All women love babies."

"But we've only got one."

"It only takes one," Lily replied as she started toward Kitty. "Especially when it's absolutely adorable."

"One baby won't fix this mess," Zac said to Dodie.

"She'll make it work if anybody can," Dodie said. She had come because, in her words, she wouldn't have missed this for the world. Zac was pleased to see she'd stopped drinking. He wasn't pleased to learn she'd found another job.

"If they're going to talk about babies, they don't need me," Zac said. "I'm going back to the saloon."

But Lily came hurrying back. "Kitty says she knows where Jack is."

"Who's Jack?" Dodie asked.

"Her husband. He was shanghaied. She wants you to go after him."

"You're crazy!" Zac said. "If I did, I'd end up sailing the China Sea at his side."

"You've got to help him," Lily insisted. "He's the father of her baby. You always said a baby must have a father."

"This isn't a simple matter of convincing a man to marry the mother of his child," Zac said. "Those people are criminals. They steal grown men and keep them prisoners for years. What ship is he on?"

"The *Sea Witch*."

"That's the most notorious ship out of San Francisco."

"She's desperately in love with him. I don't know if she could stand to lose him again."

"She can't know he's on the ship," Zac said. "She's only heard a rumor."

"Can you find out?"

"Maybe, but I can't do it here. I need to go back to the saloon. I know a few people I can talk to. Maybe we can figure something out, but I don't hold out much hope. It would take a small army to steal a man from one of those ships. You need Monty and Hen. They like fighting."

"You can do it," Lily said. "I know you can."

Zac decided there were times when Lily carried this believing he could do anything too far. She didn't realize she was talking about men who used muscle, drugs, guns, or anything else at their disposal to get what they wanted. She hadn't met their like in Salem, or anywhere else for that matter.

He was getting to be as bad as his brothers, doing one crazy thing after another all because Lily couldn't stop helping people. No matter what his objection, she always managed to draw him in. She was too soft-hearted, and he was getting too soft-headed.

He had to talk with her, make her understand he couldn't take on the support and defense of San Francisco's unfortunate women. She was turning something he'd started as a benefit to himself into a full-time job. Next thing he knew, she'd insist he start taking in fatherless children. He'd have to put his foot down. He didn't want any homeless children. He certainly didn't intend to fill his saloon with them.

But that would have to wait. Right now he had to figure out how to spring Kitty's husband. Living up to Lily's opinion of him was getting to be downright exhausting, not to mention dangerous.

* * *

Zac hadn't been gone twenty minutes when Kitty's mother came hurrying into the church. If she was surprised to see all the women taking turns holding her grandson, she didn't show it. She headed straight for her daughter.

"The *Sea Witch* is sailing tonight."

Kitty nearly fainted. She turned to Lily. Lily turned to Dodie.

"Zac can't do anything that fast," Dodie said. "I doubt he's been able to talk to anybody yet."

"But we've got to do something," Kitty said, nearly frantic. "If he leaves, I'll never see him again. I just know it."

It wasn't long before the entire gathering knew Kitty's husband, the father of her child, was residing in the hole of the *Sea Witch*. No one, however, had any idea what to do about it.

"I'm going to the ship," Kitty declared. "Maybe I can talk the captain into letting Jack go."

"You can't go alone," Lily said. "I'll go with you."

"Are you crazy?" Dodie asked. "None of you will go. You won't come back alive."

"I can't believe that's true," Hezekiah said. "This is America. People are free to go anywhere they please."

"This is San Francisco," Dodie snapped. "They don't always come back when they please."

"We could all go," Mrs. Thoragood said. "They would never dare harm women of the church."

"You'd do better to wait for Zac," Dodie advised.

"But we don't have time," Kitty said, "not if the *Sea Witch* is sailing tonight."

"I'll go with you," Hezekiah offered.

One after another, the women volunteered to go until only Dodie was left.

"How about you?" Mrs. Thoragood asked.

"I'm going for Zac," Dodie said. "Somebody's got to be able to tell the police where to look for your bodies."

"Tell him to come join us," Lily said, "but I expect we'll

302

have Jack free before he can find those men he wants to talk to.''

"Please, let's hurry," Kitty said.

Lily handed Dodie the baby. "You take him. We'll be back in a little while.''

Dodie's response made several of the women blush.

"I don't believe you," Zac said. "Not even Lily would do anything that crazy.''

"Look at me," Dodie demanded. "Have you ever seen me holding a baby?''

"Come to think of it, I haven't," Zac said, realizing that, as incredible as it was, Dodie must be telling the truth.

"They'll get killed," Zac said, heading for his office at a run.

"That's what I've been trying to tell you," Dodie shouted after him.

"What's Zac in a dither about?" Asa White, one of the regulars, asked.

Dodie explained quickly.

"Miss Lily can't go down there!" Asa exclaimed, thunderstruck.

"She's already gone, and Zac's going after her.''

"One man can't do nothing against that bunch of cutthroats.''

"It's a shame you don't have a gun," Dodie said, "You could go with him.''

"Of course I got a gun," Asa said, pulling a pistol from his belt behind his back. "I never go anywhere without it. Hey, Eric, Bob—Miss Lily's gone down to the docks. We got to help Zac get her back. Did you bring a gun?''

Each man produced a hidden pistol.

"You're supposed to be unarmed," Dodie protested.

"Are you crazy!" Asa said. "This is San Francisco.''

By the time Zac returned, half the men in the saloon had heard about Lily. They were all armed and ready to follow him.

"We're going with you to get Miss Lily," Asa said.

Cries of "me, too" echoed from all around the room.

"You said you'd need an army," Dodie said. "Well, it looks like you got one."

"I just hope we get there in time."

"I'll run ahead to the Gold Nugget," one man said. "I got a couple of buddies there who'd love to be in on this."

Before he'd gone two dozen blocks, Zac was being followed by a motley horde of a hundred men, all armed with guns, knives, and sticks. They all knew Lily, and they meant to see she didn't come to any harm. The mob continued to grow, block by block. By the time Zac reached the docks, they numbered in the hundreds. All he needed to do now was organize them into an attack force. But how do you organize a mob?

The closer her little group came to the docks, the more Lily questioned the wisdom of their decision. She sensed everyone else was feeling the same way. She could see their worried glances, the fear in their eyes; she felt the drag of their footsteps. She told herself her father wouldn't have been afraid. Neither would Zac. She wouldn't be worthy of either man if she were afraid.

But she was.

The piers extended into the bay for a quarter of a mile or more. Hundreds of ships lined their sides, their masts and smoke stacks resembling a forest in winter, many discharging or taking on cargo in preparation for their next journey. Lanterns dotted the night like giant fireflies. From every direction came sounds of activity—the soft swish of ropes, the sharp ring of metal on metal, the dull thud of heavy footsteps on hollow decks, the steady whine of a windlass, the hiss of steam.

The night air was heavy with the scent of salt, shellfish, and seaweed. The moon was so bright, its reflection could be seen on the water stretching halfway across the bay. There was very little wind, and luckily, it wasn't cold.

Lily wished Zac were here. The presence of Hezekiah and Mr. Thoragood wasn't half as reassuring as one glimpse of Zac's powerful shoulders would have been.

"I think we ought to have a plan," Lily said.

"I'll speak with the captain," Hezekiah offered. "I'm certain that given a few minutes, Mr. Thoragood and I can convince him to release this young man."

Lily hadn't been in San Francisco very long, but she knew things weren't going to be that easy. She didn't even want to think of what Zac would have said to such a notion. She still hadn't gotten used to his curses, far less their variety. She couldn't get rid of the nagging fear that one of these days Divine Providence just might let loose a little brimstone to warn Zac he was treading too close to the edge.

Lily hoped it wouldn't be the fiery kind, but she had a feeling brimstone didn't come in any other variety.

"Did you bring a pistol with you?" she asked Hezekiah.

"We don't need a pistol for God's work," Hezekiah said.

Lily remembered a Biblical injunction to beat plowshares into swords. Or was it the other way around? It didn't matter. She wasn't likely to convince Hezekiah to change his mind, but she didn't feel anyone who went around stealing grown men was going to listen meekly to a couple of unarmed preachers and a bunch of women.

They passed the first several ships. Lily didn't like the way the sailors looked at them. Neither was she reassured to see at least a dozen men on each ship. The strength of their group seemed to diminish with each stride. Lily fervently prayed that the sanctity of their errand would make up for the strength they lacked otherwise. She would rather have depended on Zac.

"There it is!" Kitty cried.

The *Sea Witch* rode at anchor at the end of the dock, a great, black hulk of a ship. Paint peeled from the sides. Gouges in the wood hadn't been repaired or repainted. The ropes that held the ship to the dock looked old and frayed. The gangplank lacked guardrails. Grease or grime covered the windows, making it difficult to see inside or for light to escape. It looked like an evil bird nesting in the water.

Lily felt a tremor of fear. She brushed it aside. She couldn't back down now. Not when they were so close.

Lily could see men moving about the deck. Others were loading cargo stacked on the docks. Maybe Jack would be one of those men.

Kitty rushed forward to the first man. He appeared to be supervising the others. Lily feared he was in reality guarding against their escape.

"Do you know a man named Jack Lofton?" Kitty asked him. "I was told he was on this ship. He's my husband. Please, I must see him."

"I don't know any Jack Lofton, lady. He ain't on this ship. Now you and your friends get outta here. We got a lotta work to do before we sail."

"Please, he doesn't want to be a sailor. He's got a baby he's never seen."

"Look, lady, I done told you, I don't know no Jack Lofton. Now get along before somebody gets hurt."

Lily could see the determination of the group waver. She didn't know if they really believed this man or if his denial was a convenient excuse to give in to their fear. She didn't believe this man would tell the truth to anyone.

"How about you?" Lily said, approaching one of the men loading cargo. "Do you know a man named Jack Lofton on this ship or any other in the harbor?"

The man looked at her out of empty eyes and walked up the gangplank without answering.

"Do you know him?" she asked a second man, but he also walked by her in silence.

"Get away!" the guard shouted. "Leave those men alone. They got work to do."

"We're looking for Jack Lofton," Lily said. "He's on one of these ships. Somebody must have heard of him."

"Nobody's heard of nobody," the big man said.

"I would like to speak with your captain," Hezekiah said,

speaking up. "Maybe he would know something of this young woman's husband."

"He won't know nothing," the guard said. "Now get out of here and leave us to our work."

"I insist upon speaking to the captain," Hezekiah said. "If you won't call him, I shall go in search of him myself."

"You can't board the *Sea Witch*."

"Then call your captain."

Lily was so engrossed in the argument, she almost missed a whispered message from a man plodding past loaded with his share of the cargo.

"Jack's chained in the hole."

Lily glanced at the man. He walked away without any sign he'd so much as looked at her. She quickly looked to where the guard was arguing with Kitty, Hezekiah, and now Mr. and Mrs. Thoragood. Apparently giving in to the pressure, he shouted for the captain.

Lily's apprehension grew when she got a look at the man who appeared on deck. He was huge, swarthy, dirty, unshaven, and dressed more like a pig farmer than a ship's captain.

"What do you people want?"

"They want to know if we got a Jack Lofton on board," the guard said.

"Never heard of him," the captain said. "Now you people get out of here."

"You have heard of him," Lily said, stepping forward. "He's chained in the hole right now."

Zac halted when he reached the docks. "We can't all go charging up at once," he said to Asa. "They're liable to grab the women."

"You can't hide this many men," Asa said, "not when they're spoiling for a fight."

Zac was thinking fast. He had just a few minutes to figure out what to do or lose control of the situation.

"Then let's give them a fight. Probably every ship at this

pier has shanghaied some of its crew. Pick out a half dozen and attack them. Then, when I give the signal, everybody converge on the *Sea Witch*. You got anybody willing to board the ship from the water?''

"Sure, as long as they don't have to stay in too long."

"Good. We'll need to take them by surprise."

"What about Miss Lily? She's a right pretty woman. No telling what some bastard would pay to have her all to himself."

Zac had been trying not to think about that. Knowing the Barbary Coast and the tastes of the men they catered to, it was exactly the kind of thing they would do.

He'd kill any man who touched Lily.

"I'll take care of Lily. You just take care of the rest."

Lily didn't like the way the captain was looking at her. If the Thoragoods and Hezekiah wanted proof that Zac wasn't evil, one look ought to convince them that compared to this man, Zac's soul was as pure as the driven snow.

"Who told you Jack Lofton was on my ship?" he demanded.

"He wouldn't give his name," Lily said truthfully. She wouldn't have told him the man's name if she'd known it. She wouldn't put it past him to kill the feeble creature.

"And you believed him instead of me?"

"You have the look of a man who makes a practice of being dishonest."

The fearful gasps of her companions were obliterated by his roar of fury.

"You dare call Rafe Borger a liar!"

Lily quaked before the blast of his rage, but she wasn't about to back down. She was certain several other unfortunate souls were also chained inside his ship.

In the silence that followed the captain's angry shout, Lily heard shouts and the sounds of combat. She prayed that whoever they were, they'd attack the *Sea Witch*.

"I merely said you have the look of a liar. Now I wish

you would stop shouting at me and send someone to bring Jack up. He hasn't seen his wife in nearly a year. He doesn't even know he has a baby."

Some of the captain's anger seemed to abate. Lily would have been more comforted if she hadn't felt it had been replaced by cunning.

"Which one is his wife?"

"I am," Kitty said, coming forward.

"Hmmm, not as pretty as the other one, but you'll do. I'll let you sail with him," the captain said. "Now what's fairer than that?"

"She can't do that," Lily said. "She can't leave her baby."

"Let her decide," the captain said.

"My good man, you can't force a woman to make this sort of choice," Hezekiah said, stepping forward.

"Who the hell are you?" demanded Captain Borger.

"I'm Hezekiah Jones, minister of God. And this is Harold Thoragood. He's also a minister."

"Two preachers," Captain Borger said with a shout of laughter. "I bet there ain't never been two sky pilots on these docks since they been built, but I ain't afraid of you." He turned back to Kitty. "You want your man, woman, come on board and see him."

Lily reached out to restrain Kitty. "Bring him up," she said to the captain.

The captain looked as though he would refuse; then he stalked over to the hole. "Bring up Lofton," he shouted.

"Oh, God, he does have Jack," Kitty murmured.

"You can't go on that ship," Lily said to Kitty. "You set one foot on that gangplank, and you'll never see land again."

"How can I see Jack and not go to him?"

"Think of your baby," Lily said.

When Kitty's husband was hauled up from the bowels of the ship, she half fainted from shock. He had a chain around his ankle. His clothes were rags, and his body seemed thin to the point of starvation. Only the bulge of his muscles indicated that the captain fed his crew well enough for them to be able to work.

"Jack!" Kitty called out.

"Kitty, is that you?" the man called back, his body no longer bent and lethargic.

"Why don't you come up here where he can see you?" Captain Borger coaxed.

"No!" Jack shouted. "He's a fiend. Leave, all of you, before he rots your souls like he has mine."

Captain Borger hit Jack a terrible blow. "You want to see your man, you got to come up here," he called to Kitty. "And you gotta bring that other woman with you."

"You dare not touch these women," Hezekiah said. "God will strike you down."

It was the guard who struck Hezekiah down. Julie fell on her knees beside his inert body.

"Bring the two women on board, Caradec," the captain ordered. It was getting hard to hear his voice over the noise from the surrounding ships. "There's trouble brewing. Let's get the rest of the cargo and get out of here."

"You can't touch these women," Mr. Thoragood protested valiantly. A blow from Caradec's fist sent him to the boards with Hezekiah. Caradec's big hand closed around Kitty's arm. His other hand reached toward Lily.

"Touch her, and I'll put a bullet between your eyes."

Chapter Twenty-four

Lily was certain that if she lived to be a hundred, she would never hear a more welcome voice. The guard let go of Kitty and turned to attack Zac.

But Zac was ready. A powerful blow to the stomach doubled the guard over. Then a sharp rap on the side of his head with the butt of a pistol sent him sprawling to the deck. Zac pulled a small pistol out of his pocket and handed it to Mrs. Thoragood. "Watch him. If he tries to get up, shoot him."

Mrs. Thoragood looked as though she'd had a live serpent thrust into her hands, but she didn't let go of the gun.

Zac turned to Lily. "Get Kitty and head toward town. There's fighting all over this dock. It'll reach the *Sea Witch* any minute."

Zac turned away without waiting to see if Lily did as he told her. She didn't. She put her arms around Kitty, who showed signs of fainting for real, but Lily couldn't leave Zac, not after he'd put himself in danger to rescue her and her friends.

"I want that man," Zac told the captain, pointing to Jack Lofton. "Let him go, and we won't bother your ship."

The captain looked at Zac with murder in his eyes. "I'll have you in chains next to him. Get up here," he shouted into the hole. "We got a fool who thinks he's going to make off with one of our sailors."

Captain Borger headed down the gangplank toward Zac. Six men rushed onto the deck of the ship through the hole and various doorways and openings.

"Asa!" Zac shouted. "It's time."

The noise along the dock continued to build, but no mob of pistol-toting gamblers converged on the *Sea Witch*.

"This is no time to be bashful," Zac called, looking around. "We've got about ten seconds before somebody hits the deck."

"It ain't going to be me," said the captain.

"Get Kitty out of the way," Zac shouted at Lily. "She can visit her husband as soon as I get through with this overgrown toadstool." He handed Lily his pistol. "If I go down, shoot him. And shoot to kill. If you don't, you'll end up as private entertainment for some son of a bitch with a very nasty imagination."

Lily accepted the gun, but refused to let herself think Zac might end up shanghaied. She would shoot Captain Borger before she'd let that happen. She lifted the gun and pointed it at the first of the men coming down the gangplank.

"Don't come any farther. I won't have a lot of cowardly thieves ganging up on my husband."

"Atta girl," Zac said, dancing out of Borger's reach. "Keep that popper aimed straight at their hearts, and we might get out of this mess yet."

Zac danced in, landed a blow to Borger's chin, and danced away before the huge man could hit him.

"He's a boxer," Hezekiah exclaimed, conscious at last. "Stay out of his reach," he called to Zac. "You can pommel him to death. But if he gets his hands on you, he'll crush you."

"I know that," Zac said, as he zipped in for another jab to the stomach and danced away again. "Just get ready to knock him in the head if I'm too slow."

"What'll I use?"

"Figure it out yourself!" Zac shouted. "I'm a little busy right now." He landed a blow in Borger's eye and just barely avoided a powerful fist aimed at his temple. It glanced off the side of his head, upsetting his balance. He fell to his knees.

"Watch out!" Lily screamed as Borger charged.

"You keep your eye on those mad dogs on the ship," Zac said, scrambling to safety. He landed a powerful blow to Borger's throat as the huge man lumbered past.

Just then a series of shouts caused Lily to look up. One of the ships had been set afire. The blaze lighted up the sky. It made it easier for her to see the look of blood lust and fury in Borger's eyes. Before she could look back, the first crewman had raced down the gangplank and tried to snatch the pistol from her grasp. She eluded him, but only for a moment. Hezekiah tried to come to her aid, but he was knocked aside almost immediately. She heard Zac's cry of rage, then something heavy hitting the dock. She only knew who it was when the man holding her released his grip and sank to the dock from a wicked blow to the base of his skull. Just then Asa White and his men swarmed over the sides of the *Sea Witch,* battering all resistance into nothing in seconds.

"That's right, wait until I've done all the work," Zac said, panting from his exertions. He grabbed Lily and pulled her to him. "Are you all right? Did he hurt you?"

"I'm fine. We've got to release Jack. Can we free the rest of the men, too?"

"That's right, don't ask me if I'm okay. I've only had to fight off two men the size of Telegraph Hill, and all you can think about is Jack Lofton."

"But I can see you're fine."

"My hands aren't fine," Zac said holding them up for

313

her to see. "It was like hitting a brick wall."

Lily dropped the pistol, which fortunately didn't go off, and took his hands in hers. "You're bleeding. Do they hurt?"

"Of course they hurt."

"You poor man. As soon as we get back to the saloon, I'll bathe them in warm water and wrap them in soft bandages."

Lily should have known better. Zac reacted like every other man. He wanted sympathy, but when he got it, he didn't know what to do with it.

"It's not as bad as it looks. They'll be just fine. We've got to get you and your friends out of here."

"Don't forget Jack."

"How can I with you shouting his name in my ear every five seconds?"

He looked around, but the fight was over. Someone had brought the captured men on deck. Asa had found the keys and was unlocking their manacles one by one. Zac collected his pistols from the dock and from Mrs. Thoragood.

"Get them on their feet," he said to Sarah and Julie of Harold and Hezekiah. "We've got to get out of here. This whole area is about to go up in flames."

Several more ships had been set afire. Kitty embraced her husband when he stumbled down the gangplank into her arms, but the other men looked lost.

"We can't just abandon these men," Lily said.

"Hezekiah and Mr. Thoragood can take them back to the church," Zac said. "Feed them, get them some new clothes, and let them sleep around the clock."

"We're not equipped to take care of so many men," Sarah Thoragood objected.

"I don't imagine they'll stay very long," Zac said. "They must have families of their own."

"They can stay as long as they need," Hezekiah said. "No one will be turned out."

Sarah and Harold Thoragood looked at each other, but

neither dared contradict Hezekiah.

"Well, come on," Zac said. "We need to hurry."

Men were racing all around them. She could see boats full of them moving silently through the water.

"Where did all of these men come from?" she asked Zac.

"The Little Corner of Heaven and dozens of other saloons," Zac said. "They heard you were in danger, and they came to help."

"But we're safe now."

"A lot of men have disappeared in the Barbary Coast, many of them brothers and friends of these men. I think they mean to find as many as possible tonight."

THE BAY CHRONICLE
San Francisco, July 27th

An event unique in the history of San Francisco occurred last night along the docks situated near Clay Street. A large number of men, apparently mostly from saloons and gambling houses in the vicinity of Pacific Avenue, attacked about two dozen ships suspected of having shanghaied men from the dives in the Barbary Coast. The mob beat the crews, released the captives, then set fire to the ships known to be using forced labor. Their captains were forced to watch before being thrown into the bay.

Although it's the policy of this paper to deplore violence, this reporter is glad to see something finally being done to curb this terrible practice of shanghaiing hapless visitors to our city and condemning them to a life chained to the bottom of some ship.

No one seems to know who or what set the events of last night into motion. But it's rumored that a woman marched down to the docks to demand the release of her husband. I've been unable to confirm this rumor, but several observers remember a striking blond woman. No one has come forward to identify her.

"Why are we moving to the hotel?" Lily asked. "You hate it there. You've never wanted to be away from the saloon."

"Because of this," Zac said, tossing the newspaper at her.

"I've already seen that, and I don't see—"

"You never do," Zac said, sticking his head out of his closet, where he was systematically removing everything from drawers and hangers. "From the moment you set foot in this town, you haven't understood anything I've tried to tell you."

"For goodness' sake, Zac, the paper doesn't say a thing that didn't happen. I'd be proud for them to know I was responsible for helping put an end to such reprehensible practices."

"See! That's exactly what I mean. You don't care if your name becomes a byword for half the city to toss around over beer and cards. You don't care if half the men in the Coast recognize you on the streets. You'd probably stop and ask about their wives or beg them to bring their babies over to the saloon so you could hold them for an hour or two."

"I can't help it if I like babies," Lily said, "and I'm not ashamed to know or be known by any man as long as he's honest and—"

"That's just it!" Zac shouted. "They're not honest. They're not honorable. You shouldn't know them or their babies."

"You know them."

"I'm a man."

"Why should that make any difference?"

"That's something else. You persist in thinking a woman can do anything a man can do. Just because everybody in Salem knows you and looks out for you, you expect the same thing to happen here. It won't. They'll be more likely to take advantage of you. Half of them would cut your throat for the price of your clothes. Can you imagine what Captain Borger would have done with you?"

"I knew you would come."

Zac understood why some men could be reduced to pulling their hair out by the handful. It did no good to explain things to Lily. She simply saw everything in a different light. So far it had proved impossible to convince her that her view of life in San Francisco was flawed. She was certain she had right on her side. She was also convinced that was going to make everything okay. Zac had done all he could to make her understand that wasn't so, but she wouldn't listen. He had no choice. He had to move to the hotel and keep her there. Maybe if she never came near the saloon again, she wouldn't get one of them killed.

"You were right when you said it wasn't proper for a man and his wife to live apart. We should have moved into the hotel the minute we got married."

Lily's smile was so radiant, he felt like a criminal for not being able to say he was moving to the hotel because he loved her so desperately that he couldn't think of being separated from her.

"Now you'd better go say good-bye to all the girls. You won't be seeing them again."

"Why?"

"You won't be coming back here."

"But surely—"

"You don't think I'm moving into that hotel so you can keep on coming here, do you?"

"But there's no reason for me to stop working here."

"Yes, there is. I'm about to introduce you to society— what I should have done in the first place. They won't let you in the door if they know you run off to a gambling saloon every chance you get."

"Will they let you in?"

"Rich men can do all kinds of things women can't."

"Especially if they're good-looking."

"It helps."

"Suppose I don't like those people?"

"You will. Besides, I expect Fern and Madison to arrive any day. Fern can take you around. She knows everybody."

317

"I thought you were going to be with me."

"I am, but I can't be there all the time."

He supposed she'd be more resigned if he told her he'd be at her side every minute, but he couldn't. He still had to take care of business. In fact, he ought to be downstairs right now.

"You're making a mess of your clothes," Lily pointed out. Two piles had fallen into each other. A third had toppled onto the floor. "You'll never be able to wear them again until they're pressed."

"I'll straighten it up later," he said as he tossed the last of the clothes on a chair with complete disregard for wrinkles. "I've got to get dressed. I should have been downstairs by now."

"I can't sit around the hotel doing nothing all day," Lily said as Zac put on a fresh tie.

"Don't worry. You'll soon have lots of new friends. You'll be going places and doing things with them." He adjusted his tie to his satisfaction, then started to brush his hair.

"I want to do something useful, not spend the day shopping or talking about somebody else's children."

"Ask Daisy. She knows—"

"Daisy's too busy to worry about me. Please, Zac, why can't I go on helping with the saloon? I was happy doing that."

Zac turned around and looked at her with a sternness she'd come to dread. "You're not returning to the saloon, and that's final." His look softened. "I know it'll be hard for you at first, but you'll soon be so busy you'll hardly believe you complained about having nothing to do." He smiled and kissed her on the cheek. "I've got to run."

"Do you want me to wait up for you?"

He took her in his arms and kissed her again. "No. I'll be late as usual. Just make sure you've got all your clothes packed. I want to be at the hotel before noon."

Whenever she was in Zac's arms, Lily could almost believe things were going to work out. He had such a satisfying way of holding her tightly against his body. For a few moments, she was his and there was no doubt about it.

She liked his kisses even better. He would begin by playfully kissing her eyelids, nibbling her earlobe, nipping her neck with his teeth. But it was never long before his lips found her mouth. The kiss would begin slowly, languorously, and then quickly change into something hot and breathless as their bodies pressed hard against each other and their tongues danced sinuously, darting, tasting, exploring. It never failed to leave them breathless.

"Now I've got to go," Zac said, holding her away from him, his breath gradually returning to normal. "Get a good night's sleep. I'll be back about six o'clock." He winked.

Lily felt all the warmth go out of the room when she closed the door behind Zac. Her life as his wife would soon be reduced to parties she didn't want to attend, a quick kiss at night, and lovemaking in the morning when she was half asleep and he was dog tired.

Zac desired her, but he didn't love her. Not really. It was time she stopped trying to fool herself. Every time something happened that seemed to bring them closer together, she'd be certain he loved her, or was on the verge of loving her, or would soon start to love her. Yet it was clear from what he'd just said that he was still setting her apart from him.

She'd thought when he came to the dock after her, when he'd fought so hard to protect her, it meant he loved her. Now she realized it was merely Southern chivalry. She should have seen that. She'd been around it all her life. Her father would have done the same thing. Zac thought he was protecting her, but he was keeping her and the saloon in separate corners of his life. She wanted all of him, but he offered only part.

Zac was just as stubborn and obtuse as her father, but he covered it up better. When her father smiled at her, he always seemed about to correct her for some misdeed. When

Zac smiled at her, she felt like committing a few extra misdeeds.

Maybe that was what had made her marry him, not her arrogant decision to save his soul. She couldn't think of that now without embarrassment. Zac had never wanted a wife. He had never wanted to be married. Her being married to him hadn't changed his behavior in the least. She wasn't even certain it needed changing.

She didn't know a thing about saving people. She had no right to assume she knew what was best for anyone else. She'd made a terrible mess of her own life. She had no reason to believe she could do better with someone else's.

There was only one thing to do. She had to leave Zac. She had to divorce him. She couldn't deny him the chance to find a woman he could love completely, one who didn't drive him crazy.

A sob escaped her throat. She didn't think she could stand it. She might have come into this marriage the wrong way and for all the wrong reasons, but it would be impossible for her to love Zac any more deeply. She didn't know how she could stand to let him go. She found she was not nearly so selfless as she had believed.

Instantly, visions of Zac blissfully happy in the arms of some beautiful brunette assaulted her mind. She saw children, a big house with a view of the bay, Zac proudly at the center of it all. It was too much. With a choking sob, she fell on the bed.

When Lily had finally cried herself out, she got up, washed her face, and sat down to think.

Zac's footsteps dragged along the corridor. He was more exhausted than usual. He had to get someone to help him with the saloon. Maybe he could talk Dodie into coming back. He certainly couldn't trust anyone else to take care of Lily. Every time he did, it was disastrous.

He also had to do something about finding Windy Dumbarton. He guessed it was time to think about hiring a Pinkerton. With the changes in his life, he didn't have time to dash around San Francisco peering into every bar and dive. He was desperate to make sure the marriage was properly registered. He simply couldn't face explaining to Lily why they had to do it all over again.

He entered his bedroom without lighting a lamp. He undressed in a hurry. He wanted to get a few hours' sleep before he had to move to the hotel. He wasn't looking forward to either Lily's reluctance or the explanations Daisy would demand of him. He'd sent her a message saying they were coming, but that was never enough for Daisy. She had to know everything.

Zac knew Lily wasn't in bed the minute he got into it. He reached across to her side but wasn't surprised when his hand encountered nothing but cold bedsheets.

He jumped out of bed and lighted the lamp. The room was empty. His clothes were no longer piled all over the chairs and sofa. He looked in his closet. Everything was neatly restored to its place. Everything except Lily's clothes. Everything of hers was gone.

He raced out of the room and was halfway down the hall before he realized he was naked. Cursing, he hurried back, threw on a robe, and practically ran to Kitty's room. He pounded on the door without regard for the dozens of girls sunk into exhausted sleep before he remembered that Kitty no longer lived in the saloon. Cursing again, he raced up and down the hall until he came to Leadville Lizzie's room.

"Go away," called an irate voice in response to his pounding on the door.

"Open up. It's Zac."

When the door didn't open immediately, he started pounding again.

"Keep your britches on. I'm coming."

The door opened a crack. A face devoid of color, hair in a purple gauze net, peered at him.

"What's wrong? The place burning down?"

"Lily's not in our room. Do you know where she went?

Has she gone to the hotel already?''

Lizzie's eyes gradually focused. When they did, her expression turned hard. "No, she didn't go to no hotel. She moved back to Bella's. She's left you.''

Zac's heels thudded angrily on the boardwalk. He could hardly believe that after all he'd done for her, Lily had left him. He'd be the laughing stock of San Francisco. The sophisticated lady's man turned out by a naive innocent from the mountains. That ought to keep people tittering for months.

All because he wanted her to move into the hotel and introduce her to society as his wife. After turning up without an invitation and trapping him into marriage, that was more than she had any right to expect.

But she wanted to stay in the saloon. She wanted to work, to feel useful, or nothing else mattered.

Well, she'd soon find that a great deal more mattered. When she did, she'd be damned sorry. She'd come to him on her knees. He'd take her back, but he'd make her suffer a little first. Nobody treated Zac Randolph like an old shoe.

Not even a female who'd managed to work herself firmly into his thoughts, waking and sleeping.

Bella was furious at being woken up in middle of the night.

"What are you doing here?'' Bella demanded. "You know I won't have men in my place at night.''

"It's morning,'' Zac pointed out. "It's nearly seven o'clock. See, the sun's up.''

It wasn't up very far.

"That still doesn't explain what you're doing here.''

"I want to see Lily.''

"Don't be absurd. She's asleep.'' Bella's eyes narrowed. "Besides, why should I let you see her? You must have done something awful to make her run away.''

"Let's get one thing straight right now,'' Zac said. He

322

was in no mood to tolerate Bella's interference. "I'm *going* to see Lily. Either I see her in your parlor and we have a nice quiet conversation, or I see her in her room whether you're screaming at me or not."

"She doesn't want to talk to you."

"I want to talk to her. She ran off leaving a lot of questions unanswered."

"You can't go around bullying people."

"I'm not bullying her, but she is my wife."

"I don't think she realizes that."

"That concerns us, not you. Now are you going to ask her to come down, or am I going up?"

Lily was in bed when Bella knocked on her door, but she wasn't asleep. She hadn't been able to sleep all night.

"Zac's downstairs," Bella said.

That didn't surprise her. She had been expecting him. "Did you tell him I didn't want to see him?"

"Sure I did, but Zac never listens to what he doesn't want to hear. I'm afraid you're going to have to come down. He won't leave."

Lily would have given just about anything not to have to talk to Zac just now. She knew it was cowardly, but it had taken all of her courage to leave the saloon. She didn't know if she had enough left to face Zac.

Lily threw back the covers and got out of bed. Who was she fooling? She'd have been devastated if he hadn't come after her the minute he found she was gone. She'd been waiting for this moment all night.

"You want me to go with you?" Bella asked.

She reached for her robe. "Yes, but this is something I must do alone. What I have to say may hurt him."

"You can't hurt Zac Randolph. Nobody can. He doesn't have any feelings."

Lily wrapped the robe around her and tied the sash. "Yes, he does. He just keeps them well hidden. People like that are harder to reach. But when you do, they're more vulnerable.''

''You couldn't prove it by me, but I guess you know him better than I do.''

''Maybe,'' Lily said, ''but I don't know him well enough.''

Lily sat down to brush her hair. She might have to talk to Zac at dawn, but she didn't have to look as if she'd just gotten out of bed.

Lily opened the door and stepped inside Bella's formal parlor with its heavy furniture and dark fabrics. It was like entering a funeral parlor. Appropriate. She was about to announce the death of her marriage.

Her heart beat a little faster when she saw Zac. He was so handsome. It was hard to believe she had actually walked out on this man, but she couldn't let herself be sidetracked by his looks. No matter how much desire he stirred in her, she was more concerned with his feelings for her.

She couldn't really judge Zac's state of mind. He wasn't dressed with his usual neatness. His eyes looked red and his eyelids sagged, but he'd been up all night in a smoke-filled saloon.

''Aren't you going to say anything?'' he asked when they had stared at each other for what seemed like a long time.

''I was waiting for you.''

''Why? You were the one who ran away.''

''I thought you'd be happier, that things would be easier.''

''It's only going to make things worse. Why did you leave?''

She might as well tell him the truth. She owed him that much. She had forced herself on him for weeks. She was the one who was at fault from the beginning. He had put up with more than any other man would have.

''Because you don't love me.''

''Yes, I do.''

He looked slightly stunned by the sound of his own words. She guessed he'd never meant to say them, but he manfully repeated them.

"I do love you."

"No, you don't. You never have. You've tried to cover it up, pretending you liked having me around, liked . . . well, you know what I mean, but even a stupid girl from the mountains will figure things out eventually."

"I do like having you around. And I do like trying to make a baby with you."

"Maybe, but that's not the same as love."

"Why not? We're married. I've introduced you to my family. I plan to take you to parties, show you around town. That proves I love you."

He didn't understand. He thought saying the words, doing the deeds, was love. He didn't understand that it had to come from his heart, not from his head.

"Now come on home and let's have no more of this nonsense."

"No."

"Why not? If you stay here, everybody's going to think something's wrong."

"Maybe that's not a bad thing. Maybe it's time we stopped pretending."

"We're not pretending. We're married."

"It might be best if we pretend that never happened."

His face turned white. She didn't know why. It seemed a perfect solution to her.

"Half of San Francisco knows we're married," Zac said. "Besides, people in society don't stay in places like this."

"I'm comfortable here. I don't think I could be happy with the kind of people you want me to socialize with."

"You don't know until you try. Besides, they're not all the same."

"Maybe you ought to forget me, let me sink or swim on my own."

"I tried that, and it didn't work."

He was right. She was always making a mess of things, then coming to him to straighten them out.

"Why did you come?" she asked.

He looked thunderstruck. "You walk out on me, and you ask me why I came after you? Wouldn't you come after me? Wouldn't you want to know why?"

"But you've known I loved you from the beginning."

"Okay. I admit I haven't been saying *I love you* at least once every hour, whispering it in your ear, acting like you're the only person in the world. But that doesn't mean I don't love you. And it's no reason to disappear without a word. I never pretended to be the best husband in the world, but I deserve more than that."

"You're right. I've messed up everything else. Why should this be any different?"

She stood up and moved behind the sofa. She needed to get her thoughts straight. She directed her gaze to the carpet at her feet. She couldn't concentrate when she looked at Zac.

"I left because there didn't seem to be anything else to do. This whole mess is my fault. I came out here without an invitation. I expected you to take care of me even though I insisted I wanted to do it myself. I wanted you to marry me even though I knew you didn't love me. I never once did what you asked. I've done nothing but defy everybody who's tried to help me, from my father and Hezekiah to you and Mrs. Thoragood."

"You don't have to keep doing it."

"I know, but I can't go back to the saloon, or the hotel. Not yet."

"What will you do?"

"I don't know, but I've got to decide for myself."

"How long is this going to take?"

"I don't know."

"What am I supposed to do?"

"Forget you ever heard of me."

"I can't do that."

"Why not? You've been trying to do it ever since I came to San Francisco."

"Only at first. Ever since then, I've thought about you a lot."

"We aren't even talking about the same thing. You're talking about working together, occupying the same room, being physically attracted."

"That's a lot."

"Maybe for a man, but not for a woman."

He looked confused, indignant. He had no idea what she was talking about.

"You've never understood women," Lily said. "You've known how to seduce them, flatter them, keep them hanging on your every word as long as they continued to interest you, but you've never known the first thing about how a woman feels. You worked with Dodie for years and never once guessed she was in love with you.

"I'm not just talking about knowing how to make a woman feel pretty and desirable. That's important, but there's much more to love than that. A woman wants to be needed, to feel her man can't get along without her, to feel a part of him. She wants him to share all of himself with her, not just a part. She wants to feel appreciated, valued because she can give him something no other woman in the world can. She wants her feelings and opinions to be important to him."

"They are."

"Zac, you haven't asked me what I thought or listened to a word I've said since I got here." Lily stopped. She made herself wait until she felt more calm. "That's not what I wanted to say. I'm not trying to blame you. I was just trying to explain why I left. I know you can't love me just because I want you to. Maybe you do love me a little bit, in your own way. But I want more. I need more. You can't give it to me. I've got to decide what I'm going to do about that."

"Do I get to help make this decision?"

"No. This is one I have to make on my own."

Chapter Twenty-five

"Daisy told me you were lovely, but she didn't tell me you were absolutely stunning," Fern Randolph said to Lily. "It'll be nice to finally have someone in the family who can give Iris a taste of her own."

When the maid had announced that Mrs. Randolph was in the parlor wanting to see her, Lily and Bella were playing cards. It seemed to be all she did these days. She had induced Bella to explain some of the finer points, even play with her. Lily assumed her visitor was Mrs. Tyler Randolph. She didn't want to see anybody just yet, but she couldn't refuse to see Daisy, not after she'd been so kind.

Lily was stunned and bewildered when a woman she'd never seen before greeted her with all the warmth of a long-lost friend.

"I'm Fern Randolph. It was stupid of me not to realize until after that young woman left that you were probably expecting Daisy."

"I'm sorry. I should have recognized you, but it's been more than four years."

"Nonsense. You had no reason to remember an old married woman surrounded by a horde of boys."

Only then did Lily remember that Fern was the mother of five energetic sons and married to Madison, who looked so much like Zac, it was unnerving.

They sat down. "I should have remembered all of Zac's family," Lily said.

"You can't. Even George forgets a nephew or a niece now and then."

"I meant the older ones," Lily said, wondering wildly why Fern had come to visit her.

"I know you're wondering where I materialized from," Fern said. "Madison has decided to move his business headquarters to San Francisco. I came ahead to look for a house. I nearly fainted when Daisy told me Zac was married. Why on earth didn't you let anybody know? The family will be gaga with curiosity."

That thought turned Lily white with fear. She had already refused to see Mrs. Thoragood and Hezekiah because she didn't know what to say to them. She had been dreading having to explain things to Daisy. She was even more at a loss with Fern.

"I can see it's the *gaga with curiosity* part that has you worried," Fern said. "You have a right to be in this family. They'll ask anything regardless of how awkward or personal. Believe it or not, the men are worse than the women."

"I don't know how to begin to explain the mess I've made of things."

"My dear, any woman who marries Zac has a superhuman task on her hands. It's only to be expected you'll make a wrong turn now and then. I really shouldn't have come here. I should have cornered the selfish creature in that saloon of his."

"It's not Zac's fault," Lily said, determined that his family wouldn't blame him for what she had done. "He's acted like a perfect gentleman from the very first. I'm the one who's made all the stupid mistakes."

"Are we talking about the same person?"

"You sound like everybody else," Lily said, flaring up, "assuming that if anything is wrong, it has to be Zac's fault. It's not Zac's fault I didn't have the good sense to stay where I belonged. Neither is it his fault that he ended up married to a woman who's not nearly as clever as she thought. Anybody else would have strangled me by now."

Fern simply stared at Lily. She made no attempt to reply.

"I'm sorry for snapping at you like that, but everybody says the most awful things about Zac. I don't pretend he's perfect, but no one else sees the good in him."

"And you do?"

"I don't see how anyone could not."

"Probably because he keeps as far away from his family as possible," Fern said.

"If everybody treats him the way they did that time in Virginia, I don't blame him."

"I think we've started off on the wrong foot," Fern said, beginning to rise. "Maybe I should leave."

Lily jumped up. "Please, no. I don't know what's wrong with me. I never used to act like this, not even when things were terribly wrong."

Reluctantly Fern settled in her chair once more. "Are things terribly wrong now?"

"Worse than ever."

"I'm a good listener. You can't live in the same house with six male Randolphs and not learn."

Lily smiled.

"You're going to have to explain sometime. Once everybody hears your name, they won't be able to contain their curiosity."

"I don't understand."

"Surely it hasn't escaped your notice that all of Zac's sisters-in-law are named after flowers. He's been running from what he calls 'flower women' for years. Everybody's going to be dying to know how you caught him."

"Unfairly."

"That statement demands an explanation."

So Lily explained. She started from the beginning and went straight through to the end. She didn't leave anything out.

"So you see, it's all my fault. If I hadn't been so foolishly certain I knew the answer to everything, none of this would have happened."

"I must say, I'm sorry Rose wasn't here to hear this. She knows Zac a lot better than I do."

"He's afraid of her. George, too."

Fern laughed easily. "Rose and George are probably the only people in the world Zac loves without reservation. He stays away from them because he doesn't want to hurt them." Fern was quiet for a moment, apparently turning a thought over in her mind. Finally she said, "I can't be sure, of course, but from what you've told me, it's quite possible he loves you just as much."

Tears sprang to Lily's eyes. She brushed them away. "Zac doesn't love me. He says he does, but he doesn't. Not really. He doesn't even want to be married."

"Oh, I have no doubt about that. Zac has fought any kind of control or restraint for as long as I've known him, probably from the first moment he drew breath. But if he's done half of what you've told me, he loves you. I know the Randolph men, and I know Zac well enough to see that."

Lily didn't want Fern to plant a seed of hope in her heart. She wanted her to say it was over, hopeless, that the sooner she went back to Virginia, the happier everybody would be. She could stand that. Barely. But she couldn't stand having her hopes raised and then dashed time and time again.

"Then it's not the kind of love I need," Lily said. "I don't want to change his life. I thought about doing that—I suppose every woman considers making her man over into one more to her liking—but I decided he wouldn't like it. But he's got to let me into his life, and I don't mean just the saloon. I mean all of it. He's trying to force me to live in a separate world from him. He tells me what to do, what to think, where to live, who my friends ought to be. That's not a marriage. It's like he owns me. That's the way my father treats my mother. I swore that would never happen to me. It's part of the reason I ran away."

"Have you tried talking to Zac, telling him how you feel?"

"Yes, but he doesn't hear what he doesn't want to hear. He's made up his mind about the way things should be, and nothing I say seems to change his mind."

"That's a Randolph through and through," Fern said. "I could tell you stories about Madison . . . But you're not interested in my husband. Suffice it to say that every male Randolph feels he has all the answers to everything."

"What should I do?"

"First, decide if you love him enough to put up with this for the rest of your life. They don't change. They may love their wives to distraction, but they're still the same hard-headed, egotistical, know-it-all beasts they were before we corralled them."

"You make them sound awful."

"My dear, I'm married to the most stubborn of them all, and I've got five boys just like him. I wouldn't trade one minute of the time I've known Madison for anything in the world, but there are times when I'd give almost anything to be big enough to beat him up."

"I feel that way about Zac a lot."

"That's because he and Madison are very much alike."

"How do you get what you want when he's determined you're not going to have it?"

"First, I make very sure of what I want and what I mean to do when I get it. Then I tell Madison. He may shout and make threats, but he won't actually stop me. If you can get someone to oppose you, so much the better. He may not think I ought to do a thing, but he'll defend my right to do it against someone else."

"But that doesn't make sense."

"Men rarely do when it comes to women. They're very good with figures and building things, but if they didn't have us to help them along, they'd never be able to find their underwear."

Lily laughed despite herself. "That doesn't sound like Zac."

"Give him time. From what he said, he has a woman doing a lot of the work for him already."

"Dodie, but she quit."

"Good. He'll fall on his face even sooner. When he does, you be there to pick him up."

Lily didn't want Zac to fall on his face; neither could she imagine being able to solve his problems. If she wanted to be his wife, she couldn't continue to do nothing but cause problems. She had to be the answer to at least one of his needs.

She thought of the hours they'd spent making love. She felt slightly guilty thinking of that first. But it had been the only time she felt truly a part of him, the only time when they didn't argue, when he didn't seem to be trying to put her out of his life.

"I guess most of the time I've been waiting for him to make the decisions," Lily said. "Whenever I haven't, I've ended up causing him trouble."

"Don't worry about that," Fern said. "You're his wife. It's your right to cause trouble."

"I don't want to."

"Don't be foolish. He's going to cause you trouble from dawn to midnight for the rest of your life. He deserves a few rough moments in return. Besides, it'll make him more attentive. It'll also make him respect you more."

"I don't understand."

"Don't waste your time trying. I told you men were foolish creatures. They're always trying to make out that we are, but they're no better. It's just that they won't admit it."

Lily had to admit Zac did have some rather ridiculous ideas. Even Dodie thought so. She doubted, though, that he would change his mind just because she wanted him to.

"Are you sure you won't move to the hotel? Daisy is worried about you."

"It'll be better if I stay here. It has nothing to do with Daisy. If I go to the hotel, Zac will think I've given in. Besides, I mean to take a job until I can make up my mind what to do."

Fern got to her feet. "Well, don't take too long. Rose and George will be coming to San Francisco in the fall. I don't even want to think of what they'll do if things aren't straightened out by then. It almost makes me feel sorry for Zac."

"But they're only his brother and sister-in-law."

"They're more like his parents. They brought him up. I think Rose feels like he's her oldest child."

Lily had no idea what kind of guidance Zac might have needed as a child, but she knew he didn't need a mother now. Whatever he did, he must do it because he wanted to. She had been party to forcing him into something against his will once before. She would never do that again.

"I know things are unsettled, but you must come see Daisy and me. I promise we won't pry. You're part of the family now. It's our right to worry about you."

"That's just it. I'm not part of the family. So far my marriage is just so much meaningless paper. Until Zac decides he wants me in his life, that he *needs* me, I'll still be an outsider."

Daisy and Fern had found Zac in his office. He felt like a cornered rabbit when Fern locked the door and dropped the key into her purse. "I'm not taking any chance on your running away until we've had our say," she said.

"You've got to do something about Lily," Daisy announced without preamble, "and you've got to do it quickly. It's sinful for that poor girl to be living by herself, working in a woman's clothing shop, when she's got a perfectly good husband who ought to be taking care of her."

Zac had always been terrified of women when they joined forces against him, especially his sisters-in-law. He couldn't curse them and drive them from his office. His whole family would turn on him. He couldn't offer to sit down and talk things out over a drink. He couldn't settle things with a fist-fight. He'd always run away before, but this time Fern had taken the key.

He was trapped.

"I've tried," he said. His throat felt dry. He considered a brandy but changed his mind. They'd probably tell Rose he'd taken up drinking. "She won't see me anymore. She said nothing had changed so there was no point in talking."

"Then it's up to you to make some changes."

"Whose side are you on?"

"Lily's."

"Great. My own family turns against me."

"I'm no blood relation to you," Daisy said, "so don't try that stuff on me. Besides, she told me what you wanted her to do, expecting her to stay by herself day after day or go off with a bunch of strangers while you go on with your fun as always."

"My *fun* is a business. It's how I make my living."

"Then let her help you."

"I don't want her helping me. It's not a proper job for a woman like Lily."

"Do you love her?"

"Of course I do. I keep telling her that, but she won't believe me."

"I mean *really* love her."

"What do you mean by *do I really love her?*"

"Is she all you think about night and day? Have you lost your appetite? Are you unable to sleep, sit still, or keep your mind on your work?"

"Of course not. What kind of idiot do you think I am?"

Come to think of it, he hadn't been feeling like his old self lately. Any of the girls could tell he couldn't keep his mind on business. As for sleep! But he'd never thought it

335

was all because of Lily. He was worried about her and irritated she wouldn't see him, but he didn't understand how she could upset his whole life just by going away.

"I guess that's the crux of the matter then," Fern said. "You can't say you love Lily if you aren't utterly miserable without her."

"I didn't say I wasn't miserable," Zac said, reluctant to confess such a weakness to anyone. "But my whole world hasn't come to an end."

But hadn't it?

"You trying to lure me back to running that saloon for you?" Dodie asked.

"I would if I could," Zac said, "but right now all I want you to do is look after things while I'm gone." He was relieved to see that Dodie was sober. In fact, she looked better than he'd seen her in a long time.

"Where are you going?"

"To find Windy Dumbarton and make this marriage legal."

"That's the first decent thing you've done in weeks. How's Lily?"

"Fine, I guess. She still won't see me."

"Maybe she will when you get back."

"Why?"

"You've changed. Not enough, but then maybe Lily isn't expecting much. Better hurry up, though. I don't know how long she means to hang around waiting for you to get some sense."

"You sound like Daisy and Fern."

"Smart women."

Zac tossed clothes into a suitcase. He couldn't stand it any longer. He missed Lily more than he could have imagined possible. He had to get her back, but first he had to make certain the marriage was legal. There was no point in getting everything else settled and having that blow up in his face. The Pinkerton had failed. It was up to him to find Windy Dumbarton if he had to search every bar and saloon west of the Mississippi.

But even as he thought of all the things he wanted to do for Lily, the promises he intended to make, he realized Lily might not want to come back. His hand paused in the act of lifting a shirt from a drawer. He didn't want Lily to leave. He wanted to be married to her. He liked having her around, and not just when they were in bed. She made him feel better. She made everything feel better.

That was love. It had to be.

He didn't want her in the saloon because he loved her. He wanted her to know only the best people because he loved her. He didn't know why she couldn't see that. What more was there?

But he had a feeling there was more. And Lily wasn't going to come back until he figured what it was.

And he would figure it out. He wasn't going to give up this easily. He might be stubborn and selfish, but he wasn't so stupid that he didn't know he'd never find anyone else like Lily.

Lily told herself that she was stupid to be talking to Zac at all, that it was even more ridiculous to attempt it while the saloon was open. He'd never managed to take his mind off cards long enough to listen to her before. She shouldn't expect things to be any different now.

But she had to talk to him. She had to find out if his feelings had changed.

At first he had come to see her nearly every day. He even woke up early one morning so he could corner her in the shop. She'd seen him coming, asked Mrs. Wellborn to tell him she was out, then ducked into the back.

Now she hadn't seen him for nearly a week. She'd spent every day of that time trying to make up her mind to go back to Virginia, but she couldn't. She loved this impossible man. That would never change. There was no point in thinking she could go somewhere else, fall in love, and settle down. It was Zac Randolph or nobody. She would not marry a man she didn't love.

She had thought she could never live with a man who didn't love her as desperately as she loved him, but the past week had caused her to question many things. It was time to wake up and face reality. Wasn't it possible that half a loaf was better than no loaf at all?

Just putting that question into conscious thought hurt. It meant giving up. It meant accepting that Zac would never love her as she wanted to be loved, that she would never find the happiness she so desperately wanted.

But wouldn't she be even more miserable without him? She had been this week. It was the longest and blackest time of her life. A dozen times an hour she'd been tempted to go to him and tell him she'd take him on any terms.

Her father had always said she should accept nothing less than one hundred percent. Her mother had said it was essential to be able to compromise. Lily didn't know which of them was right. Maybe neither was. Maybe she'd have to look for another solution entirely.

If only Zac loved her. It seemed such a simple thing to ask. She'd do just about anything he wanted as long as he'd let her stay with him. That was the one point on which she couldn't compromise. He had to let her into his world. She knew it wasn't going to be easy to convince Zac to change his mind. He had been remarkably stubborn on that issue.

She had to convince him. More than her happiness might depend on it. There was a chance she was pregnant. If she was, that changed everything.

Chapter Twenty-six

It was just like coming home to step into the Little Corner of Heaven. The familiar sights and sounds made Lily feel that everything would soon be right with her world. The number and warmth of the greetings called out to her as she passed told her the customers hadn't forgotten her. They wanted to know when she was coming back. She waved and kept going.

She was surprised to see Dodie at the table rather than Zac. She figured he was having a private game in his office.

"No need to go in there," Dodie called when Lily started toward the office. "He's not here."

"Where did he go?" Lily asked. Zac had never left his saloon, not even in Dodie's expert hands.

"He didn't say. He just asked me to watch over the place for a few days."

"Did he say when he'd be back?" She hoped nothing was wrong. Surely he would have told her if it were.

"No."

"Play or get out of the game," one of the players

growled. "You want to talk, go someplace else."

"Keep your shirt on, Chet. If you keep annoying me, I'll have you thrown out."

"Not when I'm holding the winning hand."

"Especially then. Seems to me you've been winning a lot more than you should." Dodie finished off her whiskey and signaled for another.

"You calling me a cheat?" Chet demanded.

"Not yet," Dodie replied.

"If you weren't a woman—"

"Shut up and play your cards."

Lily backed away, already forgotten in the excitement of the game. Tonight the saloon didn't look so much like fun. There was something ominous about it, unpleasant. It didn't feel the way it did when Zac was there. Maybe he was right. Maybe this wasn't a good place for her.

Lily hadn't gone far toward the door when Leadville Lizzie came running up to her.

"Please don't leave. You've got to stop Dodie."

"Why? What's wrong?"

"She's playing cards with that awful Chet Lee. Everybody knows he cheats, but they can't catch him."

"Dodie knows what she's doing. She—"

"Not tonight. She's been drinking. I don't know what's gotten into her. She didn't used to act like this, but the more she loses, the more she drinks. You've got to stop her before something terrible happens."

"What can I do? I can't just tell her to leave the game."

Lily returned to the table. She didn't know what she had intended to say, but the moment she saw the stubborn, determined expression on Dodie's face, she knew it was useless. She would not leave the game. Lily's only option was to stay until she figured out what to do.

"Can I watch?" she asked, smiling as brightly as she could at all the men at the table. "Dodie's been trying to teach me, but I've never actually watched a real game."

"Sure. Pull up a chair," one man said.

"I don't like outsiders at the table," Chet grumbled.

"I say she stays," Dodie announced.

Lily sat close enough to Dodie so she could see her cards. It took only a brief glance to know it was a losing hand. She couldn't understand why Dodie didn't throw in her cards and wait for the next deal. She ached to say something, but she couldn't talk about the cards. Maybe if she could get Dodie's attention . . .

She brushed Dodie's leg with her own.

"Sorry. I didn't mean to crowd you." Dodie didn't even look up. She continued to scowl at her cards as she moved her chair.

Lily reached over and squeezed Dodie's hand.

"You want something? All you have to do is ask one of the girls."

Clearly Dodie was beyond understanding anything in the nature of a hint tonight. Lily was going to have to find another way to help her.

Something Zac had said suddenly popped into Lily's mind. He had told her every player does something to give himself away. He said nobody ever won at poker without cheating unless he could read his opponents as well as he could read his own cards. Maybe if she studied the players' faces, she could learn something that would help Dodie.

She focused on each man's face. It didn't take her long to realize that her presence at the table made them nervous. It kept them from settling into their habitual manner. Sensing her advantage, Lily smiled as brilliantly as she knew how. She made occasional remarks and did little things to keep everybody on edge. All the while she studied the five men.

Much to her surprise, she started remembering things her father had said. He always said if a preacher was going to be of any real benefit to this flock, he had to know when someone was lying, when something was wrong even though a person put a good face on it. He had told her he watched the eyes, the mouth, the hands, any nervous movement, even the rate of breathing.

Lily was surprised at how easy it was once she knew what to look for. It wasn't long before she'd learned to read every face at the table.

Except Chet Lee's.

It seemed the more he won, the further his emotions sank out of sight. None of her tricks worked on him. He didn't want her at the table and made no bones about it. She was watching him very closely when Dodie suddenly gave out a soft moan and her head dropped on the table. She had passed out.

That was when Lily saw it. In the brief instant before she turned her attention to Dodie, she saw a tiny light of triumph far in the back of Chet's eyes. It was gone almost immediately, but she was almost certain it had been there.

"She's passed out," one of the players said.

"I've never seen that before," said another. "I thought she had a head as hard as a rock."

"What are we going to do about the game?"

"She's out," Chet Lee said. "Whoever wins the pot wins her money."

"She's not out," Lily said. She couldn't be. Dodie had a good hand this time, and she was in debt to Chet Lee for several thousand dollars. Lily was certain she didn't have the money.

"If she doesn't wake up in five minutes, she's out of the game," Chet Lee said.

Again Lily saw that gleam in the back of his eyes. It was such a tiny, fleeting thing, she hadn't been certain the first time, but she was now.

"Help me get her into Zac's office," Lily said to two of the players.

They put down their cards and virtually dragged Dodie into the office and laid her out on the couch.

"She's out cold," one said. "She ain't waking up for I don't know how long."

"She's got to wake up. She owes Mr. Lee all that money."

"Nothing she can do about it tonight, not unless somebody plays her hand for her."

"I'll play it."

The words were out of Lily's mouth before the thought could register in her brain. She was appalled at what she'd said. The men were shocked.

"You can't do that, ma'am. Zac would have our heads."

"I can't let Dodie lose all that money to Chet Lee."

"He's a good player, ma'am, the best I've ever seen except for Zac."

"Well Zac's not here. It's either me or she loses everything."

"Chet won't like it."

"I'm not asking him."

Chet didn't like it. He threatened to quit the game.

"If you do, you forfeit all the money you have on the table," Lily said.

She didn't know where she got the nerve to stand up to him. She didn't know where all this information was coming from. She supposed she'd absorbed a lot more than she realized on those nights when she'd acted as Zac's hostess, talking to the men, watching their games, commiserating with them when they lost, being pleased when they won.

She took her seat at the table and picked up the cards. "Make up your mind, Mr. Lee. The other men don't care. I don't see why you should."

She smiled even more brightly than before. She hadn't asked them, but she was certain they didn't object.

"You ever played poker before, Mrs. Randolph?" Chet Lee asked.

"No, but I think I know the rules."

The rules were simple. It was everything else about the game that was difficult. Experience was invaluable. Playing with Bella hardly counted. She would have to depend on her ability to judge odds and read her opponents.

She was scared to death. She'd never had this kind of responsibility on her shoulders. It made her realize that Zac wasn't playing cards or running a saloon just because it was fun. Winning was a serious business.

Chet Lee settled into his chair, grumbling. Lily picked up her cards and studied her hand once more. Three fours, a seven, and an ace. As she calculated the odds, she idly fingered the back of the cards. Suddenly she stopped. The backs of the fours and seven were perfectly smooth, but there was a tiny scratch on the ace. The mark was too fine to be detected by calloused hands, but her tender fingertips had felt it.

Someone had marked the deck.

She glanced up at Chet Lee. He was wearing a ring set with a large stone. No one else had anything similar. Chet was marking the deck as they played.

Lily studied the other players. She saw no sign that any of them had a strong hand. She looked straight at Chet Lee. The spark wasn't there now, only dull anger.

Lily discarded the ace and took one card. When it was her turn to bet, Lily giggled, fiddled nervously with her cards, and raised the bet twenty dollars. Everyone stared at her, but she returned every questioning look with a smile and a tiny lift of her shoulders. She was determined they would think she was a silly female in far over her head.

That assumption had the virtue of being the truth.

The betting passed around twice more. She was relieved to see two men drop out and the rest make their bets without enthusiasm. She became more confident all the time. But she couldn't get a reading on Chet Lee. She didn't *think* he had a strong hand, but she couldn't be certain. He was good. Very good. She just hoped she'd be lucky.

The betting passed around once more. Another man dropped out. Chet raised the bet fifty dollars and called. Lily met his raised and laid down three of a kind. Chet had two pairs.

Lily felt a tremendous wave of relief wash over her. But

she was determined the men wouldn't know what she was feeling. She giggled and acted surprised as she pulled the money toward her.

Chet was already shuffling the cards. He was dealing before she had counted to see how much money she'd won. Over six hundred dollars. A few more like that, and Dodie would be out of debt.

Lily picked up her cards. They were horrible. She looked up at Chet Lee. Briefly she saw the gleam flare deep in his eyes.

He was cheating, and he'd dealt himself a good hand. Everybody asked for more cards. Chet stood pat. When it came her turn to bet, she said, "I'm out," and calmly laid down her cards. Something in her voice must have communicated itself to the men. Two more tossed in their cards. Chet's three queens and two aces won him less than a hundred dollars.

"I don't think you should have to do all the shuffling and dealing," Lily said to Chet, hoping her voice conveyed innocence and not guile. "I think we all ought to take a turn."

"It's customary for one man to be the dealer," Chet said.

"But it's not fair. Lizzie," she called over her shoulder, "bring us some fresh cards. You can deal this time," Lily said to the man on Chet's right.

"I'm the dealer," Chet said.

"But if you deal all the time, I won't get to," Lily said, trying to pout. She'd never done it before, and she had no idea if she was getting it right.

One of the men said, "Aw, let's pass the deal, Chet. It won't do no harm."

Chet still looked mulish.

"Do it as a favor to me?" Lily wheedled.

Chet still looked suspicious.

"Come on, Chet. Let the little lady deal."

Lizzie brought the cards. She'd brought six packs, all unopened.

"Give one to Mr. Greene," Lily said, pointing to the man

on Chet's right. She smiled brightly. "Now we can get started."

Chet Lee looked furious, but he must have decided it would be foolish to continue to object. Besides, he'd already been a heavy winner.

Over the next few games, Lily continued to study each of her opponents until she could almost gauge the strength of his hand. She never bet when Chet Lee was the dealer. She didn't know how he did it, but he always managed to deal himself a strong hand. When she felt a tiny scratch mark on one of the aces, she realized that Chet was beginning to mark the new deck. After that she broke out a new deck every time the deal came around to her.

"Something wrong?" Chet Lee demanded angrily when she opened her third new deck.

"I like the feel of new cards," Lily said, "even if they are harder to shuffle." She shuffled with enough clumsiness to keep the men off their guard. They were so busy watching Chet and each other, it never entered their minds that she might be just as dangerous.

Over the next two hours, Lily was a steady winner. She would have been the first to admit the cards were running in her favor, but she was also very careful. She figured the odds on any player drawing a particular card. She never forgot a card played or discarded. She took that information, along with what she knew of each man's unconscious gestures and made a guess as to the strength of his hand. She wasn't always right, but she was close. She even learned that one man tended to hold on to face cards when he'd have had better luck taking whatever came his way.

As the pile of money in front of Chet decreased, his temper turned sour. The tension at the table increased. Lily was exhausted. She didn't know how anyone had the energy to gamble all night. She felt as if she could collapse in bed and sleep for a week.

Instead she increased the rate of her chatter and continued

to smile as brightly as she could. The only man who seemed immune was Chet Lee.

"Do you have to talk so much?" he snapped.

"I don't see how you can just sit there never saying a word," Lily said. "It's so exciting I can hardly sit still."

"You haven't," Chet said.

"I sure wish my papa could see me now."

"Did he teach you to play cards?" Chet asked, suspicious at her winnings.

"Heavens, no! Papa's a preacher. He'd be horrified if he could see me." She giggled again. "That's why I wish he was here. Papa turns so red when he—"

"Hell's bells, woman! Don't you ever shut up!"

"Well, if you're going to be like that . . ."

Lily placed her bet, called, and took the hand.

Chet's comment was unprintable.

"Let's take a break and get more drinks," one of the men said. He got to his feet before anyone could object. Everyone left the table but Lily.

"How's Dodie?" she asked Lizzie when she brought Lily another cup of the black coffee she'd been drinking all night.

"She's okay. She wanted to get back in the game, but I told her you were doing fine."

"I want to talk to her." Lily hurried to Zac's office.

Dodie was sitting on the sofa scowling. She didn't look so fine to Lily.

"Lizzie tells me you've turned into a regular cardsharp," Dodie said. "I taught you better than I thought."

"The cards have been running my way," Lily confessed.

"I wish I'd thought to rotate the deal and use fresh cards. The son of a bitch was cheating me blind."

Lily winced at Dodie's language.

"I'd better get back. You lie back down. You're still looking rather green."

"I don't know how to thank you," Dodie said.

The clock on Zac's desk said 2:48. Lily didn't know how much longer she could last.

"You can do that later, if I'm still winning." Lily dashed for the door. She wanted to be at the table when the men returned.

Lily's luck continued to hold, but by four o'clock her strength was fading fast. "I don't want to spoil the party, gentlemen, but I'm afraid this is going to have to be my last hand. I'm about to go to sleep over my cards."

"I wondered why it had been so quiet," Chet Lee said.

"I'm not used to such late hours. I have to go to work in the morning."

"I think you can take the day off," Chet said, glaring at the money piled before her. "I think you've got more than a day's wages there."

"This is Dodie's money," Lily said. "I wouldn't think of taking a cent."

"Let's play," Chet said, "before all this moral rectitude makes me sick."

Lily was dealt junk. She discarded everything but two hearts and asked for three cards. She nearly fainted when she received three more hearts. She held a straight flush, six high. Only a higher flush could beat her hand. She quickly tried to cover her excitement by pretending she was about to fall asleep.

"Goodness, maybe we should quit now," she said.

"No."

The single syllable told her all she needed to know. She didn't have to look up and see the gleam in the back of Chet's eyes to know he had a great hand.

"Okay, but if I start to nod, somebody poke me to keep me awake."

"Zac would kill anybody who tried," Dodie said.

Lily whipped around. "You're supposed to be lying down."

"I couldn't stand not knowing what was going on out here."

"Well, you're going to have to sit somewhere else," Lily said. "If you start looking over my shoulder, I'll be too nervous to play this hand."

"You ain't been nervous all night," Chet complained.

"I'll go sit next to Walter," Dodie said.

Lily wondered if Dodie had seen her hand. She didn't want her to give it away. But Dodie lit up one of her thin cigars and seemed interested only in talking to Walter.

The betting was steep. Several men had good hands. Before long there was four thousand dollars in the pot. Chet kept raising by increments of one to five hundred dollars a round. One by one the others dropped out until only Lily and Chet were left.

Lily was getting nervous. She knew she had a good hand. She knew Chet had a good hand. But how good? The flame at the back of his eyes threatened to burst into a blaze. Maybe she had depended on her luck one time too many.

Still, she couldn't back down. When Chet raised a thousand, she covered her shock by exclaiming loudly, "Lord have mercy! Are you trying to take all my money at once?"

"Yes," Chet hissed.

She fanned herself and chattered away. She could beat almost any hand. She dithered and chattered, then bet her thousand and raised Chet a thousand. She felt confident he would have to call or fold. He didn't have any more money. Even if she lost now, Dodie wouldn't owe him anything.

"It's a good thing I came prepared," Chet said. He reached inside his coat and pulled out a thick wad of bills. He peeled off a thousand and raised her another thousand.

Lily felt perspiration threaten to pop out on her forehead. She didn't have another thousand. She had only four hundred. If she couldn't meet his bet, she would have to forfeit. She felt desperate.

"Why, Mr. Lee, shame on you. You know I don't have that much money. It's not nice of you to raise me when you know I can't equal your bid."

"That's part of the game, ma'am. If you can't stay with the pace, you have to fold."

"But I can't just fold and give you all that money. Why, goodness gracious, I'd have nightmares just thinking about it."

"It's pay or fold, ma'am."

"I'll cover my wife's bets," a deep voice said from behind Lily. "She'll match your thousand and raise you a thousand."

Lily nearly jumped out of her skin at the sound of Zac's voice. A hundred different emotions clamored for primacy. Relief won. Zac was there. Everything would be all right now. No matter what happened with this hand, no matter what he said to her or Dodie, everything would be all right.

Zac was there.

"You can't lend her money," Chet objected.

"If I'm correct, the marriage contract says what's mine is hers," Zac said. "I'm just bringing it to the table."

"We had an agreement. You could only use the money on the table."

"But you bet money that wasn't on the table," Lily pointed out. "If you interpret the rule strictly, than you can't meet my bet, and I win by default."

Chet was cornered, and he knew it.

"You can borrow some money if you need it," Lily said, magnanimously. "I don't mind."

"I don't need to borrow."

Chet bet a thousand and raised two. Zac equaled his two thousand and raised him two more. Chet was clearly sweating now. "You broke the rules, damn you. That pot ought to be mine."

"Maybe somebody will lend you the money."

"Sorry," the men around the table said. "We ain't got that much."

"How much do you have?" Lily asked.

"Fifteen hundred."

Lily took five hundred from the pile and handed it back

to Zac. "Now you can equal my raise and call."

Chet suddenly broke out into a smile. "This will teach you a lesson, ma'am. Once you get your victim on the prongs of your pitchfork, don't let him off. I got four aces."

He spread them out. With a loud laugh he reached for the money.

"I believe that's my money," Lily purred. "My cards may be little, but they pack the house full." She laid down her straight flush.

One of the men let out a crack of laughter. "Well, I'll be durned. Four aces beat by five little ones. I never seen the like."

"You cheated," Chet shouted.

"No, you did," Lily replied calmly. She could say that, knowing Zac stood behind her. As long as he was there, she could do just about anything. "That's why I insisted we rotate the deal. It's also why I changed cards so often. You were marking the aces with that big ring you're wearing."

"You saying I cheated?"

"Yes."

"I'm saying it, too," Dodie said. "I just wasn't smart enough to catch you."

Chet jumped to his feet. "I ain't taking that from no man."

"Chet, Chet," Zac said in a gently chiding manner, "can't you tell these are women?"

"Damn you," Chet growled, "you've made fun of me for the last time."

He started to reach inside his coat, but before he could extract whatever he was reaching for, he was looking into the business end of a double-barreled derringer.

"If you want to keep that hand, you'll take it out of your coat very slowly, and it won't have anything in it."

Chet lowered his hand to his side.

"I don't know why I've put up with you for so long," Zac said, "but I don't mean to do it any longer. As of this moment, you're banned from the Little Corner of Heaven.

If you attempt to force your way in, I'll have you thrown into the streets.''

Chet Lee was so furious, his face was dark and mottled.

"I'll get you back for this, damn you," he shouted. "I'll get you both back for everything."

"If you want to leave here with your arms in working order, I suggest you do it before you say anything else," Zac warned. "I've had a very long and frustrating trip, and I'm in just the mood to take you apart piece by piece."

Chet was mean, vicious, and in a rage, but he wasn't fool enough to go up against a derringer pointed at a spot between his eyes.

"This is not the end," he said, backing away. "I swear I'll get even."

Chet left the saloon at a stumbling run, bumping into tables and chairs without apology.

"You," Zac said sternly, looking directly at Lily, "into my office. You've got some explaining to do."

Chapter Twenty-seven

"I'm coming, too," Dodie stated. "This is all my fault."

"You weren't playing poker with the biggest cheat in town."

"I was, and I was drunk to boot. Lily saved my bacon."

Zac glared at Dodie. "Both of you, into my office now!"

Zac's heart was still beating too rapidly. He hadn't gotten over the shock of entering the saloon and seeing Lily in the middle of a poker game with nearly twenty thousand dollars on the table. He got light-headed just thinking about it. People got killed for far less money than that.

He hadn't even known she could play poker.

What was she doing here, and why was it that every time he turned his back, she got into trouble? She was going to give him grey hair before he was thirty. If he'd had any doubts before, they were erased. He had to get her completely away from the saloon.

Even if it meant selling out.

That thought had haunted him all the way back from Virginia City and his abortive attempt to locate Windy Dumbarton.

"Now let's have this story from the beginning," he said as she closed the door to his office. He directed his gaze at Dodie. "I assume you were the one to teach her to play poker."

"I asked her to," Lily said.

"When?"

"All those mornings and afternoons while she sat here waiting for you to wake up," Dodie said. "She would do it by the hour."

"I wanted to find out what was so fascinating," Lily said, "what could keep you and hundreds of other men glued to the table half the night." She massaged a crick in her neck. "I don't see how you can keep it up till dawn. I'm so sleepy I can hardly hold my head up."

"That's because it's after four o'clock, and you've been up all day," Zac said. "But that's getting away from the subject. What were you doing at that table?"

"I came to see you," Lily said. "I decided it was time we talked."

"Why couldn't we talk any of the times I tried to see you?"

"I wasn't ready."

"But you are now?"

"Yes."

"That sounds like a cue for me to leave," Dodie said.

"We'll skip that part for a moment," Zac said. "Tell me about the poker game."

"I let Chet Lee sucker me into a game too deep for me," Dodie said. "When Lily came in, I passed out."

"You've got better sense than that," Zac said. "You know Chet would kill you if you didn't pay him."

"I wasn't thinking."

"Dodie had a real good hand," Lily said. "That's why I took her place. I couldn't let her lose."

"But why did you keep playing?"

"I wanted to get her money back. Besides, you told me all about studying people, looking for the little signs that give them away. I did, and it was easy to tell when they had a good hand."

"She had the good sense to rotate the deal and keep using new cards so Chet couldn't mark the deck," Dodie said.

"But why did you keep playing?" Zac repeated. "You could have lost even more."

"I wasn't losing. I was winning," Lily said. "It was fun. I liked being able to beat those men, to prove I wasn't just some silly woman. Besides, Chet Lee made me mad. I wanted to take as much of his money as I could."

Zac felt his heart sink. He had waited too long. Not only did Lily know how to play poker, she enjoyed it.

He had only himself to blame. He'd spent so much time gambling, insisting it was perfectly all right for him to keep doing it, why shouldn't she think it was okay for a gambler's wife? She had absolutely no understanding of what it could mean to her.

"I was playing the last hand when you came in," Lily said.

"You still could have lost everything."

"I know. You don't know how grateful I am you arrived when you did."

"What would you have done if I hadn't arrived?"

"Asked some of the other men to lend me the money."

"They would have," Dodie said. "They adore her."

That was it. He'd be damned if his wife was going to become the darling of a bunch of gamblers. He certainly wasn't going to have them falling over themselves to lend her money. He could just hear Rose now!

"Okay, Dodie. You can go back outside, but I want to talk with you before you leave." He had to get to the bottom of this sudden return to drinking. It worried him more than he wanted to admit.

"If it's about the drinking—"

"It is, but it's about something else, too. Now leave us

alone. Lily and I have a lot to work out.''

''Don't you yell at her.''

''I probably will, but I won't hurt her if that's what you're worried about.''

''I never thought you'd do that,'' Dodie said. ''But if you've got to yell at somebody, yell at me. She did what she did tonight for me. I ought to take the blame.''

''Don't worry. This isn't about the poker game.''

''But it is,'' Lily said when the door closed behind Dodie. ''It's about that and all the other things you've told me not to do.''

''Yes, I guess it is, but it's all my fault. I should have realized from the first you couldn't be left on your own. It was stupid of me. No, it was selfish. I was only thinking of what would be the most comfortable for me, what would upset my routine the least. I never once thought about you.''

''You thought about me all the time,'' Lily protested. ''I worried you sick.''

''I worried *after* things happened. Never before. If I'd been a decent husband, none of this would have happened. But I wasn't trying to be a husband. I was just trying to keep things the way they were. I realize now that's impossible.''

''What do you mean?''

''Don't look so frightened. I don't mean anything terrible. I just realize that being married involves more than trying to make a baby.''

''I like that part.''

Zac smiled. He liked that part, too. He hadn't been able to stop thinking about it since she moved out of the hotel. His body was ramrod stiff with the tension accumulated during this seemingly endless period of abstinence. Now it was all he could do to keep his hands off Lily. But he knew, nice as it was, that it wouldn't fix what was wrong between them.

She looked so small, so frightened, so alone. He walked across the room and took her hands into his. ''I like that part, too. I don't mean to stop. It's just that there's more.''

"What do you mean?''

"Well, the first thing is to get you out of this saloon.''

"I don't want to go back to the hotel. I'd rather stay at Bella's.''

"I don't mean the hotel or Bella's. I mean a house of our own. A home.''

He could see Lily's eyes light up. He was an idiot not to have understood this before now. Every woman wanted a home. It was just men who thought houses were a burden. For a woman they were as essential as the very clothes she wore.

"Where is it? Can I see it?''

He couldn't help smiling. She was adorable when she got excited. She forgot everything—his being mad at her, their awful marriage—and the innocence shone through like a single star in an empty sky. It was times like this when he wished he could give her the whole-hearted love she wanted so much. Well he couldn't, so there was no use berating himself about it. At least he loved her enough to make the changes that were necessary to her happiness.

And his.

He'd gotten used to having her around. She never bored him. No two days were ever alike. She was a lot of trouble, but much to his surprise, he didn't mind it. Now that he had made up his mind what he needed to do, he didn't mind that either. It had been a wrench at first, but he was relieved at how quickly he had gotten used to the idea.

He kissed her on the end of her nose. "I haven't picked out a house. I thought you might like to do that. You could get Fern to take you around. I imagine she's seen half the houses in San Francisco by now.''

The excitement suddenly dimmed. "Aren't you going to help me decide?''

"I've got a thousand things to do here. Besides, picking out a house is a woman's job. I wouldn't know what to look for, but Fern will. Madison makes her move every few years. Just make sure there's plenty of hot water in the bathroom.''

Zac was surprised to see the animation go out of Lily's expression.

''I don't want a house if you mean to stay here.''

''I don't,'' he assured her, relieved to know the source of her worry. ''We're going to live in the same place, both of us, all the time.''

She looked relieved. ''When can I start looking?''

He laughed. He couldn't imagine why he hadn't done this before now.

''Tomorrow if you like, but there's something else I want to talk about first.'' He took both her hands and pulled her over to the sofa. They sat down. ''I want us to get married again.''

''What!''

She looked stunned. He should have expected that. It was a strange request; it would probably seem even stranger because he couldn't tell her the real reason for the second marriage.

''I want to get married in a church.''

''Why? We had a perfectly good marriage in the saloon.''

''I know, but I'm ashamed of it. If I hadn't been in a temper, I'd have done everything differently.''

''I guess all of us are a little to blame.''

''Maybe, but there's no reason we can't fix it. You can have a big church wedding with a white dress and dozens of bridesmaids. All my family will want to be there. They won't believe I'm married until they see it for themselves. You will want to invite your family.''

Her face fell. ''They won't come.''

''You won't know unless you ask them. Anyway, I want to have the biggest wedding this town's ever seen.''

She was still dubious.

''You can ask Fern to help you plan it. She doesn't have a daughter of her own. I know she'd love to do it.''

''But I'll feel silly—''

358

"We can invite everybody from the saloon."

"You wouldn't!"

"I certainly would. These girls are more my family than just about anybody else."

"You're sure you want to do this?"

"Absolutely sure. I've been thinking about it for days. Actually for longer than that."

"You really want to marry me in front of all those people?"

"Of course. What man wouldn't?"

"But I'm always getting you into trouble."

"We get out of it again. Both of us, together."

"Do you mean that—the together part, I mean?"

"Yes."

"For always?"

"Absolutely."

"You're sure you don't regret it?"

"Positive."

And he didn't. That much at least was the truth. "Now you'd better be getting to bed. I'm surprised you can keep your eyes open."

"I'm not going back to Bella's."

"But you're exhausted."

"You said we'd be together. I think we ought to start right now."

Zac let himself smile, but he didn't dare say a word. If Lily had any idea how much he wanted to go to bed with her, she might think that was the only reason he was making these changes. It wasn't, but it sure was a good place to start.

Lily lay awake long after their lovemaking was over. Zac didn't love her. He had held her close and kissed her hungrily, been tender and sweet, passionate and caring, but he never once said he loved her. He had never been wilder or more uninhibited than tonight. If ever his true feelings could have slipped past his guard, it would have been tonight.

They didn't. There was nothing to slip past.

She couldn't understand it. He was doing all the right things. She felt certain he was doing them for the right reasons. How could he not love her? If he did, why didn't he tell her?

She always came back to the same answer. No matter how strong his feelings for her might be, they were not that strong. He would be her husband, buy her a house, father her children, take care of her every need. But she hadn't been able to tap the deep well of emotion inside him. She knew it was there. It was evident in the passionate way he lived life. Why couldn't he be passionate about her? Why couldn't he share *himself* with her, not just his possessions?

She wondered if it was possible for Zac to love anybody deeply and truly. Maybe he had never learned to love because they'd gone about this all the wrong way. She had never given him time to search deeply inside himself. She had forced him to marry her while he thought he barely liked her.

She used to think she was fortunate that he had accepted the situation with good grace. Now she knew she should never have married him until he loved her so much he couldn't think of anything else. But marriage had come before love. Maybe he didn't feel anything else was required.

Lily had even begun to wonder if it was possible for anyone to love her the way she wanted to be loved. Maybe she was looking for a kind of love that didn't exist. Now that she thought about it, she didn't know if she'd ever see it. Her parents certainly didn't feel that way about each other.

She sighed in disappointment. How could everything feel so right and so wrong at the same time!

It would be so easy just to give up and take what she was offered. It was so much more than most people ever found. She felt ungrateful. She certainly couldn't go looking for a house and start planning a wedding, then change her mind.

She had to make up her mind, and she had to do it soon.

But first, she had to make certain about the baby.

Zac lay staring at the ceiling. He was feeling pretty good about the way things had turned out. He wished he could have found Windy Dumbarton. He hated not having that first marriage recorded. It was like an accusing finger pointed at him in secret. One day someone would find out, and there'd be hell to pay.

He wasn't sorry, though, about getting married again in a church. Marrying Lily in that secretive way was just another thing he'd done that he was ashamed of now. He hoped he wouldn't do any more things like that. He intended to be more responsible in the future.

He smiled in the dark. Responsibility had always been a dirty word. He'd done everything in the world he could to avoid it. Yet somehow he found himself responsible for a wife and a saloon full of women. This wasn't what he had in mind just a few months ago, and it surprised him that he was content for it to be so now.

He looked at Lily, lying asleep beside him. It was difficult to comprehend the difference she had made in his life. In him. He wasn't the same person, yet he didn't think he was essentially different. Other people were going to think he was. That was okay. Like Monty said, a man had to learn to do a lot of things differently when he got married.

Monty was crazy about Iris. Zac wished he could feel that way about Lily. Sometimes it surprised him how strong his feelings were, but they fell short of that all-consuming passion he saw in his brothers.

Maybe he wasn't capable of that kind of love. His father had never loved anybody but himself. It was only reasonable that one of them would end up being like the old bastard. He just wished he hadn't had to be the one. It should have been Madison. He was as cold as a fish except when it came to Fern. Say one word to upset his wife, and you'd better start making out your will real fast.

Zac envied his brothers being able to love like that. He hadn't wanted to at first. Then when he tried, he couldn't. He guessed he did love Lily. It just wasn't the whole-hearted feeling he expected to feel, that he wanted to give her. He was sure it could be mighty uncomfortable at times, but anything that could turn Jeff into a human being must be pretty wonderful as well.

He knew Lily loved him utterly and completely. He felt guilty that he couldn't return her feelings in equal measure. She deserved to feel loved and treasured, to feel that for one person at least she was the most important person in the universe.

Well, she was to him. If that was true, he must love her. He didn't feel the earth move or his heart stop beating. He just felt pleased and contented. He guessed crashing thunder and flashing lights weren't for him. He would never experience the joys, or the agonies, of a grand passion. He was disappointed, but there was no use crying over what couldn't be changed.

Maybe he couldn't give Lily the grand passion, but he could give her everything else. He'd give her so much, she wouldn't have time to realize she was missing anything. And if he was lucky, he'd learn how to love her as much as she loved him.

Madison stared at Zac as though he had lost his mind. "You're asking me for a job?"

"Yes. I hate ranches, so that lets out the twins and George. I want nothing to do with Tyler's hotels—even if Daisy could stand to be in the same room with me for more than five minutes—and I couldn't work with Jeff if my life depended upon it. I figure you and I are pretty much alike. We ought to get along okay."

"I thought you were married to your saloon. The last time I talked with you, you said—"

"I know what I said, but I wasn't married then. Can you imagine one of your snooty matrons oozing up to Lily at some fancy party and asking, 'And what does your husband do for a living, my dear?' She's bound to say, 'He runs a gambling saloon in the Barbary Coast!' ''

Madison chuckled. "I'd give a thousand dollars to be there."

"I don't want my wife being the butt of your entertainment, or anybody else's," Zac said. "She's got to have a respectable husband, somebody she can be proud of." Zac swallowed, then plunged ahead. "That's the reason I'm selling the saloon and giving up gambling."

Madison stared at his youngest brother for the space of several minutes. Then he got up, opened a cabinet, took out a bottle of brandy, and poured some into a glass, which he handed to Zac. "Here, drink this, then repeat what you just said."

Zac smiled as he waved the glass away. "I suppose it is a bit unexpected."

"It's a damned shock," Madison said. "Have you told George?"

"No. I'm waiting to tell him about the wedding at the same time."

"Fern told me you were doing the wedding over. Are you sure you know what you're doing?"

"Yes. If I'd known a little earlier, all of this could have been prevented."

Madison drank the brandy himself, then settled back into his chair. "I'll give you a job," he said. "I always thought you'd be good in business. You've got the right instincts. It's a lot like gambling anyway, only more respectable."

"And for larger stakes."

"Much larger," Madison said, sobering. "You realize I'm going to ride you hard? You're not going to get any breaks just because you're my brother."

"I don't want any. I'll pull my weight. If I can't, I'll leave on my own."

Madison shook his head in disbelief. "I wouldn't have believed this conversation if I hadn't been sitting right here.

You've got to bring this wife of yours over. I've got to see the woman who could put the handcuffs on you. Does she know what a devil you are?''

"That's just it. She thinks I'm damned near perfect. She nearly attacked the preacher's wife for criticizing me."

"Is she all right in the head?"

Zac laughed. "She's just as blind as Fern."

"If she's only half as good as Fern, you got more than you deserve."

"I got a lot more."

Bella's dark parlor was absolutely the wrong setting for the news Lily had just heard.

"I can't imagine why Hezekiah should want to marry me," Julie Peterson was saying, "but he swears he does."

"I'm sure Hezekiah knows his own mind," Lily replied, all the while fearing he must have lost it completely. Only a short time ago, he'd been certain Julie was a woman of easy virtue.

"But he's a minister, and I've worked in a saloon."

"Hezekiah won't care about that." And he wouldn't. He might allow himself to be swayed once in a while, but Lily had never doubted the purity of his heart.

"But other people will. I couldn't stand to have anybody say terrible things about him because of me. Can you imagine what Mrs. Thoragood will say?"

"He won't care, and neither should you."

"I can't help being worried. I don't know how to be a minister's wife."

"Don't worry. You'll learn. Hezekiah will help you."

"But I can't always be hanging on him. Would you mind terribly if I asked you? You know all about it already."

Lily almost laughed at the irony of the situation. She who knew all about being a minister's wife had married a gambler. Julie, who had found sanctuary in a saloon, wanted to marry a minister. Surely Fate had played a joke on both of them.

"I'll do anything I can to help. When are you getting married?"

"I don't know. I've told Hezekiah we've got to wait a year."

"Why so long?."

"It's a terribly big step for both of us. I have to make sure I can do this. It's not going to be easy for Hezekiah, either. Some congregations won't accept me."

"Why not? All they'll see is a pretty young wife and her devoted husband."

"Hezekiah says he wants to stay in San Francisco. He wants to help young women the way Zac does."

"I think that's wonderful. Now I suggest you go find Hezekiah and tell him you really don't want to wait a whole year."

"You think I should?"

"I think a month will be plenty."

"You've got to promise to come to the wedding. I couldn't think of getting married without you. None of this would be happening if you hadn't rescued me from that man."

As they said their good-byes, Lily consoled herself with the knowledge that at least one good thing had come of all the foolish things she'd done in the past months. Julie could look forward to her wedding knowing her husband loved her.

Lily told herself she was being foolish not to feel the same way, but she couldn't. She was certain she was pregnant. Her time of the month had always come with unfailing regularity, never varying more than a day or two. Now she was more than two weeks late. She was sure.

This should have been one of the happiest moments in her life. She wanted to be Zac's wife more than anything else in the world. She wanted his baby. Yet she spent hours every day trying to keep from bursting into tears.

She was caught. It was no longer a question of what she wanted to do. She had to think of her child. That child would need a father. She had no right to deny it the privilege of growing up with two parents. Besides, she knew how Zac felt about fatherless children.

There could be no more indecisiveness. She couldn't even consider leaving him. She had to stay. She had to be his wife. It infuriated her that her decision should make her want to cry. She was acting stupidly. Zac was everything a woman could want in a husband—handsome, rich, determined to do everything he could to please her. She reminded herself for the thousandth time that she had no one to blame for her situation but herself. She had known Zac didn't love her when she married him.

She was extremely fortunate that he now seemed happy and eager to be her husband. He had changed his whole life because of her. He couldn't possibly have any doubts. She was the only one who wanted more.

Well, it was about time she stopped acting like a child and faced up to the fact she was a very lucky young woman. With ninety-nine percent of their relationship nearly perfect, it was foolish even to think of rejecting it for the one percent that was missing.

She sat down to write Zac a note telling him she'd been acting foolishly these last weeks. She'd be happy to marry him again in the biggest wedding in the country if he wanted. She was very proud to be his wife and wanted everyone to know it.

She knew such a note would bring him rushing over, suspicious at her giving her in. But she would have time to get her feelings under control, to look like she was the happiest woman in the world.

She owed him that much.

Chapter Twenty-eight

"We'll have the reception here at the hotel," Daisy was telling Tyler. "You can make everything as fancy as you like, but I don't want you anywhere near that kitchen the entire time."

"I have to make sure everything is prepared properly," Tyler objected. "This is my brother's wedding, and half of San Francisco society will be here. Everything's got to be perfect."

"If your chefs can't manage a reception by themselves after all this time, you need to fire them. I repeat, you're not to go near that kitchen. And don't think you can sneak by me. I intend to set the children to watch you."

"They're only three and four."

"Perfect ages. They haven't yet learned they're supposed to lie for their father. You're incorrigible, Tyler. Sometimes I think I want to go back to that mountain cabin and be snowed in all winter. If you ever had to choose between your kitchen and me, I'd be raising those children on my own."

Tyler grabbed his wife as she turned away from him, turned her around, and engulfed her in his embrace. "It wouldn't be an easy decision, but I'd give up cooking for you."

"Well, I wouldn't want you to do anything like that," Daisy said, returning her husband's embrace. "You'd probably waste away to nothing."

Tyler nuzzled his wife's neck. "Not if I was too busy to think about the kitchens."

Daisy giggled. "Not now, Tyler. The children will be here in half an hour."

"Can you think of a better way to spend the time?"

Daisy couldn't.

"But she can't want us all to be in the wedding," Madison said. "That'll be six of us."

"She knows exactly how many brothers Zac has. What's more, she wants all of her sisters-in-law to walk down the aisle as well," said Fern.

"Good lord. It'll be a mob. Nobody will see the bride."

"They'll see Lily," Fern assured him. "We'll be in blue. She'll be in white."

"Well, since it's the last time, I guess I can stand it."

"Brace yourself. That's not all. She wants Zac's nieces to be flower girls."

Madison let out a hoot. "Elizabeth might do just fine, but George's twins and Monty's Susan will turn it into a circus."

"No, they won't, not if I have anything to say about it."

Madison knew that was no idle threat. After dealing with five sons each day, four girls ought to be a snap. Well, maybe not a snap. There was nothing about George's twins or Monty's daughter that was easy. Beautiful they were. Terrors they were as well.

"She wants the boys to carry her train."

"My God. Does she know how many male Randolphs there are?"

"Precisely. She wants William Henry and Jordy to be ring bearers."

"This is going to be a nightmare. I just hope we all live through it."

"You will."

"Maybe we should move back to Denver."

"How about Kansas?"

"And have you revert to wearing pants and that abominable sheepskin vest! Never. I'm keeping you where you have to wear a dress to look presentable."

"Good. I'm not planning to move from this house until they have to carry me through the door," Fern declared.

"How about me carrying you upstairs?"

"I can walk, thank you."

"But it's much more fun if I carry you."

Fern didn't walk.

George was working over his accounts when a scream from Rose sent him racing to her sitting room. When he reached the doorway, she was standing in the middle of the room, holding a letter in her hands.

"Did anyone die?" George asked.

"Zac is getting married," Rose said, "for the second time to the same woman."

"What?" George had never known what to expect from Zac, but this was beyond the limit.

"He got married in a private ceremony, but now he wants a proper wedding," Rose explained. "He wants us to stand up with him. He wants the children to be in the wedding, too."

"All of them?"

"William Henry is to be a ring bearer, and the girls are to be flower girls."

"The twins are a little old for that, don't you think?"

"Fourteen's not too old. I'll have to telegraph the school to make arrangements to send them to San Francisco at once. Thank goodness William Henry hasn't started West

Point yet. I doubt they'd let him off. He can travel with Jeff.''

''He might prefer to come on his own. He is big enough, you know.''

''Accept it, George. My children will never be old enough.''

A little girl of eight years came running into the room. ''Mama, was that you screaming?'' she asked.

''I wasn't screaming. I was just surprised.''

''She was screaming,'' George said, grabbing his youngest daughter from behind and giving her a hug and kiss.

''You're going to be in a wedding,'' Rose said. ''Would you like that?''

''Whose wedding?''

''Your Uncle Zac's, if we can believe his letter.''

''Who'd marry him?''

''See what you've done?'' George accused his wife.

''A very nice young woman,'' Rose told her youngest child. ''And you're never to repeat a word I've said, on pain of being trampled by a million longhorns.''

''Papa said we don't raise longhorns anymore. He says they don't have enough beef. We raise Herefords.''

''All cows are the same to me,'' Rose said, dismissing such an unimportant distinction. She paused. ''I can hardly believe it's been nineteen years since I came to this ranch. I can still remember Zac peeping though the door that first horrible day. He was such a darling little boy.'' She turned to her husband. ''Do you remember how proud he was when he got his first pair of chaps?''

''But Uncle Zac hates cows,'' Elizabeth reminded her mother.

''He didn't then. He couldn't wait to ride with his brothers. Anything to be grown-up.''

''But you said Uncle Zac never grew up.''

George laughed delightedly. ''She's got you there.''

Rose was nettled. ''Sometimes he still acts like it. Now, we've got to go to San Antonio immediately. Both of us need new clothes. Fern says it's going to be the biggest wedding of the year. I can't imagine how she got Zac to agree to it."

"At least I'm not pregnant," Laurel said as she supervised the packing for her family.

"Would that mean we could stay home?" Hen asked as he kissed the back of his wife's neck.

"No, and stop that. You're setting a terrible example for the boys."

"On the contrary, I'm setting a good example. I want them to know exactly how to go about it."

"There are certain things that don't need practice. You certainly learned fast enough."

"But practice is more fun."

Laurel took her husband's hands and put them behind her back. "It's up to you to make sure Adam and Jordy understand they've got to behave properly while they're in San Francisco. I'll be mortified if they show up at the wedding wearing spurs and boots."

"I still think it would be better to leave them here."

"I agree, but Lily wants them in the wedding. Apparently, she's hoping this will help heal the breach between Zac and the rest of the family."

"It won't."

"Well, I'm going to do my best to help her," Laurel said. "I still believe one of those Blackthornes would have killed you if Zac hadn't shown up in that ridiculous dress."

A nurse came out of the house carrying a little girl in her arms. Three boys, ages six, five, and two, followed close behind.

"You sure you won't need more help?" Hen asked.

"Helen and I can handle the children. You just take care of Jordy and Adam."

"I think you've got the easier job."

"I know I have. Are you sure it's a good idea to let them ride?"

"The only way you'll get them to behave for that long is to wear them out first."

"How soon before we get there, Daddy?" A four-year-old girl with flame-red hair looked up at her father. "We've been on this train an awfully long time."

"We'll get there tomorrow," Monty said to his daughter.

"I want to go home."

"We've only just left."

"I don't like trains."

"It's a lot better than going by horseback," her mother said. "Trains don't get tired like horses or have to be fed and watered."

"I still don't like trains."

"Don't talk so loudly," Iris cautioned. "You'll wake your sister."

Monty could never get enough of the sight of his wife holding either of their daughters. It was still a miracle to him that these energetic creatures were his children, that he had been part of creating anything so vital, so beautiful. They had their mother's red hair and his blue eyes. They were perfect, and he loved them so much that at times it was almost painful.

"Are we going to stay in Uncle Tyler's hotel?" Susan asked.

"Yes," her mother replied. "And you're not to run up and down the halls."

"Will Sandy and Carter be there?"

"Yes. All of your cousins are coming."

"They'll run up and down the halls."

"Fine. Let your Aunt Fern worry about them. Just don't let me catch you running after them."

Susan considered that for a moment. "That doesn't seem fair."

"You're going to be in your Uncle Zac's wedding. It's very important that you be on your best behavior."

"Is Helena going to be in the wedding?" Susan asked,

looking at the year-old child asleep in Iris's arms.

"No. She's too little."

"What am I going to do?"

"You're going to be a flower girl. You'll wear a pretty dress and spread rose petals all over everywhere."

"I can't believe he's going to have all these children in the wedding," Monty said. "It'll be a zoo."

"It'll be worth it just to see the woman who finally managed to put her brand on the last free Randolph." Iris looked at her husband, grinned, then turned to her daughter. "Of course, it won't be half as hard as catching your father. I tried to hook him with a herd of cows, but he wouldn't bite. I had to chase him all the way from Texas to Wyoming."

"Is that a long way?" Susan asked.

"It seemed like it then."

"You go to the desk and make sure our rooms are ready," Violet said to Jeff as their carriage came to a stop before the Palace.

"You'll need help with the children."

"I can handle the children just fine. It's seeing about the rooms and the baggage I can't handle."

"You should have told me you were expecting before we left. I'm sure Zac would have understood."

"You should have assumed I was pregnant," Violet said with a laugh. "It seems I have been from the moment I married you. I think it was easier being a housemother. At least I didn't get them until they were at least ten."

"We still don't have to go."

"Of course we do. I wouldn't have missed this even if I were due the day of the wedding. This is your last brother. Aren't you curious about the bride?"

"I guess I am. I remember that child from her visit several summers ago," Jeff said. "It never occurred to me then that she would be the one to marry Zac. He treated her exactly like a younger sister. Here, hold Tom's hand while I help the girls down."

"Look, Mama," her son said, pointing up at the covered roof that seemed hundreds of feet in the air.

"I'd better not," Violet said after only a glance. "It'll make me dizzy. Does your brother always have to build such extravagant hotels?" she asked Jeff.

"I didn't think anything could top the one he built in Denver, but this certainly does."

"Can I go with Papa?" Tom asked.

"That's right. You men run off and leave us women to struggle along as best we can."

"Men don't take care of babies," Tom said.

"Now I wonder where he learned that," Violet said, eyeing her husband.

"William Henry told me," Tom announced. "He said babies was women's work."

"You're off the hook this time," Violet said to her visibly relieved husband, "but you wait until I see William Henry. I'll teach him to poison my child's mind."

"I think we'd better go see about the rooms before you say anything else," Jeff said to his son. "You sure you don't need help?"

"Catherine's asleep, and Dorothy's nodding. I just need to be able to put them to bed soon. I want them well rested before the wedding rehearsal."

"Why have you been getting drunk?" Zac asked Dodie.

She had just entered his office. She had closed the door, but hadn't had time to sit down.

"If you called me here to talk about my drinking, I'm walking right back out that door."

"I didn't, but it's something I need to know."

Dodie didn't move. "You tell me what you want. If I think it's any of your business, I'll tell you why I get drunk."

"You going to sit down?"

"Should I?"

"Yeah."

Dodie settled herself into a deep chair. "Aren't you going to offer me a brandy?"

"I was hoping you wouldn't want one."

"I don't get drunk on brandy, Zac. Just whiskey."

Zac and Dodie locked gazes.

Maybe he was making a mistake. Maybe Dodie was the wrong person. He didn't know why she had fallen apart, but he couldn't afford to take the chance she would do it again. Too much would be riding on her shoulders.

"Do you want a brandy?" he asked.

"No, but it was nice of you to ask." She flashed a brilliantly insincere smile. "Now, what was so important that you actually got yourself out of bed before noon?"

Zac walked in front of his desk and perched on the corner. "I'm making some changes in the way I live," he said. "Getting up before noon is only the beginning."

"It's about time," Dodie said. "Now if you can just get yourself to bed before dawn."

"I plan to do that as well. But as you can guess, that leaves no one to look after the saloon."

"Don't look at me. I'm not staying up all night for any man, especially so he can go to bed with another woman, even if it is his wife."

"It's important the saloon keeps going. There'd be a lot of people out of a job if it closed. Think of all the girls who'd still be on the street."

Dodie got to her feet. "You're not going to rope me into going to work for you again by making me feel guilty, Zac Randolph. I don't ask anybody to take care of me, and I'm not taking care of anybody."

"I'm not asking you to take care of anybody, just keep the saloon open and running."

"No." Dodie started to the door.

"Would you do it if it was your place?"

Dodie stopped in her tracks, then slowly turned around. "Explain what you mean by *your place*."

"It's one of the changes I'm making. I'm getting out of the gambling business."

"You're doing this because of Lily?"

"I have to. It's no kind of life with one of us awake while the other is sleeping. She doesn't belong in a place like this. As long as I own it, there'll be no way to keep her out."

"Damn! You really must be crazy about her after all."

"I guess you could say I'm not as clever as I thought, but I finally realized Lily couldn't shape her life to fit mine. She would try—Lord knows we saw ample evidence of that—but it's not right, and I know it."

"You can't know how relieved I am to hear you say that. I've been feeling guilty over insisting you marry her. I was certain you were in love with her but would never see it unless somebody gave you a push."

"Well, you gave me a push all right. It took a little getting used to, but now I'm happy you did it. Now about that drinking."

"I guess it is important," Dodie said, looking away. She started fiddling with a small statuette on the table next to the sofa. She kept her back to Zac.

Dodie walked over to the window and looked out at the bay. "I could handle your not loving me as long as there wasn't anybody else. I even thought I could handle it when I saw you falling for Lily. But I was wrong.

"I didn't realize that until after you got married. That's why I quit. I couldn't work around you with you married to someone else. That's why I started drinking again. I had stopped until you asked me to watch the saloon while you went looking for Windy."

She turned around to face him. "I realized when you were willing to take three days off to go look for Windy Dumbarton that you really did love her."

She looked at the floor. "That was the final blow to my hopes that maybe . . . somehow . . . Anyway, it was rougher than I thought. I got drunk again, but only that one night."

She took a deep breath and looked him in the eye. "I'm

over it, finally. I haven't had a drop since. It hasn't been easy, but I can finally say I'm happy for you. I hope you have the best of everything.''

He didn't know what to say now any more than when Dodie first told him she loved him. He wondered how many times he'd done or said something to hurt her. They were beyond counting, he was certain.

He crossed the room and took Dodie's hands in his. He held them tightly. ''I'd have been very proud to have you for my wife.''

''Except for the fact that you didn't love me.''

''I'm not worthy of you, Dodie.''

''Don't give me that.'' She jerked her hands, but he wouldn't let go. ''That's what every man says when he's trying to wiggle out of something, hoping he can get the hell out before a woman starts crying.''

''Well, I do mean it. I'm not worthy of you *or* Lily.''

''You're damned right,'' Dodie said, her eyes gleaming with moisture. ''But handsome bastards like you are always getting things they don't deserve.''

Zac kissed her on the cheek. ''You've been the greatest friend I ever had. I couldn't have run this place without you.''

''Oh, hell! You know how much a woman hates it when a man says he wants them to be friends.''

''I'm sorry, but there's nothing else I can do. I love you dearly, but not—''

''I know, you love me like a friend.''

''Yes.''

Dodie wiped her eyes. ''Well, I guess that's something. Now before I start to cry, you'd better tell me how you expect me to finance buying this saloon. Knowing your liking for sharp deals, I don't expect you to give it to me.''

Zac peeped out into the church and grimaced. He wondered if it was possible to cancel a wedding after the organ had started playing. The Randolph side of the church was packed with the cream of San Francisco society. Daisy and Fern had really put themselves out to make certain everybody of importance was there.

It was the bride's side that worried him. It was filled to bursting with nearly every man who had ever set foot inside the Little Corner of Heaven since Lily arrived. And the girls and the staff. Lily had invited everybody.

He was certain there hadn't been such an ill-matched gathering since every animal who could run, climb, or crawl had packed themselves inside Noah's ark.

The church was filled with the exception of one pew reserved for Lily's family. Lily had insisted that Fern use it for other guests. Fern was equally insistent that it would be held in reserve until the last minute. "You never know about trains," she had said. "They don't always arrive on time."

The trains had arrived, but Lily's family hadn't. She had tried to pretend it didn't matter, but Zac knew it did. He didn't look forward to the confrontation in the least, but one of these days he was going to have words with Isaac Sterling. Zac wasn't going to have his wife made unhappy just because her father had decided to be churlish. He was a Virginian. He had manners. It was time he learned to use them.

"It's time to start," Mr. Thoragood said to Zac. The two men walked to their place in front of the altar.

Zac considered the church too dark and gloomy, but Fern had insisted it was the only church big enough for a Randolph wedding. Grey stone absorbed most of the light the stained glass windows let in. Dark wooden pews and choir stalls and deep red carpets and hangings added to the somber effect. Fern had tried to brighten the atmosphere by the liberal use of candles and white ribbon, but Zac thought it still looked like the bottom of a cave.

But once his family started down the aisle, he forgot about everything else. It was a truly magical moment, and even he could sense it. They came in pairs, each brother with his wife on his arm. It wasn't the usual way, but Lily had insisted. George and Rose were first. From oldest to youngest.

Zac had never thought of himself as a sentimental man, but he couldn't help feeling a little strange inside. It was impossible not to think back nineteen years to when George and Jeff had returned from the war. The six oldest were married now, and eighteen of their twenty-two children would soon be marching down the aisle.

They were good men, tall and straight, proud of their accomplishments, proud of their wives and families. For the first time Zac felt part of them. He no longer felt like the boy struggling against his older brothers. He was a married man about to be welcomed into the fraternity of married men by the people who mattered most to him.

His entire family—even the babies—had come to the church.

He watched as Jeff's Dorothy and Monty's Susan started down the aisle. They were very serious about their job of spreading the rose petals evenly down the long aisle. Zac expected that if Elizabeth Rose hadn't been between them, Aurelia and Juliette, following impatiently behind, would have run over them.

It came as something of a shock when Zac saw William Henry. The boy had grown as tall as his father and looked so much like George that it stunned him. When had the brat had time to grow up so much?

Jordy was a year younger, but he, too, looked like a young man. Zac decided he would have to start seeing more of his family. He had missed too much of their lives already. He hoped they wouldn't ignore him the way he had them. He'd been mortified to have to confess to Lily a few days earlier that he'd never seen Hen's three youngest children.

Dodie. She looked as nervous as a cat in a dog pound, but he had never seen her more radiant. From the moment Lily asked her, she hadn't stopped insisting that she couldn't possibly be the maid of honor. But Zac was certain Lily couldn't have done anything that would have made her happier.

Dodie arrived, and Julie Peterson started down the aisle. Lily had insisted on two maids of honor. Julie did look lovely—no wonder Hezekiah had fallen in love with her—but she couldn't hold a candle to Lily. In a few minutes, they'd all see. His Lily would outshine every woman in the church.

That included Iris!

He thought of his eleven nephews, nervously waiting outside the doors to carry Lily's train. He hoped they didn't stumble over their feet. He wanted everything to go perfectly. He wanted this to be a day Lily would remember with happiness for the rest of her life. Maybe he couldn't give her the kind of love she longed for so much, but he would damned well give her everything else.

Whatever happened, Zac was going to make sure he never let her out of his sight again. He felt a shiver of dread run all through him every time he thought of what could have happened on that dock if he hadn't arrived on time.

He couldn't stand it if anything happened to Lily. If the way he felt when she ran away to Bella's was anything to go by, there wouldn't be anything left to do but shoot himself. He'd be too miserable to go on living.

There'd be no point in getting up before noon if he couldn't see her smile, hear her quote her ridiculous father, or find somebody else for him to take under his wing. She was an essential part of his day, of everything he did, of his every thought. He couldn't even think of himself as an individual any longer. The two of them had merged in his mind until they had become one unit made up of two inseparable parts.

All at once he had so much he wanted to tell her, things he'd never told anybody, thoughts he'd kept to himself because they seemed too foolish to utter. None of them seemed silly anymore because he knew Lily would understand.

Then, as he stood there waiting for the doors at the back

of the church to open, Zac finally understood what Lily had been talking about. He finally understood what could turn Madison and Jeff, two of the most unfeeling men in the world, into charming, devoted husbands and lovers. The love they felt for their wives was so important to them, so essential to their existence, that it simply transformed them.

Just as his love for Lily had transformed him.

He hadn't turned his life upside down because he thought he ought to, or because he thought he must to make Lily happy. He'd done it because he wanted to, because he simply couldn't imagine doing anything else.

All because he loved Lily.

And he did love her, *really* love her. With his heart, his soul, his mind, his whole body right on down to his toes. He was so full of it, he was sure it showed on his face, the same lovesick expression he'd seen on his brothers' faces time and time again.

But he didn't care who knew. He was crazy about her, so crazy about her he wanted to yell it out to everybody, especially Fern and Daisy. He hadn't been left behind. He was just as good as anybody else. No Randolph was going to make a bigger fool of himself over his wife than he was.

Zac knew his family would probably think he'd lost his mind, but he didn't care. He wasn't the same man who had looked down at that ace-high spade flush two months ago. Then no power on earth could have gotten him to attend a wedding such as this, much less be its focal point.

Now he couldn't wait to marry Lily, and he didn't care who watched. He was proud of her. He wanted to show her off to his brothers, to his family, to the whole world.

Zac felt a great weight lift from his shoulders. He loved Lily. He *really* loved her. He knew it was real because he could feel it. He couldn't wait to tell Lily. She had looked troubled and unhappy recently, all because he was too dense to see what was staring him in the face. Why else would he have sold his saloon and taken a job with Madison?

He was tired of waiting. He was impatient with the whole

proceedings. He wanted the wedding over so he could tell her. He wanted to see the frown disappear, the wrinkles at the corners of her eyes smooth into a happy smile. He wanted to see her as happy as he felt at this very moment.

The organ swelled again, and the guests craned their necks to get the first glance of her, but the doors stayed closed. Lily didn't appear.

It was those boys. They must have gotten the train balled up. Or pulled it off. Anybody should have known it was ridiculous to ask eleven boys to do anything together, especially when their name was Randolph and they ranged in ages from four to fourteen. He wondered how long it would take Lily to get things straight again. He hoped it wouldn't be long.

He knew that as far as the rest of the world was concerned, she was already his wife, but he'd never felt married. He wouldn't have even if he'd had the marriage recorded properly. His heart hadn't been in it that day.

Everything was different today. He didn't care how much discomfort he had to endure. If it would make Lily happy, it would be worthwhile. Besides, he was looking forward to his new life. He was a gambler, and change was always a gamble. Being Lily's husband was the best gamble of all.

Zac was aware that too much time had passed for a simple mix-up to be the cause of the delay. Fern and Daisy were looking at each other with worried glances. The guests were beginning to fidget. He couldn't imagine what was wrong, but something definitely was.

"Don't worry," Mr. Thoragood whispered. "Sometimes brides get so nervous, they're afraid to open that door. But once they do, they're just fine."

Zac knew that wasn't it.

He wanted to go find her, but he knew he couldn't. It was unheard of for the groom to go running down the aisle to fetch the bride.

But as the seconds ticked off, it was clear somebody was going to have to do something. Rose and Fern were holding a whispered conversation. Fern handed Rose her bouquet. But before she could take a single step, the doors at the back of the church burst open. Instead of his bride, an enormous man flanked by two equally large young men burst into the church.

"Ye sons and daughters of the Devil!" he intoned in a voice that sounded as though it had been honed by years of speaking from mountaintops, "bow your heads and pray for your salvation. But before you do, you miserable sons of Satan, somebody had better tell me what you've done with my daughter!"

Chapter Twenty-nine

The vestibule looked more crowded than the sanctuary. Eleven young male Randolphs stood waiting nervously, certain they were somehow responsible for things going wrong.

"She never came out of that room," Madison's oldest son told Zac. "We waited here just like Mama said, but she never came out."

"Are you the Zac Randolph who calls himself my girl's husband?" Isaac Sterling demanded.

"Of course," Zac replied, heading toward the bride's room. "Do you think I'd be dressed up like a French waiter if I weren't?"

He went down a short corridor, turned right, and entered a room littered with boxes and tissue paper. Lily's veil and train lay on a table, waiting for her to put them on. Her street clothes hung neatly in an open cupboard. A deck of cards lay scattered on the floor. One card, the jack of spades, remained on the table.

Lily was gone.

Fear threatened to numb his brain, but Zac fought it off.

He had to think. He had to figure out what had happened to her.

At first he thought she had run away because he didn't love her, but Lily wouldn't have left without telling him, certainly not at a time like this. She was impulsive, but only when it came to helping others. No, somehow, for some reason, she'd been forced to leave. But why?

Immediately he thought of Captain Borger. They had freed his crew and burned his ship. But Borger would be after Zac, not Lily.

Isaac Sterling bulldozed his way into the bride's room. "Where is Lily?" he demanded, his eyes blazing. "What have you done with her?"

"It's a little late to start worrying about her now," Zac growled. "As soon as I find her and we get this wedding over with, I've got a few things to say to you. Until then, get the hell out of my way."

"Do you know where she is?" a soft-spoken woman asked.

Nobody had to tell Zac the woman was Lily's mother.

"No, and I can't figure it out with all these people asking questions."

Dodie pushed her way in, adding to the confusion. She looked around, her expression one of shock and bewilderment.

"She's gone," Zac said. "Disappeared."

"Have you any idea why?" Dodie asked.

"All I can think of is that ship's captain, but it can't be him. Who else could hate Lily?"

"Or have a grudge against you," Dodie said.

Zac moaned. "That could be half of the city."

"What were these instruments of Satan doing in a room with my daughter?" Sterling pointed to the cards.

"Can't you stop worrying about sin for five minutes?" Zac demanded, furious.

"She was playing cards to calm her nerves," Dodie said.

"I can't imagine why the cards are on the floor," Zac

muttered absently. "Everything else is in perfect order."

Zac and Dodie's eyes met.

"She did that intentionally!" Zac exclaimed. "It's supposed to tell us something."

"Only a fool looks to cards for help," Sterling thundered.

"Be quiet, Isaac. Let the man think."

He was quiet. Zac figured it was from shock that for the first time in his life, his wife had told him what to do.

"What can she be trying to tell us with the knave of spades?" Dodie asked.

"Chet Lee!" Zac exclaimed, certain he knew who had kidnapped Lily. "He's not only a black knave—he has reason to hate me, you, *and* Lily."

Zac darted past Reverend Sterling and dashed into the church. "Lily's been kidnapped," he called to his brothers.

As they started toward him, he addressed the guests. "Stay where you are, folks. I'll have her back before long."

"Who's got her?" Asa White, who was seated close by, asked.

"Chet Lee."

He thrust a gun into Zac's hand. "Here, you'll need this."

"What do you want us to do?" Hen asked Zac.

"Follow me. I think I know where he's taken her. I need you to make sure he doesn't sneak out."

"I'm afraid I came without a gun," George said. "I never expected to need one in church."

"None of us are armed," Madison said.

Suddenly a dozen or more guests were in the aisle, pressing pistols of various sizes and descriptions on the brothers.

"Damn," Monty exclaimed, his eyes gleaming with pleasure as he accepted a snub-nosed pistol and a long-barreled Colt. "My wedding wasn't half this much fun."

Out of the corner of his eye, Zac saw Madison and Rose take Lily's father in hand. That was one less worry. By the time he got back, they ought to have him broken to halter. He hoped Tyler and Jeff could convince the guests to wait.

After all this trouble, he didn't want to come back to an empty church.

Zac ran out of the church ahead of everyone. He headed straight for one of the cabs waiting to take the bridal party to the hotel for the wedding reception. "Head to the dock on Clay Street," he ordered. He climbed into the carriage.

"You're not leaving us behind," Monty said as he and Hen piled in behind Zac.

"Then you've got to keep up," Zac said, too worried about Lily to consider his words.

"We may be thirty-five," Monty said, "but sitting astride a horse every day keeps us in better shape than bellying up to a gambling table."

"Where are we going?" Hen asked.

"I think he's taken her to the docks," Zac said. "The only thing he can do is try to get her on a ship. He's got to know that if he keeps her anywhere in the city, she'll be recognized."

The brothers said very little during the drive to the waterfront. Zac kept berating himself, thinking if he'd married her properly in the first place, this would never have happened. He'd have sold out long ago, that disastrous game with Dodie would never have taken place, and he'd be trying to figure out how to coax Lily up to bed in the middle of the afternoon.

The cab stopped before a drab, wood frame building fronted by a covered boardwalk. The back of the building extended out over the water.

"What's the inside like?" Hen asked as they jumped out of the cab.

"There's a big gambling hall downstairs with some offices. The girls have rooms upstairs."

"Those kind?" Monty asked, curiosity dancing in his eyes.

"I'll search the rooms," Zac said. "You take the offices and keep everybody off my back."

They burst through the door. Hardly anyone in the saloon

took notice. Zac headed straight for the bartender. "Did Chet Lee just come through here?"

"I ain't seen him all day," the man replied and turned away.

Zac reached across the bar, grabbed the man by the collar, and jerked him off his feet. He banged his head on the bar.

"I'll ask you once more. Did Chet Lee just come through here with a woman in a wedding dress?"

"Now that you mention it, I do think I saw him go past," the man said.

"Which way did he go?"

"I didn't notice."

Zac banged his head on the bar again. This time he split the bartender's lip.

"Upstairs," the man managed to gasp.

"This place has more escape routes than a gopher town," Zac told Hen. "See if you can keep most of them covered."

Zac ran up the stairs three at a time. He started throwing open the door to each room as he came to it. He left a trail of screaming women and shouting men behind him. He didn't slow down until he came to a locked door at the back of the building. He didn't hesitate. Using his foot, he kicked the door at the lock. The soft wood splintered. The door swung open, revealing a narrow stairway.

Zac bounded down two flights of stairs half a dozen steps at a time. They ended at another closed door. Unlocked, it opened into a room that seemed to be a basement storage area. Zac heard muffled sounds of a struggle coming from beneath the floor. He found the trap door almost immediately. He threw it open just in time to see the door at the other end open.

The light coming through the doorway framed Chet Lee and Lily in a struggle.

"Lily!" Zac shouted as he catapulted down the dark stairway, "I love you!"

Lily ceased to struggle for a moment, and Chet pulled her away from the door and shut it behind him. He locked it.

Zac hit it with a crash, but it was much stronger than the inside doors. It held.

"What did you say?" came Lily's muffled voice.

"I said I love you," Zac shouted, then stomped the door with his foot. It still held, but he heard the wood begin to give. Twice more he hit the door. Afraid he would injure his foot and be unable to run after Chet Lee, he threw his shoulder against it. It gave way and Zac tumbled out, hitting the ground at the edge of the bay.

Zac scrambled to his feet to see Chet and Lily standing near a boat. Chet held a gun to Lily's head.

"Don't come any closer," Chet said.

"You may as well give it up," Zac said. "You're not going anywhere. If you harm one hair on her head, I'll kill you."

"I've got a gun."

"I've got two of them," Zac said, pulling the pistols out of his pockets. Zac started walking toward Lily. "Let her go."

"Stay where you are."

"Give it up, Chet," Zac said, his pace never slowing. "You can't win."

"Let me have him," Monty said. He'd come around the west side of the building.

"I'm the best marksman in the family," Hen said, approaching from the opposite side. "I can pick him off any time you say the word."

Finding himself suddenly facing three men with guns, and all escape on land cut off, Chet looked wild-eyed. He struggled to drag Lily into a boat pulled up on the shore, but he couldn't control her and hold on to his pistol.

"Come on, Chet," Zac said, only a few yards away now. "I admire a good bluff, but you're bucking an unbeatable hand. You've sometimes been an unwise gambler, but you've never been a stupid one."

"Get in the boat," Chet said to Lily. "Get in, or I'll shoot Zac."

Zac started forward.

"Don't bother," a voice said from somewhere above them. "I can still shoot the pips out of a playing card. I guess that's good enough to hit a coward's back."

It was George. He was on the pier, about ten feet above their heads.

Chet whipped around, loosening his hold on Lily. She broke away and fell to the ground. Chet swung around, horrified to find himself exposed to the aim of four guns. Blind fury flared in his eyes, and he swung his pistol toward Lily.

A fusillade of gunfire filled the air, and Chet Lee sank to the ground, his body riddled with bullets.

"He came into the room just after Dodie and Julie left," Lily told Zac as they traveled back to the church. "I was playing cards to keep from being so nervous. I had dealt only one when he cornered me."

"The jack of spades."

"I couldn't think what to do. No one would hear my screams over the organ. I knocked the other cards on the floor, hoping you'd figure out what I meant."

"I call that very good thinking. So was falling down. But I'm afraid it's muddied your gown."

"I don't care about my gown as long as you meant what you said."

"You mean the part where I shouted *I love you?*"

Lily smiled shyly. "Yes, that's the part."

"I meant every word of it," Zac said. "I had to be crazy not to figure it out before."

"Are you sure?" Lily asked. "I mean, are you *really* sure?"

"Maybe this will help convince you."

When Lily emerged from Zac's embrace, slightly more rumpled, she sighed and leaned back against the seat cushions.

"We'll have to call off the wedding. I've ruined my dress."

Panic held Zac in its iron grip. After getting this far, they couldn't stop now. "Nobody will notice."

"Of course they will," Lily said, pointing to a huge stain. "Besides, I imagine everyone will have left by now."

With a terrible sinking feeling, Zac realized that he was going to have to share with Lily the secret he'd hoped to take to his grave. If he let the wedding be cancelled now, he'd never arrange another one without telling everybody what he had done. Lily might not kill him—he hoped she wouldn't—but he knew his brothers would. He guessed he was going to find out if she really loved him after all.

"I've got a confession to make," he said. "Please don't say anything until I'm finished."

"Is it that awful?" Lily asked.

"Worse. We're not married."

"What?"

"We're not married. I had Windy Dumbarton perform the ceremony and fill out all the papers but not register them. I didn't believe you would want to stay married to a gambler," he said, rushing ahead. "I was sure that after a few days you'd change your mind. As long as the marriage wasn't official, all we had to do was pretend it never happened."

He lowered his head. He was afraid she might hit him and he wouldn't see the blow coming, but he couldn't stand to look into her eyes and make such a confession.

"I knew almost from the beginning that it wouldn't work," he went on, "that I didn't want it to work that way. I tried to stay away from you. Only you started talking about making a baby, and I couldn't help myself. I tried to find Windy, but I couldn't. I've worn myself ragged and a Pinkerton besides. I've been in places I hope never to see again, but the damned man has disappeared off the face of the earth.

"I can't tell you how sorry I am for what I did. It's been driving me crazy for weeks. It would serve me right if you never spoke to me again. But I love you. If you left me now, I'd have to follow you around for the rest of my life."

He looked up. Lily glared at him.

"I'd make a sorry spectacle waiting at doors, hanging around outside your rooming house, following your cab, haunting the place you worked. You'd be embarrassed. It would upset my family, too. I'd probably take to drink."

Lily didn't say anything, but she must have been really angry. She was shaking.

"Besides, I don't know how I can explain it to your father and Hezekiah. I think they'd probably kill me before I got the chance."

Lily dumbfounded him by laughing.

Zac was confused, relieved, and slightly irritated. "It's not funny. I've nearly gone crazy looking for that damned Windy, worrying you'd find out and never speak to me again. I racked my brains for a whole week to come up with an excuse to have a second wedding."

Lily stopped laughing. "Do you really want to marry me again?"

"Of course I do. Do you think I'd go through all this if I didn't? This time when I make all those promises, I want to mean them."

"You don't have to do it again if you don't want to. We're really married."

"No, we're not. I just explained."

"Windy gave *me* the marriage papers. He said he was emigrating to Australia and had to give them to somebody. He registered them before he left. I've got the marriage certificate, all properly signed and sealed."

Zac felt as though the air had been knocked out of him. He'd been driving himself crazy for nothing. He was married. Lily wasn't going to leave him. His family wasn't going to disown him. He was going to come out of this with a whole skin.

Dodie always said he led a charmed life.

"I've got a confession of my own to make," Lily said.

"I should have told you earlier, but I didn't know how you'd take it."

Zac didn't like confessions. They did funny things to the pit of his stomach.

"We're going to have a baby," Lily said.

Zac wasn't certain he could take any more shocks. "You mean we . . . all those times . . . are you sure?"

Lily nodded.

A sudden thought came to Zac, and he felt his stomach take another of those nasty dives. "You aren't staying with me just because of the baby, are you? I mean, if you weren't going to have a baby, you wouldn't want a divorce, would you?"

"I'd never want to leave you for any reason. I was only afraid if I stayed, I'd keep you from finding somebody you could really love. I know we did it all wrong, but you're not sorry, are you?"

"No. Being in love is great. It's just getting there that's hell."

The guests were still in the church when the bridal party returned. The general feeling was that no one wanted to miss the end of this bizarre afternoon. No society bride had been kidnapped before. One matron was overheard to say she hoped it wouldn't become the fashion.

They did the procession all over again, just like the first time except for a few changes. The front pew on the bride's side was occupied by the bride's mother and brothers. Her mother cried. Her brothers looked uncomfortable.

Someone had managed to obtain a new supply of rose petals. The flower girls were delighted.

The bride entered on cue, her train faultlessly managed by eleven handsome young Randolphs. She was given away by her father, who was heard to say later, as he accepted his second glass of champagne at a sumptuous reception at the Palace Hotel, that they generally managed these things without so much fuss back in Salem.

The groom was impeccably attired. The bride's gown was snagged in places and muddy, but no one seemed to care, least of all the groom. Despite the unexpected contretemps, he seemed to be in the best of spirits. However, now and then he would suddenly frown and start muttering about shipwrecks on windy deserted islands inhabited by cannibals. One guest asked the bride how there could be headhunters on a deserted island.

The bride just smiled.

Author's Note

Well, friends, this is end of the stories about the Randolph family. At least for now. Some gave me a few more headaches than others (Tyler was so much trouble I threatened to tell my editor he'd died in a cave-in), but I thoroughly enjoyed writing these seven books.

I couldn't possibly move on to something else without thanking a few special people. To my agent, Natasha Kern, who listened to my garbled version of the series over the phone, and could make enough sense out of what I was saying to tell me to stop the book I was working on long enough to write up a proposal. To my editor, Alicia Condon, who liked the proposal enough to buy it and who saw that I got great covers from first to last. To my family, who saw too little of me and heard too much about the Randolphs. To Karen and Lois, who never hesitated to tell me when I'd done something stupid, and to Lesley, who gently pointed me in the right direction.

But most of all, my very special thanks to the hundreds of readers who've fallen in love with the Randolph family and written to tell me about their favorite bride, favorite brother, or ask if I would do a book about a favorite secondary character. I believe Salty and Hope got the most requests, but I think my choice would be Dodie. After putting up with Zac for all those years, she deserves somebody really nice.

Thank you for the holiday greetings, the gifts, and the poetry. But most of all, thanks for those wonderful letters that keep coming and coming and coming. There can't be any better way to finish up a day than by reading three lines, or three pages, from a reader who's fallen in love with my characters or who found the answer to a problem in her life in something that I've written. You make me feel that I do something very special when I sit down to write.

For Phyllis Vyskocil, whose letter arrived on my desk without an envelope, thanks. I love every word you wrote.

And now my new project. I've already started work on a series I'm calling *The Cowboys*. It's built around a group of orphans who grow up on a cattle ranch in Texas. I hope you will grow to like these boys as much as you have the Randolph brothers.

Please feel free to write me at P.O. Box 470761, Charlotte, NC 28226. A SASE would be appreciated.

LEIGH GREENWOOD'S
SEVEN BRIDES
Laurel

Although Hen Randolph is the perfect choice for a sheriff in the Arizona Territory, he is no one's idea of a model husband. After the trail-weary cowboy breaks free from his six rough-and-ready brothers, he isn't about to start a family of his own. Then a beauty with a tarnished reputation catches his eye and the thought of taking a wife arouses him as never before.

But Laurel Blackthorne has been hurt too often to trust any man—least of all one she considers a ruthless, coldhearted gunslinger. Not until Hen proves that drawing quickly and shooting true aren't his only assets will she give him her heart and take her place as the newest bride to tame a Randolph's heart.

_3744-0 $5.99 US/$6.99 CAN

LEIGH GREENWOOD

"Leigh Greenwood is a dynamo of a storyteller!"
—*Los Angeles Times*

Jefferson Randolph has never forgotten all he lost in the War Between The States—or forgiven those he has fought. Long after most of his six brothers find wedded bliss, the former Rebel soldier keeps himself buried in work, only dreaming of one day marrying a true daughter of the South. Then a run-in with a Yankee schoolteacher teaches him that he has a lot to learn about passion.

Violet Goodwin is too refined and genteel for an ornery bachelor like Jeff. Yet before he knows it, his disdain for Violet is blossoming into desire. But Jeff fears that love alone isn't enough to help him put his past behind him—or to convince a proper lady that she can find happiness as the newest bride in the rowdy Randolph clan.

_3995-8 $5.99 US/$7.99 CAN